SILVARUM

BOOK I: FROST

For Eddie, Oli, and Ava.

Never stop dreaming.

SILVARUM

BOOK I: FROST

BY

DEAN KUHTA

ELVELON PRESS

Silvarum, Book I: Frost is a work of fiction. Names, characters, places, and incidents either are the product of the author's imagination or are used fictitiously. Any resemblance to actual persons, living or dead, events, or locales is entirely coincidental.

ISBN 10: 0-692-89087-4
ISBN 13: 978-0-692-89087-5

Published by Elvelon Press.

www.silvarumbook.com

Printed in the United States of America.
Book design by Dean Kuhta.

10 9 8 7 6 5 4 3

FOREWORD

Every faithful reader of fantasy knows the elements that make up an exceptional quest story the way they know the feel of their favorite novel in their hands: a call to action that cannot go unheeded, characters who must band together to face the looming threat, a journey into the unknown, on which the protagonists will confront magical creatures both malevolent and benign, unexpected tribulations that thwart our heroes at every turn, and a final, epic showdown in which good succeeds in triumphing over evil in a way that makes all the mental, physical, spiritual, and emotional anguish of the journey worth it.

Dean Kuhta's *Silvarum* contains all of these elements and more, and does so in a way that has the reader turning pages as quickly as possible to see what happens next while simultaneously dreading the culmination of each chapter because it means they are one step closer to bidding farewell to Marie, Mckenzie, Roger and the other vividly rendered characters trekking through the pages of Kuhta's wonderful book.

I first discovered Dean's work when I went trekking myself, not through the Whispering Hills or the Shadow Mountains, but through the dealer's room at NecronomiCon in August 2017. A beautiful black-and-white ink illustration of a woman walking along a deserted path, her head cocked strangely and the tentacle of some unearthly creature poking up from the pool of water on her left caught my eye, and I was overcome with the need to speak with this artist who could say so much with a single black-ink drawing while posing countless other questions with the very same print.

Dean and I struck up a conversation, I purchased "She Was Swathed in Sorrow," the illustration that had so struck my fancy, along with another gorgeous and enigmatic print entitled "Windowpane," and a few months later was polishing a short story to contribute to Issue #2 of Dean's newly-resurrected magazine, *Outpost 28*. It was working on this issue together that solidified our tremendously rewarding professional relationship, but it was a mutual love for storytelling aesthetics—be they in the form of a novel, short story, or visual art—that laid the foundations for our friendship.

And speaking of the different mediums of novels, short stories, and visual art, *Silvarum* somehow manages to capture Dean's skill in all three. The novel includes more than a dozen of his signature, masterfully detailed illustrations, as well as an appendix of maps, notes, and artifacts featured in the story, yet these are just the supplemental materials to his dynamic tale. *Silvarum's* narrative also showcases Abigail Somberlain, a character who made an appearance in what seemed to be a short story in Issue #1 of *Outpost 28*. "Little Lonely Girl" followed the immediate aftermath of a young violinist killed in a car crash on her way home from a recital, leaving the reader to imagine their own conclusion for the ethereal, pint-sized protagonist. This ghostly, Gothic tale ended up being a teaser for a *Silvarum* side plot, effectively inviting *Outpost 28* readers to dive into *Book I: Frost* and learn the fate of little, perhaps-not-so-lonely Abigail.

In its entirety, *Silvarum* is an eight-part story that sees a group of plucky teens pursue the runestones of Nexxathia in order to defeat a foe first taken on by their parents and uncle when Trelinia, Benjamin, and Brian were the teens' age. The multi-generational narrative is propelled along by atmospheric prose, deftly-weaved suspense, the most colorful cast of characters encountered in a fantasy series in recent memory, and an impending battle that makes Frodo's struggle against Sauron's legacy and Gollum's teeth on the edge of the Cracks of Doom look like a mere dress rehearsal.

Though there is no shortage of familiar fantastical tropes in the world Dean Kuhta creates, these tropes are employed just enough to give readers a sense of comfort before the author twists and breaks and forges them from scratch with dragon fire and hexadecimal systems into something extraordinarily new.

Good writers know the history of the genre in which they write and give readers a story that sits neatly on synapses previously created over the course of consuming countless fantasy plots and adventure series. The very best writers craft tales that may appear, at first glance, to be the tried-and-true, but that ultimately take their readers on a journey that creates entirely new synapses, synapses that are the equivalent of brilliant, miniature explosions that rip open the minds of their readers, expanding their tastes and capacities for magic so that when they eventually close the book in question, they will never experience fantasy in quite the same way again.

In other words, enjoy the world of *Silvarum*, and relish in the experience of having your mind blown.

Christa Carmen
April 7, 2019

TABLE OF CONTENTS

Book I SILV

Emerald
Bay

Pa

Kadiaphonek

The Wondering
River

Gnoll
Cave

Thorndale

PROLOGUE

"The woods seem somber," said Verdie.

"They're the same damn woods they've always been," replied her brother Taso. He expelled a dramatic sigh, pausing along the trail.

"You promised you weren't going to chicken out on me again. Are we going, or do you want to turn back?"

"No, we're going. We must. I'm not scared this time."

A chorus of brittle leaves trembled in the night breeze. The bony fingers of ancient oaks pointed into the darkness, beckoning the travelers to continue. Crickets chirped amidst the call of a distant whip-poor-will.

Verdie snapped to attention at each sound.

"Are you sure?" asked Taso, laughing.

"Yes."

They advanced along the forest trail as it curled around clusters of sycamores and dipped through mist-enveloped creek beds. Their pace was confident, yet they remained observant. The woods were indeed a familiar environment to both, yet the purpose of this errand was of an unusual nature.

"Tell me again what I'm supposed to do while you're inside?" asked Verdie.

"All you have to do is be my lookout," he replied. "Like a sentry, you know?"

"I know what a sentry is. I'm not stupid."

"I'm glad to hear that, because it's a simple job. Just keep an eye out for that groundskeeper. There shouldn't be anyone else around this time of night. Plus, it won't take me long. I'll pop in and out before you know it, and then we'll have our prize."

"How much do you think it's worth?"

"That depends on the buyer. That one vendor from Gravesend said he'd give me two hundred gold for it. But then Lonzo claimed that if we can get it to him before he closes tomorrow, he'd pay three seventy-five. He's full of shit though. He can't possibly think I've forgotten what he pulled on Victor last summer."

"Was that the mix-up with the little mechanical device?"

"Yea, but it wasn't a mix-up at all. Victor let Lonzo borrow the device for the weekend so he could analyze it, and then the guy conveniently loses it." Taso made air quotes with his fingers.

"We go into this other shop in Kad a week later and see the damn thing sitting on the shelf. It still had the little scrapes on it from when Victor tried to open the case."

"I've never trusted that guy. So, if we can't count on him, do you think two hundred will be enough? Can you haggle with that other dealer?"

"I can try, but he's a stubborn old geezer. I do trust him, though. He's a lot more familiar with this type of technology than I am, and if he says it's worth that much, then I believe him."

"But is two hundred enough to get Karl back?"

Taso took a sip from his water pouch and wiped his mouth. "I hope so."

They continued along the trail in silence. The faint glow of Taso's lantern was their only light. It bobbed from side to side as he held it aloft. The hum of the crickets blended with the hoot of an occasional owl. A heavy downpour from the previous day had left the forest musty and damp.

They entered the eastern edge of Blackwood Forest and soon flanked the gentle slopes of Maple Hill. Verdie peered up to its crest and saw strange shapes in the mist. Ancient standing stones and peculiar monoliths protruded from the turf. She had seen the structures on several occasions in the daylight, but something about them this evening seemed off. Their shapes and angles were wrong. Verdie focused her eyes into the gloom.

"Hey," said Taso, pinching her arm.

She leapt with a panicked squeak.

"Goddamnit, don't do that!"

"I thought you weren't scared out here."

"I'm not, but cut that shit out, will you?"

"Sorry," said her brother. "I looked back and you weren't there. What are you doing?"

Verdie composed herself and motioned toward the grassy dome that emerged from the canopy.

"What am I looking at? The trees?"

"No," she replied, pointing to the shapes on the hill.

The shapes were gone. Maple Hill itself was gone.

"There were stones up there," she muttered.

"What?"

"The statues on Maple Hill," said Verdie.

"I know the place."

"It was right there a second ago and I saw weird things on it. Strange shapes."

Taso was losing his patience. "Right. I don't see anything like that now, so it must have been the mist or something."

He turned back to the trail and held up the lantern.

"Let's get going. We're not far now."

Verdie hesitated, uncertain of her perception. She glanced

back to the phantom hill, shook her head in confusion, and then trotted up the trail to her brother.

"Can I ask you something?" Taso said once he heard the leaves crunching behind him again.

"Sure."

"It's about Karl."

"Okay."

"Even if we do sell this thing for enough money, and they actually give him back, how the hell are we going to explain all this to Mom and Dad?"

"I have no idea. I haven't thought that far ahead. I'm still struggling with the fact that our little brother's been kidnapped, and it's our fault."

"That's not exactly true."

"Really? We left Karl with her, and now he's gone. How's that not our fault?"

"We don't know for sure that she did it. Why would our teacher be involved with something like this?"

"I saw her do it. She passed him off to some other lady and they disappeared into the crowd. The expression on Karl's face still haunts me. He was so scared and confused. For God's sake, he's only five."

"I'm going to kill them," said Taso.

"Who?"

"The bastards who took him. I'm not letting them get away with this. I don't care how tough they think they are. Once we get Karl back, I'm going after them."

"All right, but let's focus on our current ordeal, okay? I can barely comprehend what we're about to do, let alone fight some strange adults."

Taso looked back at his sister with raised eyebrows. "I thought you'd try to discourage me."

"Why would I? I want the people who did this punished just as much as you do, but a bunch of kids are going to have a hard time. If you really want to go after them, we'll need help."

"Can I see the letter again?" asked Taso.

"Why? You know what it says."

"Just give it to me. There's a description of the device and I need to look at it for a second."

Verdie took a crumpled piece of paper from her pocket. "Here."

"Thanks," said Taso, holding it up to the lantern.

The flickering light revealed a few paragraphs of text and a roughly drawn map. Several symbols and cryptic notes were scattered around the edges.

"Did you find it?" asked Verdie.

"Yep," said Taso. He blew out the lantern and crouched behind a fallen tree stump.

"What's wrong?"

"We're here."

***

A gentle rain fell as Taso and Verdie examined the mausoleum. Its stonework was crumbling and ancient. A grand pediment was held high by a cluster of Corinthian columns. Hieroglyphs were carved into the surfaces, but from this distance they appeared diffuse and elusive. To either side of the structure was a scattering of well-kept gravestones and statues. Several bouquets rested before the stony epitaphs of departed loved ones. A break in the clouds revealed the pale flush of a waxing crescent amid the overlap of distant fir trees.

"Are you ready?" asked Taso.

"No, but we have to do this for Karl."

"That's the spirit."

Taso stowed his lantern in his backpack and crept around to the edge of the tree stump.

"This place is definitely active, but I don't see any signs of that creepy groundskeeper."

"His name's Jarvis," whispered Verdie. "I remember him from when we were little. I used to see him in town occasionally when Mom dragged me around on her errands. He would always tip his hat and smile. He's not that bad."

"Maybe, but I doubt he's going to throw a party if the two of you are reunited now."

Verdie rolled her eyes. "Let's get this over with."

With a final glance to either side of the trail, they dashed across the wet leaves and into the cemetery. The fabric of their cloaks brushed against the dimpled stone of the main structure as they sought shelter in its shadows. Taso eased around the corner of the mausoleum to look through the space between the front columns. He peered into the darkness for a moment and then climbed onto the portico.

"Wait," said Verdie.

Taso scaled the side and disappeared.

"Shit." Verdie crouched back down to the ground and frantically surveyed her surroundings. The rain had picked up and the deep rumble of distant thunder mingled with the swell of blowing leaves. Verdie felt a sudden emptiness in her stomach. A sense of dread washed over her. She wanted to get away.

"Psst," whispered Taso from above. He poked his head between the columns. "Where are you going?"

"I don't like this plan anymore. Something's not right."

"What are you talking about? It's fine. The front door is unlocked. Stay here and keep a look out and I'll be right back."

Verdie stared back at her brother with terrified eyes. "Please, Tas. Let's get out of here and come back tomorrow during the day."

"Goddamnit, no," he said with a flash of rage. "You were too chicken shit to do this during the daylight yesterday. What makes you think you're going to be brave tomorrow? We'll get caught during the day anyway. Now stay here and keep watch and quit being such a damn baby."

Taso vanished again without another word.

Verdie sunk into the shadows of the outer wall and raised her hood. Why did he have to always yell at her like that? She took a deep breath and watched the trail and surrounding tree line. The tapping of raindrops on leaves melded with the sound of swaying branches in the wind. She forgot about the unpleasantness of her current situation for a moment and absorbed the calming sounds.

Clank. Clank. Clank.

Verdie spun to her left at the noise.

"Taso, is that you?"

There was no response.

She waited a few more moments and then called out again. Still nothing.

The emptiness in her stomach was unbearable. Her heartbeat raced, and her vision faded around the edges. It was another panic attack for certain.

"Not now," she said. "Please not now."

She thought about her little brother Karl and how scared he must be at this very moment. Where did his captors have him? Was he locked in a room? A cage? Was he in pain? Whatever horrors he was experiencing were infinitely worse than some noises in a little graveyard. She needed to be strong for him and do her part. Verdie blinked away her trepidation and looked back to where she had heard the clanking. She cocked her head and listened.

Clank. Clank.

There it was again, but not as harsh as the first time.

Verdie tip-toed to the back corner of the structure and slowly peered around the corner. She laughed to herself.

A broken water pump handle knocked against the rusted face of its central casing.

"Jarvis won't be happy about that," she said as she turned around.

She knelt in her hiding spot and continued her sentry duty. The rain and wind had stopped, and the lingering moan of thunder was barely discernable in the distance. The crickets resumed their previous chorus.

Verdie examined her surroundings again. The trail that faded into the forest. The looming oak trees with their bony fingers. The wet leaves and grass that covered the small plot of graves. She sighed and looked up at the dark space between the mausoleum columns. *Taso should be back by now.*

A face looked back at her, but it was not her brother's.

"Fuck!" she screamed and scrambled to her feet.

"Girl! What are you doing there?" shouted an old man. It was the groundskeeper.

"I…I'm…I," stuttered Verdie. She was frozen with fear.

"This is private property. Get out of here now or you'll be in some real trouble."

"I can't," she said.

"Whatcha mean you can't? Be gone!"

"My brother's inside and I can't leave him."

"You're grave robbers then?" sneered Jarvis. "You know what the punishment is for robbing graves? Death."

The old man pulled a dagger from his belt. "Stay right where you are, little lady."

Footfalls smacked upon the front steps as Jarvis raced around the structure. He was dreadfully nimble.

Verdie spun on her heels and sprinted in the direction of the broken water pump. The saturated turf impeded her pace and caused her to kick up bits of dirt and mud. She slipped to one knee but managed to catch herself and continue forward. The enraged breathing of the groundskeeper was right behind her.

She raced around the back wall and paused at the adjacent corner. She had two options for escape. Option one was to burst through the tree line and run like hell through the forest, abandoning her brother and probably ruining the only real chance they had at obtaining enough money to save Karl. The second option was to descend into an open cellar that resided to her left and led to God knows where. Verdie only had a few seconds to make her decision before she had to confront option three. Hand-to-hand combat with a crazy old man wielding a blade. Unsure if she was making the right decision, she leapt into the cellar, slamming and latching the door behind her.

Her new environment was pitch black. She reached into the stale air for a wall or anything solid to guide her path. Behind her the locked cellar door rattled, muting the shouts of the groundskeeper. He would surely run around to the front entrance and continue his pursuit, but for the time being, she was safe.

Verdie stepped forward into the unknown. Her boot knocked into a metallic case, spilling tools across the dirt floor. She hopped away from the clatter, brushing against the solid stone of a wall. With both hands, she followed its coarse texture until her fingertips met the grooves of a doorway. She turned a handle and entered a torchlit chamber.

Stacks of coffins lined the walls and floor. Across the room, an open passageway beckoned. From its mouth radiated a series of disconcerting sounds. Tormented cries for mercy amid the taunts of malicious laughter. One of the voices sounded like Taso. Verdie navigated between the caskets and descended a flight of stairs.

She reached the bottom and gasped. Her brother lurched forward on his knees, streams of blood flowing from his mouth and nose. Standing over him loomed a tall man. In the torchlight, Verdie noticed a thin, crimson scar that ran vertically from his eyebrow down to the middle of his cheek.

The man looked up and examined the girl.

"Is this the brave sister that you were mumbling about?" he said as he propelled a heavy boot into Taso's stomach. The boy sobbed in pain and vomited.

The man casually stepped away from the mess. "Well, she certainly doesn't look like she's going to save you. As a matter of fact, she looks positively terrified."

Verdie had succumbed to the most extreme panic attack of her young life. All logic and perception had evaporated from her current reality.

"Grab her."

Powerful hands pulled Verdie from the steps and held a dagger to her throat. The stench of ale flowed from her assailant's smirking mouth. Resistance was impossible in her current state. She went limp and could only observe in terror.

"Before we part ways," said the scarred man, unsheathing his long sword. "I wanted to commend the two of you, whoever you are, for your attempted gallantry this evening. Although you couldn't possibly have had any understanding of the device you sought to retrieve from this tomb, you were helpful in our efforts to acquire it. Your brother had located the artifact before my companions and I arrived, so that saved us a little time. And you, of course, were crucial in distracting that annoying Jarvis."

Harsh laughter emanated from within the chamber.

The scarred man shrugged at the absence of a response from either Taso or Verdie.

"Very well," he said, raising his sword.

"Wait," said Taso.

The man hesitated. "What is it?"

Taso spit a wad of blood onto the floor. "I want to say something to my sister first."

"By all means," replied the man.

"I'm sorry, Verdie. I'm sorry I yelled at you earlier. You didn't' deserve that. I love you."

The scarred man nodded with approval. "Well said."

A single swing sheared Taso's head from his body. Blood erupted from the exposed cavity as his corpse fell to the floor. His arms twitched for a moment and then were still.

Verdie did not scream.

"Interesting," said the scarred man as he approached.

Verdie would meet her fate with the blade after all. The sensation as his sword's tip punctured her chest and sliced through her aorta was painful on a level that she could not process. A deep melancholy washed over her with the realization of her impending death. The man who clutched her from behind yanked her head back and dragged his blade across her exposed jugular. As she slipped into oblivion, Verdie's final thoughts were of her brother Karl and her parents.

PART I
THE WOODS

CHAPTER I

THE RUNESTONES

"Grab my hand," said Roger.

"Pull me up, my foot slipped," replied Marie.

"I'm trying," he said. "Quit whining so much and take my hand before I get bored and leave you dangling up here for the rest of the day."

Marie grunted and extended her hand. Her brother grasped it and pulled with all his strength. Emerald and amber leaves spilled through the canopy of the elm tree as she brushed herself off.

"Your turn, Mckenzie," said Roger. "Please don't take forever like your sister. My arm's sore now."

"Poor baby," replied Marie.

"I'll only be a second," said Mckenzie. "Watch this."

"Wow, you're almost as good a climber as I am."

"Almost as good?" she said as she ascended the branches.

"You forget who you're talking to, little brother. I could beat you to the top of a tree any day of the week."

"Sure," he said. "All right, let's do what we came up here to do. Get the pens and role of parchment out."

Marie groaned. "Why are you so bossy today? Did Mom take away your allowance again for not keeping that stinky little pig pen you call a room clean?"

"No," replied Roger. "And I'm not being bossy, you're just too slow. Now hurry up before Mr. Bluestream catches us up here."

"He doesn't care if we're in his tree on another one of your silly adventures, Roger," said Mckenzie. "Stop picking on Marie and let's just try and have some fun for a change."

She turned and winked at her little sister.

"Thanks," said Marie.

"Anytime."

"Fine," said Roger. "Marie, may I pretty please with sugar on top have the parchment and a pen from your backpack?"

"When you ask nicely like that, yes you may."

The teenagers crawled to the edge of a gnarled branch and peered out over the valley. The summer sky was a brilliant blue over the village of Thorndale.

"I've never seen the town from this perspective," said Marie. "How many people do you think live here?"

Roger unrolled the parchment and organized his map-making supplies. "I'd say around five hundred or so."

"No way," replied Mckenzie. "I know for a fact that there are a hundred and forty-four villagers. Were you paying attention in class the other day? Mrs. Roberts taught us all about the people and history of Thorndale."

"Of course he wasn't paying attention," said Marie. "He was probably day-dreaming of fighting goblins and ghosts with his little wooden sword."

"Or climbing into trees on a perfectly gorgeous Saturday morning," said Mckenzie.

"Actually," replied Roger, not bothering to turn. "The reason we're in this tree is to complete the assignment Mrs. Roberts gave us. Were *you* paying attention? We each have to create a detailed map of the town. And my sword isn't wood. It's a finely polished, White Oak short sword."

The girls giggled.

"Good grief," said Mckenzie. "Whatever you say. And we already finished our assignments, for your information. Marie and I went to the library and looked in books to study the village as normal people do."

"That's not normal," replied Roger. "I'm making my map the right way. The adventurer's way. Merkresh taught me that the best method to make a map is to explore the actual area and experience it yourself. What you guys did was cheating and doesn't count."

"Not that Merkresh again," said Marie. "Is that where you've been hiding out these days? He's a weird old man. Mom says that we should stay away from him."

"Why?" asked Roger. He turned around to face them. "Merkresh is very intelligent, and he's been everywhere on great adventures. You should see the maps and drawings and neat stuff in his shop."

"Mom didn't say why we should stay away from him. She just did. Maybe you should ask her yourself."

"I'll do that. Now for the love of the Great Forest, can

you two please let me finish my map in peace?"

"Certainly, great adventurer Roger!" replied Mckenzie. "Come on, Marie. Let's climb over to the other side and leave bossy pants to his maps and wooden swords."

"It's White Oak!" he shouted.

***

"Whose house is that?" asked Mckenzie as she pointed to a gathering of neatly tended farmhouses. A thin sliver of blue smoke curled up from one of the stone chimneys.

"That's the Leaftail family's house. And next to them are the Rawthornes. Do you know the new girl, Arina?"

Mckenzie nodded.

"They moved into town a couple weeks ago," said Marie. "It's just her and her father, but she seems pretty nice. She likes magic at least."

"Is she as good as you are with magic?"

"She's way better actually," replied Marie. "She did this trick the other day where she made a little garden gnome come to life. Do you know the statue in the middle of Mr. Greatmane's garden? Arina waved her wand around and the gnome started blinking and looking around. I totally screamed."

"That's amazing," said Mckenzie.

"That little guy walked around the garden for a minute and then she turned him back to stone. It was wonderful. She laughed and said that she had named him Phillip. I have a feeling she was only playing around, though. I could tell she's really advanced with magic."

"Do you know where she and her dad moved from?"

Marie thought for a moment. "She told me that they used to live in a village called Briargulch. It's somewhere deep in the forest, but I've never heard of it or seen it on any maps. She said they moved here because her dad got a new job at the hospital with Dr. Skybeam."

"Her dad's a doctor?"

"Yes."

"Then maybe he can help me with a potion that's been giving me trouble. It's a healing potion. Well, it's supposed to be a healing potion. Actually, all it does now is turn things purple. I asked Frederick to test it out for me, and his arm turned a funny shade of purple for an hour. Why it turned purple is a mystery to me, but he said it didn't hurt or anything."

"Poor Frederick," replied Marie. "He always ends up being your test subject."

"I know, right?" said Mckenzie. "But he's a good sport about it. I'm surprised that he hasn't grown a tail or gone blind after all the stuff I've made him drink."

"He likes you. That's why he's a good sport. You think he enjoys being turned weird colors or have disgusting warts grow on his face for the fun of it?

"Frederick? He's only twelve years old."

"He's fourteen. And I'm pretty sure he has a crush on you, so maybe you should tone down the medical experiments and be a little nicer to him."

"Point taken," said Mckenzie. "I'll have to find another willing participant. Does Roger have any other goofy friends?"

"Mckenzie!" replied Marie with a grin.

"I'm kidding."

The sisters laughed as they peered out over the bustling

village. Roger mumbled and cursed to himself on the other side of the massive trunk. A gust of wind had almost blown the roll of parchment out of his lap.

"Anyway," said Marie, "I bet Mr. Rawthorne will be able to help you. I haven't talked to him that much, other than a few hellos, but he seems friendly enough. I'll ask Arina for you. We're supposed to hang out tonight."

"I wish I could hang with you guys, but Mom wants me to help her with some things around the house. Chores on a Saturday? Why tonight?"

"Because she's lonely and just wants to spend time with you. Since she and Dad separated, I don't think she's been handling the solitude very well."

"You think so?" asked Mckenzie.

"I do," said Marie. "She seems really sad lately. Haven't you noticed?"

"I haven't been around that much."

"Well, I have been," said Marie. "And I've noticed that she's depressed. Now that Dad's gone on this trip of his, she's even worse. She's been pacing back and forth and checking the mailbox a hundred times a day."

"When was the last time he sent us a letter?"

"About a month ago."

"A month? That's not good. He was sending them once or even twice a week."

"I'm sure Dad's fine, and I'm not too worried," said Marie, "but Mom definitely is. If I were you, I'd spend some time with her tonight and help her with chores or whatever it is she wants you to do. All these recent changes have messed her up, and I think she wants to talk to you about them. You two used to always talk about important stuff together."

"I guess you're right," replied Mckenzie. "I've been so consumed by my projects and adventuring that I haven't been around much this summer. It's nice to be with you now, though. Even if we're just sitting up in this tree."

Another gust of wind blew through the limbs of the elm as Roger shouted out more curse words. The girls grinned and rolled their eyes.

"Hopefully you can stick around longer this time," said Marie. "Good things always happen when the three of us are together. You know that, right?"

"I do," replied Mckenzie. "And I'm going to be around more often. As a matter of fact, there's something I wanted to talk to you about."

"Really? What is it?" asked Marie. She sat up and stared back at her sister.

"I have an idea for another adventure through the woods, and I wanted to know if you'd like to join me this time."

"I'd love to. Where are we going?"

"Into Blackwood Forest."

"That place is haunted."

"I know it is, but I found something on my last trip," replied Mckenzie. "A symbol that references a person or creature that lives in there."

"What did you find?"

"A runestone. Do you know what those are?"

"You mean the drawing in Mrs. Roberts' class? The one hanging up on the wall above her desk. It has a picture of a stone with a weird symbol carved into it."

"Right. She sent me to find this runestone."

"What? You guys are working together?"

"We are. She studies history and archaeology in addition to being a teacher, and she's been sending me out on these hikes to find old artifacts for her. She even gives me a silver coin for each artifact that I bring back."

"Wow," said Marie. "But why in the world do you need me to go? I've never gone on a long hike like that before. At least not outside of Thorndale Woods."

"Because you know magic. And, like you said, when the three of us are together good things happen."

"Three? You mean you're going to ask Roger to come?"

"I already have, and he's agreed. He can be grumpy and annoying, but he's a decent adventurer. Even though I tease him about his sword, he's actually good at using it. I once saw him knock down a giant mole rat with it."

"This is exciting," exclaimed Marie. "The three of us on a dangerous adventure together. But Blackwood Forest? Aren't you scared to go in there? Does Mom even know about this idea of yours?"

"Not yet," replied Mckenzie. "Maybe tonight is the right time to talk to her about it."

"Talk to her about it?" said Marie. "You mean ask for her permission to go? I'm sure the answer will be 'no way,' or 'how crazy do you think I am, young lady?' She might even get upset with you about the previous trips."

"I wouldn't be so sure."

"What do you mean?"

"I haven't yet told you what I found on the runestone to make me want to go into the forest."

Marie turned and stared out across the village. A cool

breeze swept through the limbs of the tree while the cries of a lone crow pierced the distant hills. A door slammed somewhere down in the village. She turned back to her sister.

"Is it something to do with Dad?"

"Yes."

"Oh my," replied Marie, raising a hand to her mouth.

"There are a few smaller symbols on the back of the stone I found," said Mckenzie. "Mrs. Roberts deciphered one of them based on an old book she has. She said the symbol means *Gothkar.*"

"What in the world is a Gothkar?" asked Marie.

"I have no idea, but look at this."

Mckenzie pulled a worn piece of paper from her pocket and handed it to her sister.

"It's a letter from Dad."

"One of the last he sent," replied Mckenzie. "Read the final paragraph."

Marie held the paper up to the morning sunlight and read the lines aloud.

In the morning I'm headed into Blackwood Forest to find Gothkar. I'm hoping that he'll be able to tell me more about this iron key Brian left me. I'll also ask about the fate of the last runestone. We shall see. Based on my encounter with him when we were kids, he wasn't known for his hospitality. I'll write again after I talk to him. -Ben

The sisters looked at one another.

"Dad was supposed to be on a trip for business, but this sure doesn't sound work related to me," said Marie. "Now he's caught up with these runestones too? What is this iron key he mentioned? And was he referring to Uncle Brian?"

"I have no idea," replied Mckenzie. "But there's a bigger story in motion here, and it clearly has something to do with these mysterious runestones."

"What should we do?"

"I think we should talk to Mom tonight and let her know what I've found," replied Mckenzie. "Maybe she'll tell us more about this secret trip Dad went on. I'd also like to visit Kaldor at the library. Mrs. Roberts said he may be able to translate the other two symbols."

"That spooky old owl?"

Mckenzie smiled. "He's an intelligent creature and knows a great deal. He'll probably be able to tell us about the Blackwood Forest and this Gothkar character."

"All right," replied Marie. "Let's go and see if Roger's finished making his map yet or if he's fallen out of the tree."

CHAPTER II

WIND THROUGH THE LEAVES

"Welcome back, girls."

Trelinia Woods smiled through a circular kitchen window that overlooked the foyer hallway. Puffs of steam billowed from an array of bubbling pots and saucepans as she perfected the finishing touches of their supper. She watched as her daughters stumbled through the front door and dropped their backpacks on the floor.

"How'd the map-making adventure go?" she asked.

Marie pulled off her mud-caked boots and socks and let out a sigh of relief. She unwound her bun, letting the long, red hair fall to her shoulders.

"It went okay, but I'm exhausted," she said as she wiped a river of sweat from her brow and plopped herself on the hallway bench. "We walked forever today."

"It was definitely entertaining," said Mckenzie. She eased

off her boots and backpack and stretched out on the floor at the base of the front door.

"Entertaining?" replied their mother. "Let me guess. Was Roger up to his usual antics?"

"You could say that again," said Mckenzie as she locked her hands behind her head and stretched her legs out to their full length. She noticed a small hole had formed at the tip of one of her red socks and proceeded to wriggle her big toe through it.

"I hope you two are hungry," said Trelinia, disappearing from the window to return to the kitchen.

"I'm starving," Marie said.

Trelinia removed a copper pot of stew from the stovetop and carefully ladled the contents into three bowls. Using a wooden tray carved with intricate designs, she carried the bowls of stew out to the dinner table. The clinking of silverware and glasses danced through the hallway as she set the placemats. A comforting aroma of basil and thyme filled the house.

"Supper is almost ready. Please leave your muddy boots in the hall and throw those nasty socks in the washer. Wash your hands before you come to the table, and there's a basin in there to soak your feet. But be quick about it!"

"Yes, ma'am," they replied.

Mckenzie kicked off her sock with the hole and eased herself up from the floor. Marie slowly stood from the bench and followed her sister to the bathroom at the end of the hallway. They both moaned from the soreness in their feet.

"Can you hand me that lavender soap?"

"Sure," replied Mckenzie.

Marie whispered as she scrubbed the dirt and grit from her fingernails. "Are you still telling Mom about the runestone?"

Mckenzie wiped her hands and hung up her towel. "Of course. Don't you think it's time we found out what Dad has really been up to?" she asked.

Marie nodded in agreement while she dried her hands and sat on a stool next to a clawfoot bathtub. She raised her sore feet and gently lowered them into a steaming basin of milky water.

"That feels amazing."

"I hope he's not in trouble," said Mckenzie.

"Trouble?"

"I was thinking while we were walking home, and I'm concerned about this Gothkar character he mentioned in his letter. Who is this guy? What is he?"

"What is he?" asked Marie. "You mean, is he something other than human?"

"Yes, or even worse. I can't imagine anything pleasant living alone in the Blackwood Forest. Based on the few maps that I've seen of that place, there are all kinds of weird and creepy things in there. Graveyards, castles, and other haunted stuff."

"That sounds like the last place I'd ever want to live," said Marie. "But it seems like Dad has met this fellow before, whatever he is. Isn't that what he said in his letter?"

"Apparently. When they were kids."

"Exactly. This Gothkar person was a kid once too, right? That kind of sounds encouraging. Monsters and ghouls aren't typically children, are they?"

"Good question," replied Mckenzie.

The sisters gazed in silence at the steaming liquid and drifted into their troubled thoughts.

***

"How was school today?" asked Benjamin Woods as his children grabbed their coats and walked out the door.

"It was good," replied Roger.

"Bye, Mom," said Marie.

"Goodbye, dear. What are you guys doing tonight?"

"The usual routine," said Benjamin. "But I think we'll go on a big walk too. The weather is lovely this evening."

"A big walk?" said Mckenzie. "We're too old for those."

"Seriously?" he replied. "You're going to complain about big walks? When did walking with your dad stop being fun?"

"Since forever ago," replied Mckenzie.

"I see," he said. "Yes, Trelinia, we'll be grabbing a bite to eat and then taking the dreaded big walk together. See you later."

Trelinia laughed. "See you in a few hours."

After dinner, they headed over to the park. Mckenzie and her father stood on the crest of a hill as Roger and Marie raced down a grassy trail and yelled at the birds.

"Dad," said Mckenzie.

"Yes?"

"Why did you and Mom really split up?"

***

"Hurry it up, slowpokes," said Trelinia from the dining room. "Did you fall asleep in there? The stew's getting cold."

Mckenzie blinked out of her memory. "Sorry about that. We're on our way."

"Oh, Mom. It looks wonderful," said Marie when they finally sat down.

Vermillion linen covered the dinner table. In the middle

of a lace setting stood a large, crimson candle. It was adorned with silver highlights and encircled with green fir clippings that Trelinia had gathered that morning when she checked the mail (for the third time). Twinkling candlelight filled the room with a cheerful glow. Porcelain dinner plates gleamed atop emerald-green placemats. The bowls of stew were still miraculously steaming, despite the amount of time that the sisters had spent recovering in the bathroom. Normally, there were four places set, but this evening there were only three. Trelinia expected Roger to be in later that night, plus he had mentioned that he wanted to visit Merkresh. The old man was going to inspect his map.

"This looks spectacular," said Mckenzie. "What did we do to deserve such a fine meal?"

"Thank you, my loves," replied their mother. "I felt like doing something special for a change. It's been so long since all of us have sat down for a meal together. And I feel like I haven't seen you in weeks, Mckenzie."

Trelinia paused and gazed into the golden candlelight. "To be honest with you, there's something important I wish to speak with you girls about."

Marie and Mckenzie glanced at each other.

"But first, let's eat," she exclaimed, sitting up straight and placing her napkin on her lap. "I know you're both starving. Tell me all about today's adventures. I want to hear what sort of mischief Roger was up to."

The sisters stirred from their uneasy silence and began to eat. Marie dug into her stew as if she had not eaten in days.

"Well," said Mckenzie. "Our grand and marvelous quest began by climbing up to the top of that old elm tree on the edge of Mr. Bluestream's property. You know the one with a clear view of the entire valley and village?"

"Yes, I know the one," replied Trelinia.

"We spent a few hours up there, at least," said Mckenzie. "Roger spent most of the time on one side of the tree, cursing and grumbling with his map, while Marie and I sat on the other side chatting and looking out over the valley. The sound of the wind through the leaves was lovely."

"When it wasn't being disturbed by Roger's cursing," said Marie through a mouth full of stew.

"Indeed," replied Mckenzie. "Once he finished drawing his silly map, we climbed back down. When Marie and I reached the ground, we looked back and couldn't find him anywhere."

Marie giggled at the oncoming explanation.

"Well, what happened?" asked their mother.

Mckenzie cleared her throat dramatically and continued.

"As we searched around the base of the tree, we looked up to behold our dear brother's pants hanging from a branch by one of his belt loops."

"My goodness. Are you serious?"

"Yes, indeed. His pants were dangling in mid-air from a giant tree branch. Minus Roger, of course."

"Good grief," replied Trelinia. "How in the world did he manage that?"

"I can't even begin to imagine, Mom. But I do know that Marie and I watched him run like the dickens down the hill and through a field of pumpkins. He escaped into the forest."

"I'm pretty sure that he was covering his nether region with that big, goofy map he had been working on all day," said Marie. "Proving at the very least, that his map-making skills are useful for something."

They burst into laughter. Mckenzie spewed a fountain of milk clear across her place setting and onto a piece of tree clipping. Marie snorted and howled with such ferocity that she had to struggle to prevent bits of stew from squirting out of her nostrils.

"Bless his heart," said Trelinia as she settled down from her own fits of laughter. "We mustn't tease him about this, you understand? Promise me that you won't. Roger is extremely sensitive about these types of episodes."

She paused to wipe away the tears with her napkin.

"We won't," said Mckenzie. "It's just so ridiculous how he always gets himself into these situations."

"I wouldn't be surprised if a squirrel or some bird has already made a home out of his britches," said Marie.

"All right, ladies, that's quite enough," replied Trelinia. "We've had a good laugh at Roger's expense. Let's give him a break, okay?"

The girls eventually relaxed their fits of laughter with only the occasional outburst and uncontrollable giggle.

"Marie," said Trelinia after a few moments. "Would you please run to the cupboard and fetch me the container of salt? I forgot to refill this shaker."

"Yes, ma'am," she replied as she wiped her mouth and set the napkin in her chair.

Trelinia took a sip of her drink and turned to Mckenzie. "So, my dear. Where have you been off to so often this summer? I'd really like to hear all about your adventures. Are you still working with your teacher? Mrs. Roberts, right?"

"You know I've been working with Mrs. Roberts?" asked Mckenzie.

"Of course, I know. I'm your mother. What I'm not clear on is exactly where she keeps sending you."

"You know about my other trips too?"

Trelinia grinned.

Mckenzie cleared her throat. "Mrs. Roberts and I have formed a sort of partnership over the past year. She's been studying artifacts that relate to her research and sending me out to look for new specimens."

"What's her area of research?"

"Don't you know?"

Trelinia raised her eyebrows.

"I'm sorry. I can't believe that you already know about this. I was actually planning on telling you about it tonight. I've been stressing out all afternoon."

"I'll be honest with you. I've known Mrs. Roberts for many years. Since we were kids."

Mckenzie shifted in her chair.

"Your teacher went to the same school as your dad and me. That seems like such a long time ago."

"Mom," yelled Marie from the kitchen. "There's no salt container in this cupboard. I've searched every shelf."

Trelinia stirred. "I'm sorry dear, can you please run to the cellar and check for me? I may have left it down there."

"Yes, ma'am," replied Marie.

"In addition to updating me on your progress at school, Mrs. Roberts and I still keep in contact on a personal level from time to time. She told me all about your partnership, and just so you know, I think it's a wonderful idea."

Mckenzie let out a sigh of relief.

"However, my dear," said Trelinia in a serious tone, "I

would very much appreciate it if you'd communicate to me when you're venturing out of the village borders. You do realize that many places outside of Thorndale aren't safe, right?"

Mckenzie squirmed in her chair, lowering her gaze to her plate. "Yes, ma'am. I know."

"Where exactly did you go this time?"

The girl muttered something unintelligible.

"I couldn't hear you. Can you please speak up?"

"The old graveyard."

Trelinia put a hand to her mouth. "You went into that graveyard alone? What were you thinking?"

"I was fine," replied Mckenzie, surprised by her mother's dramatic reaction. "It's only a graveyard. I don't understand why you're so upset."

Trelinia lowered her hand and placed it in her lap. "You weren't fine, young lady. You have no idea of the danger you put yourself in by leaving the village alone and venturing into that dreadful graveyard."

"What's wrong with the graveyard?" asked Mckenzie.

"I found it!" exclaimed Marie in triumph as she carried a giant container of salt into the room and plopped it on the table. Silverware and plates rattled under its weight.

"Sit down," said their mother, harshly.

Marie surveyed the solemn expressions of her sister and mother. "What's wrong?" she asked.

Trelinia took off her glasses and placed them on the table. She rubbed her eyes and let out a long sigh. Mckenzie motioned for Marie to get back into her chair.

After a few moments, Trelinia looked back up and smiled at her daughters. She gazed at each of their faces in turn and nodded her head as if in silent conclusion. She acknowledged to herself the significance of this moment. It was the ending of one stage of their lives and the beginning of another.

"Girls, I think it's time that I tell you the real reason why your dad has been away."

CHAPTER III

LITTLE LONELY GIRL

Cold. Dark. Confused.

Abigail opened her eyes. Darkness. A gloom of sovereign purity wept with primordial silence.

"Where am I?"

She blinked her eyes and strained to make out shapes in the void, but there was nothing. Only the darkness. Only the cold. Awakened to the absence of light and devoid of any sense of direction was disorienting. Was she standing? Floating? Lying in her bed? Was she dreaming? Her eyes danced in all directions, desperate to make sense.

Abigail struggled to move and quickly realized that she was lying on her back on a painfully hard surface. Stone perhaps. She tried to sit up.

"Ouch!" she cried as the rough texture of stone slammed against her forehead. A stream of blood ran past her eyebrow and down into her eye. Her lashes blinked madly.

She immediately raised her hand to wipe away the blood and feel the severity of the gash, but her arm would not move. A terrifying panic swept over her. She pressed her hands to either side and felt more stone and more cold. Stone below, stone above, and stone to each side. She was trapped.

"Help me!"

She screamed in utter panic, but her cries fell muted and toneless in the enclosed space. Every inch of her being quivered. She was sweating and frantic. Her breathing became so intense that she was confident she would soon fall into unconsciousness and fade into impenetrable oblivion. She ceased her struggling and wondered how being unconscious could be any worse than her current situation.

Think.

Abigail focused her eyes into the abyss. Into the infinite chasm that swallowed her being. Into her new existence.

Think!

She closed her eyes and focused. In her mind's eye, she saw shapes. The shapes were fuzzy and diffuse at first, lacking volume and form, yet familiar and comforting. She focused harder, and colors slowly emerged from the shapes. Blues, greens, a girl's pink dress, a man's black tie, framed against the ironed creases of a white, button-down shirt. The shapes were standing and clapping. They were whistling and shouting. They were smiling. Yes, it was coming back to her now. She had been standing on a stage looking out into a crowd of cheering people. Her violin recital.

The memories poured through her mind. They carried her thoughts over a waterfall of cascading images.

Faster...

A crowd of clapping parents and students.

Faster...

The shouts of congratulations and praise.

Faster...

The feeling of achievement and happiness.

Faster...

Laughing with her mother in the car ride home.

Faster...

The disturbing screech of rubber against asphalt.

Darkness.

Abigail abruptly opened her eyes and beheld the darkness once again. The void grinned back at her, mockingly. The silence cradled her confused senses. She understood now. The cold. The darkness. The confusion.

She was dead.

***

A thick blanket of sorrow enveloped Abigail with the harsh realization of absolute emptiness and defeat. She shivered under its deathly weight. Tears welled in her eyes and pulsing orbs of crimson disappointment dripped from the forsaken boundary that confined her to the stone coffin. Her new home. The void of death. The final resting place for her tired bones, wrapped tightly within the infinite ages of ghosts and frigid memories. She could sleep now, giving herself willingly to the whispering lulls of the grinning slumber. Her sixteen-year journey among the living was over. Her mom was gone. Her life was gone. She was dead.

"No," said Abigail.

She opened her tearful eyes and glared with hatred into the mocking gaze of the stygian darkness. Foul fingers grasped and clawed at her consciousness. They implored her to succumb to the immeasurable embrace and inevitability of eternal solitude.

"No!" she screamed. Her guttural vocalization leapt from her lips with frightening intensity, saturated with passion and determination. The sound ripped through the void, spinning and twirling, forcing a path through the bitterness. The ghostly fingers grasped and reached for the sound but faltered. They exploded into a blinding storm of countless snowflakes, drifting and falling along the pastoral breeze of Abigail's memories. A faint cry echoed in the depths of the chasm. The boundary had been broken.

She clasped her hands into tight fists. Knuckles cracked, and tendons moaned as an empowering surge of blood rushed up through her face and into her brain. Energy flowed through her limbs, and she felt the warmth filter through her veins. It covered her body with confidence and rejected the frigid clutch of the deathly blanket. With all her remaining strength, Abigail thrust up her hands and forced open the lid to her coffin.

A pale sheet of frozen light burst through the threshold of the falling cover and draped across Abigail's sensitive eyes. The muscles in her face fluttered and cringed. Her teeth grated. Icy puffs of breath streamed from her cracked lips as she raised herself with both hands and climbed out of the casket.

"Do dead people breathe?" asked Abigail as she stood in the middle of a cramped mausoleum. "Do they feel pain and bleed?"

The crypt was dreadfully cold and ancient. Thin fingers of

pale light crept between cracks in the wall's decrepit masonry and illuminated sections of the stone floor. A spider scurried across the crumbling stones and disappeared through a crack in the base of the opposing wall. Thick cobwebs covered every angle and corner of the room.

Abigail slowly turned her head and surveyed the contents of the shadowy crypt. Situated against the far wall, veiled in a gossamer gown of fine webbing and dust, stood a wooden pedestal. Her joints cracked and popped as she walked across the stone floor to investigate.

Atop the pedestal lay a moldy, leather-bound book, shrouded in eons of dust and decay. Iron hinges cradled the binding and a massive lock impeded further analysis of the tome's contents. With a brush of her hand, Abigail swept away a layer of the gray dust to reveal a peculiar symbol on the cover. Carved into the cracked leather, beckoned a pair of overlapping circles. In the middle of the circles peered a single, lidless eyeball. She bent down closer to the symbol to get a better look. The eyeball blinked twice.

"Shit!" she cried, falling back to the stone floor.

A beam of frosty blue light emanated from the eye and searched throughout the room. A whisper, as faint as falling snowflakes, groaned from the pages of the ancient book.

"Who has awakened me?" asked the voice.

Abigail gasped for breath. She shuffled backward on her hands, bumping into the edge of the open coffin. The blue light paused its searching and slowly lowered until it met the girl's frightened gaze.

Calm.

Abigail blinked. She felt at ease.

A soothing orchestra of cathedral bells drifted through her thoughts and carried her from the depths of the mausoleum to the mountainous heights of a snow-covered forest. The contrast from dark to light stunned her perception. In the hazy distance, she perceived a solitary figure that walked among the trees. Now visible. Now hidden.

Abigail walked to the shrouded figure. Her bare feet left soft prints in the snow as she wandered deeper into the silent embrace of the enchanted woods. She approached the figure and paused. Snowflakes fell softly and silently as they faced each other.

"Mom?" asked the girl.

Her mother stood in the falling snow and smiled.

"What's happened? Where are we?" asked Abigail.

"Look at me, child," said a voice.

The snow began to fall harder as her mother turned and disappeared into the forest. She was gone.

"Mother, wait," said Abigail.

"Open your eyes," replied the voice.

Abigail blinked. The snow-covered forest dissolved into a spinning flurry of confusion and light. She opened her eyes and found herself back in the spiteful grasp of the ancient crypt. The blue eye glared up at her from the book's cover.

"No," she cried. "What's happened to me?"

"You are dead," replied the voice.

"Dead? How can I be dead? I'm standing here bleeding. I'm talking. I just saw my mother. That's not being dead."

"And what do you know about death?" it asked. "The life that you knew before is over. What you perceive as death is but a new beginning. The next phase of the endless journey."

Abigail looked down and studied her hands. The wrinkled lines in her palms that she knew so well were still there. The freckle on her left pinky finger remained. They were still her hands. They appeared normal, whatever normal meant in this new reality. Abigail placed her right palm on her chest. Her heart was beating. Its rhythmic pulses echoed softly in the frigid air of the crypt.

"Do you see?" asked the voice.

"See what? I don't understand."

"That you still exist. Your body, the beating of your heart, and the thoughts in your mind. They all still belong to you, yet you are here now."

"Where is here?"

The voice paused. The blue light dimmed slightly.

"Answer me," said Abigail.

"The answer lives in my pages. You must find the key."

"The key? What key? Who are you?"

"I am the Novemgradus," it replied. "I am the mist that always swirls. I am the fog that envelopes myth and legend."

"What does that mean? I don't understand," she replied.

"You will, my child. In time, you will learn."

Abigail stared at the book in silence.

"Find the key and unlock my pages. Within their chapters, you will find your answers. Go now, my child. Go."

The ancient voice faded into a flapping gust of wings.

A door, previously hidden amidst the shadows of the frostbitten crypt, slowly creaked open and revealed a crumbling stairway. Abigail ascended the steps to the unknown.

CHAPTER IV

STEAM AND BRASS

"Hello?" asked Roger through the front door. "Merkresh, are you in there?"

There was no reply. Only the wildlife and wind responded to his repeated knocks. A battalion of crickets sang their evening cadence as a cool breeze blew through the lane. Wind chimes hummed softly from the house across the street.

Roger looked down at his pants and shook his head. How had he fallen out of that stupid tree like that? He could not remember but was certain that his annoying sisters were going to harass him about it for days to come. Probably years. Even his best friend Frederick had teased him when he showed up with that map wrapped around his waist. Could they be blamed for their mockery? It had truly been a ridiculous sight. At least Frederick had let him borrow a pair of old pants, even if they were two sizes too big.

The boy turned to the door and knocked three more times. Still nothing. "Good grief," he said under his breath. "I've been waiting out here long enough."

Roger slowly eased the door open and gazed inside. The interior was dark and musty, reminding him of his grandmother's attic. He heard a faint clatter and clanking of activity deeper inside the shop.

"Hey, Merkresh. It's Roger," he said again, a bit louder. "We were supposed to have an appointment tonight at seven to look at my map. Remember?"

Roger pulled out a brass and mechanical timepiece from his breast pocket. Its face and hands were set within the industrial patterns of a worn cogwheel. He flipped open the polished cover and checked the time. It was 7:34 p.m. After all, Merkresh was terribly old and forgetful and probably just overlooked their appointment. There was no harm in letting himself in. Roger nodded at this reasoning and stepped inside the shop.

Rusted hinges creaked and moaned as he pushed the door open. As he stepped inside, the boy noticed that none of the interior candles had been lit. Only a faint glow from the street lanterns filled the room. The dim light revealed a ghostly impression of the irregular shapes and angles that cluttered the surroundings. He slipped inside and stood perfectly still in the middle of the room. He listened.

Tap. Tap. Shwoooosh.

Ding. Pop.

He tilted his head and focused on the sounds. His hearing was enhanced by the lack of light in the room. The bangs and clanks originated from downstairs.

Pop. Pop. Creeeeeeck.

The second set of noises called his attention to an area at the far end of the room. It was darker in that direction. Roger unstrapped his backpack and knelt on the floor. He unbuckled a leather pouch and felt inside. A folding pocket knife? There was no use for that right now. Fishing line? Nope. Something sticky and small and round? Definitely not. He did not even want to know what that thing was. He felt around some more. It was in there somewhere. Yes, that was what he was looking for. His green glow torch. It was fashioned in a similar style as his timepiece. The design was industrial and fatigued, accentuated by a riveted, brass outer shell and a metal mesh that covered the glass face.

Roger fastened up the pouch (he stuffed the knife in his pocket because every adventurer knows the value of having one handy). He slung on his backpack and cranked up the torch's dynamo. As he switched on the light, the room immediately came alive with a greenish shade of form and structure. He temporarily forgot about the noises from downstairs and stared in wonder at the fantastic objects that filled the shop.

Shelves and shelves of leather-bound tomes crowded the four walls. The enormous collection of books was stacked both horizontally and vertically, filling every possible nook and cranny. Perpendicular to the bookshelves glared glass cases, each one crammed with whimsical shapes and alluring devices. Most were mechanical in nature and were covered with dials and buttons. Other objects highlighted a patchwork of brass fittings, wood paneling, and copper tubing. Several of the specimens were constructed of electronic components.

Roger saw an assortment of mechanical masks in one of the crowded cases. He stared in awe at their complexity and artistic design. Six of the nine masks contained large tubes that curved up from a grated mouthpiece and connected to a rectangular apparatus at the back. Was it a breathing filter of some type? All the masks contained round eyepieces. Some extended out from the face, while others sat flush against leather linings and brass fittings. A mask on the second shelf featured a nose piece in the shape of a long beak, like some mechanized bird. Chrome rivets peppered the polished straps and linings that encompassed the curious designs.

One of the masks caught Roger's attention and curiosity. Situated on the top of the case, next to a mechanical glove, glared an unusual contraption. On its crest sat a leather top hat. Like most of the other masks, it contained the filter hoses, circular eye lenses, and brass gadgets.

"But why the top hat?" asked Roger. He would have to ask Merkresh about its purpose.

In the green light, the glass cases reflected and permeated an ethereal glow throughout the showroom. Capricious shadows danced upon the objects as Roger moved his glow torch and shifted his attention from one wonder to the next. It was an experience of sensory overload. He turned from the masks and surveyed the other side of the room.

Numerous shelves of books and cases stood on this side. Instead of masks, however, these glass displays were filled with weapons of war. There were firearms of all types and sizes, crossbows, and long swords. They were all mechanized and as elaborately artistic and impressive as the masks. A tremendous composite bow, as tall as Roger, hung above one of the cases. Its technical characteristics were absurd. Gears, pistons, and tubing created a brass tapestry along the bow's limbs.

Roger walked to a rack of longswords. As he crossed the floor, his right boot kicked a hard object that emitted a buzzing sound. He froze in place. All was silent except the chirping crickets from outside. Even the weird sounds from downstairs were gone. He hesitated for another moment and then continued to the display of blades.

The boy had visited Merkresh's shop a hundred times, yet on each occasion, his mind raced with thoughts of adventure and mystery. Each visit was a privilege that offered a brief glimpse into an alien world that was filled with enchantment and life. Being exposed to this amount of knowledge and technology was infinitely more interesting than sitting in a boring classroom every day learning about fractions and long division. The books written in mysterious tongues and symbols, the inexplicable artwork that hung on the walls, and the steam-powered devices. Where did Merkresh obtain all these outlandish curiosities? Over the years, Roger had asked about his travels countless times. Merkresh always smiled in return, proclaiming that one day he would speak of his astounding adventures. Roger wondered if that day would ever come.

He reached into his breast pocket and rechecked the time. Roger let out a shriek of terror as the green glow of his torch shined onto the timepiece. A giant spider sat on his forearm. It was the size of his hand and had eight thin legs that were tapping and searching. He shook his arm in a frantic motion to get it off, but it did not budge. He waved his arm even harder. The spider was attached to his shirt sleeve and was not going anywhere. Roger pointed the torch back on the monstrosity and realized that it reflected the green light. He focused his eyes and examined it carefully. The spider was made of brass and metal. Delicate gears and pistons connected to each of its eight legs. The main body contained miniature dials and sensors. Eight glass eyes, all black as pitch, peered from its head. It was not a real spider at all. It was a machine.

"Click! Get off Roger's arm right now," said a voice from the darkness.

A buzzing hum emerged from the spider's gears as it turned its head toward the command. It hopped from Roger's arm and scurried across the floor.

A sharp mechanical twang pulsated through the walls and illuminated a multitude of gas-powered lanterns. The chamber glowed with new life and color. A figure stood across the room from Roger. It was clad in a gray cloak, a vest with many pockets, and a mechanical glove. The individual also wore a mask that contained large eye lenses, an elaborate magnification device, and an acoustic feature that resembled a miniaturized brass horn. Each component was covered with intricate gears and piping. The mechanical spider was perched on the figure's shoulder.

"Is that you, Merkresh?" asked Roger.

The figure reached up with its mechanical glove and turned a white knob below one of the rubber hoses. Jets of steam hissed from either side as he slowly unbuckled several leather straps and removed the mask. The venerable face of Merkresh Warington smiled back. His long, white beard and bushy eyebrows complemented the brass composition of the steam-powered equipment.

"Hello, lad," he replied. "What brings you by my shop on this fine evening?"

"I thought we had an appointment at seven. You said I could show you my map, and you'd give me some feedback."

Merkresh rubbed his beard thoughtfully. "Oh dear," he replied. "I'm sorry, Roger. You're right, of course. I completely forgot about our appointment. I've been locked away in my workshop all day. There's just so much to do."

Roger shrugged and smiled. "It's okay, Merkresh. I can come back another time if you're too busy now." He reached down and switched off his glow torch and turned back toward the front door.

"Heavens no," replied Merkresh in protest. "Our meeting will still be honored. As a matter of fact, I'm very excited that you're here." The old man thought for a moment and continued to fiddle with his beard. "Let's review the accuracy of your map, as we intended, and then I'll give you a demonstration of the project I've been working on. I could use your feedback as well. Does that sound like a plan?"

"That sounds perfect."

"Very well," replied Merkresh. "Now, let's see if we can find some empty table space to inspect your map."

They glanced around the clutter-filled room. Every inch was occupied by some gadget, device, or book.

Merkresh frowned. "This will not do at all."

He placed his mask and mechanical glove upon a stack of books and opened a brass panel filled with knobs, switches, and colorful dials.

"I've not used this thing in ages, but I believe this turns it on," he said as he flipped two switches and turned four dials.

Motors clanked and murmured within the ceiling and floor. Jets of white steam shot out from a matrix of copper tubing along the nearest wall. Roger stared in wonder.

"I'll be surprised if this still works," said the old man.

Three slots in the ceiling slid open and revealed long rubber hoses that snaked and searched through the air. Each hose contained a brass funnel at the end that produced sharp sucking sounds. They crept and twisted toward the center of the room. An industrial crank table sat near Roger. It had been previously concealed due to the enormous number of blueprints, notes, sketches, and other assorted clutter. The hoses encircled the table in unison and sucked up all the papers and objects.

Shwooomp!

Shwuuump!

Shwaaamp!

A polished metal surface, pockmarked and bruised from decades of use, glimmered up at them. The table's chrome crank wheel and heavy-duty steel legs mirrored the industrial theme of the workshop.

Merkresh clapped. "I'm amazed that gizmo still works after all these years."

"Where are all those things going?" asked Roger.

"Wait," replied the old man. "It's not over yet. This is the best part."

Roger followed the bulges and lumps of the objects in the tubes as they disappeared into the ceiling. The hoses themselves then escaped back through the slots. More steam vents whirled above their heads as metallic clamps opened and closed in rapid succession. The boy and the old man stared upward.

Merkresh motioned with his index finger for Roger to watch the wall on the opposite side of the room. The boy twirled around while still staring straight up and then tilted his head to focus on a massive bookshelf. Like everything else in the room, it was the personification of disarray. Gears and pistons produced a sharp clank, and then each of the shelves receded into the wall and out of view. Some of the books and papers that sat near the edge of the shelves fell to the floor. Merkresh grunted at this observation and scribbled into a small notebook.

As each cluttered shelf was pulled back by conveyor belts into the wall, a new shelf, perfectly organized and tidy, slid into its place. They all contained neatly folded scrolls, papers, and blueprints organized and set into metal bins, and leather-bound books that were set upright in alphabetical order by author.

"Wow," said Roger. "That was incredible."

Merkresh tapped a pencil onto his notebook and shook his head. "It does work fairly well, I suppose, and I'm certainly impressed that it still functions after all these years. Apparently, I haven't used it to clean up this place in a long time. Nevertheless, I think I'm going to have to log a couple of defects."

"Defects?" asked Roger.

"Those items shouldn't have fallen off the shelves like that, for one. I could probably integrate some metal netting along the edge that would pop up and catch any outliers." He scribbled some more notes into his small book and grumbled to himself. "Secondly, the sorting algorithm doesn't seem to be calibrated correctly anymore. I'm sure you noticed that the books are in reverse alphabetical order based on the fourth letter of each author's last name."

Roger scratched his head and stared at the old man.

"Aww, who cares anyway," said Merkresh as he threw the notebook and pencil over his shoulder. "What's really important is that we now have a clean table to unfurl your map on. Bring her here, lad, and let's have a look."

Roger unstrapped his backpack once again and carefully

took out the map. He unfolded it and they each took an end. Merkresh grabbed a random book *(Cruniac's Principle of Elastic Modulus and Transverse Isotropy, Vol. 89)* and placed it on his edge to keep the map flat. Likewise, Roger set another leather-bound tome *(Essential Adiabatic Theorems and Quantum Perturbations, 13th Edition)* on his end.

"Excellent," said Merkresh. "This will do nicely."

As the old man leaned over and studied the details of the topography and geographic elements, the mechanical spider crept down along his arm and hopped onto the parchment.

"Hey there, Click," said Merkresh.

The spider raised itself upon its eight limbs and expelled a series of motorized squeaks. A rotating dish antenna spun in circles as the mechanical creature danced and sang.

"Where did you get that thing?" asked Roger.

"I built him from scratch, of course. It took me a whole weekend. His name's Click. Isn't he cute?"

Roger peered at the brass arachnid and grimaced.

The old man snickered at his expression. "You're not a lover of spiders are you, real or mechanized?"

"I'm afraid not," replied the boy. "I had an unpleasant experience with one of them when I was younger."

"I see," replied Merkresh. "Click won't bug you. He's more like a survival knife than a real spider. If you're ever in a pinch, this fellow will be able to get you out of it."

"What can he do?" asked Roger.

"All kinds of fantastic things, but we don't have time to get into the details now. Instead, let's review this magnificent map of yours, shall we? There's still so much to do."

Roger motioned to his illustrated map and described the

major landmarks of Thorndale and its surrounding countryside.

"Basically, I focused on the main streets and avenues of the village and then worked outward to the isolated locations."

"A very logical technique," said Merkresh.

"Here's the main street with all the shops and stores. As you can see, I've labeled each shop's function and owner. Then extending out from the central marketplace, I've attempted to catalog each house along with the family's name. This is my neighborhood and here's the smaller one on the other side."

He tapped on the specific locations. Click moved out of his way each time. His motors and pistons buzzed with activity.

"Over here's the schoolhouse, the main park, town hall, the post office, the library, the grocery store, the hardware store, hospital, your shop, the bank, and Leaftail's Bakery."

"Very nice," said the old man.

"Finally, I chose to implement a border around the local area here." He pointed toward a dotted line that encapsulated the entire village, nearby woods, and streams. Beyond its boundary was much less detailed. "Having never been beyond this border myself, the rest of the map is a work in progress."

Merkresh nodded with approval. "This is fantastic work, my young friend. Not only have you illustrated the shops, homes, and natural features with the skill of a master artist, but you've also accurately incorporated the basic principles of cartography."

Roger smiled.

"Can you please tell me what those three principles are?" asked the old man.

"The fundamental purpose of cartography is to articulate the geographical information of an area graphically."

"Correct."

"The first principle is beauty," said Roger. "The second is accuracy, and the third is communication."

"Well done," said Merkresh.

Click hopped up and down in the center of the map and chirped his mechanical applause.

The old man walked to the opposite side of the map and bent down low to study the upper corner in detail. An elaborately drawn ink legend contrasted against the yellow-beige tint of the parchment. It was illustrated in the shape of an eight-pointed star, with a face in the center, and encircled by eight symbols.

"Roger. The compass rose that you've depicted here is rather spectacular. Where did you come up with these symbols?"

"A compass rose? Is that what it's called? I've only ever known of it as a legend. For depicting the four directions of a compass. I guess I got a little creative in my interpretation."

"A little? This is wonderful. A compass legend is also known as a Rose of the Winds or a Star of the Sea. The eight-pointed rose that you've created here was historically used to portray the eight principal winds. They include the four cardinal directions: north, east, south, and west."

"And the four intercardinal ones, right?" asked Roger. "Northeast, northwest, southeast, and southwest."

"Exactly," said Merkresh. "You're really improving with your cartography knowledge."

They turned back to the map and continued to study its contents. The old man examined the compass in detail.

"But tell me," said Merkresh, "where exactly did you get the idea for this design?" He tapped his finger on the symbol located between the north and northwest points. It was a triangle encircled by a ring at its center.

"Oh, that one?" replied Roger. "I saw it in a dream not too long ago. It's actually supposed to represent a giant pyramid that has a gold ring orbiting its center. It sounds silly, and it's kind of hard to explain, but the golden ring is, in my dream at least, constantly spinning around the pyramid. There were eight other objects that formed the shape of the pyramid, but I felt that adding them would be too complicated. I wanted to keep the design simple, and I thought it might look neat as a little symbol on my map."

"Roger," said Merkresh, dumbfounded. "That place you dreamed about is real."

CHAPTER V

PATTERNS IN THE MIST

A gray sky frowned upon the North Gate. Pockets of fog hung in the nearby fields and crept up from the dark chasm that encircled the castle walls. A group of gate guards gathered at the end of a lowered drawbridge and peered out into the gloom of the early morning light. Puffs of icy breath escaped their lips as they quietly spoke to one another.

"Can you tell me more about these people we're waiting for?" asked a young guard named Belris. His nervous eyes danced upon the road as he anticipated the approaching caravan.

Sergeant Brian Woods, an older, grim-faced guard, worn down by decades of battle and adventure, spat a wad of liquid onto the muddy road. A bit of rancid juice dangled from the knotted mess that he called a beard.

"They're not people. They're monsters."

The sergeant paused in mid-speech and pressed a finger

to one side of his nose. As he blew, a stream of gray-green snot sprayed out of the other nostril.

The young guard cringed in disgust and then stared in mild fascination down at the wad of bubbling spit and goo. It had attracted a group of insects and flies. He shifted the heavy sword that hung from his belt and looked up into the fog.

"What exactly do you mean by monsters?"

"Exactly what I said," replied Brian. "They're horrible, and awful, and hideous, and any number of other negative adjectives you can think of. What more do you need to know about them to perform your duties?"

Belris cleared his throat. "Yes, sir. What I meant to ask was, what is it about these creatures specifically that makes them so horrible? Are they horrible looking, or horrible sounding, or do they smell horrible?"

"One moment, private," said Brian with a raise of his hand. He motioned to another guard who stood behind them near the gatehouse.

The gate guard trotted across the bridge, his heavy armor jingling with each stride.

"Yes, sir," he said.

"Corporal," said Brian. "Where do we stand with the riflemen I requested?"

"Sir, they're in place and ready atop the curtain wall."

"All of them?"

"Two, sir."

"Two? I requested six. Why would we only have two?"

The corporal stirred and cleared his throat. "Captain Hamonet felt this exchange only required two riflemen."

"Did he?" replied Brian. "Well, I hope Captain Hamonet

has made the correct decision for a change. It would be a shame if there was trouble and we required the firepower. Remember what happened last time?"

"Yes, sir," replied the corporal.

Brian thought for a moment and then shook his head in frustration. "Fine. Return to your post and wait for my signal. Our guests should be arriving presently. When I wave to you, open the gate to let the captain and his guards out to greet them. Do you understand your orders?"

"Yes, sir."

"Very well, corporal."

The gate guard turned without another word and dashed back to his post. His heavy boots echoed against the wooden planks of the drawbridge.

Brian turned back toward the mist-enshrouded road and gazed out into the emptiness. Two riflemen? Seriously? On top of that, he had only been provided a handful of fighters for the encounter. This strategy had become a dangerous pattern. Brian Woods had observed in recent weeks the relaxed posture of this castle outpost and its apathetic leadership. Trade with these creatures had become much more frequent and lucrative over the past year, but it did not justify a decrease in strength during minor encounters such as these. Hostilities had subsided only a few years ago. It was still vital to maintain a show of force, regardless of the insignificance or scale of the engagement. Brian recalled when he first arrived at the castle...

"Anyway," said Belris. "What's so horrible about them? Where do they come from? What do these things look like?"

Brian snapped out of his reverie and glared.

The boy took a few awkward steps backward in surprise.

"For heaven's sake, private," said Brian. "Isn't it a little early in the morning for history lessons? I would really love to explain to you the ins and outs of these monsters that we're standing here waiting for, but honestly, I'm freezing cold and exhausted." Brian stamped his feet and rubbed his hands together to try and generate some warmth. "Maybe if you scare up a hot cup of coffee, I might pursue this conversation further."

Another guard that stood just behind them chuckled in agreement. "Aye," he said. "And don't forget that I take mine with a little cream and two spoons of sugar."

Belris winced at the sergeant's rebuke. "Forgive me, sir, but I'm just a bit anxious this morning. I tend to ask a lot of stupid questions when I'm nervous."

"I noticed," replied Brian.

"Ah, yes," said the young guard and let out a forced laugh. "As you are aware, I was just recently posted to the North Gate, and I've heard about our dealings with these creatures, of course, but I really don't know much more. Is there nothing else that you can tell me?"

Brian expelled a loud sigh. He realized that he was not going to escape this mindless conversation by ignoring the young man or making more jokes. He would have to ease this fresh recruit's fears by answering his questions. This was one of the responsibilities that he had recently been given. Right? To manage and maintain the defense and morale of the castle walls. Of course, answering questions about what they were waiting for would more than likely cause the boy to be even more fearful. Why did Count Zaran insist on sending these kids with no experience out to defend the main gate? Unfortunately, Brian knew the answer to that question. Veterans were in short supply.

Those with any real combat experience had been reassigned to fight on the Northern Front, or they had been lost during one of the count's numerous expeditions into Nexxathia.

Brian raised his eyes out of the muck and looked back at the young guard. He took a deep breath and scratched at his beard. Although he hated to admit it, he had to acknowledge that he was just as scared of these creatures as this boy. Brian had engaged with these beings on multiple occasions. Engaged them in battle. He knew firsthand what they were capable of and the amount of fear that they could inflict on most ordinary men.

Brian wiped a dangling strand of brown spit from his beard and grinned. "All right, lad. Do you want a history lesson? In the few remaining moments that we have before these things arrive, I'll tell you whatever you want to know."

Belris smiled and stepped a few paces closer.

"Thank you, sir," he said as he adjusted his chest plate. "First of all, what are these things actually called? I've only ever heard of them referred to as the Tombspawn."

"They call themselves Nexxathians. We refer to them as Tombspawn because that's where they come from. Deep within the tombs and subterranean crypts under the horrible city of Nexxathia. Regardless of their name, however, they're truly hideous. I wasn't joking with you earlier. If you haven't seen anything like them before, I warn you, it will be a shock."

"I haven't, sir. And I do believe you," replied Belris. "The only creatures I've ever seen were the flying reptiles from the Eastern Swamps, and that was from a great distance. We were stationed high in the cliffs and could barely see them flying and circling from afar. I also saw a group of wild Preevnu during my first patrol, about six months ago, I think."

Brian frowned. "How old are you, private?"

"I just turned eighteen in August, sir."

"This will certainly be an experience that you'll not soon forget. Preevnu are slow and stupid and easy to tame. These Nexxathians, on the other hand, are cunning and deliberate. They're devious. They also possess an ability that's superior to our weapons of steel and fire. They use thought."

"Thought?" replied Belris.

"Aye. They use thought as a weapon. For those who are weak-minded, or fearful, the Nexxathians can paralyze with a thought, leaving them frozen as victims for the other things."

"Other things?" he asked. "What other things?"

"There are a few types," said Brian. "Not all Nexxathians use thought weapons. Some are regular fighters, like you and me. They're still extremely dangerous, but they don't seem to possess the power of the others. Then there are the creatures that are like priests, or holy men. I'm not entirely sure what you call them. I've only seen one or two of their kind before, but they're hideous, and they use magic."

"Magic?" replied Belris. He pulled back the hood of his cloak and wiped away a line of sweat. "Why didn't they tell me any of this during my training?"

"Hey," said Brian. "You wanted to know all the details. You're going to have to deal with that and still do your job. Is that clear? Now pull yourself together, private. You'll be fine."

Belris gulped and took a deep breath. He tried to control his breathing. "Yes, sir. I just need a few more moments, and I think I'll be all right."

Brian released his gaze upon the young man and turned back to the road.

"Unfortunately, you don't have a few more moments," he said. "Something is approaching from the mist."

Belris turned from the sergeant and peered into the fog. A chill silence washed over him as he strained his eyes on the swirling haze. Shapes emerged. All his previous thoughts were immediately erased. His breathing quickly picked up again, and he felt his temples pound with fear. His heart rose into his throat as he started to panic.

A shape emerged from the fog, then two. Cloaked figures rode upon animals with many legs. Hoods concealed the riders' heads as they sat upon high saddles. Another figure was perched from a similar seat atop an enormous gray-green reptile. The creature's neck was so long that its head was hidden within the heights of the gloom. Only two red eyes could be discerned in the darkness. Other obscure figures walked or glided ominously on either side of the beasts. Wisps of white fog quietly swirled over the road as they broke through the foreboding veil.

The encounter had transpired too quickly for Belris. He desperately strained his mind to process what he was witnessing. Never in his eighteen years had he seen, or even heard of, beings so abnormal and terrifying, or float in such a bizarre manner. He yearned to be far away from this miserable road. He wanted to be safe at home, causing trouble with his older brothers, or teasing his sisters as they played with their dolls. At that moment, his thoughts were so confused and uncertain, that he could not even remember how he had brought himself into this situation. Belris glanced to his side, noticing the sergeant's stare.

"Collect your wits, boy," he said between clenched teeth. "Do not show your fear to these creatures. This will be over soon enough."

Brian Woods raised his hand to signal the corporal at the gatehouse. The clinking and strain of heavy chains echoed across the bridge as the main gate door was raised. It bellowed a deep boom, locking into its upright position.

Flanked on either side by two knights, each armed with elaborate broad swords and heavy suits of decorated plate armor, Captain Hamonet cautiously walked toward the edge of the drawbridge. Wooden boards creaked and moaned under the stress of their heavy boots. The three men reached Belris and Brian and halted. They stared into the mist at the approaching caravan. The captain's hand rested eagerly upon the hilt of his sword, and his fingers twitched in anticipation. Like Belris, he was boyish and untested. Barely a man, he had been quickly promoted through the ranks because of his family name, rather than his leadership ability or skill in battle. As with most of the assembled gate guards, he had not had dealings with these creatures before. They watched as the last form emerged from the mist.

Thirteen of the ghoulish figures gathered at the end of the drawbridge and stood motionless. Six were saddled atop colossal, blue-gray spiders. Chaotic legs tickled the puddle-filled road as hundreds of arachnid eyes peered mockingly back at the guards. Two adjacent figures, clad in purple robes, were mounted on the backs of hideously large, reptilian beasts. Their prehistoric necks towered over the humans. A curious collection of skulls dangled from iron chains.

The spider riders were mounted warriors. They sat low on the backs of the arachnids and clasped blades of obscene shape and sharpness. Green liquid dripped from the tips of their weapons, sizzling into the mud with each drop.

Belris gazed along one of the ghastly necks until he met the stare of two red eyes. Puffs of crystal-blue mist emanated from nostrils high above. The remaining figures were on foot at the head of the group. They were clad in flowing cloaks, two of which pulled a covered wagon.

Captain Hamonet cleared his throat and addressed the caravan. "Well met, travelers. What news do you bring from the Northern Lands?"

His feeble voice was lost in the fog. The Nexxathians made no response. Disturbing clicks issued from the spider's jaws and legs. The young captain turned to his guards in confusion. At that moment, one of the massive reptilian necks slowly lowered its head to the ground. Its rider emerged from the saddle and casually walked along the neck to the muddy road. It strode confidently to the front of the group, standing before the captain and his men. A large hood concealed its face.

"Pray tell, mine captain," said a voice that was both high pitched and horribly deep. Several of the gate guards positioned along the parapet gasped aloud in terror. "For, although we have clearly presented to you in plain view the substance you desire, I fail to see the lightdust that is owed to us. I only see fusty men and children before me."

The captain was too startled by the creature's hideous voice to process the insult, nor did he have a clear understanding of the intent of the question. His head pounded. A murky veil of uncertainty blanketed his thoughts and dulled his reasoning.

"Sire," he replied after an anxious moment. "We felt a proper reception was appropriate before we brought forth the goods." He rubbed his eyes painfully. "It's our custom to greet our guests openly and exchange news to…"

The voice interrupted the captain's faltering monologue with a long hiss that ended in disturbing, cackling laughter.

"Nay, human. We care not for your customs, nor your shallow hospitality. We have traveled many leagues, over stone and wood, through space and time, to acquire what we are owed. Bring it hither and let us be done with your company."

"As you wish," replied the captain. He motioned over his shoulder toward the open gate. Two guards pushed a wooden cart across the bridge. The sound of its spinning wheels pierced the captain's perception. He grasped at consciousness and felt the world slip away.

CHAPTER VI

THE LICHGATE

Abigail Somberlain ascended from the mausoleum steps and faced a cloudless sky. The stark contrast between the crisp air and stale tomb tormented her senses. Her skin crawled from the bite of the wind and her eyes burned under the sunlight's unyielding embrace. She raised a thin arm in defense of its gaze. As she reached the top step, her bare feet met the crunch of snow and stone, and she halted. She slowly lowered her arm and felt the gentle kiss of tears upon her cheek. Did they fall from burning eyes, or was she shedding tears of sadness? Probably both. She rose from the darkness of her previous life into the blinding haze of a new existence.

The sensory onslaught of her new setting receded, and Abigail could faintly make out shapes in the gloom. She rubbed her eyes and blinked. Through her tears, she perceived Gothic structures that were ancient and crumbling. Abigail stood amidst an enormous cemetery. She was adrift in an ocean of countless tombstones, statues, and cenotaphs. Leafless oak trees, crooked and malformed, congregated in confused groups throughout the surrounding deathscape. Their gnarled branches moaned and cracked in the wind.

Before her feet unfurled a cobblestone path, spotted with patches of dusty snow. It twisted past her and curved gently downward, between rows of steps and Corinthian columns. Withered grasses and moss covered the bordering slopes. Abigail peered from the crest of a hill surrounded by thick weeds, decaying tombs, and ivy-covered monuments. Within the clutter, she could still appreciate the expansive scale of the landscape through gaps in the path and spaces between the marble. Golden reflections sparkled from the pyramidal tips of distant obelisks.

The mournful cries of dingy birds filled the sky. They flew in aimless paths, perching upon the contorted limbs of dead trees and the cracked corners of ancient pediments. Their lamentations echoed against stone altars, Doric capitals, and ornately decorated triglyphs.

"So, this is death," she said to the wind.

The birds answered her with retorts of malice. She stared back at them with an expression as stoic as the stone walls and sculptures that surrounded her. Abigail rubbed her eyes and took a deep breath. The frosty air filled her lungs and cleared her thoughts. She took another breath. Then another. She glared up at the birds. "Fine!" she cried. "I'm a ghost. What am I supposed to do now?"

Her piercing shouts startled the birds. They ceased their aerial disputes, landing on tree limbs and marble monoliths. Some perched upon the weather-stained crowns of weeping statues, while others rested atop the iron pickets of fallen gates.

Abigail shook her head with indifference and focused her attention back to the cobblestone path. It was the only reference in her new environment that provided a sense of direction. A purpose. *A future.*

"Which way should I go?"

She turned her gaze to the left and scanned the path. A mosaic of dirty snow mingled with the shadow-shrouded stone and grass. Rotted masonry lay strewn across a section of path that crested the hill. She surveyed the trail of moss-covered stonework back along the cobblestone. A fallen birch tree had destroyed the oxidized copper roof and columns of a ghastly sepulcher.

Abigail looked toward the right. The path curled a short way between structures and tombstones and then tumbled back down the hill. There were no visible obstructions, and the drifts of snow were lighter and sporadic on this side. She nodded her head and decided to follow the path to the right.

"I may be a ghost," said Abigail, "but I should really do something about these bare feet."

She looked down and wiggled her toes. Abigail realized for the first time that she was adorned in a white dress of exquisite beauty and elegance. She reached up and felt a lace bust and delicate sleeves that extended just beyond her elbows. The needlework was finely detailed and embellished with Venetian highlights and flowered embroidery.

The gown was luxurious and expensive. She had never worn anything of its kind during her living days. Abigail pictured her mother picking this dress out, spending a fortune so that her recently deceased daughter could be laid to rest in beauty. The image of her grieving mother produced a stream of tears, and she struggled to hold them back.

"I must go on," she said.

Her dress had suffered damage during the departure from the coffin and ascent out of the crypt. Blood from the gash on her forehead had dripped to her chest, drying into a constellation of crimson stars. The juxtaposition of delicate lace and blood formed a peculiar visual effect. Furthermore, the bottom-most portion of the dress's hem was caked in mud. She reached behind her and felt that a section of the fabric was torn. Abigail faintly recalled scrambling backward on the crypt floor, bumping into a sharp corner. The memory was as cloudy as a forgotten dream. She shook her head in frustration, continuing to try and make sense of her situation.

"Where am I supposed to find shoes?" she asked. "I doubt there's a store for ghosts in one of these crypts that I can walk into and place an order."

She giggled at the absurd thought. It was the first smile or laugh since her awakening within the dreadful coffin. The feeling was pleasing and warm. For a brief instant, it countered the freezing wind and frosty stones beneath her toes. She decided at that moment that she was going to try and laugh more. If she could still enjoy her sense of humor, even if she were now a ghost or spirit or whatever, then she was going to use it to her advantage. At the very least, it might provide her a fleeting sense of warmth within all this frozen misery.

Abigail reasoned for a moment. If she awoke into this deathly existence still wearing the clothes that she had been buried in, perhaps there were other lost souls in a similar situation. And maybe some of these fellow ghosts had been buried with shoes on. Comfortable, warm shoes. However, if she decided to steal the shoes off a dead person's feet, would she then be considered a grave robber? Or, because she was now a guest of the cemetery, did she still have to follow the same laws of the living? Being a ghost was already proving to be more complicated than she had ever imagined. She looked back down at her cold feet and weighed the options. Freeze to death (could she die again?), or partake in the thievery of ghostly footwear?

Her focus now was to find a pair of shoes, and preferably a warm pair of socks, at whatever the cost. She figured that this was her current purpose in life (in this case, death). Otherwise, she would have to find a place to keep warm for the night or climb into her original crypt. That option was unacceptable. The path to the right would be her starting point. Whatever happened based on that choice, she would have to deal with it.

Abigail craned her neck to locate the position of the sun, shielding her eyes from its bright rays. The glaring orb hung somewhat overhead. She had a fair amount of time to scavenge before the cemetery became colder and darker.

"Let's move feet," she said, starting down the path.

She soon reached another solemn crypt. The outer walls and steps were choked with long weeds and thorny brambles. Its heavy door stood ajar and was splintered with deep cracks. Abigail could squeeze through one of the fissures and check around inside for shoes, but there was something unusual about the entrance that held her back. The feeling was odd. An uneasy sense of being watched overcame her. She leaned forward and tried to peer into the darkness. The sensation was overwhelming. She stepped away from the door and continued toward the right, away from the crypt.

As she made her way to the edge of the hill, both sides of the path opened to the horizon. The vastness of the cemetery was unhindered to Abigail. A labyrinth of alleyways, marble walls, and ancient tombs sprawled before her. As she focused on the distant horizon, it became evident that there was a thin line that wrapped around and encompassed everything. A pale mist hovered just beyond the border that gradually blended into the blueness of the sky. Shady oak trees and untrimmed bushes obstructed portions of the line from her view, but it became clearer the more she focused, that the line was indeed a fence. She traced the wall to the left and saw a sizable gate.

"That's my destination," she said with a nod.

Abigail continued to walk along the lane down the hill. Now and again, to avoid patches of snow or sharp rocks, she had to hop from stone to stone, or tiptoe along soft beds of gray moss. She kicked at lanky mushrooms or twigs that obstructed her path. Abigail extended her arms to keep her balance. It soon became a game of how long she could stay on the patches of moss before losing her balance and falling back to the path.

Hop. Hop. Pause. Hop. Hop. Kick. Hop. Hop. Pause.

She performed an involuntary dance along the moss and stones, and it was almost fun. On one of the pauses, her arms still outstretched, Abigail laughed from the enjoyment. Then she saw them and froze. The hairs on her arms and neck stood straight up. A pair of black boots sat atop a tombstone.

Abigail immediately dropped to one knee. She snapped her head to either side and quickly scanned her surroundings. There was nothing. Only the wind and the blowing grass. She felt incredibly exposed and vulnerable out on the cobblestone path. She needed to find cover and find it fast. A decomposing tomb and an oak tree with thick limbs beckoned to her left. To her right was an open field of graves and tombstones, one of which contained the mysterious pair of boots. Keeping as low as possible, Abigail dashed across the path toward the oak. She reached it with open hands and cowered behind its far side. With her back pressed against the rough bark, she waited and listened. The wind whistled through the bare branches.

Abigail eased her head around the tree to study the boots in detail. She blinked in anticipation. A strand of long hair fell in front of her eyes as she peeked around the side. She blew it out of her face in desperation and looked across the path.

A young girl stood next to the boots.

"Holy shit!" exclaimed Abigail, flinging herself around the tree and sliding to the ground.

She sat numb and paralyzed. Her mind wanted to wriggle like a worm into the center of the oak and curl up into a ball. To her dismay, she even considered running back to her coffin and falling into a deep sleep. She wanted to do anything to escape this moment and feel safe again.

She concentrated on her breathing.

Inhale. Exhale. One.

Inhale. Exhale. Two.

She opened her eyes and focused on the objects that were in her immediate field of vision. She made a mental list of them. The ancient stone walls of the tomb. Grasses blowing in the wind. A twisted tree limb with curled branches.

Abigail listened and constructed another list of all the sounds. The wind through the branches and grass. The chirps of a solitary cricket. A cry from a bird high above.

The listing technique had helped her, and she felt more relaxed. Her breathing returned to normal, and she was thinking clearly again. Abigail took another deep breath before she stood and turned. Instead of looking around the tree cautiously, like she did the first time, she whipped around as fast as she could and peered across the path.

The girl was gone.

The boots remained.

Abigail scratched her head as she stared at the tombstone and boots. Had she even seen the girl? If she had not, then who put the boots there? And most importantly, why would a random pair of boots be set out like that as an offering, unless someone or something knew that she needed them? It was highly unlikely that some other person had been taking a stroll along this path and decided to take off their boots and conveniently leave them. But then again, what did she know? She had just arrived in this bleak landscape, and for all she knew, abandoned black boots on the tops of tombstones could be an everyday occurrence. Abigail rolled her eyes at the ridiculous theory. In all probability, the boots had been left for her.

She realized that she had a decision to make. She could flee immediately and hope that whatever was following her left her alone, or she could put the boots on and trust that they had been provided for her with positive intentions. She leaned against the oak tree and stared at the tombstone across the path.

There was no reason to believe that this entity, virtuous or evil, was going to stop following her. She had briefly seen the image of a young girl. That seemed significant because if it had appeared as a giant monster with tentacles and claws, then she would have panicked and run away screaming. In contrast, perhaps it was evil and merely trying to fool her by presenting itself as a young girl. Abigail was terrified by whatever it was, but she did not feel a sense of malice from it. Trusting her instincts had worked in her previous life. She would trust them now.

She pushed herself off the face of the oak tree and slowly walked toward the boots. As she crossed the path, she glanced to either side and checked her surroundings. Still nothing. Abigail stepped off the stones and into the long grass of the field. She cautiously crept up to the tombstone. They were black combat boots. One boot had thick, pink shoelaces and the other had black and white checkered ones. The tips were scuffed and worn, but otherwise, they seemed to be normal, and they even looked like they would fit her feet. She reached out with a finger and touched one. It was solid. It was real. She picked up one of the boots and noticed a balled-up sock inside.

"She left me socks too?" exclaimed Abigail.

If this was an evil, malevolent being, intent on eventually doing her great harm, then it was sure off to a dull start. Or an effective one, depending on your perspective.

She reached into the boot and pulled out the sock. It was dry and soft. Abigail turned to her right and noticed a stone coffin that she could use as a bench. The ground was frozen and muddy. It would be comforting to sit down and catch her breath, especially after this latest scare.

She grabbed both boots, walked over to the coffin, and hopped up. Abigail unraveled the socks and slipped them on. They reached the middle of her calf. She extended her legs in front of her and wiggled her toes in the socks. She then put on the boots and tied them with double knots. They fit perfectly.

Satisfied with her new footwear, Abigail stretched her arms behind her and leaned back onto the lid of the coffin. She let out a long sigh. The afternoon sun beamed upon her face for the first time during this disheartening new reality. It warmed her soul. The crows and ravens had returned to the sky. They cawed and croaked in the distance. Abigail leisurely kicked her feet off the edge of the coffin and gazed at the horizon. She listened to the wind blow through the grass as long shadows fell among the obelisks, mausoleums, and trees. She searched again for the gate. There it was. She could see it perfectly from her stone perch that overlooked the cemetery.

She sat up straight and froze. At the base of the gate stood a small figure. It was the girl.

Abigail stared. She did not feel a sense of terror this time. Instead, she felt a sudden longing to engage the girl. She wanted to talk to her. The girl was the only other person that she had encountered during this nightmare. Abigail rubbed her eyes and looked again. The girl was still standing there.

She hopped from the coffin and walked down the path in the direction of the gate. Abigail tried to keep an eye on the girl as she progressed, but it was difficult due to the clutter of the cemetery. The twisted trees and pointed steeples blocked her view. She lost the girl completely as the path fell into a shallow valley. With her new boots, Abigail could run without the worry of harming her feet. She raced to the top of the next hill.

As she approached the gate, she could see that the girl was still standing there, motionless. Abigail saw her each time there was a break in the moving scenery. The cobblestone path snaked and curved between trees and monuments as she continued to run toward her destination. A group of ravens, startled by the clatter of her boots, squawked their disapproval.

Iron fence tips peeked over the summit of the final hill. As she reached the crest, Abigail stopped and looked. The girl had disappeared again.

"For crying out loud," she said.

Abigail slumped forward with her hands on her knees and tried to catch her breath. She stood straight after a few moments and walked down the hill for the final approach.

From her original viewpoint on the hill, the gate and fence had appeared as a thin black line. Standing directly in front of them now, however, Abigail realized their true proportions and intensity. The fence stood at least three meters tall. It was constructed of thick posts, iron panels embellished with scroll markings, and large hinges. The gate was made of solid ash beams and a pitched roof with overlapping clay tiles.

Abigail walked to the lichgate and peered through the tunnel. A dreary haze lingered beyond the threshold. It was like looking into nothingness. She followed the gray void straight up until it gradually and seamlessly merged with the blue sky. The sensation caused her to lose her balance. She took a deep breath and then walked through the tunnel to the outside world.

SMACK!

She smashed into an unseen barrier. The impact propelled her backward and sent her sprawling onto her backside. Abigail moaned from the shock and sat up.

"You can't get out that way," said a voice.

Abigail spun around and found herself face to face with the young girl.

"My name's Penelope. But you may call me Penny."

CHAPTER VII

LOG ENTRY 377

"Your dad isn't on a trip for work."

The girls remained silent, staring at their mother.

"This whole thing is rather complicated," said Trelinia. "I'm just going to start from the beginning and try my best. I've never had to tell this entire story before, so please be patient with me. Okay?"

Mckenzie and Marie nodded their heads in unison. The golden candlelight illuminated their perplexed expressions.

"Where should I begin?" she said as she shuffled in her chair. "The Woods and Drake families have, shall we say, a type of ability that other families don't. Everyone back to your great-great-grandmother, that's five generations ago, have all possessed these skills. The women and men, from both sides of the family. Drake being my side and the Woods line being your dad's."

"What kind of ability?" asked Marie.

"All different kinds. Some of us have a heightened sense of awareness in certain situations. Others can perform processes that generate a beneficial outcome. And even others can exhibit exceptional physical feats that are above and beyond the ordinary individual."

"Come on, Mom," exclaimed Mckenzie. "You're talking about magic."

"Yes, dear. I'm talking about magic."

The sisters looked at each other and smiled.

"All the members of the Woods and Drake families, for the past five generations, have had a particular magical power of some kind or another."

"But we know this," replied Mckenzie. "Marie is already proficient with magic, and I've been using healing spells for a few years now. Even Roger has his outlandish talents with technology and science."

"And that's wonderful, Mckenzie. Believe me when I tell you that I know exactly what you three have been studying because I've been following your progress. But what do you know about my abilities, or your father's abilities, or even your Uncle Brian's magic?"

"Dad's abilities?" asked Marie. "What type of magic can he do?"

"Probably the most unusual of all of us," replied Trelinia as she cleared her throat. "Your dad can see and communicate with people who've passed over into the spirit world. He can even travel into their unseen realm."

"You mean ghosts?" asked Mckenzie.

"Yes. Traveling into their dimension is more complicated than a normal spell, but he can go there and interact with them."

"Is he there now?" asked Marie.

"Not exactly, but you're pretty close. We'll get back to the details of your dad's journey soon. But first, I want to talk with the two of you about these abilities and why you have them."

Trelinia sighed and shook her head in frustration.

"We should've communicated to you children about your magical abilities much earlier in your lives than this, but we've been putting it off. For that, I apologize. Your dad and I have come up with every excuse in the book to justify not addressing the situation. We're guilty of hoping the problem would go away if we just ignored it."

"What problem?" asked Mckenzie.

Their mother gazed into the candlelight. The girls stared at her with anxious anticipation.

"The problem of the runestones," she replied.

"The runestones!" cried Mckenzie. "I knew it."

Trelinia chuckled. "I wouldn't get so excited about them if I were you. The runestones are a dangerous business and should be taken seriously."

"I do take them seriously," she replied.

Mckenzie jumped out of her chair and ran back to the foyer to retrieve her backpack. Marie looked at her mother and shrugged. The two sat and waited patiently until the sound of Mckenzie's footsteps clamored back down the hallway.

"Look, Mom," she said as she flew back into her chair and held out an object wrapped in cloth. "This is what I found in the graveyard. It's one of the magic runestones."

"What graveyard?" asked Marie.

"One moment, dear," said Trelinia. "Let me take a look at this stone your sister found and then I'll tell you about that."

She held the stone and bounced it up and down. Trelinia nodded to herself and then closed her hand, gripping it tight for a moment. The girls watched intently as she opened her palm and flipped the stone over with her other hand. She studied the three small symbols inscribed on its surface.

"This is not a runestone," said Trelinia.

"But Mrs. Roberts said it was," replied Mckenzie.

"Of course she did. That's what she's supposed to say."

Mckenzie frowned. "What in the world are you talking about? Why would she lie to me?"

"The runestones aren't something you can just snatch up on a leisurely weekend stroll and run back home with. They're protected by powerful forces. Sometimes they're guarded and watched over by peaceful beings, but this time they're not. In fact, all the runestones are back in the hands of dangerous and evil powers. And that's the problem."

"How many of these runestones are there?" asked Marie. "There's a picture at school that shows only one of them."

"There're eight runestones in total," replied their mother. "The others are called companion stones. That's what you have here, Mckenzie. They're sort of like clues or guides for finding their parent stones. The parent stones are the ones that possess real power."

"That sucks," said Mckenzie. "I really thought that I'd found an actual runestone. All that work for nothing."

"What did you mean when you said that Mrs. Roberts was supposed to say that this was a runestone, when in fact, it sounds like she knew it's not?" asked Marie.

"That's an excellent question," replied Trelinia. "She told you that this is a runestone because she, and everyone else, didn't want you, or your sister and brother or any of your friends to go off on some crazy quest to try and find the real ones."

"Why?" asked Mckenzie.

"Because of the extreme danger involved. Do either of you have any idea of the threats that are lurking just outside the borders of Thorndale?"

Mckenzie looked at Marie. "Sure we do. We kind of have an idea, right?"

Marie nodded.

"There's the Blackwood Forest and those giant spiders Roger and I saw two summers ago. And then there's that creepy graveyard that I went into last weekend."

"Is that it?" asked their mother.

Trelinia rubbed her forehead and thought for a few moments. "Look, girls, the reason you don't know anything else is that your dad and I, and a few others in town, have tried very hard throughout your lives to keep it that way. Part of the reason is that's our role as your parents, but mostly, it's because we didn't want you to have to do what we did when we were your age. We'd hoped that it wouldn't have to come to that again. But, as life has a way of surprising you when you're least prepared, it seems that history is on the verge of repeating itself."

"All right," said Mckenzie. "You're going to have to be specific and tell us what it is that you are going on about. What is it that you guys did when you were our age? Out with it!"

Trelinia chuckled. "Well now, that's precisely the sort of attitude that your father and I have always been afraid of. But you're right. Both of you deserve to know the truth. So here it is."

***

"There are eight runestones," said Trelinia. "Frost, Fire, Light, Shadow, Technology, Nature, Life, and Death. Hundreds of years ago, in 1184, my great-great-great-grandfather, Dr. Edric Drake, first discovered their existence during an archaeological expedition in a distant mountain range, far to the north, called the Shadow Mountains. His nine-person team of archaeologists, scientists, and geologists were there to conduct research and collect data about the natural resources of that desolate, Arctic region. They expected to find a bunch of minerals and metals and other useful substances, which they did, but they also found something else buried in the ice and permafrost. They found the ruins of an ancient civilization within the depths of an evil and hideous city. For weeks, Edric and his team explored the ruined monuments, hallways, and marble rooms of that dreadful metropolis. They'd become so obsessed with their discovery, that they abandoned their previous project."

Trelinia took a sip of water and thought for a moment before she continued.

"During that time, the team had been documenting and recording all their discoveries and findings, as proper scientists should. They cataloged and drew diagrams of every building, street, and room that they encountered. They were even relaying their data back home at least once a day. The team made detailed descriptions of the bizarre architecture, the surreal artwork, and inscribed pages and pages of data regarding frightful spells and mysterious incantations. That's when the runestones were first found. They'd exhumed a burial chamber, deep within the bowels of the city, that contained eight large coffins laid out in a square in the middle of the room. On the lid of each coffin was encased a runestone. This discovery was phenomenal, obviously, but they were still unable to decipher or understand any of the ancient writing or symbols on the stones or in the many books they'd discovered. That's until they found the Watcher's Pyramid."

"The what?" asked Mckenzie.

"The Watcher's Pyramid is what they called it. It was a stone monument in the center of the city that contained four languages carved into its sides. There was one language on each face, and they all recited the same thing. Because one of the passages was understood by a team member who studied ancient languages, it enabled them to decipher the texts they'd found and then the runestones. This was the moment when the team began to make real progress. All of these stunning developments were being transmitted to their associates back home. Scientists, archaeologists, philosophers, and everyone else in the scientific community, were all going wild with excitement. An entirely new civilization had been discovered in a region of Silvarum that was, up until that stage, deemed inhospitable to life. At some point, soon after that, about a month after they had first discovered the ancient city, all communication with the team was lost. Dead silence. No more data transfers, letters by ship, nothing. The team had completely vanished."

"Did anyone go back to look for them?" asked Marie.

"Yes," she replied. "A year later, in fact. As you might imagine, there was a lot of commotion and drama after they lost all communication with the team. For many months, the people back home debated and argued about whether to send another expedition to find out what had happened."

"Why would they debate it?" asked Mckenzie. "Wouldn't they just go up there right away as soon as they lost contact?"

"You'd think so, yes," replied Trelinia. "That would've

been sensible. The reason they didn't immediately race up there was due to the incredibly disturbing nature of the team's final messages. To be frank, the people back home who were listening to these daily transmissions were frightened."

Marie felt the hairs on the back of her neck stand up. "What do you mean?"

"It's difficult to explain in my own words. The concepts are rather technical. It'll be easier and make more sense if I just show you. I'll be right back."

Trelinia got up from the table and left the room.

Marie looked at her sister. Mckenzie's expression was filled with confusion and anxiety.

"What are you thinking?"

"I'm not sure. This is way more complicated than I ever imagined and to be honest with you, I'm not really excited about where this story is going."

"Me neither," replied Marie.

Trelinia walked back into the room and placed a massive book onto the table. It produced a thump upon the mahogany surface, expelling a puff of dust from its ancient pages. As she opened it, Marie observed a curious design on the cover. It was made of two overlapping circles that formed a lidless eye.

"Here we are," Trelinia said as she turned to one of the first pages. It was a table of contents. She ran her finger down the list of passages as she read them aloud one by one.

Drake Expedition, Jan. 13, 1184. Base Camp Provisions, Jan. 17. Initial Survey and Core Samples, Jan. 21. Copper and Nickel Findings, Feb. 2. Cave Exploration.

Trelinia tapped her finger on a passage at the bottom of the page. **April 21, Runestone Translation. Page 610.**

She lifted a swath of pages and flipped them over in one go. That put her on page five hundred and eighty-eight. She licked her thumb and quickly flipped through the remainder of the pages and began to read the entries aloud.

"All the log entries that I'm about to read were originally transcribed from audio transmissions sent daily by Dr. Edric Drake. All right, here we go."

Entry 371, April 21, 18:34 – As recorded in journal entries 89 through 90, the WM (edit: Watcher's Pyramid) has enabled Profs. Multon and Eldridge to successfully transcribe pages 735 through 887 of volume 465-P. This was the volume that was discovered in tomb 87-B on February 11. The resulting incantations, read aloud by myself in burial chamber 41, and observed by Prof. Dwyer, have thereby resulted in the subsequent unlocking of the mysterious mechanism that constrained the runestone on coffin 01. It should be noted that a significant energy phenomenon, in the form of electrostatic discharge, was observed from the remaining seven stones upon removal of the stone 01A.

Entry 372, May 3, 11:22 – With the assistance of Dr. Carrell, I've been successful in extracting the remaining seven runestones (02A, 03A, 04A, 05A, 06A, 07A, 08A) from each of their mechanical housings. This was accomplished by the complete transliteration of volume 465-P. Multon and Eldridge have been working straight through the night for the past few days to accomplish this formidable task, and I'm certain that they're in need of some much-deserved rest. As a matter of fact, I believe they're both sound asleep in the next tent as I record this journal entry. Another important observation worth documenting is that once all the runestones were removed from their casings, Prof. Dwyer reported that a previously undocumented object had been seen within the southwest district of the city. Furthermore, the object appeared to demonstrate the ability to hover and spin in mid-air. We're planning to investigate these peculiar mechanics tomorrow once we all get a little more sleep and food.

Entry 373, May 5, 02:59 - The floating structure that was previously mentioned (hereafter referred to as R71-X), was in fact hovering and spinning above the surface of courtyard 17-B in District 13. Its rate of rotation was calculated to be eight r/min. A group of us, which included Profs. Dwyer and Eldridge, Dr. Carterson, and I all observed this curious phenomenon. Contrary to our current understanding of the laws of gravity, R71-X didn't exhibit the usual characteristics of matter in 3-dimensional space. The object itself is composed of sixteen individual tetrahedrons and 32 triangular faces, 24 edges, and eight vertices. These are characteristics of objects that conform to 4-dimensional geometry, and the group is obviously confused as to how it can exist in our reality of three dimensions. Prof. Eldridge posited that R71-X might be held airborne by an unseen and unheard propulsion system within its interior. Magnetism was another theory considered. Unfortunately, we're unable to observe with a reliable level of accuracy any such system of propulsion, whether through visual or auditory observations. What we could observe on R71-X, however, were the nine symbols evident on its triangular faces 20 through 29. The symbols, at least eight of them, appear to correlate to the eight symbols carved into each of the runestones found in chamber 41. The ninth symbol on face 29 is yet to be deciphered. It's been designated as rune 01B. Profs. Multon and Eldridge will continue to analyze it in an effort to understand its meaning and relation to the other eight runestones.

Entry 374, May 5, 13:18 - Tragic news. Prof. Multon has died. During the analysis of rune 01B, what appeared to be a grievous accident occurred while they were studying the object. Prof. Eldridge reported that R71-X displayed a matter transference while Prof. Multon was in its proximity. R71-X transformed instantaneously, according to Prof. Eldridge, from a 16-cell hexadecachoron polytope to a 24-cell icositetrachoron. The result of this matter transition engulfed Prof. Multon, and he was lost inside the structure. We're postponing all research for the time being to ascertain the cause of this horrible accident and to try and understand the physics involved. I'll be notifying Prof. Multon's next of kin immediately.

"Mom," said Marie. "I don't understand what he's talking about. How did the man die?"

"I still don't really understand all of this technical stuff either. And I've had this book since I was your age. What I've learned, is that this floating object they found was able to change its shape in the blink of an eye. This poor fellow, Multon, was just too close to it when it changed."

"You're saying that thing sucked him up somehow?" asked Mckenzie.

"Well, that's one way to put it. A more accurate way of explaining it would be to say that his state of matter phased with the structure. In a sense, he became part of it. Kind of like when you drop an ice cube into a glass of warm water. The solid water of the ice cube will melt and change into a liquid, merging with the rest of the water in the glass."

"You mean Multon turned into water?" asked Marie.

"Of course not," she replied. "Just let me continue. I haven't even got to the bad parts yet."

"Oh my," said Mckenzie.

"Wait a second, Mom," said Marie. "I just realized how bad I have to go to the bathroom. Can we please take a break?"

"Of course. I have to go as well."

"Me too," said Mckenzie.

They jumped up out of their chairs and raced to separate bathrooms. When everyone finally returned, Trelinia commenced with her narration.

Entry 375, May 5, 20:51 - Prof. Multon was buried in an icy grave on the Western Ridge. Since we didn't actually have his remains, we elected to bury some of his most cherished possessions. It was a morose occasion, as most of the team had known and worked with the good man for many years. We're all disheartened by the loss. He is survived by his wife and five children. No one is in the mood to conduct research today. We'll see about tomorrow.

Entry 376, May 8, 08:55 - The team's spirits have been lifted substantially by the discovery of a completely different area of study from what we've been obsessed with over the past few weeks. Dr. Mulgrew, the team's senior geologist, has discovered a thick deposit of diamonds near the base of the Eastern Ridge. A multitude of volcanic rocks and lamproites have been excavated and have thus yielded fine specimens. Even gold has been found. The entire team is now focused solely on this unexpected turn of events. This is, after all, the real purpose of our expedition. Since the death of Prof. Multon, interest in the further study of the ancient city has faded. We've requested that future expeditions take over the research from where we left off. In any event, we're more focused on the gemstones and the party of sorts that has been planned this evening to celebrate our new-found breakthrough!

Entry 377, May 10, 03:38 – I record this journal entry with my sanity in doubt. I'm not certain as to what I've just witnessed, yet for the sake of keeping a record of these disturbing events, I'll attempt to articulate the details in as clear and unemotional a manner as humanly possible. I'm confident that I'll fail at this task. During the night, Prof. Multon returned to the camp. At least, something that appeared to be Prof. Samuel Multon returned. As we were all celebrating our recent discovery of the gemstones, standing outside our tents and talking to one another, a faint figure approached us slowly from the southeast. Since all remaining team members were present and accounted for, we were immediately frightened and reacted defensively. Capt. Stevens, who's always carrying a sidearm, attempted to confront the intruder. As the figure approached the glow of our lamplight, however, we were all stupefied by the appearance of our departed colleague, Prof. Multon. He looked completely normal at that point. Dr. Susan Dexter, God rest her soul, was the first person to call out to what she believed to be her old friend. I recollect her final words being something along the lines of 'Sammy, you're okay!

You survived!' or something of that nature. The sequence of events that followed was too fast and confused to completely register, yet their imagery will be burned into the fabric of my thoughts for the remainder of my living days. The figure of Prof. Multon turned toward Dr. Dexter and propelled a geometric shape, somewhat similar in form to R71-X, into her chest. She disappeared. I'm unable to explain in words the physics of the action as it moved and spun through the night air, let alone the visual dynamics of the object itself. Nonetheless, I can, and will always remember the dreadful sound that Dr. Dexter made when she was absorbed into that illogical shape. I refuse, however, to inscribe a description of those sounds into words here. Capt. Stevens immediately screamed and fired at the figure of Prof. Multon. The bullets, instead of penetrating his body or missing him entirely, appeared to freeze in place. They orbited his torso in the form of a bright accretion disk of light. Multon then instantly transported himself directly onto the form of Capt. Stevens. Again, there were the ghastly sounds. I can't explain it any clearer than that. One moment Multon was standing in one spot with the disk of light orbiting him, and the next he was instantly standing in the location of Capt. Stevens. At this point, everyone went into a crazed panic. People were running in all directions. Some into their tents and others out into the snowy darkness. I simply froze, unable to move or scream. I watched in horror as the image of Multon, who stared straight at me, transformed from his human form into a geometric shape of preposterous dimensions and then proceeded to fold in on itself and vanish. I'm aware that my words are inadequate in communicating these illogical events. Unfortunately, I'm now exhausted and have no energy. I can barely keep my eyes open and my thoughts together. My head is now hurting terribly, and I see strange things. Numbers. Shapes. Colors. I must find sleep.

Trelinia looked up from the book and peered into the faces of her daughters. Marie stared with sadness, while Mckenzie held an expression of anger.

"That was awful," said Marie. "All those poor people."

"I know, dear," replied their mother. "But it's important that both of you hear exactly what happened next. These last few log entries will explain everything."

CHAPTER VIII

STEREOGRAPHIC PROJECTIONS

"What do you mean that place is real?" asked Roger.

"The pyramid with the orbiting disk of light," replied Merkresh. "It's an actual place. I've seen it. I've been there. And as a matter of fact…"

He leaned over the eight symbols again and studied them intently. "Astonishing. Each of these symbols that you've drawn around your compass are all real."

"They're just scribbles I made from my imagination," replied Roger. "I don't understand how they can be real."

"Nor do I, lad," replied Merkresh as he stared off deep in thought. He nodded a few times and shook his head back and forth as if arguing with himself.

"Are you certain that you've never seen these symbols before?" asked the old man. "Maybe in books, or maps, or artwork? What about somewhere else in the village?"

The boy shook his head. "No, I swear I haven't. I saw them all in the dreams that I've been having lately. I don't even know what they mean."

"What about at your school?"

"My school?"

"Yes, of course. Your teacher is Mrs. Roberts, I believe. Is there anything in her classroom, like a map or drawing, that depicts these symbols?"

Roger rubbed his chin and thought. "Actually, now that you mention it, I do think there's an illustration near her desk that's about archaeology. It has a diagram of an excavation site on it and other images of artifacts. There are some pottery and tools and some old ruins." He visualized the poster in his mind. "I remember that one of the artifacts on the poster is a stone with a strange symbol on it. But it's not labeled, and it doesn't have a description near it like all the other pictures."

Roger pointed to the symbol between the south and southeast points on the compass. "It's that one."

Merkresh smiled and nodded. "I thought so. That's the Rune of Frost."

"The Rune of Frost? But I didn't know that."

The old man turned toward the boy and studied his facial expressions and body language. After a moment, he patted him gently on his shoulder and smiled. "I believe you."

Roger exhaled and felt at ease again.

"But if what I believe you've achieved is indeed true, that you've successfully perceived all eight runestones through your visions, then you and I are due for a long talk."

"What kind?"

"The kind of talk where I finally explain to you in detail

everything you've ever wanted to know about my life and travels. Of my adventures to distant lands. How I acquired the fantastic devices and technology that you see in this room. And the real story of the runestones that were found in the ancient city of Nexxathia and my role in that epic adventure."

The boy gasped and stared back with his mouth open. He was both shocked and excited.

"Oh yes, I was aware of each time you asked about my travels over the years," said Merkresh. "Or when you asked me how I collected these outlandish curiosities, as you often refer to them."

"If you remember all those times," asked Roger, "why didn't you answer me?"

"Because you weren't ready yet. I'm afraid you needed to prove your worth to gain the knowledge of the runestones. Do you really think I'd tell this to just anybody and give away all my best secrets?"

"And you think I'm worthy enough now? Because I've come up with these symbols on my own?"

"Maybe. You're certainly off to a fantastic start, that's for sure. But there's still one more test that I need you to take to validate what I think you are. If you pass, then, like I said, we have much to talk about. Now follow me down to my workshop. Onward friends!"

Roger and Click followed Merkresh to the mouth of a dark staircase. The boy extended his hands to each side to keep his balance while his fingers followed the grooves in the wall.

"Watch yourself here," said Merkresh as they descended.

Roger angled his head to the right and safely maneuvered beneath a rusted pipe. He grinned to himself, impressed by his quick reflexes and agility. Similar to his skills in climbing trees and traversing creeks, Roger considered himself a master adventurer. He peered back up and smiled at the pipe as he continued to descend the stairwell.

"And here too," said the old man.

SMACK!

The stinging kiss of metal smashed against the boy's forehead as he turned toward the old man's voice. The low boom echoed in the passageway.

"I've been meaning to move that pipe out of the way," said Merkresh. "Sorry about that."

A hefty bump began to grow out of Roger's scalp.

"I'll get you something for that impressive knot as soon as we arrive at my workshop."

"Thank you. I'm going to need it."

At the bottom, Roger turned to his left, past a full display of plate armor, and entered Merkresh's workshop. The area was sizable but not as massive as the room upstairs. Oil lanterns hung from the walls, illuminating a collection of desks, worktables, and laboratory gear. The hiss of steam-powered devices and bubbling liquids radiated throughout the chamber. The old man scurried around at the opposite end of the room, examining a shelf of colorful bottles and jars.

"Just a moment," he said. "I'll be right there."

Roger swiveled his head and surveyed the landscape. The section on the left was devoted to mechanical and technological endeavors. Racks of spanners, ratchets, and tiny bits of brass and copper tubing covered the metal shelves and tables. The opposite space was a mélange of carpentry projects. Wood dust blanketed every table, bench, and cabinet. Piles of curly shavings crowded the corners. On a woodworking table lay an assortment of rulers and protractors, chisels, carving knives, and saws. Roger breathed in the sweet aroma of pine, cedar, and cherry. The back of the workshop was filled with the laboratory equipment of a mad scientist. A metal table contained an outlandish collection of glass tubing, erratically shaped flasks, and gas burners. On the back wall hung wooden racks that held beakers, cylinders, and funnels. A porcelain crucible, as well as a mortar and pestle, were on display amidst a field of brightly colored powders.

"Here we are," said Merkresh as he returned. "Rub a bit of this on your head. The swelling will go down in no time."

The old man handed the boy a clay bowl filled with a green, gooey substance. Roger scooped up a sample.

"That stinks!" he cried, covering his nose.

"I know," replied Merkresh. "But it works, I promise. Go ahead and slap a nice dollop onto your forehead."

"Can't I just put a bag of ice on it?" he asked. "What's in this stuff? It smells like the ass of something that's been dead for a hundred years."

"Indeed. That's actually one of the ingredients."

Roger gagged.

"It works, I swear," said Merkresh. "I use it every time I bump my head coming down those stairs."

"Wouldn't it be easier to just move the pipe?"

The old man shrugged. "Probably."

Roger grimaced at the goopy ointment in the bowl. He scooped up a heftier blob this time and carefully rubbed it onto his head. His initial instinct was to cry out from the pain, but he instead realized that the green goo relieved the discomfort. It was invigorating. A tingling sensation buzzed throughout his body.

"See," said the old man. "What did I tell you?"

"Wow, you were right. The pain is completely gone, and the bump doesn't hurt anymore."

"Excellent," replied Merkresh. "Now, please follow me this way." He motioned to an assortment of mechanical devices that stood on the left side of the workshop.

Situated next to a metal workbench and a wall of tools, stood a quizzical contraption. A wooden pillar, two meters in height, was capped by a glass enclosure. Inside, resting directly on top of the flat surface of the pillar, sat the most bizarre object Roger had ever seen in his life.

"What's that?" asked the boy.

"That's a polychoron," replied Merkresh.

"A what?"

"A polychoron. A polyhedriod. A 4-polytope. Don't they teach geometry in school anymore?"

"Of course they do," replied Roger. "But I've never heard of those weird names before. They teach us about spheres and cubes and pyramids. Stuff like that."

"That's something, at least. However, all those names you recited are three-dimensional objects, right?"

"Sure, I guess so."

"Very good," replied Merkresh. "Do they also teach you about two-dimensional geometry?"

"You mean like circles, squares, and triangles?"

"Yes, indeed. What can you tell me about the relationship between a square and a cube?"

Roger stared at the old man for a moment and then turned toward the polychoron in the glass enclosure.

"No," replied Merkresh, shaking his head. "That thing

has nothing to do with the question. You know the answer. You just have to think about it in terms of dimensions."

The boy inadvertently rubbed the bump on his head.

"Ouch!" he cried. "That's still sore."

"Then don't touch it. It still needs a few more days to heal. The stinky ointment only reduces the pain and enhances the healing process. Now, please concentrate on the question. This is relevant to the point I'm trying to make."

Roger lowered his hand and looked back at the old man. As exciting as it was to hang out in his workshop to learn new concepts and be exposed to all these alluring technologies, he sometimes felt like he was taking a test in school. This was one of those moments.

"Well?" asked Merkresh.

"The relationship between a square and a cube is that a square is a two-dimensional representation of a three-dimensional cube," replied the boy.

"Very good. Understanding that, what would you say is the next higher representation of a three-dimensional cube?"

Roger turned back to the polychoron again and pointed. "That weird thing?"

"Yes," replied Merkresh. "A polychoron is simply a three-dimensional representation of a four-dimensional object."

"What do you mean by four dimensions? I thought there were only three?"

"It's another spatial dimension beyond the normal three, generally called spacetime. The others, of course, are comprised of height, width, and depth. You already know this concept well because of your knowledge of longitude, latitude, and altitude."

Roger nodded and continued to listen.

"When the fourth dimension is applied, we're essentially adding another coordinate axis to the existing three."

Merkresh scratched his beard and thought for a moment. "This next part is probably brand new to you, and might be confusing, so just bear with me. I'm sure you'll get it."

"I'm trying," said Roger. "Is all of this math stuff going to be on the test I still have to take?"

"In a way," he replied. "But I'm not going to give you some silly exam that you will be graded on. I'm just trying to teach you some basic concepts so that you can better understand that object over there when you have to deal with it."

"That's good. I thought you were giving me the test right now. I'll try to relax and focus more on what you're attempting to teach me."

"That would be constructive, thank you," replied the old man. "Now, where was I?"

"The fourth dimension."

"Because we mere mortal human beings must accept the fact that we can only perceive a three-dimensional universe, it's therefore difficult for us to accurately perceive four-dimensional objects in their truest sense. For example, the retinas of our eyes are actually two-dimensional receptors that capture the light from three-dimensional objects. Our brains then accurately simulate these three-dimensional objects by filling in the missing details like shading, depth, and foreshortening. Are you still with me?"

"Yes, please continue."

"Since our eyes can only perceive up to three dimensions, we have to engineer a way to visualize four-dimensional objects in three dimensions."

The old man motioned toward the polychoron. "The

technique for visualizing four-dimensional objects in three-dimensions is called projection. This is the same concept as the original question I asked you earlier. Do you remember what that question was?"

"What's the relationship between a square and a cube?"

"Correct. Projection is known as dimensional analogy and can theoretically be used to visualize any two dimensions. It's a clone of an n-dimensional object in n minus one dimension."

"Can you do it with fifth-dimensional objects?"

"Outstanding question!" exclaimed Merkresh. "Of course you can. That's what the n represents in the basic premise. Technically, you can go up to as high a dimension as you want, but that's far too advanced for us at this stage."

Roger nodded.

"The polychoron that you see in the glass case is what's known as a higher-dimensional polytope net. It's basically the folded-out version of the real object. For example, if you took a paper cube and unfolded all the sides, you would have a two-dimensional representation of that object."

"I think I see what you mean," said Roger. "The shape in the case is the unfolded, three-dimensional version of its four-dimensional counterpart, which we are unable to see because our eyes can only account for three dimensions."

"Well said," replied the old man. "I don't think I could've explained it better myself."

"What if someone could construct a device that enabled our eyes to see a real object in four-dimensional space?"

Merkresh smiled and handed Roger the mask that he had been wearing earlier. "You'll never guess what I made."

CHAPTER IX

GAZING UNTO THE STARS

"Catch him!" cried a gate guard as Captain Hamonet collapsed.

Brian grasped him under the pauldrons, guiding his limp body gently to the drawbridge. The grinding of their plate armor screamed through the dense fog.

"Well anon," said the hooded figure. "What has befallen the young captain? Has he become ill?"

Evil laughter erupted from the group of Nexxathians.

The horrified gate guards turned their attention from their fallen leader to the cruel tone of the guttural voice. Brian crouched next to the captain, checking his pulse and vital signs. He was unconscious but breathing normally.

"Help me get his helmet off," Brian said.

The two knights bent down and raised the captain, setting him in a sitting position against the wooden cart. Brian carefully pulled off the helmet. Set within a mail coif, the young man's face was deathly white and cold. Beads of sweat covered his forehead and poured down his flushed cheeks. Brian pulled a rag from a pouch on his belt, gently patting the streams of perspiration.

"Come," said the mocking voice. "We do not have all day to wait on this knave. Roll your captain aside and allow us to complete this transaction. The morning draws late."

Brian ground his teeth in anger, struggling to ignore the being's insults while tending to his fallen captain.

"Patience, sire," he replied with his back turned.

Brian placed his hand against the young man's forehead. It was burning hot. "Please allow me to assist my captain. We'll complete the trade directly, and you and your group will soon be underway."

"What did you say?" asked the Nexxathian. "Who is this brigand that speaks to me in such a manner with his back turned? Rise and behold me with thine eyes."

Brian continued to wipe the captain's forehead with the rag, ignoring the shrill commands.

"Corporal," he said. "Hurry to the gatehouse and fetch some water. The captain's burning up."

"You there!" cried the voice. "I command you to turn around and face me. Do not ignore me."

"ENOUGH!" shouted Brian with his mind.

He stood and turned, the aggressiveness forcing the Nexxathian to step back two full paces. There was an immediate flurry of movement and commotion from the group of cloaked figures and reptilian creatures. They ceased their raucous laughter, yelling in outrage. The gate guards were too frozen with fear to respond. They gawked in wonder at the sudden confrontation.

"What did you say?" it replied. "How dare you."

"I said enough of this madness. You will mock my captain no longer, and you will refrain from using mind control on my men," he replied. His lips were motionless. Brian Woods communicated to the creature with his thoughts alone.

The Nexxathian took another confused step backward. The fighters atop the spiders cried a series of orders and charged forward. Belris strained his astonished gaze toward the cloaked figures that stood at the front of the group. Bright orbs of blue light formed in their palms while an electric crackle increased in volume.

As the spider's freakish legs splashed through the puddles to attack, the leader of the Nexxathians raised his hand. The riders immediately stopped in their tracks. They were so close that they caused chunks and droplets of mud to splash upon Belris' greaves and tasset. The blue orbs were also extinguished with a wave of the figure's purple cloaks.

The Nexxathian tilted its head, studying Brian with a new-found appreciation. Its wicked voice was notably more relaxed, yet it expelled an ominous chuckle. "Human. How are you able to speak to me thus?"

Belris and another guard looked at each other with blank expressions. They had not heard the sergeant utter a single word.

Brian stared at the creature and did not respond, neither by voice nor telepathy. His face was on fire with anger, his hand resting nimbly upon the hilt of his sword.

"I see," replied the Nexxathian, turning to address the cloaked priests. "This human possesses the gift of mind speech. This is a most interesting revelation. Would you not concur?"

"A very interesting revelation, indeed lord," they replied.

The Nexxathian leader whispered something unintelligible

to the priests and then calmly turned to address the sergeant.

"What is your name, valorous sir?"

Brian relaxed his aggressive posture. He eased the tension in his shoulders and modified his stance to one more suited to civil conversation. The fire that had burned in his veins during the intense exchange subsided. He took a deep breath.

"My name is Sergeant Brian Woods."

"And mine is Lord Mordok," replied the Nexxathian with a respectful nod. "We are honored by your presence and are truly concerned for the unfortunate state of your young captain. Now then, may we please commence with the exchange of goods, Sergeant Woods?"

Belris and the group of gate guards looked at each other in turn with confused expressions.

"Indeed, we may, lord," replied Brian. "If you would allow me to check on the status of my captain's health, I'll have him situated, and then we may proceed."

Lord Mordok nodded. "As you wish."

Brian bent down next to the captain.

"What's happened, sergeant?" asked Captain Hamonet.

"You fainted, sir."

"I can hardly remember," he replied. "One moment I was motioning for the cart and the next I was awash in an ocean of confusion and color."

"Can you stand?"

The young man nodded.

"Help me get the captain to his feet," said Brian.

The two knights supported the young man as he slowly stood, bracing himself against the cartwheel. As he rubbed the back of his head, he surveyed the two groups of figures.

"What's the situation? Is there trouble?"

"No, sir," replied Brian. "There was a bit of conversation with our guests, but everything is in order now, and we're ready to make the exchange."

"Very well. Please proceed with the transaction."

Brian motioned for the guards to bring forth the cart. Likewise, Lord Mordok signaled to the priests to present their wagon. As the two groups converged, and the wooden carts touched end to end, heavy tarps were thrown back to reveal the contents of each party.

The human's cargo consisted of a single chest. An orderly collection of twenty-one metallic devices were arranged within the case. Each device featured a glass portal that exposed its contents. Brian noticed a white light softly pulsated from within.

The Nexxathians presented their chest. Iron brackets perched perpendicular to its lid and were straddled by thick straps and buckles. A bronze lock and keyhole were fixed in the center.

"Open it and show these folk," said Lord Mordok.

"Aye, lord," replied one of the priests, unlocking the case.

"Gold?" asked Brian.

"Just as your own Count Zaran requested."

Lord Mordok peered into the human cart and counted the metallic devices. He shook his head in disgust.

"Nay, this sum is not sufficient," he exclaimed. "The contract did state thirty-four instances of lightdust. This trade is not acceptable."

Captain Hamonet cleared his throat, attempting to stand straight. One of his arms still rested on the cartwheel. "My lord, Count Zaran directed me to explain that twenty-one devices were all the castle could produce this month. As an incentive, he will gladly increase the amount to fifty-five upon our next trade."

"Incentive?" mocked Lord Mordok. "Nay, human. We do not recognize incentives and we thus honor the contracts with which we commit to. If it be true that you do not possess the full amount of thirty-four, then you shall not receive the order of the gold substance you so desire."

Lord Mordok turned and whispered to one of the cloaked priests. The figure nodded, removing thirteen gold bars from the chest. They clinked together as he dropped each bar into a bag. The entire group watched this process play out in silence.

"There now," said Lord Mordok. "This amount is more suited to our current situation. Would you not agree?"

"But, lord," replied the captain, "that's not enough gold. Count Zaran will not accept that amount."

Lord Mordok bowed low, sweeping his hand across the face of his flowing cloak. "Then our business this morning is thus concluded, gentlemen. I say valorous day to you."

He turned from the humans, motioning for the caravan to disembark. The spiders and dinosaurs turned their thunderous bodies in the muddy road.

Captain Hamonet took a step forward, watching as the wagon creaked along the drawbridge. His face was stretched with pain and uncertainty. He glanced at his men, observing how they stared at him with pitiable and disgusted expressions. The captain swayed in troubled thought as he glanced from the caravan to the mist-covered road.

"Lord, wait a moment," he said.

The caravan halted. Lord Mordok slowly turned, his cloak whipping around him in a wave of purple.

"Aye, captain. Have you changed your mind?"

"I have. The sum of twenty-one will suffice."

"Very well," replied the Nexxathian, laughing.

As his deliberate display of satisfaction concluded, Lord Mordok raised his hand. The priests pulled the wagon back along the bridge, exchanging the gold and chest of metallic objects.

"Is there anything else you require of us on this cold, gray morning?" asked Lord Mordok.

"No, lord," replied Captain Hamonet. "That is all."

With a snap of his cloak, Lord Mordok turned without another word. The group of gate guards watched in awe as one of the colossal dinosaurs lowered its head, allowing him to climb its neck to the saddle. The beast let out a piercing cry as it turned and bounded into the gray mist.

CHAPTER X

DEAD WINTER DAYS

"Hello. My name's Abigail."

Penelope smiled. The young girl was clad in an outfit the likes of which Abigail had only ever seen in history books, or during school field trips. Her clothes and features were timeworn. Upon Penelope's head sat a white, cotton cap. Her blonde hair was wrapped in a bun and tucked beneath lace and ruffles. She wore a burgundy waistcoat with long, wool sleeves and silver buttons that ran down the center. Her dress consisted of a gray gown and petticoat with a skirt and bodice. The lower half of her legs revealed black stockings and leather boots with brass buckles. Around her back fluttered a green cloak and hood.

Penelope extended her hand.

"Thank you," said Abigail as she pulled herself up.

"You're welcome. Do you fancy the boots and socks?"

Abigail looked down at her feet, wiggling them inside the

combat boots. "They're perfect. I love them. Did you put them on the gravestone for me?"

"Aye. I hope I didn't frighten you too much back there, but you seemed to be uncomfortable in your bare feet."

Abigail smiled. "I *was* frightened, actually. Thank you for offering them. I was about to go searching around in these tombs to find something to wear."

"I know," replied Penelope. "That's why I set them out for you. To save you the trouble. This isn't exactly an area that you want to blindly roam around in. Especially during this time of day and especially if you're new here."

"I really appreciate your help."

Penelope lowered her gaze. "I apologize again for scaring you, but I haven't encountered another person in a very long time. I wasn't exactly sure how I should approach you. The last thing I wanted to do was to come running up to you as soon as you walked out of your tomb."

"That was probably a good idea," said Abigail. "I'm sure I would've freaked out. Was it you that I felt watching me through the cracks of that crypt door?"

"Yes. That's where I heard you complain about your bare feet. I was sitting around the corner on some steps when I heard your shouts."

Abigail chuckled. "I knew I felt somebody watching me."

"I'm sorry for spying on you."

"Oh, I'm not upset. I'm just reacting to my ability to sense things. I was always good with perception, so I'm glad I still have it in this place."

"I'm happy to hear that," said Penelope.

Abigail looked at her surroundings. The sun was low in

the sky and cast long shadows across the cobblestone path.

"Where are we?" she asked.

"We're in the cemetery."

"No, I mean where is this place?"

Penelope sighed. "You realize *what* you are, right?"

"A ghost?"

"Yes."

Abigail felt a profound sense of disappointment upon hearing the confirmation of her death. A part of her still hoped that this was all a dream or a mistake.

"I know exactly how you feel," said Penelope. "I walked out of my tomb just as you did. The only difference was I had on these warm shoes and stockings."

Abigail snapped out of her thoughtful gaze and chuckled.

"How long have you been here?"

"I'm not sure. I don't think time works the same way in this place as it does where you came from. But I still remember when I arrived here."

"When was that?"

"December twenty-fourth. Sixteen hundred and nine."

"What?" gasped Abigail. "You've been in this cemetery for four hundred years?"

"I don't know," she replied. "I guess so. What year was it where you came from?"

"Nineteen ninety-one. I'm from San Francisco."

"San Francisco? I've never heard of that place."

"I guess you wouldn't. It wasn't named that in your time."

"I'm from a settlement called Jamestown," said Penelope. "Have you ever heard of it?"

"The Jamestown settlement in the state of Virginia?"

"I'm not sure what a state is, but I think that's the same one. Virginia was called a colony when I lived there."

"That's amazing. It's like going back in time."

"And for me, it's like going into the future. See what I mean about time in this place?"

The girls stood together amongst the ancient mausoleums and crypts. A chilly wind blew through the tangled branches of the oaks that lined the path. Wisps of sparkling snow curled around their feet, settling in drifts along the base of the gate. Two ravens called to each other from the snow-covered heads of distant statues. Abigail shivered.

"I know where we can get you a warm coat."

"That'd be great. Is it always freezing here?"

"Aye, unfortunately," replied Penelope. "There are a few spots in the cemetery where you can find a wee bit of warmth, but most of the time it's just cold like this. That's why I try to sit outside under the sun most days. As long as I've ever been here, though, it's always been snowy and bleak."

"It's always winter?"

Penelope nodded.

"That really sucks," replied Abigail.

"Sucks?"

"It means when something isn't good."

"That's funny," said Penelope. "It does sucks here."

"No," replied Abigail. "It sucks here. Not, it does sucks here. Try again."

Penelope took a deep breath and screamed at the top of her lungs. "IT SUCKS HERE!"

A murder of crows screeched in disgust, flying off from nearby branches and rooftops.

"IT SUCKS HERE!" they screamed in unison, erupting into a fit of laughter.

Abigail turned toward the lichgate after a few moments, pointing. "Is that invisible barrier I smacked into preventing us from leaving the cemetery?"

"Yes. At least, until you're ready to leave."

"What's that supposed to mean?"

"As I said, I've been here for a very long time. In that time, I've only ever known one other person. Another ghost. She was older than you and me, like the same age as my mum was when I was alive. For a long while, she was like a mum to me too, to be honest with you. Even more so. After many years together in this place, however, she eventually left through that gate and never returned. I've been alone ever since."

"How old are you?" asked Abigail.

The girl chuckled. "According to the year you just said you arrived from, I guess I'm almost four hundred years old."

"No, I mean how old were you when you died?"

"Oh," replied Penelope. "I was sixteen."

Abigail gasped. "I'm sixteen years old too!"

Penelope smiled.

"How did you die?" asked Abigail, realizing her brashness too late. "I'm sorry, that was rude of me to ask. You don't have to talk about that if you don't want to."

"It's all right," replied Penelope. "I don't mind." She stared into the foggy horizon beyond the tunnel as the limbs of a black oak scratched at a section of iron gate.

"I remember always being hungry," she said in a somber voice. "We were always hungry and always thirsty. The settlement was already in bad shape when I arrived. I was a passenger aboard the third shipment of settlers and supplies from England. That was in the fall of sixteen hundred and nine."

"You're originally from England?" asked Abigail.

"Aye, London."

Penelope cleared her throat and continued. "When we arrived, the existing settlers that had already been there for two years, mostly men and boys, were desperate and starving. There was hardly any clean water due to the marshy land, they weren't able to farm much food, and they were constantly fighting with the local Powhatan. Trade with the Powhatan, which had been their primary source of food and supplies since the founding of the colony, had almost entirely ended by the time I arrived. I never learned why, but I remember hearing tales about an incident that happened between Captain Smith, Pocahontas, and her father, Chief Powhatan."

"You knew Pocahontas?" asked Abigail.

"Aye. I met her a few times. She was about my age. She used to come to the settlement and bring us food every once in a while. How do you know about her?"

"I learned about her, John Smith, and the Jamestown colony in school," replied Abigail.

"I see," said Penelope.

"I'm sorry to keep interrupting you," said Abigail, "but this is so fascinating. Please continue your story."

"When we finally arrived on the third ship during the fall, the settlers were facing a drought in addition to all of their other problems. And our arrival, without the amount of supplies that they desperately needed, only added to the number of mouths that had to be fed. Also, Captain Smith had been in some sort of accident shortly after we arrived, so he sailed back to England.

That left the colony without any leadership or direction. At that point, things really started to get worse. Because the Powhatan refused to trade with us anymore, we couldn't get much food. Even Pocahontas stopped coming by. Whenever a group of men went beyond the walls to hunt or trade, they'd get killed or captured by the natives. All of us inside the colony were scared to death and began to panic. Folk started eating the few horses that were left, their own pets, and even rats. Once winter arrived and the snows began to fall, the colony was in complete chaos."

Penelope paused, staring out into the rustling trees and blowing snow. A gust of wind swelled through the skeletal fingers of the oaks. They creaked and scraped within the waning light of the late afternoon. She raised her hood to block out the chill and continued her tale.

"I saw people do terrible things. Folks who were starving and desperate. Even close friends that I'd known for years and sailed with across the ocean from England. All they were trying to do was survive. All they wanted to do was to go on living, but it was awful. I think my perception of humanity changed for the worse on that final, ominous day. I witnessed with my own eyes what regular folk are truly capable of when they've run out of options. When they've run out of hope. I remember at the very end, during the howling winds of a fierce snowstorm, that I'd crept away and hid inside the blackened shell of a burned-out house. I bundled myself up in a dark corner and just waited for the end to come. I'd be lying to you if I said I wasn't hoping for death. I prayed for it. I'll never forget the sound of the wind as it moaned through the trees that final night. It was chilling. It was beautiful. The next instant I opened my eyes and found myself in a tomb in this cemetery."

Abigail gazed at Penelope with a new-found sense of respect and admiration. She wiped the tears from her eyes. "I'm sorry that happened to you, Penny."

The girl turned her gaze from the distant trees and smiled in return. "Thank you," she replied.

CHAPTER XI

HALLWAYS OF MOONLIGHT

Entry 378, May 12, 17:43 – Everyone else is gone. I don't know for sure if they're dead or lost in the mountains, but I do know for certain that I'm the only person that remains in this camp. I've slept for the past twenty-four hours now. My head is much clearer, and I don't see the bursts of color or other disturbing images as often. However, there's one image that I can't get out of my head. The pyramid with the golden, spinning disk of light. It's a consistent picture in my mind. I'm also feeling a strong urge to hike back up to the ruins and investigate. I think the answers to this disaster may be found 6d756c746f6e there. Perhaps that's where the others have gone. I'm going to rest for the remainder of the day and tonight and then I'll attempt a trip up to the city in the morning.

    Entry 379, May 14, 07:35 – Strange things. I saw so

many strange things during my hike up the mountain and above that dreadful city. As planned, I made the trip up the trail at first light. I followed the path and tracks that myself and the rest of the team had 456c6472269646765 made on all our previous expeditions over the past few weeks, but I immediately noticed sets of new tracks. Illogical tracks. They made absolutely no sense to me whatsoever. Some of the impressions were like shallow, spherical indentations in the 4477796572 snowy trail. These bizarre tracks followed parallel paths on both sides of our previous foot traffic all the way up to the ruins. Other tracks were like convex indentations in the snow. They were exactly the opposite of the other types.

"Mom," said Marie.

"Yes, dear," replied Trelinia.

"Why are you reading those numbers and letters in the middle of his sentences?"

"Because that's exactly how Drake relayed his log entries. The number and letter sequences would just come out of nowhere in the middle of his speaking. Keep listening, and you'll see what I mean."

"You mean he was actually saying the numbers and letters out loud?" asked Mckenzie.

"Yes."

Trelinia took a quick sip of her drink and continued. "This is where I left off from the previous entry."

They were exactly the opposite of the other types. I counted eight distinct paths in the snow that were all similar to this phenomenon. I finally reached the ruins at 23:35 that evening under a full moon. As I stood on the ridge that overlooks the city, I could clearly make out a group of new objects hovering over different districts. Not surprisingly, there were eight of these objects, all evenly spread around the city in four groups of three so that they formed a square. This formation was identical to the way the tombs were situated in burial chamber 41. They all seemed to spin and hover about six meters 43617272656c6c above the buildings and monuments. I'm not yet sure that I'm prepared to make the correlation that I fear to be true, but I'm close. I simply need more data, but I'm doubtful that this is all just a coincidence. As I peered down into the city, I could plainly see the similarities of the eight objects to R71-X. They were all hovering, four-dimensional, geometric forms that took the shape of a rotating, 24-cell icositetrachoron polytope. I also witnessed an entirely new, previously undocumented object. Spinning and hovering about 60 meters in the sky and directly above the central focal point of the eight 4d756c67726577 polytopes, was the most unreasonable, implausible, and irrational spectacle I've ever witnessed in my scientific life. Even in my dreams, I couldn't have envisioned such a ludicrous demonstration of physics and nature. I'll try my best to describe in technical terms what I beheld as I stood at the edge of that snowy ridge. I've also made several sketches of the structure and its details in my field notebook. The main object that was hovering roughly 60 meters directly above the eight 436172746572736f6e objects appeared to be a 120-cell hyperdodecahedron. I'm convinced now that it is, in fact, the physical manifestation of the ninth symbol, symbol 01B, that was observed by the team on face 29 of R71-

X. Attempting to accurately describe its appearance in words is difficult, if not impossible. Please refer to my sketches for a more accurate visual reference. Mathematics is always the most successful method for describing these complex types of geometric objects. Nevertheless, the object at the apex of the formation was comprised of 120 dodecahedral cells. At each edge of the object, known as the vertex, four of these cells joined together, producing an absurd visual effect. Based on my previous observations and calculations with R71-X, I'll speculate that O1B's rotational speed was close to eight r/min. Protruding from the top of O1B, and extending upward until it vanished into the atmosphere, was a continuous current of radiant 446578746572 energy. I was able to accurately observe this phenomenon due to the clear night sky. Without the proper instrumentation, however, I was unable to detect what other forms of electromagnetic radiation the stream was ejecting, but in terms of visible light, the color of the energy stream was a bizarre combination of purple, green, and yellow. The colors appeared to shift and twist around one another as they shot upward. In addition to the vertical beam, there were also eight individual energy beams, all red, that stretched downward toward each of the eight polytopes closer to the city. Each of these eight beams met at a single focal point at the bottom and center of O1B. This design, combined with the other beams of energy that connected each of the eight objects at the base, constructed a massive pyramidal shape. Orbiting around this pyramid of energy beams and rotating shapes, was the most incredible object of all. A glowing, bright accretion disk of golden light spun with tremendous speed around the red beams of energy. The disk gave off a faint hum as it orbited the structure. Again, I was only aware of the visual light, but even so, the formation of the energy that extended from O1B to each of the smaller objects was perplexing. Instead of traversing a straight line, the downward light appeared to be warped in numerous places, like 7374657656e73 it was being bent around a collection of unseen objects. This bending of the light phenomenon did not disturb the structure of the overall preposterous composition that I observed. I'm now painfully aware that the collection of these shapes and objects and interconnected beams of energy are, in fact, the same image that has been pulsating inside my mind for days. It is the pyramid with the spinning disk of light 6261726360C6179. It has found me.

"All of this weird technical stuff is making my head hurt," said Marie. "I don't understand anything you're saying."

"It's almost over, honey," she replied. "This next entry is the last one ever to have been received from the expedition."

"Thank God," said Mckenzie.

Trelinia took a deep breath. "There wasn't the usual log entry number or date and time with this last one. It just began like this. All right, here it goes."

Multon011001100111001001101111011100110111010DexterO1100110011010010111001001100101

"Wait a second," said Mckenzie. "What is that? What in the hell are you reading?"

"This is the last entry," replied their mother. "This is exactly how it's transcribed. Look."

She pointed to the words and numbers on the page. Both

girls jumped up out of their chairs and examined the log entry. Mckenzie popped out of her chair so fast that it fell over and hit the floor.

"What's all that?" she asked.

"It goes on like this for a while. Each person's last name on the team is followed by a series of ones and zeros."

"Why?" asked Mckenzie. "What's it mean?"

"I'll tell you in a second," replied Trelinia. "First, let me skip past all this gibberish and get to the next interesting part. After the final name and numbers, it continues like this. There's also a note next to the passage that states the voice in the final recording was spoken in a demonic tone."

Beholdeth, the eight runes of Aza'zel art linked again. And alas, the most wondrous city of Nexxathia is thus reborn anew. Through the plunderage and defilement of our masters' tombs hast a seed of hatred birthed upon the realm of Silvarum. The eight shalt thus wipeth clean the ignorance of thy blasphemy. Aza'zel is waking!

Trelinia stopped reading and looked up from the book.

"That's all of it?" asked Marie.

"That's it," she replied. "That's the last thing anyone ever heard from the Drake Expedition of 1184."

"Who said that last weird passage?" asked Mckenzie.

"Like all the other log entries, it was spoken by Dr. Edric Drake, but obviously, that doesn't sound like something he would say. The theory is that, when he made that final transmission, he had either gone crazy, or he had been overcome by a power from the runestones. Most people believe that he'd been possessed by an evil entity from Nexxathia."

The girls looked at their mother in silence.

"I have a bunch of questions," said Mckenzie after a few moments. Marie nodded her head furiously.

"I bet you do," replied Trelinia. "Let's hear them."

Marie spoke first. "For one thing, what do the first sets of numbers mean? Where he was randomly saying them within the middle of his sentences?"

"Because of the bizarre structure and randomness in each entry, at least they initially believed them to be random, the alphanumeric sequences took a while to be decoded by the scientists back home. Not because they could not figure out their meaning, but because they originally ignored them altogether. They were interpreted as nonsense, the mutterings of a clearly deranged individual. What they eventually figured out, however, was that they were all sequences based on a numeral system called hexadecimal."

"What's that?" asked Marie.

"It's a number system based on sixteen characters. They include zero through nine and the letters *a, b, c, d, e,* and *f.* When you combine them into specific sequences, you can encode all types of information. I bet you'll never guess what the scientists found those perplexing sequences to mean."

"What are they?" asked the girls at the same time.

"They're the last names of each team member."

The sisters gasped.

"Drake was reading off each of his team member's name in hexadecimal. The scientists that analyzed this data postulated that he was actually unaware of this behavior while he was doing it. In previous entries, he'd mentioned suffering from visions of color and numbers and other disturbing images. They believed that this was another type of vision."

"So why does it matter?" asked Mckenzie.

"The fact that he was calling out the names of his missing team members, through an encoded numerical system, implies that he was being controlled by an outside force. It might also have been a clue to anyone listening to the transmissions. Other than that, the scientists at the time were unable to determine a conclusive explanation. Now that I think about it, however, I do remember one interesting theory that talked about the weird number sequences being part of a larger puzzle. There was a scientist a few years ago that made a stunning breakthrough with the mystery."

"What did he find out?" asked Marie.

"It's a she, actually. Her name is Dorothy Tompkins, but she goes by the nickname Dot. Anyway, she's a Tullek that lives in the city of Kadiaphonek."

"And what about all those ones and zeros you were reading at the end of the last entry?" asked Mckenzie. "The sequences that followed each name?"

"Good. Now you're starting to put the pieces of this mysterious puzzle together. As you pointed out, each team member's name was followed by a long sequence of ones and zeros. This follows another numeric system, called binary. They basically mean on or off. Where hexadecimal is a base sixteen system, binary is a base two system. When they decoded these sequences and matched them up with the others, you'll really never guess what they found all of it to mean."

"What are they?" the girls asked again.

"They're the names of the eight runestones."

"What? That's crazy!"

"Here's what was finally decoded from Drake's final set

of bizarre log entries and the hexadecimal and binary sequences. Prof. Multon is Frost. Prof. Eldridge is Fire. Prof. Dwyer is Light. Dr. Carrell is Shadow. Dr. Carterson is Technology. Dr. Mulgrew is Nature. Dr. Dexter is Life. Capt. Stevens is Death."

"What do you mean that Multon is Frost and Mulgrew is Nature?" asked Marie.

"Each member of the expedition has been transformed into the creatures that the runestones once entombed. Multon is now a dragon called Lord Mortis that protects the Rune of Frost. Mulgrew is a warlock called Thulcandra that protects the Rune of Nature. The other six are all different types of monsters with different powers and are all equally horrific. They each protect their specific runestone in different locations throughout the realm of Silvarum. What the scientists and others of that time came to realize, to their horror and dismay, is that, because the Drake Expedition desecrated the original tombs and stole the runestones from their sacred burial chamber, each of them was then punished by being absorbed by the power within the ancient city of Nexxathia."

Mckenzie rubbed her eyes, shaking her head. "Mom, are you seriously saying to us that there are eight of these monsters still alive today and roaming around Silvarum?"

"Yes, that's exactly what I'm saying to you."

"And how can you possibly know this?"

"Because your dad, your Uncle Brian, and I had to defeat five of them when we were your age."

CHAPTER XII

CAAT v1.2.13

"Are you telling me that this mask can really see four-dimensional objects in their actual forms?"

"Put it on and find out," said Merkresh.

The boy examined the glove. It was an impressive meld of digital technology, steam-powered engineering, and artistic form. For the amount of hardware that was attached to it and the intricacy of its design, it felt surprisingly light. Roger bounced it up and down in his hands several times. Much of its construction consisted of several interconnected sections of dark-brown leather. Each of the components were fortified with brass rivets that reflected the lantern light of the room. The feel of the mask's skin was pliable and satisfying. It reminded him of the leather chair that was tucked away in the corner of his father's study. He lifted the mask and breathed in a mixture of fresh leather and oiled metal.

As he had briefly observed upstairs, Roger now studied the main components of the mask in detail. They were comprised of the air filter, the giant eye lenses, the visual mechanism, and the cone-shaped auditory apparatus. Each example of technology was exorbitantly intricate and fascinating. The filter cartridge was a multi-layered, spherical box that protruded from the location of the mouth. It was fabricated from dark metal and contained holes of varied sizes. Two cross-sectioned, flexible air hoses extended out from either side of the cartridge. They wrapped around both sides of the mask toward the back and connected to a metal box that was located just above the base of the neck.

The eye lenses were equally massive and engrossed most of the area of the front of the mask. Shiny, brass frames, fitted with silver rivets, surrounded and secured the glass of each lens. The glass was murky green and flashed emerald highlights as Roger moved the mask in his hands. An elaborate collection of optical instruments, in the form of colored lenses and visual enhancements, was attached to the left eyepiece. Each adaptable lens could be individually flipped up or down over the central apparatus. A web of copper switches, knobs, and calibration dials engulfed the device.

The acoustic enhancement was a miniature copper horn attached to a small aperture on the right ear. The open mouth of the mechanism was aimed forward and could be adjusted and calibrated by several brass gears and cogs. Three clear tubes curled from the end of the horn and disappeared into the side of the mask.

Roger lifted the mask above his head and slowly slipped it on. It fit like a glove. The soft skin cradled his facial features, and the scent of the leather and metal was intoxicating. He blinked a few times to adjust to the new perspective. The view through the eye lenses allowed for a clear and unobstructed display of his surroundings. The emerald-tinted glass of the right eye produced a blanket of green, while the left lens processed objects into a three-dimensional crispness and fidelity.

"Wow," gasped Roger as he turned his head and looked around the room.

"Are you reacting to the impressive view of the Eyeculus 2584?" asked Merkresh.

"Yes. Is that what you've named it?"

Roger's voice generated a mechanical tone as he spoke through the mask's mouthpiece.

"For now," replied the old man. "What do you think?"

The boy continued to spin around. "Honestly, the name sounds pretty bad. What if you just called it the Eyeculus and took off the 2584 part?"

Merkresh chuckled. "That actually sounds much better. I like it. The Eyeculus it shall be."

"Cool," replied Roger as he turned to the glass enclosure.

"That thing doesn't look different, though," he said.

"That's because you haven't even turned the mask on," replied Merkresh.

"It turns on?"

"Of course it does. Reach up and press the button that's below the aperture over your left ear."

Roger felt for the button. As he pushed it, three distinct actions occurred within the mask. The first was the sound of a high-pitched twang immediately followed by a low hum. The vibration of the sound sent a gentle shockwave throughout the layers and components of the mask. The second action was that the acoustic device on his right ear activated and he could hear everything with stunning clarity and sharpness. The pops of bubbling liquid within a beaker near the back of the workshop. The tip-tap of Click's brass legs as he crawled around a table of tools in the woodworking section. As he began to filter through all the sounds, Roger could even make out the chirping of crickets through the windows upstairs. The third action, however, sent the boy's senses into a virtual mind spin. Both eye lenses flickered on. The right lens switched from an emerald-green haze to a crystal-clear screen. A blue HUD awoke along the borders of the right lens. Streams of data began to flash and display upon the glass. *Power, Range, Tracking, Time,* and *Target* were a few of the data headings that he could read.

"Holy shit!" gasped Roger. "This thing's computerized."

"You bet it is," replied Merkresh.

Roger peered through the left lens. The 3-D effect was apparent, but there was no other noticeable change.

"What's wrong with the left lens?" asked Roger.

"Nothing. I have one more toy to show you."

The boy turned and saw that Merkresh was holding out the mechanical glove that he had been wearing earlier.

"No way," said Roger.

"Yes way. Put it on and try it out."

Roger took the glove and eased it onto his right hand. It fit up to his elbow. Buttons and dials covered its leather and brass body. He wiggled his fingers into place and felt sensors at the tips of each finger.

"Are you ready for a quick overview of the controls?" asked Merkresh.

"Are you kidding me? This is the coolest thing ever."

"The sensors on your fingertips control everything in your mask and the glove. There are so many code combinations, however, that I have had to develop a program that will display all of them and their functions on your heads-up-display. I am way too old at this point to remember all the combos. There are about a thousand distinct functions that you can choose from. Tap your index finger three times and your thumb once to display the list."

Roger tapped the combination with his fingertips. Instead of the control program being displayed, a 3-D grid popped onto the screen, and a computerized female voice spoke to him.

"Plasma pulse online," she said. "Please lock onto the requested target and fire when ready."

"Oh no!" exclaimed Merkresh. "Quick, press your index finger three times, and then your thumb twice to disengage it."

Roger fumbled with the glove as he tried to process the instructions and remember the difference between his index finger and thumb. He tapped the combo, and the green grid and voice disappeared.

"Good grief," he said. "What in the world was that?"

"Sorry about that," replied Merkresh. "I told you that my memory is not as sharp as it used to be. That was a plasma weapon, but I don't think you're ready for that yet."

"This thing has weapons too?"

"It has all kinds of features. I'll train you on the weaponry later. For now, let's focus on the basics like turning things on and off without blowing up my workshop."

"Good idea," said Roger.

"Let's try that again. This time, tap your index finger two times and your thumb two times."

Roger executed the combo and immediately saw a new heading from the menu bar at the top of the screen that read *Master Control.*

"It worked. I can see the master control program."

"Great. When you move your hand in the air, you should also see an arrow pointer on your screen that follows you."

Roger moved his hand in circles and watched for the arrow on the screen.

"I see it!"

"Now, whenever you want to select something from the menus, just press your index finger one time. When you want to execute a program or function, all you have to do is click twice with your index finger. Got it?"

"I think so. Should I select the master control program and then run it?"

"Yes, please," replied Merkresh.

Roger twirled his gloved finger in the air and carefully maneuvered the pointer up to the menu bar. He felt like a symphony conductor guiding a stage of musicians through the layers of a dramatic crescendo. As he clicked on the *Master Control* menu item, a drop-down list of additional options was displayed. They included *List, Custom, Search,* and *Help.* Roger thought for a moment and then clicked on the *List* item. Another sub-menu dropped off to the right side of the main menu and displayed the first ten options in alphabetical order. These included *ActvARS, ActvAVR, ActvEar, ActvEar01, ActvEye, ActvEye01, ActvCAAT, ActvJARP, ActvLogs,* and *ActvMod7.*

"I can see the first ten functions," said Roger.

"Splendid. Do you see the one called Activate CAAT?"

"Yes, but it says ActvCAAT."

"That's the one. Click on that."

"What do the other functions do? What's ActvMod7?"

"ActvMod7?" replied Merkresh. "No, don't worry about that one right now. I'll tell you about it some other time. For now, please just execute the CAAT program."

Roger moved the cursor down to the function and then selected it. Yet another submenu was generated. It displayed the values: *2-1, 3-1, 2-2.*

"There are a bunch of numbers and dashes now."

"That's the combo for executing the program with your finger pads. Want to try and guess what they mean?"

Roger peered at the series of numbers and dashes on his heads-up-display and mumbled to himself.

"I'll give you a hint," said Merkresh. "Your thumb is designated as location one, your index finger is location two, and so on. Your pinky finger is location five."

"Oh, cool," replied the boy. "I think I get it."

He tapped his index finger once, then his second finger once, then his index finger two more times. The charming female voice returned to the speakers inside the mask.

"Good evening. Please provide the required combination of the function you wish to execute."

"Wow," said Roger.

"Say hello to your new friend, CAAT."

"Does that stand for something?"

"Computerized Assistant and Auditory Technology."

"Cool. Does she respond to voice commands too?"

"Not yet, I'm afraid," replied Merkresh. "She can only interact with the glove combos in this version. I was almost finished with implementing her voice recognition functionality, but as you'll see in a moment, I recently became completely distracted by another breakthrough. CAAT is only version 1.2.13. Her version 2.0 will have a VR interface. I promise."

"She's super cool already," replied Roger.

"Let's try something more advanced, shall we?" asked Merkresh. "From the master control menu, click on the search option and type in the letters *e-y-e-c-u-l-u-s*."

Roger moved the pointer back to the menu with *Search* and pressed his index finger once. A text box opened.

"Wait a second," he said. "How am I supposed to type with this glove on?"

"Good question," replied Merkresh. "It might be helpful if I teach you that now. It's really easy. All you have to do is tap all your fingers once at the same time to bring up the keyboard. Tap them all again to get rid of it."

Roger tapped his fingers all at once. A virtual keyboard was displayed in the center of the eye lens.

"I can't believe how cool this thing is."

"Thank you. It still has a few defects to work out, but it's definitely fun to play with. Now that you have the keyboard up, all you have to do is point and click on the specific key to type. Unfortunately, you must hunt-and-peck for the time being. At some point, I'll have the other glove finished, and you'll be able to type with both hands."

With the text box still opened, Roger twirled his fingers around in the air and typed out the letters *e-y-e-c-u-l-u-s*.

"Do I need to click on this looking glass icon?"

"Yes, click it. That executes the search."

"Searching," said CAAT.

An hourglass animation popped up next to the text box.

Tiny bytes of sand fell through the top of the hourglass and piled up at the bottom. After a few iterations of falling sand, a results set was displayed on the screen.

"Search complete. 376 results found," she said.

"That's a lot for Eyeculus," said Merkresh. "Try filtering the search. Click on the refine button and then type *m-a-g-n-i-f-y*."

Roger typed in the refined search term.

"Searching," said CAAT.

More bytes of sand.

"Search complete. Three results found."

"Much better," said Merkresh. "Can you please read the results out to me?"

"Sure. It says EyeculusMagnify01, 02, and 03."

"Very well."

The old man peered across the room. "Click, where in the world are you?"

The mechanical spider was in the process of spinning a huge web between an assortment of glass beakers and tubes. Upon hearing the old man's voice, he looked up and produced a loud mechanical chirp.

"There you are," said Merkresh. "Stay still a moment if you don't mind. I want to show Roger something, and then you can carry on with your web making."

Click chirped in acknowledgment.

"All right, Roger. If you'd please focus your attention to Click across the room."

The boy turned and searched for the spider in his web.

"I see him."

"How well can you see his features from here?"

"Not very well. He just looks like a teeny bronze blob."

"Wonderful. Now if you'd please select the search result for EyeculusMagnify02 and retrieve its combination."

Roger moved the pointer over the appropriate selection and clicked. It displayed the combo: *4-1, 5-1, 1-2*. He slowly and carefully tapped out the sequence with his fingertips.

"Eyeculus magnification level two initiated," said CAAT.

Roger gazed across the workshop in the direction of Click. The left eye lens swiftly cycled through the selection of adapters and then focused in on the mechanical arachnid. Where before he could only see the basic shape of the spider's bronze and metallic form, with the enhanced magnification of level two, he could now easily make out the exact number of teeth on each of his cogwheels and gears.

"Wow," exclaimed Roger. "That's so much better."

"How does our friend look now?" asked Merkresh.

"I can see the scratches on the brass of his smallest gears. I can even see the hydraulic levers and pistons extending up and down along his legs as he moves."

"Perfect. Are you feeling more comfortable with the basic operations of the mask and the glove?"

"A little better, yes. But I want to keep going. What else can you show me? Can we shoot the plasma gun now?"

"Not yet," replied Merkresh. "We'll get to all that soon enough. Not to worry. However, I do think you're ready to take that test I mentioned earlier. Please reset the magnification back to level one and take a look over here."

CHAPTER XIII

WARINGTON CASTLE

The last beast disappeared behind the veil of fog. A swirl of mist encircled the creature's tail as it vanished into the haze. The men stood at the end of the drawbridge, listening to the procession of deep booms as the footfalls faded into the hills.

"That could've gone better," said the captain.

"It certainly should have," replied Brian Woods.

"Watch your tongue, sergeant."

"My tongue, sir, was the only thing that saved you and the rest of us from harm this morning," he replied. "You should be more appreciative."

The knights and other guards cringed at the directness of his open criticism and hostile attitude. Their helms twisted back and forth between the men's tense words.

"Turn and face me, sergeant," replied Captain Hamonet.

Brian spat a glob of liquid onto the road.

"Yes, sir," he said, snapping to attention.

Captain Hamonet grinned. His beady eyes and weak chin quivered with arrogance and self-importance.

"Count Zaran warned me about your direct nature and aggressiveness. You have quite the reputation around here, don't you? It's plain for me to see now, but would you care to elaborate on my actions this morning?"

"I'd be happy to elaborate," replied Brian. "Simply stated, you don't belong out here on the wall. You displayed doubt and cowardice toward the Tombspawn, and they immediately took advantage of it. That's precisely what they prey upon. Fear and weak-mindedness. Once their leader, Lord Mordok, sensed those traits in you, he forced his will upon your mind, and you eventually fainted. Simple as that. If I hadn't intervened and taken control of the situation by countering his belligerence and earning his temporary respect, then we might all have been in a great deal of trouble."

"Rubbish," exclaimed the captain. His eyes were wide and manic. "I fainted from exhaustion alone. From dehydration and the fatigue of the numerous missions that I've performed for this castle over the past week. It wasn't due to anything that hideous creature did to me. And as far as your heroic and courageous performance, I witnessed nothing of consequence from you. All you did was stand there and gawk, like the rest of this worthless rabble."

"You didn't witness anything of consequence because you were knocked out cold on your ass," replied Belris. All heads snapped in his direction. One guard let out a hushed giggle.

"What did you say, private?" asked Captain Hamonet, glaring at the boy. "I don't recall asking for your irrelevant input or disrespectful comments. I swear, if you say another word, you'll march yourself straight up to the keep and stand before Count Zaran himself."

"It's true, though," said Belris. "Sergeant Woods said or did something to the Nexxathian that scared it. It was only after he confronted him that they began to cooperate and trade. They were just playing around with us until you fainted."

"Silence your insubordination," said the captain. "I told you I didn't faint because of that monster." His voice was shrill and desperate.

Brian Woods shook his head in disgust, interjecting with a relaxed voice. "You're free to believe what you will, captain, but the fact remains, you aren't qualified for the task of confronting these beings out here in the open. To interact with them, you must be able to first stand up to them. The private is correct. This is all just a game to the Nexxathians. All they want to do is fight and kill. Only when you confront them with an equal footing, will they show you a pittance of respect and do business with you. As I said, captain, you're just not suited for a task of this nature."

The captain jerkily turned his enraged expression toward the calm voice. His face and eyes convulsed with scorched fury, while his thin lips curled up as tight as a drum. He blinked wildly as he tried to control himself and regain a sense of composure. After several deep, exhaustive breaths, Captain Hamonet sneered, expelling a bizarre cackle.

The men frowned and looked at each other in confusion.

"I see," he replied as the disturbed laughter concluded. "I'm truly sorry to hear that you feel this way about my leadership abilities, Sergeant Woods. Your superior, however, disagrees with your keen analysis. He believes that I'm perfectly suited to command such a task. Now, what sort of disrespectful comment do you have to say to that?"

Brian Woods spat another blob of juice onto the road and looked into the captain's eyes. "Then I would say that my superior is just as unsuited for the job as you."

Gasps escaped from the guards.

Captain Hamonet laughed sardonically. "Indeed, sir. I expected you to say as much. Fortunately, you'll soon have the opportunity to express your disdain for his leadership skills straight to his face. I invite you to have a chat with Count Zaran in his throne room upon the conclusion of this most enjoyable conversation. Or shall I say, you are commanded to stand before him. I'm confident that he's looking forward to speaking with you once again."

"Fine," replied Brian.

"I'm sorry, I didn't catch that last part. What did you say?" asked the captain, dramatically turning his ear toward the sergeant in a sarcastic gesture.

Brian clenched his teeth. "I said, yes sir."

"Outstanding," replied Captain Hamonet as he turned and addressed the other guards. "This morning's trade is thus concluded, gentlemen. Report back to your posts immediately."

The men grumbled and dispersed from the drawbridge.

"Not so fast, private," said the captain. "You'll follow Sergeant Woods up to the keep and stand before Count Zaran as well. I must say that I'm delighted to hear how well you respond to his inquiries. He has a reputation for, shall we say, being extremely creative during his interviews. No doubt that your answers will be as courageous and valiant before his gaze as they were toward mine. If we're fortunate, maybe his Uncle Amfridus will be in attendance. Now that would be a treat."

Belris turned a sickly shade of white at the thought of standing before the count in his throne room. He looked over at Brian Woods with an expression of panic and dread. The man shrugged.

"Fantastic," said Captain Hamonet with a caustic chuckle. "We're all set then. Gentlemen, if you'd be so gracious as to hand over your weapons to these fine men, I'd be much appreciative. Guards, please then escort our two guests up to Count Zaran's chambers. Onward to the castle keep!"

Captain Hamonet, Brian, and Belris marched along the drawbridge and under the iron portcullis of the North Gate. Soft waves of murky water lapped against the lichen-covered stones of the moat below. As they cleared the gatehouse and stepped onto the muddy grass of the outer bailey, Belris turned his head and watched as the gate dropped to its closed position, bellowing an ominous moan.

***

Warington Castle was an extraordinarily large stone and wood fortification for that region of Silvarum. It overlooked the countryside atop the high moorlands of the Northeast Province and sat nestled between the gray grasses of the Whispering Hills and snow-covered summits of the Shadow Mountains. For hundreds of years the castle had served as the northernmost outpost for defending against the evils that slithered and crawled out of the bowels of the mountains.

Baron Ulric Warington, along with his three sons Giraud,

Gualterius, and Raimond, originally built the castle in the year 1190. This was a mandated project, ratified by the citizens to construct a defense directly proportionate to the impending threat posed by the evil of the dreaded city of Nexxathia. The dark forces that were unleashed upon Silvarum by the Drake Expedition of 1184 caused a massive buildup of castle outposts and other defensive fortifications. Eight mighty castles, including Warington, were swiftly constructed and strategically positioned along the northern borders of the realm. A dense network of roads and byways connected the castles to their lower cities, providing an efficient system of resupply and sustainability. This solid defensive strategy served the kingdom well for many years and resulted in numerous victories.

In the year 1220, Baron Ulric and his son Giraud and thirty thousand other citizens perished from an outbreak of bubonic plague known as the *Shrieking Lady*. The defenses along the northern border began to crumble and weaken. Because of the devastating death toll, the Nexxathian horde took full advantage of the softened defenses and, commanded by the fire demon known as Vexx, swept through the breach and attacked several southern cities. The battles fought during this grim period are for another chapter in this tale. Suffice it to say, however, that once all was said and done, and the ashes of war had settled, Baron Ulric's other son, Gualterius, had recaptured and assumed command of their castle. He and his brother Raimond had once again rebuilt its fortifications to their former glory and strength. Gualterius, having been the oldest of the surviving two brothers, ruled behind its stone walls until his death.

During his tenure within the gates of Warington Castle, Gualterius himself bestowed three sons upon the realm. Their names were Gualterius II, Merkresh, and Amfridus. They were noble offspring, learned in the arts of warfare and virtuous chivalry. Both Gualterius II and Merkresh, upon fulfilling their training obligations as squire and page, were anointed their knighthoods by the prime age of twenty-one. They served their castle proudly by defending Silvarum against the ever-present threats and evils of Nexxathia.

Amfridus, on the other hand, had elected to pursue a much more sinister career path in life. At a tender age, he had become infatuated with the Dark Arts, specifically the nebulous realm of witchcraft and necromancy. While his two older brothers were learning the highborn skills of falconry and equestrianism, young Amfridus was creeping within dark corners and damp cellars, perfecting ancient spellcraft and studying demonic magiks. He had withdrawn entirely from his family and the rest of society during the time of his brothers' accolade. Amfridus the Corruptor, as he was dubbed early on by estranged family members and fearful villagers, can still be seen skulking and lurking within the castle's most ancient and forgotten corridors. During the witching hour, his cloaked silhouette is often framed against the blazing backdrop of a full moon, scrambling along the curtain wall on some devious errand. He has become a living ghost, creeping and conspiring within the castle's hallways of enchanted ebony.

Upon the arrival of their father's death in the year 1301, Gualterius II assumed command of Warington Castle and its surrounding estate and lands. For his gallantry during the war of 1299, the monarch chose to promote him to the rank of count. His brother Merkresh, freshly knighted and eager for more battle, had recently been summoned to aid in the ongoing fight against

Silvarum's enemies far away in the south. Amfridus, however, remained hidden within the shadows of the castle, enhancing his wicked studies and weaving his cunning webs. Over the years, he had begun to quietly assist his older brother in matters of policy. Land grievances between quarreling villagers, punishments for local criminals, and the constant expansion of the family's wealth and power were a few examples of Amfridus' growing influence. Where the rest of his family had renounced his noble status due to his meddling in the Dark Arts, Count Gualterius II had embraced his younger brother's vile talents. Together they began to use these powers to spy upon, bribe, and deceitfully influence other unsuspecting noble families and villagers within their province. As they began to cultivate their wealth and success through their deceptive game of corruption, the brothers became even more emboldened. They soon found themselves devising treacherous deals with rogue groups of humans, villainous tradesmen of various species and breeds, and even doing business with their hated enemy, the Nexxathians. A foul storm of decrepit malevolence had saturated Warington Castle, ushering in a new generation of evil.

In the year 1320, Count Gualterius II had his first and only son. His name was Zaran Maximillian Warington. He was a rotten and insidious child, short-tempered and impatient. From a youthful age, he watched intently and studied the unscrupulous behaviors of his father and uncle. He learned through their example how to treat others cruelly and how to bend the will of the weak and powerless. In addition to having a black and hateful heart, young Zaran was a brilliant strategist and soldier. It was a deadly skillset. He soon demonstrated these talents upon the battlefield by leading successful raids into the neighboring kingdoms and countries. Unsanctioned and largely unaware by the monarch in the south, that was dealing with its own political and wartime conflicts, the remote castle outpost was essentially left alone. Thus, the Warington heraldry began to wage its private campaign of outright invasion and subjugation across the surrounding landscape.

At the age of twenty-one, like his father, Zaran had been anointed his knighthood. Unquenched and bored by his effortless assaults upon the nearby human realms and territory, the young warrior soon found himself thirsty for a much larger chalice of conquest. He had his sights set on the mysterious powers that flowed from the domain of the Nexxathians, a hidden realm that lay deep within the Shadow Mountains and below the ghoulish city of Nexxathia. During his various battles, Zaran had observed the magical abilities and sorcery of these beings firsthand. Mind control, levitation, and palm-projected orbs of blue energy. He wished to understand and obtain these unusual abilities for himself. Why should his family be satisfied with the Northern Province, when they could use this untapped magic to achieve so much more?

Amidst the melancholy alleyways and cobblestone streets of Warington Castle, whispered voices spoke of a mysterious power that bubbled and frothed within the depths of the subterranean city of Nexxathia. Zaran, along with his corrupt father and sorcerous uncle, was determined to discover this factory of dark magic. To accomplish this lofty task, however, they chose to pursue their exploration methodically and patiently, through deception and trade, rather than direct confrontation. This thoughtful methodology ran contradictory to their instincts of domination and rapid destruction. Count Gualterius II thus escalated their existing relationship with the Nexxathians by enabling open commerce. Caravans from both species began to shuttle goods and precious materials between their two cities. This collaborative trade agreement, though uneasy and often irritable, lasted for years.

Count Gualterius II died in 1350 from unknown causes. Some believed that it was due to a heart condition, which had plagued him his entire life. Others, including his brother Amfridus and some of his closest advisors, speculated a more perverse motivation. The exact reason for his death was never fully ascertained. Nevertheless, his son Zaran, now thirty years old, was swiftly elevated to the command of Warington Castle. Within a few years, the monarch had promoted him to the rank of count. And thus, Count Zaran Maximillian Warington began his reign of corruption and hatefulness upon the northern landscape. He continued to receive dark guidance and advice from his warlock uncle. Likewise, he maintained the open business relationship with the Nexxathians. The deeper he delved and the closer he came to obtaining their evil secrets, the farther Count Zaran drifted from his family's former virtues and honor.

***

The late morning sun beamed down upon the bustling market square and interior grounds of Warington Castle. The fog had all but burned off, and pockets of blue sky began to shine high and crisp amongst the puffy clouds. Wisps of dusky smoke curled up from a blacksmith's forge as men clad in gray tunics and dirty faces sharpened blades and tempered steel. A master carpenter, flanked by apprentices, nailed together and polished the finishing touches of an order of furniture. Colorful tents and decorated stalls, filled with fragrant herbs, spices, fish, and steaming breads, crowded every stone wall and corner. Citizens of all types and classes talked, laughed, and shouted with one another amid the flurry of commerce.

Captain Hamonet motioned for their group to halt at a muddy intersection. He signaled to his knights, conversing with them in hushed voices. Belris shuffled his feet and turned to observe a group of youngsters yelling and chasing each other in a grassy courtyard. He frowned, wishing he could be one of them. To enjoy the grass and the sun without a care in the world.

Brian Woods spat a wad of brown juice upon the muddy ground and watched a chandler hang up a line of freshly dipped candles.

"Oy, you there," said a haggard voice.

Brian turned and peered down at the pockmarked face of a scraggly peasant. An enormous wart surged from the end of his crooked nose. The man wore a burgundy tunic and ankle-high britches. Both were covered in colorful patches and mud stains.

"What do you want?" replied Brian.

The man grinned. His rotted and cracked teeth glistened in the sunlight. "Oh, nothing really. I'm just here enjoying the sights and sounds of the day. The chirping of the bitsy birdies and the warm sun on me face."

"That's nice," replied Brian, turning back to watch the candle maker.

"Would you know," said the man after a few moments, "that I happened to see some unusual sights and overhear some rather interesting comments earlier this morning. And they ain't have nothing to do with no birds or weather."

"That's fascinating. I'm very happy for you."

"Thank you," said the man, clearing his phlegm-filled throat. "I'm called Hubert the Wise. I'm considered a rather skilled collector of information in this part of the castle. It's a pleasure to meet you. And your name is?"

"My name's fuck off," replied Brian. "I'm not interested right now in making your acquaintance, and I could care less about your bird stories or other talents."

Hubert smiled. "I'm very sorry to have bothered you."

Brian Woods looked over at the captain and his knights, wondering what they could be whispering about. They seemed exceedingly excited about the topic, whatever it was. Each man pointed and gestured to illustrate his inputs and opinions. Brian hoped it did not have to do with the mind trick that he had played on Lord Mordok. But, considering how bad the morning had gone thus far, it probably did.

"How about this?" asked the peasant. "What if I was to tell you that, in between enjoying the chirps of the teensy birdies and the warm sun, I've also been watching and listening to you."

Brian glared at the man. "Are you kidding me?"

"Now it seems like I have your attention," said Hubert. "And I'm not kidding you."

"Hubert the Lies, is it?" asked Brian.

"Wise. Hubert the Wise."

"Of course it is. Now, Hubert. I believe I just stated to you, less than three seconds ago, that I wasn't interested in hearing your stories and I don't care about what you have to say. Do you remember any of that?"

"Aye, I remember all of that, sir."

"Do you also notice that I'm wearing the armor of the

gate guard and carry the rank of sergeant?"

"Yes, sir. I notice all of those things too," replied Hubert. "Very impressive, indeed. However, I also see, and this is the really interesting detail, is that you're not carrying your own sword at the moment. That gentleman over there is holding it. This fact leads me to believe that you and your young mate there are in a bit of trouble. Is this assessment correct?"

Brian Woods glanced around at the bustling crowd. This last statement caused him to suspect that something much more devious was at play. No longer did this seem like a simple case of an annoying peasant and his innocent chit-chat.

"Don't worry, sergeant," said Hubert with a wicked grin. "Me mates are well hidden. At least for the time being. Whether they remain that way is entirely up to you."

Brian peered at the man and said nothing.

"Now, the real reason that I came over here to talk to you was to convince you to help out me and my friends. We have recently acquired information that we think is profitable."

"Good for you and your friends."

"It's good for you as well, sir."

"Oh really? And why is that?"

"Because by not revealing the valuable information that we have acquired, to your captain over there, for example, you'd be in better shape than if we did. As a show of our generosity, we would, therefore, be obliged to sell you this information for a meager fee and be done with the matter. How does that sound?"

Brian chuckled. "What exactly is this valuable information that you think you have?"

"It's a bit of valuable information that we think…"

"You said that already," said Brian.

Hubert expelled a shrill laugh and cleared his phlegmy throat again. He coughed up a wad of green mucus, spitting it onto the ground.

"Easy there, sergeant. Don't get upset with poor Hubert. I was just about to let you know that I gathered this valuable information while I was watching you outside the gate earlier this morning. I was peeking through my wee peephole in the wall. Aye, I even seen how you stood up to that cloaked rascal out there on the bridge. And then how you and the young captain was hootin' and hollerin' at one another."

"So what," replied Brian. "Why should I care about what you think you saw?"

Hubert stepped closer, lowering his voice to a whisper. His breath stank of alcohol and fish.

"Because through my secret peephole in the wall I could tell that you used the mind-speech on that cloaked fella. Yes, you did. Don't go and tell a lie to Hubert. I see everything that goes on out there on that bridge. And I've lived in Warington long enough to spot when someone has that type of talent. I also know how valuable that talent can be to the right person."

Brian backed off a few paces.

"And there's something else that I noticed out there on that bridge. I saw how you seemed shy about divulging that special talent of yours to your mates. Would I be correct in guessing that you've been trying to keep that detail a secret? Why would that be? All you have to do is purchase this teeny bit of information from me, and I promise you, I won't tell a soul."

"My dear Hubert," said Brian in a calm voice. "I'm going to ask you politely one time, so perk up those rat ears of yours and listen. Here's what you're going to do. You're going to quietly turn around and slither away. You're then going to forget that you ever threatened me. If you choose to disregard this cordial request, well, then that'll be your problem. Again, if you don't do exactly what I've just asked of you, then I promise you'll be dealing with the consequences of your choice for the remainder of your miserable life. How does that sound?"

Hubert's eyes lit up like two glowing embers as his yellow teeth stuck out in delighted astonishment. The raucous laughter that gushed from his mouth spewed forth a cackling array of mucus-filled sputters and uncontrolled wheezes. Several nearby villagers turned toward him, cringing.

"How dare you speak to Hubert the Wise like that! Do you know who I am? I'm a collector of valuable information. I'm an important person in Warington. Now I'll tell you what I'm going to do. I'm going to march right up to your captain there and tell him exactly how I saw that you can…"

Hubert clutched the sides of his head, emitting a series of high-pitched screams. His face was frozen with a disturbing expression of surprise and fear. The cracking of his nose and cheekbones pierced the air as his limp body slammed to the muddy ground, face first. Air bubbled around his submerged head for a moment, and then Hubert the Wise was silent.

Brian Woods turned around and continued to watch the candlemaker hang his candles.

CHAPTER XIV

EVENFALL

The sun had almost set. A small sliver of waning light remained on the horizon and a cloudless sky, sparkling with silver stars, imbued a smooth transition from blue to deep purple. A sapphire canvas framed their silhouettes as the girls walked along the hill.

"How did you die?" asked Penelope.

Abigail sighed, slowing her pace. "We were on our way home from my violin recital when it happened. My mom and I had just left school. We were talking and laughing and reflecting on how well everything had gone with the concert and solos. I'd been practicing my piece, my solo, for a month straight. Every night, after dinner and homework, I would sit in the living room and practice my part over and over again. My mom, bless her heart, would always watch and listen to every note while I played for her. I'd become pretty good at it, but I was still so nervous about the idea of playing on a stage in front of all those people.

She thought that if I performed for her and got used to it, that it would help me when I had to do the real thing. She did that for me every night. For an entire month, she sat there and smiled and encouraged me and told me that I would be perfect no matter what happened. The evening of the concert I was so unbelievably nervous that I couldn't even think straight. I felt sick and dizzy, and I wanted to jump up and run out of that place. But then I saw something. I saw something that made all of that fear go away in an instant."

"What did you see?" asked Penelope.

Abigail cleared her throat and continued. "We were only moments away from going on stage. I mean, like seconds. My head was overflowing with anxiety, and my whole body was shaking. I didn't know if I could go through with it. But then, as we stood there waiting on the side stage, I glanced over through a break in the curtains and I spotted my mom in the crowd. She was sitting in the third row from the front. She couldn't see me, but I had a perfect view of her face and the expression it held. My mom seemed so proud. She was sitting on the edge of her seat with a giant smile on her face. All I could see in her eyes was love and encouragement and happiness. Happiness for her daughter who was about to go on stage and face one of her greatest fears. And no matter what happened, whether I missed a note or felt embarrassed, the look in her eyes assured me that I would be perfect. And that's all I needed. In that instant, I let go of all my manufactured anxiety. All my doubt. I walked out onto that stage, and I conquered my fear. And when we all stood there at the end and bowed before the audience, the only thing that I could see, the only thing that existed in the entire universe for me, was my mom's proud eyes."

Abigail took a deep breath and gazed out into the frosted twilight. The portraits of misshapen trees swayed gently against the embrace of the approaching night.

"On the ride home all that happiness was destroyed. One moment we were talking and laughing and the next was pure darkness and silence. The transition was instantaneous. I mean, it was like a light had been switched off. I remember hearing the scream of tires and an awful, crunching impact. Then it was all over. Darkness. There was no pain or anything, it was just all black. And then like you, the next time I opened my eyes, I was in my coffin."

Penelope smiled, placing her hand on Abigail's shoulder. "Thank you for telling me that story. Your mum sounds like she's a truly amazing person."

"She really is. But I can't even imagine the pain she's been going through since it happened."

"She is feeling pain but try to imagine this instead. She still loves you. And even though she's grieving over your death, I'm sure that she'll always remember those same experiences that the two of you shared. The same ones that you just told me. Like sitting there each night and practicing your solo or being at your recital and supporting you as you faced your fear on that stage. Those are the memories that you'll cherish when you're alone in the darkness. Believe me, I know."

"You're right. But everything is still so fresh and painful in my mind. It's like it only just happened a few hours ago."

"The confusion of dying will begin to pass over time," replied Penelope. "It's strange to say, but after a while, you'll actually get used to the idea of being dead. Of being a ghost. Think of it this way. You're only a ghost from the perspective of a person who's alive. Do I look like I'm dead or an apparition to you as we stand here on this hill and have a conversation? No. But to a person who's alive and not of this time and space, we certainly would, if they saw us at all. Anyhow, all I'm saying is that you'll figure all this death stuff out eventually."

Abigail smiled. "I've never thought of it that way before."

"The pain of losing your mum won't go away as quickly," said Penelope. "I'm sorry to be so honest, but it's true. At least for me, it has. That pain will be with you for a while. What's important is how you choose to deal with all that sorrow."

"And how have you dealt with it?"

Penelope sighed. "Truthfully, not always so well. When I first arrived in this place, I didn't have anyone else to talk to for ages. I did a lot of crying and a lot of wandering and a lot of sitting on those steps and staring out into the nothingness."

"Other than that woman, there wasn't anyone else?"

"No," she replied. "I mean, there're plenty of dried up corpses in these crypts and tombs, but just try to get one of them to strike up an engaging conversation. It ain't going to happen. And yes, before you go and ask, there were a few times when I pretended that some of them were alive so that I could talk with something that sort of resembled a human being. Talking to birds and trees got old fast."

"I wasn't actually going to ask you that, but since you volunteered the information, I probably would have done the same thing. At least you didn't dress them up and set them in chairs and pretend they were your family and friends, right?"

Penelope stared back at her.

"Wait, you actually did that?"

"Look, that's what I mean by not always handling things

well," replied Penelope. "I can't even believe I'm telling you this. Let's see how well you behave after wandering around in a freezing cemetery all by yourself for four hundred years. You end up doing some weird stuff."

"I'm sorry. I didn't mean to make fun of you or hurt your feelings," said Abigail.

"It's fine," she replied, smiling. "It was a long time ago anyway, so I guess I can laugh about it now. Besides, I've made another friend since then. I'll introduce you to her soon."

"What?" exclaimed Abigail. "But before you said there wasn't anyone else here since that woman left you. What other person are you talking about?"

"That was mostly the truth," replied Penelope. "The new person arrived this morning, right before you did. I knew her when she was alive."

"What?"

"You'll see," said Penelope. "Come on. Let's head back up the hill to where you found those boots."

"What else did you do after you arrived here? Did you try to get out?" asked Abigail as they walked up the hill.

"Of course. One of the first things I did was come down to this gate, just like you did, and try to walk out."

"Did you bounce off the barrier too?"

"What do you think?" asked Penelope. "Would I still be hanging out in this miserable cemetery if I didn't?"

"Yeah, I guess that was a dumb question. But didn't you say that the woman you knew before was able to walk through it? Why was she able to? Where do you think it leads?"

"Aye, I watched her walk through it and disappear, but I have no idea where it leads to, or where she went."

Abigail stopped walking and looked at Penelope with a thoughtful expression.

"Penny, did you ever see a book in your crypt when you first awoke here?"

The girl stared back at her, hesitating. "I don't think so. What kind of book are you talking about?"

"It was really old and leathery, and it had a big lock on it."

"Nay. I don't remember anything like that."

"And there was a voice," said Abigail. "There was a weird voice that talked to me from an eyeball on the book. I know this must sound crazy to you, but just listen."

"I am listening. And aye, it sounds crazy."

"I don't remember anymore what the voice said, but I do recall that I had a vision. Like, it somehow sent me from the crypt up into some snowy mountains. I saw my mom walking in the woods."

"Really?" asked Penelope. "I definitely never experienced anything like that here. What do you think it means?"

"I have no idea," replied Abigail. "My mom never said anything back to me in the vision, but now I'm wondering if that whole experience was supposed to let me know that she actually died in the car accident too. I'm so confused."

"Whatever it means, I'm sure you're going to figure it all out, but it's going to take a while. You just got here, and there's no way you're going to find all the answers right now. I know it's painful and confusing to have lost your mum and everyone else you have ever known but trust me, it'll get easier over time."

"How long did it take you to get over it?"

"Over the pain and loss? You don't ever truly get over those things. All you can really do is confront them and accept them, but at the same time appreciate and remember all the moments you shared with the folks you loved while you were alive. Those memories will never die. Not from a snowstorm or a car accident. And in a way, neither will you. You'll always be alive within those unbreakable memories of you and your mum. They are yours for eternity."

Abigail smiled. "There's one thing that's come out of this whole mess that I am sure of."

"What's that?" asked Penelope.

"That you and I are friends now. It sucks that we had to die to meet each other, but I'm thankful now that I know you."

Penelope laughed. "Aye, we are friends. We just had to both become ghosts first. How funny is that?"

The two girls laughed together as they stood on the path. The sun had dropped beneath the horizon causing puffs of icy breath to escape their mouths as they talked. Penelope scanned the darkness.

"What is it?" asked Abigail, sensing her anxiety.

"We need to get indoors now."

"What? Why?"

"There are things that come out once the sun sets."

"What kind of things?"

"Just follow me, and I'll tell you when we're safe inside. God, I can't believe I lost track of time like that."

Penelope immediately turned, rushing back up the hill.

"Wait!" cried Abigail.

As the last whisper of light vanished beneath the murky horizon, every object and form within the cemetery became enshrouded under a veil of gloom. The mausoleums, tombstones, and weeping statues all depicted a new sense of foreboding.

"This way," said Penelope.

"Where are we going?"

"To a safe place. It's just across this field."

They carefully navigated through a maze of open graves and fallen headstones. Lanky grass and thorny bushes choked the aisles. Abigail's dress became snagged on an outcropping of brambles. Penelope hopped up and down anxiously as she waited for her to pry the fabric loose.

"We're almost there," she said.

"How much further?"

"It's right up ahead."

As they maneuvered between the final rows of tombs, Abigail could still hear the constant hum of the crickets. Even over her labored and stressed breathing, their melodic verses were distinct. However, there was another sound amidst their chirping that caught her attention. As she listened carefully, she could make out a new sound. It was deeper, like a long, drawn-out howl. Abigail stopped and listened.

"What're you doing?" cried Penelope.

"Can you hear that?"

"We don't have time to stop. It's not safe."

"What's that noise?"

Abigail strained her eyes into the dusk, peering across the field. There was a shape, hovering. It was barely visible, yet she perceived the faint outline of a figure. It glowed an ethereal blue and was shrouded in a translucent, flowing cloak. Shredded strips of fabric dangled as it floated above the cobblestones.

"Please, Abigail. We must go."

"What is that thing?"

"Something terrible."

The apparition thrust its arms toward the girls, emitting a sorrowful wail. It was unlike any sound Abigail had ever heard in her living days. The howl was drowned in layers of sadness and pain that penetrated the marrow of her bones. Two red eyes flashed within its hood as the phantom floated across the field.

"It's coming for us!" cried Abigail, running.

To her dismay, she fell into the muddy mouth of an open grave. Abigail screamed from the sudden disorientation, flinging her arms in a desperate attempt to catch her fall. She slammed against the bottom of the grave with terrible force.

"Are you all right?" asked Penelope from the surface.

Abigail coughed up dirt as she tried to catch her breath. She had landed on her side but did not seem to have suffered any serious damage. Only scrapes and bruises. She raised herself and surveyed her surroundings. The interior of the grave was pitch black and damp. The rich scent of fresh soil filled her nostrils.

"I think so," she replied.

"Try and jump up. That thing is still coming."

Abigail slowly stood, craning her neck skyward. From her vantage point in the grave, she saw Penelope peaking over the edge of the grassy rim, framed by the night sky and sparkling stars. Everything else around her was black. She stepped toward one of the slimy walls, reaching for something to hold onto and climb. As she walked, she felt the crunch of round objects under her feet. She extended her hands as she met the wall and felt the rough texture of dirt and the shoveled gouges of frozen soil. It was a clean dig, without any obvious handholds or roots.

"Try and grab my hand," said Penelope, lying on her stomach and extending her arm over the edge.

Abigail stood on her tiptoes. "I can't reach you."

"Then jump up."

Abigail bent her knees and vaulted toward Penelope's grasping hand. Their fingertips grazed for an instant, but gravity sent her plunging back down into the pit. As she hit the ground again, her right foot caught one of the round objects and caused her to tumble onto her side. The same side that she had initially fallen on. This time it hurt.

"Please try again," said Penelope. "It's right there!"

As she lay sprawled on the floor of the grave, Abigail had an idea. She felt on the ground around her for one of the round objects. Her fingers scraped against something solid, and she immediately pulled. The object produced a sucking sound as she released its grip from the mud. She turned it around in her hands, quickly realizing what it was. The eye sockets. The exposed and cracked teeth. It was a human skull. She eased herself up and placed the skull at the foot of the wall. Abigail knelt again and felt for more. The floor of the grave was carpeted with human skulls. She grabbed three more from the mud, dropping them into a pile against the wall. She backed up to the other side of the pit.

"Here I come!" she shouted.

As Abigail dashed toward the wall, the wailing phantasm dropped into the grave behind her, extending its ghostly fingers. Its howls were deafening in the enclosed space. Abigail propelled herself off the pile of skulls, stretching her arms above her head. Her joints and muscles screamed from the tension. Penelope grasped Abigail's hand and pulled her to safety.

They scrambled through the final row of tombstones and across another cobblestone path. A mausoleum stood before them. Corinthian columns and twisted oaks flanked its entryway and carved pediment.

Abigail turned and looked as they ran up the steps. The apparition had crept out of the open grave but paused just before the path. It hovered above the ground, continuing to extend its bony fingers. A chilling laugh emanated from its hood.

"What's it doing? Why did it stop?"

"They can't cross that path."

Penelope pounded against the door three times. A series of unlocking clicks and grinding metal gears echoed from within. The door creaked open, drenching the girls in candlelight as they slipped inside.

The apparition hovered above the cobblestone and stared as the door closed behind Abigail and Penelope. It watched for a few moments, then slowly turned and vanished into the cemetery.

CHAPTER XV

TRAIL OF INSECTS

Benjamin Woods leaned against a lamp post across the street from the *Smoking Wizard*, picking at his teeth with a fingernail. He watched the throng of citizens rush by him in all directions. They bustled along the cobblestone sidewalks on errands or important business, as a myriad of others congregated amidst the countless food stalls and vendors that lined the narrow streets, winding alleyways, and flagstone plazas. The patrons chatted, laughed, and yelled to one another as they haggled and bartered over an eclectic assortment of food products, artifacts, and curiosities.

The city of Kadiaphonek overflowed with a wide variety of wondrous citizens. It was a haven for adventurers and quest seekers. There were plenty of humans, of course, but most of the city's residents were a combination of humanoid species and other exotic life forms, none of which remotely resembled a human being. Some of the main species included the Tulleks,

Xekals, Krii, and the Stryrax. These groups were considered humanoid because they were bipedal, had two arms (the Krii had four), one head, and communicated through spoken languages. They generally had two eyes and ears, although the Stryrax, a reptilian species originally from the Southern Wetlands, had six eyes and a long tail. The aforementioned beings were about as close to human as you could expect to find in this part of Silvarum. Kadiaphonek was situated in the middle of the realm between the tamed lands of the south and the haunted forests of Blackwood. The city's harbors and docks nestled right up to the dreary shores of the Wondering River, which served as the natural barrier between the two distinct lands. Travelers who chose not to cross through that vast enchanted forest either settled permanently in Kadiaphonek or remained for a while, eventually pursuing the much longer journey north through the Whispering Hills and into the Shadow Mountains.

Kadiaphonek's exotic inhabitants, in contrast to the humanoids, were much more colorful and outlandish. They were all sentient beings, in their own right, but were vastly different in form, function, and appearance. There were the Preevnu, a spider-like organism, about two meters in height, that featured brilliant, turquoise wings. Then there were the menacing Qugron. A colossal, horned serpent that slithered along the streets with a massive tail and stood at least six meters. They had horns protruding from their heads and scaled hoods that extended below their necks. Another species was the Muurx. Essentially, they were floating eyeballs. Their bodies were composed of a single eyeball, roughly a meter in diameter, that was wrapped in a diffraction cloak. Depending on the viewing angle, the cloak would display an array of different colors. It opened in the front, allowing the large eye to blink and peer around at its surroundings. Atop the main eyeball body, sat a smaller eye, which was typically enveloped by a hood. Both eyeballs could peer in different directions at the same time as they hovered above the ground. The Muurx communicated and interacted through an advanced form of holographic projection. Colored beams of light, transmitted from either eye, could transpose language and symbols onto the air molecules directly in front of them. It was a delight to watch the illuminated conversation among a group of Muurx once the sun set. Finally, there were the Brol. In terms of strangeness and peculiarity, these characters transcended all others. Like the Qugron, they slithered along with slick, scaled bodies, standing about four or five meters. Where they differed, however, was with their many pulsating and twisting tentacles. They continually probed their surroundings as they snaked and crept along. Additionally, their giant heads contained seven luminous eyes, a long pointed nose, that was typically covered in warts, and a curly beard that covered their pronounced chins. The Brol spoke perfect English with deep and aristocratic accents.

Kadiaphonek enjoyed another characteristic that differed from other cities and municipalities in the region: its outlandish public transportation system. Where most towns and villages in Silvarum chose to exercise their modes of transport through the traditional use of horse-drawn carriages, wagons, and cable cars, Kadiaphonek operated on an entirely different level. Dinosaurs, giant insects, over-grown arachnids, flying reptiles, and other bizarre creatures were the preferred method for moving about the labyrinth of streets and avenues. The beasts carried out their civic tasks as well as, or commonly faster than, their conventional counterparts. Residents waited at covered bus stops for a ride atop the magnificent Kyrashk or the fantastically odd Labzhir. The former was a massive beast that towered to the height of twelve meters. Kyrashk had six legs and an immense tail that slithered along the street. Commuting citizens used its huge tail to climb aboard a row of comfortable seats situated on its back. The Qugron and Brol rarely used this manner of travel, due to their large and bulky bodies. However, they did often take advantage of another type of transport that was more suited to their needs. The Pteryxtodons were winged lizards that lifted citizens by leather straps and harnesses, carrying them to all of the city's neighborhoods. The flying beasts had large wings, around five meters from tip to tip, that were formed by thin membranes and leathery skin. Muscular arms were attached to the front of each wing and contained three curved digits. The most prominent feature of the Pteryxtodons was their elaborately decorated crests. They were backward-pointing, blade-like structures that sat atop narrow skulls. Widely varied in design, color, and length, the crests were often decorated with spots or other curious patterns.

Finally, there were the Brachiosaurus. They were the city's most popular mode of transportation, for obvious reasons. Their long necks and thunderous footsteps were a formidable sight. Only the wealthiest citizens, who had patiently endured months on a waiting list, could enjoy such transport. There was nothing like booming through the city streets atop one of their mighty backs while citizens on the ground scrambled for safety. Unfortunately, the beasts were a constant headache for the city maintainers and utility services. Potholes and cracks in the streets were a constant dilemma. Nevertheless, the citizens loved their dinosaurs and would never consider replacing them.

179

Benjamin spat another fingernail onto the sidewalk as he waited patiently for his childhood friend, Gothkar, to depart the *Smoking Wizard*. Unlike his aggressive and strong-willed brother Brian, Benjamin was more of a reserved and thoughtful type. Not to say that he was shy, because he certainly was not. It would be more accurate to describe Benjamin as introspective and analytical. He tended to think more about what he was going to say before he said it, especially in social gatherings with more than a few people. Benjamin often found himself being the observer of situations, rather than the center of attention. This pattern perpetuated until Benjamin became a teenager. It was at that time that he stumbled upon his magical abilities.

***

During the summer of Benjamin's thirteenth year, his uncle Arthur Woods had succumbed to a brain injury suffered two years earlier. He had fallen down his basement stairs while carrying an armful of boxes. Arthur had been Benjamin's favorite uncle. The type that, when you had the pleasure of spending time with during family gatherings, would always have a dirty joke or outlandish story to tell. "Hey there, little man," he would always say when he saw young Benjamin. One of his talents was his ability to perform magic tricks. Benjamin's favorite trick of all was when his uncle would pull a silver coin from his ear. The boy knew that it was not real magic, but he loved the performance of the illusion and the interaction with his uncle.

After the terrible accident, Uncle Arthur was never the same again. Although he had fought tirelessly and bravely for a year to regain his ability to walk, his speech and dexterity never fully recovered. Benjamin saw his uncle two more times before he died. During both of those visits, Uncle Arthur performed his beloved magic tricks, even though he had to painfully struggle through each movement and syllable. "Hey there, little man. I'll see you next time," he was eventually able to articulate.

As the family stood before Arthur's coffin during the funeral that summer, Benjamin thought about how much he missed his uncle's magic tricks and jokes. He desperately tried to understand how someone so positive and generous, so full of life, could be inflicted by an injury so cruel and relentless. How his uncle's free-spirited personality could be wiped clean because of a fall down a flight of stairs. As the warm, summer breeze blew through the elms amid a backdrop of blue sky, it occurred to Benjamin that his uncle's personality had not changed at all. Regardless of the brain damage, or the slurred speech, Arthur's essence had remained intact. The spark that ignited his marvelous personality had been perfectly evident through his determination and refusal to surrender to his injuries. In fact, his uncle had achieved something more profound, especially within the mind and memories of his nephew. Arthur's determination and courage had influenced the boy's outlook on reality and his appreciation for life. Benjamin smiled with that realization as he gazed across the cemetery on that luminous day.

As the family departed the gravesite, Benjamin had asked his father if he could remain a few more moments to contemplate on his own. His father had approved with a hug. Benjamin stood alone at his uncle's grave, silently thanking him for the invaluable lessons that he had learned from the bitter experience. He peered into the bright sky and wondered where his uncle's essence was now. Had it extinguished from existence upon his death, or did it persist, absolved from the restrictive confines of its human shell, now free to experience the universe in its purest form?

"Hey there, little man," said a voice from behind.

Goosebumps flared from Benjamin's arms at the sound of the familiar voice. The hairs on his neck stood on end. With wide eyes, he slowly turned to behold the image of a figure that should not exist in his reality. It was his Uncle Arthur. He stood before Benjamin, as real as the grass and trees, dressed in the same suit that he had just been buried in.

"I told you I'd see you again," he said. His speech was as perfect and fluid as it had been before the accident.

Benjamin blinked wildly, rubbing his eyes. "This can't be real," he said. "I'm just dreaming."

"You're not."

"But you died," replied the boy, struggling to breathe, and too frozen with fear to run away. "I just watched them bury you."

"You're right. I did die."

"Then how am I able to see you?"

"Because of your magical abilities."

"My what?"

"I don't have much time to explain, so I'm going to make this quick," replied Uncle Arthur. "I've come to tell you about the magnificent gift you possess. It's a type of magic that allows you to see and communicate with dead people. You must understand and accept this ability of yours. You're going to need to use it very soon."

"This isn't happening," said Benjamin, shaking his head with disbelief. "You're not real."

"I understand how frightening this must be for you, but I am real. I'm as real as you are, just in a different dimension. Try to imagine it as the same place as you are now, but in a different space and time. Your magical abilities allow you to act as a bridge between our two realms. As a result, you're able to see people who've passed on. In time, you'll even be able to cross over into this dimension. I have a task for you, little man. Seek out a boy your age called Gothkar Maalik, a troll who lives on the edge of Blackwood Forest, near Kadiaphonek. He possesses the skills to assist you with your impending quest."

Benjamin stared at his uncle's ghost, bewildered. His eyes were seeing, and his ears were hearing, but his mind had thrown up a defensive wall, rejecting the illogical stimuli. He felt a tidal wave of blood and heat rush into his face. The anxiety crashed over his brain, causing his peripheral vision to go black and his legs to become shaky. He was passing out.

"There's something else I wanted to do one more time before I finally go," said his uncle. "If you'll permit me."

The boy remained silent.

Uncle Arthur held up and presented his empty palm. He flipped it from front to back twice and then stepped closer to Benjamin. He gently grasped the boy's ear, pulling his hand back to reveal its contents. In his open palm lay a silver coin. Benjamin looked at the object and then at his uncle. The final, hazy image he perceived before passing out was the smiling face of his Uncle Arthur, grasping the silver coin in his hand and crying.

"Thank you, Benjamin," he thought he heard him say.

***

Benjamin had run out of fingernails to chew, so he simply stood still, gazing out into the flowing spectacle of busy citizens, floating eyeballs, stomping dinosaurs, and slithering monsters. He reached into his shirt pocket and pulled out a brass timepiece. Its face and hands were set within the industrial patterns of an old, worn cogwheel. He and his son, Roger, had constructed two identical timepieces last winter as a project while they were cooped up inside from the snow. His two daughters, Mckenzie and Marie, by contrast, could not have cared less about their technical or scientific endeavors and hobbies. Apparently, the nerd genetics only flowed through the males in the family. Nevertheless, it had been a wonderful weekend spent with his son. They had worked together to design and construct different gadgets and gizmos. As he held the timepiece in his hand now, however, Benjamin thought about his children and how much he missed them. He wondered how much longer this journey would keep him away from the people that he loved.

He flipped open the polished cover, checking the time. It was 8:30 a.m. According to a Stryrax vendor called Nejareeth, whom he had questioned earlier this morning, Gothkar would remain inside the *Smoking Wizard* until at least 9 a.m. Allegedly, based on Nejareeth's keen observations over the past few months, Gothkar frequented the tavern every morning until that time. Benjamin had a few more moments to waste, but he needed to eat something. The grumbles in his stomach urgently informed him that he required something substantive and a refill on his coffee. His dirty fingernails would no longer suffice as an acceptable breakfast.

Benjamin snapped shut the lid on the timepiece and placed it back into his shirt pocket. He took a deep breath and then glanced around his immediate surroundings for something quick to eat. Within his swarming city block alone there was a multitude of culinary options to choose. There were bubbling cauldrons of soups and stews, colorful curries with intense spices, and kabobs filled with grilled meats and steaming vegetables. Shouting street vendors and exotic food stalls lined the sidewalks. Their embers and purple smokes bellowed forth mouth-watering aromas and smells. Benjamin licked his lips as he stepped from the cover of his lamppost and onto the main sidewalk.

"Hey, watch it," said a Tullek as it scurried by.

"Pardon me," replied Benjamin, backing off the sidewalk. He watched in amusement as the tiny humanoid kicked its feet and vanished into the ocean of larger legs and bodies.

Tulleks were a gnome species that lived in the hollowed-out innards of ancient, twisted oak trees. There was a large district in Kadiaphonek devoted specifically to their habitat and ecosystem. It was called Prugglehusk. The Tullek neighborhood was filled with hundreds of old oak trees that were intertwined by lantern-lit streets and firefly infested walking paths. The trees and the Tullek residents shared a special, symbiotic relationship. The wee folk did not just live inside the massive oaks, they lived with them. Each oak tree was an actual member of the family that lived inside. It had a face and could talk, and most of them had long bushy beards that were made of tangled lichen and gray mosses. The oaks were members of an ancient race of tree-men known as the Elvelon. Their Tullek companions generated sustenance for them through an elaborate system of aqueducts, as well as large, bountiful gardens to feed their roots with nutrients. In turn, the Elvelon provided sturdy homes and security for the gnome families.

Adult Tulleks only reached a meter in height. They were commonly dressed in colorful, woodsy, and rustic outfits. This was due primarily to the fact that their favorite professions were farming and gardening. Blue work shirts and red suspenders, purple pants with bright patches on the knees, and brown or black work boots. Their attire was unquestionably common but undeniably functional. Most of the male Tulleks grew curly beards that they tucked into their pants as they busied themselves on errands throughout the city. Some of the elders still wore the pointy-brimmed hats, resembling pint-sized wizards.

Benjamin turned his attention back to the sidewalk and aggressively surveyed his selections. His hungry eyes quickly fixated upon a promising food stall situated at the opposite end of the block. This time, before wading out into the river of foot traffic, Benjamin tried to time his entrance with more grace. He watched for specific patterns in their steps while he ticked off a metronomic cadence in his head.

Step. Step. Step. Step. Step. Step. Go.

Thrusting himself into the deluge, he was rapidly carried away like a piece of driftwood caught in a swift current. Benjamin had to pump his leg muscles furiously to keep up with the pace. It dawned on him that he was walking on the streets during the heart of Kadiaphonek's rush hour. Citizens commuted to work, while for the past hour, he had stood on the sidelines, gnawing at his fingernails.

The food stall that Benjamin had focused on approached quickly on his left side. Because of his position within the river of bodies, Benjamin needed to deviate from right to left, against the grain, and pop out of the congestion. Unfortunately, as his legs continued to circulate blood through his muscles at an unreasonable rate, he had no idea how to accomplish that task. A screeching Pteryxtodon provided the solution. It swept down above the crowd just ahead of him, dropping an enormous Brol onto the sidewalk. The horde of commuters, although painfully accustomed to this type of daily occurrence, were, for whatever reason, ill-prepared on that occasion. The Brol's flailing tentacles whipped and thrashed around him as he plummeted awkwardly to the ground. Citizens who were caught within his immediate landing zone expertly maneuvered and jumped out of the way to safety. Two unfortunate Muurx, however, who were distracted by their complicated conversation, were not as nimble. The blubbering Brol crashed down on top of them, enveloping the pair beneath its layers of scaly flesh. Waves of impact concussions radiated throughout its massive body. As it finally settled itself and straightened out its beard, the Brol calmly lifted part of its backside, allowing the two bewildered Muurx to scramble away.

"My sincere apologies, gentlemen," said the Brol in a haughty accent. "Please forgive my unfortunate interruption."

As the Muurx hovered away, wobbling and careening from the impact, they projected a red symbol in response. Essentially, it was their version of the middle finger.

Benjamin chuckled to himself as he took advantage of the chaotic aftermath. A temporary corridor had been cleared within the traffic due to the evacuation of the panicked commuters. As the crisis dissolved, Benjamin scrambled to the opposite side of the sidewalk. The food stall stood right in front of him.

"Pork buns! Get your steaming hot pork buns!" said the Krii vendor. His four arms masterfully assembled the barbecue-pork-filled buns while also serving customers and washing dishes.

Benjamin stepped into the line. There were two types of buns being served. The first type was a soft bun with a white exterior. The second was golden brown and glazed.

"I'll take three of the steamed, please," said Benjamin.

"That'll be nine copper," replied the Krii vendor. "Pork buns! Pork buns! Get your steaming hot pork buns!"

Benjamin handed him the coins.

"Here you are," said the vendor as one of his right arms tossed three buns into a bamboo steamer. Another arm handed the steamer to Benjamin while his other limbs immediately went back to work to serve the next customer in line.

"Do you serve coffee?" asked Benjamin.

"No coffee here," he replied. "Coffee across the street at Groppler's stall. Pork buns! Steaming hot pork buns!"

Benjamin peered across the street for the coffee stall. Through the onslaught of rushing commuters and crashing Brachiosaurus, he could barely make out the tents on the other side. Benjamin turned to his left and observed the crosswalk at the end of the block. It would be easier to cross there, rather than attempting the insane strategy of bulldozing his way straight through the commuters, dinosaurs, and insects. Regardless, he would still need to step back into the river of bodies. Benjamin took another bite from his pork bun, weighing his options.

"The time!" he cried, spitting bits of barbecued pork out of his mouth. He had lost track of time since he stepped out of the shadows on his quest for food and coffee. Benjamin snatched the timepiece and flipped open the cover. It was 8:55 a.m.

"I can still make it," he muttered.

Benjamin popped the last pork bun into his mouth, preparing to step back onto the sidewalk. Before he had made a single step, however, he froze in his tracks and stared.

"Hello, Benjamin. What a surprise to see you again," said his friend Gothkar, nibbling on a fluffy, white pork bun.

CHAPTER XVI

DRAGONS AND WITCHCRAFT

"You did what?" asked Mckenzie.

"We killed five of those monsters," replied her mother. "Let me tell you, your dad and I were ferocious when we were your age. And don't even get me started about your Uncle Brian. He's on a whole different level of ferocious."

"Give me a break, Mom," she replied. "We're supposed to believe all this? Just because you've been reading a bunch of weird passages from some old book and filling us with fairy tales. Now you want us to accept that you and Dad were actually demon-slaying teenagers?"

"Yes, I expect you to believe it. Because it's true."

Mckenzie frowned, turning to her sister. "What do you think about all this? Do you believe any of it?"

"I guess so. Why would she make it up?"

"She lied about the true nature of the runestones."

"That was for your protection," replied Trelinia. "I've already apologized to you for why we kept the details a secret. Now listen to me. I need the two of you to believe that what your dad and I did really happened. Until you do, there's no way you're going to be able to face this daunting task. I'm not making this stuff up, and this isn't a joke. If my words aren't enough to convince you, perhaps these will help."

Trelinia flipped to the back of the enormous book and withdrew a tattered envelope. She pulled out five black and white photographs, aligning them neatly on the table.

"Holy shit!" said Mckenzie, standing. "Are those the five monsters that you guys killed?"

"Indeed they are, young lady," replied her mother. "I'll excuse your dreadful language on this occasion because of these extraordinary circumstances."

"I'm sorry. Please go on."

Marie giggled.

"We took these group shots after we defeated each boss. Even though it appears that the body has been destroyed, the lifeforce of the runestone is never truly dead. It retreats for years, probably within Nexxathia, and then always returns stronger."

The sisters stared at the five grainy photographs. Each image captured the teenage versions of their parents and uncle, all posing around the slain corpse of some hideous creature.

"Is that a giant robot?" asked Mckenzie.

"That's Sutekh," replied Trelinia, tapping on one of the photographs. "It guarded the Rune of Technology."

"How did you defeat something as frightening as that?" asked Mckenzie.

"With great difficulty. Not only was it a terrible monster

to fight, but just getting to it was a nightmare. We had to solve all kinds of ridiculously complicated and dangerous puzzles on the way to its lair."

"Is that a real dragon?" gasped Marie.

The second photograph in the sequence depicted the group standing around the severed head of a massive dragon. A young Brian Woods stood with his right boot propped upon the dragon's head, raising a blood-soaked sword in victory.

"That was the dragon that defended the Rune of Light."

"Why did you cut its head off?" asked Mckenzie.

"That was your uncle's idea. I told you he's ferocious."

"That's one grim image," said Marie. "The fact that all of you are smiling and look so happy while standing in a pool of blood makes it even darker."

Trelinia chuckled. "You're right. Looking at it again after all these years, it does seem unsettling. But you girls must realize everything we'd been through up to that point to understand how relieved and amazed we were to still be alive. That was the second boss we'd defeated."

Mckenzie rubbed her forehead. "I guess I believe you, Mom. I just can't fathom how this is our actual reality. Our family has been mixed up in this madness for hundreds of years, and my own mom and dad went on a quest to fight monsters."

"It's indeed a harsh reality to come to terms with, but it's a reality that you both have to accept. Believe me, all of us felt the same way when we learned of this as teenagers. Nevertheless, the three of us were specifically chosen, based on our magical powers, to complete this colossal quest. We had to travel to all the corners of Silvarum to locate and confront the five protectors of the runestones. There were many adventures along the way."

"And you promise to us that you, Dad, and Uncle Brian actually fought all five of the monsters in these photographs?" asked Marie.

"Yes," replied Trelinia. "I swear to you. But it wasn't just us. Many people helped along the way. This was a tremendous undertaking during that time. Countless individuals with all sorts of skills and talents helped us reach our ultimate goal. It took us many years to accomplish what we did, to defeat those monsters, but in the end, we were successful."

"Did you actually kill all of these things?"

"No, we didn't kill any of the true evil. That's the horrible truth and why they're still a threat. It's the whole reason why we're talking about this now. I'm not even sure if they can be killed, to be honest with you. At least in the sense that we understand death. These beings, these creatures that were spawned from Nexxathia, are unlike any other lifeform on this planet. They're multi-dimensional entities and aren't living in our reality to begin with. All we did was defeat their hosts and temporarily take back the runestones."

"What are the names of the monsters you had to fight?" asked Mckenzie.

"We fought Loex, Vexx, Sutekh, Thulcandra, and Queen Natassja," replied Trelinia.

"What in the world?" said Marie. "Those are their names? What about each one being a member of the Drake Expedition?"

"They're not the members of the expedition anymore. They only used those people and their lifeforce to transform back into their true alien forms. What they are now is the real thing. And they're anything but human beings. They're all terrible and evil creatures with deadly abilities."

"And one of the protectors is a dragon?" asked Mckenzie. "Are there really dragons in the world? I thought they were just made up fairy tales that parents told their kids at bedtime."

"Honey, have you listened to anything I've said for the past few hours? Look at the photographs. These creatures are not from our world. And yes, one of them is a dragon. As a matter of fact, two of them are dragons."

"What?" gasped Marie. "I can't fight a single dragon, let alone two."

"That's exactly what I thought when I was your age and confronted with this unimaginable responsibility," replied her mother. "You know what? Even though I was scared to death and had no idea what I was supposed to do at the time, I trusted in my family and my friends and all the other people that helped us. Because of that, I could believe in my powers and abilities. It was the only way we were able to defeat them. The fact that we all believed in ourselves. I'll tell you the secret right now. All it takes is the courage and confidence to believe in yourself, and you can defeat anything. Even dragons."

"That's wonderful advice," replied Mckenzie, "but how in God's name am I supposed to defeat an army of alien, multi-dimensional monsters, when all I can do is make a bunch of crappy healing potions? They don't even heal anything. All they do is turn things purple or give people warts."

Trelinia laughed. "I don't have the slightest clue, dear. But I imagine that there's a lot about yourself that you're going to figure out during this quest."

"This quest?" replied Marie. "You mean it's already been decided that we're going? You're saying that the three of us have to do what you did and fight these monsters?"

"Unfortunately, you're going to have to do more than we did. We only had to find and defeat five protectors. Compared to the current state of the runestones and the strength of the enemy, we had it easy. This time around, because of the number of runestones that have been stolen back, the three of you are going to have to find and defeat all eight."

The girls sat motionless, staring back at their mother with blank, confused expressions. The gravity of the words that she had just uttered had not fully processed within their young brains. The concepts had not yet had enough time to be analyzed and cataloged into their proper states of fear and anxiety.

"I'm afraid it gets worse," said their mother. "Back when we had to fight them, we still retained three of the runestones and their respective powers. We had Frost, Shadow, and Death. Luckily for us, the combination of those three runes produced a potent magic. They have them all now. This means, not only do you not have the runes' powers to use against them, but the creatures will undoubtedly use them against you and anyone else that tries to retake them. Their power is growing by the day."

"This is hopeless," cried Marie, flinging her head into her hands while expelling a dramatic sigh.

"There's one more unfortunate detail," replied Trelinia. "Now that they've reclaimed all eight runestones, they'll be able to summon the ninth protector: The Dream-King. The most powerful entity of them all."

"The who?" replied Mckenzie. "Does this nightmare ever end? How many of these monsters are there? And who is this Dream-King fellow?"

"It's their master. Their supreme deity. It exists between the dimensions of life and death and space and time. If they've summoned it, which we're almost certain now that they have, then it'll attempt to construct the pyramidal formation over Nexxathia that Edric Drake described within his last coherent transmission. Through the power harnessed from that 4-dimensional construct, the Dream-King will be able to inflict unimaginable damage upon Silvarum. This time, it may be the end of us all."

Mckenzie shook her head with frustration. "Okay, Mom. Let's just say that I believe all the fantastic things that you've told us over the past few hours. I can't say that I understand much of it, but for the sake of argument, let's just pretend for a moment that I do. And let's also say that I have the proper courage and confidence and all that other stuff to fulfill this unbelievable task. Please tell me then. What are we supposed to do now? How can we possibly defeat these things?"

Trelinia took off her glasses again and rubbed her eyes. "That's a good question. I'll be honest with the two of you right from the start. Your quest is going to take a very long time to accomplish. At this point, we only have a plan to take back the first runestone. The Rune of Frost. Beyond that, we're not sure."

"You keep saying *we*," replied Marie. "Who is that?"

Trelinia nodded in acknowledgment.

"It's a group that includes me, your dad, your Uncle Brian, your teacher Mrs. Roberts, Steven Rawthorne, a girl named Penelope Crofts, and Merkresh Warington. We're the council that was formed to hide and protect the runestones and to determine the best course of action for when they were stolen again."

"Mr. Rawthorne?" asked Marie. "Arina's dad?"

"Yes, the very same. They just moved from Briargulch."

"I had plans with her tonight. How's her dad involved?"

"He's the most recent protector of the Rune of Shadow. Your friend's father is a mighty wizard."

"What? Arina told me that he's a doctor."

"She told you the truth. We all must earn a living too, you know? Just because we possess magical powers doesn't mean that they pay the bills. Why do you think your dad owns a grocery store? Anyway, none of that is important right now."

"Are you referring to that weird, old man that Roger is infatuated with?" asked Mckenzie. "Merkresh?"

"Yes, but please let me finish explaining Mr. Rawthorne's role in all of this before I get into Merkresh's life story."

"Fine, sorry."

"Thank you. Now, Steven Rawthorne has been the most recent guardian of the Rune of Shadow. Since our quest thirty years ago, when we used it and the other stones to defeat the five protectors, he was chosen to watch over it and keep it safe. Unfortunately, and we haven't figured out how this happened, the Shadow Rune's location was recently discovered and stolen. Even worse, his wife Stephanie, a fellow warlock…"

"Stop!" shouted Mckenzie.

Trelinia froze at the outburst, gazing at her daughters.

"Did you just acknowledge that you're a witch?"

"Yes, I guess I did."

"I knew it," said Mckenzie. "All these years I've suspected that it was something like this. All the weird and unexplainable things that I've noticed you do, but never asked about or called you out on. It all makes perfect sense now. A witch though? Really Mom?"

"Technically I'm a warlock," she replied. "You knew that I had magical powers, just like you do. So, what's so awful about that? And forgive me for pointing out the obvious, my dear, but look who's been trying to perfect her healing potions? Who else do you think dabbles in potions and healing? Warlocks!"

"That's enough from the two of you," said Marie. "Our mom's a warlock. So what. We're literally debating how to fight dragons and robots from another dimension, and the two of you are sitting there arguing about healing spells. Give me a break."

"Thank you, Marie," replied their mother. "I couldn't agree with you more. May I please continue now?"

"Fine," said Mckenzie, folding her arms in protest.

"What happened to Arina's mom?" asked Marie.

"It's not good," said Trelinia. "She's been taken."

"What? Who took her?"

"We're not sure yet. It has to be someone who's gained intimate knowledge of our secrets for hiding the runes."

"No disrespect intended," said Mckenzie. "But losing all eight runes isn't exactly keeping them secret."

"We understand that," replied Trelinia. "We all knew that the stones couldn't remain hidden from them forever. They were going to recover them all eventually. The fact that we were able to recapture five of them during my quest was nothing short of a miracle. We're dealing with other-worldly powers, and this isn't the first time that members of our two families have had to venture out into the wild and fight this enemy. It's basically been our legacy. Now, it's simply your generation's turn."

"Can you please just tell us what the council's plan is?" asked Mckenzie. "What are we supposed to do?"

"Yes, of course," she said. "We only have a plan to take back the first rune, the Rune of Frost. Recovering this one will be the most challenging because you'll not have the other runes and their powers to aid you in the battle. However, once you defeat Lord Mortis and take back the runestone, you'll become stronger. Then, after each rune that you acquire, you'll get even more powerful, and so on. Unfortunately, the power that you gain will be proportionate to the strength of the subsequent protector. In other words, each boss gets harder as you advance. When you eventually have all eight runestones and must face the Dream-King in Nexxathia, the three of you will be unbelievably powerful. But, as I said, that won't be for years to come. So let's just focus on one rune and one boss at a time."

"You're assuming, of course, that we'll actually defeat this Lord Mortis guy," said Marie, "and he won't just kill us and eat us for breakfast."

"I am assuming that. That's part of the whole believing in yourself idea that I was trying to explain to you girls earlier. You *will* defeat him. You *will* take back the Rune of Frost. You must believe that."

The sisters rolled their eyes.

"Here's the plan for Frost. Here's how the three of you are going to reach Lord Mortis and then defeat him. There are three distinct components to this plan, so I'm going to just address them one by one. First of all, your dad and your uncle were dispatched months ago to scout out the state of affairs between here and throughout Blackwood Forest, and to prepare the road for your departure. Friends of ours have already been alerted to your forthcoming quest and are waiting to hear from you, should you need their assistance. You'll certainly not be without help during this adventure. Your Uncle Brian has been stationed at a place in the north called Warington Castle. We've believed for some time that the people in charge there, led by an evil man called Count Zaran, have been up to no good and that they're in league with the evil forces of Nexxathia. Your uncle's mission is to uncover the corruption that's infiltrated that castle and put an end to it. As for your dad, his task is even more complicated and uncertain. He's been sent on a journey to seek out his old companion, Gothkar, who lives in Blackwood Forest. Gothkar will then assist your dad in passing over and entering into the Tombworld. Once there, he'll meet up with one of our council members, Penelope Crofts, and begin the process of harnessing an ancient power that lies within the realm of the undead. This power, long hidden within the depths of that phantom world, will be invaluable once the three of you have to face each of the rune guardians."

"Is this girl, Penelope Crofts, a ghost?" asked Marie.

"Yes. She's very old, and she's been in the Tombworld for centuries. She, along with another ghost, helped your dad and the rest of us during our quest thirty years ago."

"What's the next part of the plan?" asked Mckenzie.

"The second component involves Merkresh. His story and involvement with the runestones, in general, is epic and legendary and far too complicated to go into now. Suffice it to say that he's the most powerful of any of us. A while ago, one of you asked if there was anyone who'd ever ventured back into the Shadow Mountains after the disaster of the Drake Expedition."

"I asked that," said Marie.

"Merkresh was a member of one of those expeditions. He's mostly responsible for why they recaptured all of the runes during his quest."

"But how's that possible?" asked Mckenzie. "Wasn't that over a hundred years ago? How old is Merkresh?"

"Ancient," replied Trelinia. "He's the second oldest son of Gualterius I, who ruled Warington Castle until he died in 1301. Merkresh was even a famous knight in his youth."

"A knight?"

"Yes, and not only that but the wealth of knowledge and technology that he obtained from the remnants of Nexxathia have allowed him to construct some fantastic contraptions and weapons over the years. That's where the second component of the plan comes into play. Merkresh is going to train Roger with an arsenal of marvelous devices that'll aid you on your quest."

"If Merkresh is this legendary fighter, who helped save Silvarum, then why have you always told us to stay away from him?" asked Marie.

"We thought you guys were just too young to get caught up in all of his bizarre projects and adventures. Merkresh is a wise and honorable person, but he also has a remarkable ability to project his energy and enthusiasm onto others and influence their actions. We simply didn't want you to be exposed to all that yet. Roger, however, has demonstrated his technical and scientific aptitude over the past few years and has naturally gravitated toward the old man. Your dad and I decided that it was a relationship that Roger could benefit from and should pursue for two reasons. One, because it was an effective way for him to build up confidence. He's full of potential, but he's still unsure of himself and lacks the conviction that we know he's capable of. The second reason was for Merkresh to pass down his vast knowledge to a new generation."

"And the third component of the plan?" asked Marie.

"Ah, yes," replied Trelinia. "The third part of the plan is where your mom the warlock gets involved."

Mckenzie rolled her eyes.

"In the time that remains before you must depart on your great quest, I'm going to train you girls in arcana, spellcraft, and healing. You'll be masters at how to properly gather the required ingredients while traveling throughout Silvarum. Everything from Bloodroot to bat poop, you'll have the catalog memorized."

"Gross," said Marie.

"Because I promise you, once you get out there on your own and into the wild, it'll be vital that both of you know the difference between the toxic plants and roots like Ghostvine and Ironstem. Your lives, as well as others, will depend on it. I'm also going to teach you how to create spells and potions from scratch and even how to modify and enhance old ones that have been passed down through our family. With the knowledge that I'm going to teach you, the two of you should be well prepared for the journey to face Lord Mortis."

"Have all the Drake and Woods women been warlocks?"

"Most of us," she replied. "Arcane magic has skipped a few people, but for the most part, it's been our specialty."

"So how long do we get to train? And when do we have to start on this quest?" asked Mckenzie.

"That's difficult to answer at the moment. I've been expecting a letter from your dad about his meeting with Gothkar. That letter hasn't yet arrived. We wanted to time your departure from Thorndale with your father's entrance into the Tombworld. Since we don't know his status, we could delay your departure a few months, or send you off sooner than we planned. Either way, the group, minus your father and uncle, needs to reconvene as quickly as possible to discuss the next steps."

"You think we have a few months until we have to go?"

"Maybe. Or it could be as soon as a few weeks. We'll have to see how your dad is doing and what the group thinks."

"No way," exclaimed Marie. "A few weeks is too soon."

"You'll be ready, my love. Don't forget that you have friends and family members that are aware of your quest and will be helping you all along the way. There's plenty of time for all of us to prepare for the long journey. More importantly, though, I have saved the best thing for last."

"You mean for the plan?"

"Yes. Wait here a moment, and I'll get them for you."

Trelinia stood and walked out of the room. The sisters sat in silence, thinking about all the outlandish things they had heard throughout the evening. Marie glanced at the large clock above the mantel. Its hands read 11:13 p.m. In that time, they had transformed from carefree children to hopeful dragon slayers.

After a few moments of silent contemplation, the sisters watched as their mother walked back into the room, placing two mysterious objects on the table.

"Are those what I think they are?" gasped Mckenzie.

"If you think they're magic wands that have been passed down from generation to generation to fight against the evil powers of Nexxathia, then yes, those are exactly what they are."

"Wow," exclaimed Marie. "Can I pick one up?"

"Of course you can. They're yours now."

Both wands were roughly thirty centimeters in length and possessed vastly different designs and characteristics from one another. The simplest of the two was carved from the ancient roots of a hardwood called Black Oak. Its handle was smooth and dull and slightly thicker around its end cap than the remainder of the wand. The opposite end was curved and ended in a thin tip. The other wand, a heat-tolerant hardwood called Black Birch, was much more elaborate and decorative. Like its companion, the wood was spiraled and black. The differences, however, were evident in its intricately carved handle and the crystal mounted at its tip. A brilliant, purple amethyst sphere was set amidst a carved mounting that resembled twisted roots.

"These are so cool," said Marie as she picked up the curly wand (the sisters referred to it as the curly wand for the rest of their lives). She held it above her head, waving in wide circles.

"Careful!" cried her mother. "You can't wave it around all crazy like that."

"Why?" asked Marie, throwing it back to the table.

"Because it's a magic wand, silly. You have the innate ability to summon the magical powers that live within it. Even now, the wand is attuning itself to your lifeforce. Based on what you were thinking at that moment, you could've easily blasted a hole through the ceiling by waving it like that."

"Seriously?" gasped Marie.

Mckenzie burst into laughter.

"Indeed," said Trelinia. "You must learn to respect these wands. They're unbelievably powerful tools that can destroy as well as heal. Not to worry, though. I'll teach you both everything you need to know. Besides, Marie, that's not your wand. That one belongs to your sister."

Mckenzie's eyes perked up as she reached out with an open palm. "Gimmie," she said.

Marie slapped the curly wand into her hand.

"So what," said Marie. "This other one looks even better and stronger than yours. It has a cool, purple gem on it, and yours just looks like a little twig."

"Actually, the wands are the same in terms of strength. They just specialize in different magic. The curly wand is used for natural magic like healing, alchemy, and astral forces. The purple wand is used for elemental magic like fire, ice, and shadow."

"Yeah," replied Mckenzie, smirking.

Marie stuck out her tongue.

"Oh dear," said their mother. "I can see that you two are worn out and cranky. Let's get some rest now and try to let it all soak in. All right? We'll continue talking through all this business in the morning."

"Can we start our training too?" asked Marie.

"I think that's a fantastic idea," replied her mother.

"What about a yummy breakfast before we get started?" asked Mckenzie. "That way our tummies will be nice and full and ready to learn some real magic."

"Certainly," said Trelinia. "I suppose the two of you have earned it after having to endure all of my grim storytelling and witchery revelations tonight. I'll even let you guys sleep in for a bit while I prepare a breakfast feast. We'll have some scrambled eggs, bacon, biscuits, and grits with butter. And how about some pancakes? The kind that you two loved when you were little girls. The ones with chocolate chips."

"Yes, please!" they shouted.

"That sounds fun," said Trelinia. "But then we need to get to work. There's much to prepare for."

"That's the best plan I've heard all night," said Marie.

CHAPTER XVII

A SOOTHING GLANCE

Nadia Drake rose to a standing position, brushing the dirt away. It was too fast. She reeled as blood rushed through her veins in pulsating waves. The rolling sensation washed over her face and brain like a tidal wave of crimson light and heat. Her mind. Her soul. Her being. They were battered against the rocky shores of time and space. She took a step backward. Dizziness. Sorrow.

Breathe.

A curtain of heartache swept over her with the burning realization of absolute emptiness and loss. She shuttered under its unyielding weight. Tears welled in her eyes while spiraling orbs of scathing sadness dripped from the rocks of the forsaken shore that confined her to this moment. This life.

A hand tugged at her leg.

A child? Her child.

Her daughter.

Nadia opened her eyes and looked down at the precious face. The girl was saying something. Screaming something. The words fell flat and toneless beneath the crashing waves of her endless grief.

For him, I will do this.

She reached down, touching her daughter's shoulder. The sensation was instantaneous. The crashing waves receded from the shore, and her mind felt at ease. The mother had comforted her daughter. The daughter had comforted her mother. There was balance. The water was still again.

A different voice called to Nadia.

She turned to see her husband rushing toward her. His expression was fraught with concern and anguish. He grasped her by the shoulders and held her upright. He was her support. Her monolith. She smiled, nodding slowly.

My family. My home.

The three figures embraced each other as they looked down at the grave that Nadia had just finished filling. Their son's final resting place. A towering menhir bore their family symbol along with the boy's name, Joseph Drake. Smaller rocks were lined neatly along the grave's edge.

Her daughter had set a single flower at the base of the monolith. It was trumpet-shaped and purple, having a short stem and leafless. A mountain flower that she and Joseph had always brought back during their long treks into the mountains with their father and uncles. It was a purple gem for the eons. An unbreakable bond between sister and brother.

Nadia raised her free hand and studied the dirt that had accumulated under her cracked fingernails. The same dirt that now cradled the body of her son. Her firstborn. Her love.

Where are you?

A cool, morning breeze rustled through the forest leaves and grasses as a golden beam of sunlight broke through the canopy, resting upon the standing stone. The warm ray passed through Nadia's raised fingers and reflected off the rocky face of the monument. The shadow of her hand and arm stretched vertically along the center of the menhir. Reaching. Soothing.

Mother, can you hear me?

Nadia perceived a faint whisper, as soft as the wind.

Remember the purple gem.

Her husband stirred, motioning for them to leave. It was time for the family to depart from the burial ritual and begin the long journey home. She acknowledged him with a nod and looked down at the face of her daughter. She was smiling now, reassured. Nadia kissed her on the head.

"Mother," said Trelinia Drake.

"Yes, Trel?"

"What happened to you? Were you sick?"

Nadia peered into her daughter's eyes, running her fingers through her hair. "I was dizzy for a moment. I was tired from the digging and the ceremony, but I feel better now."

Trelinia smiled. "I was worried about you. You looked like you were going to faint."

"I'm fine now, my love. I promise."

Nadia noticed her husband waving for them farther down the trail. "Come, Trel. We can talk during the walk home."

This pleased Trelinia. She jumped up and grabbed her mother's hand, trotting by her side as they began to descend from the cemetery.

Nadia looked back a final time at her son's resting place.

A sliver of amber sunlight remained on the monolith. It flickered for a moment and then gently faded from existence.

Goodbye, mother.

***

A wide, alpine valley unfolded before the family as they emerged from the depths of the forest. Clear sky beamed upon sloping grasslands and flower-filled meadows. Clumps of ash, beech, and oak trees spilled from mountain ridges, nestling within the rolling boundaries of the lush landscape. On either side of the valley rose the jagged, snow-tipped summits of the Ethereal Peaks. Stony arms stretched and clawed toward the cumulus clouds that hung in the heights above.

The family walked in a line along a neatly tended path that curled down the mountainside. At the front of the company strode Nadia's brother, Nicolai, the great hunter. He was clad in tough animal skins and wrapped in a sturdy, grass overcoat fastened together with bone needles and sinew stitching. His hiking boots were a combination of tightly packed grasses, bear hide soles, and cordage constructed from soaked basswood fibers. Around his waist, he wore a leather belt made from Preevnu hide. It contained pouches that allowed him to carry essential survival items such as flint, tinder, and a variety of plants used to treat minor wounds.

From a belt loop hung one of his two primary hunting tools: a copper axe. Fashioned from polished beech wood, the handle was lashed with leather cording and featured a pure copper axe head fortified with birch tar. The second hunting tool, his most prized possession, was a yew longbow. Across his back was strung a quiver filled with arrows made from ash and fletched with turkey feathers. The arrowheads were shaped and chipped from flint.

Behind her brother walked her father, a smelter and tool craftsman. By his side strode her mother, a gatherer of medicinal flora and a pottery maker. The remainder of the family included her younger sister, a gatherer and tender of livestock, and her uncle, a farmer and herdsman. Nadia's husband walked behind them, bringing up the rear of the company. The family dogs ran free among the grassy fields and outcroppings of trees as the group gradually made their way down the path.

Nadia looked out across the expanse of green and sighed. A golden eagle cried in the distance as it soared high above the valley floor. The scent of pine needles and grass filled the afternoon air. Rocks crunched under their feet.

"Mother," said Trelinia once again.

"Yes, dear."

"May I ask you a question about this morning?"

"Certainly."

The young girl kicked a rock down the trail, hesitating.

"What is it, Trel? You may ask your question."

"What happens when we die?" she whispered.

Nadia smiled. "There's no reason to be ashamed. You're in the company of family."

Her uncle turned toward them, winking as he adjusted the straps on his backpack.

"That's a thoughtful question," continued Nadia. "That you would be so inquisitive makes me proud of you."

Trelinia smiled up at her mother.

"May I ask you a question in return, young lady?"

"Yes," replied Trelinia.

"What do *you* think happens when we die?"

The girl stopped and peered out over the vista. She raised a hand to shield her eyes from the sun and pointed toward the horizon. Deep shades of crimson saturated the mountain peaks while long shadows crept across the valley floor.

"Can you see those two eagles flying in the distance?"

Nadia turned and strained her eyes against the brightness of the sky and valley.

"I can see them."

"Then that's my answer."

Her mother raised an eyebrow. "We become eagles?"

"Maybe eagles. Maybe grass. Maybe the wind. Or maybe we continue as we are, just in a different form."

"That's an intriguing idea," replied Nadia. "What then would you say to those who believe that when we die, we're simply given back to nature? That we cease to exist."

Trelinia thought for a moment, continuing to gaze out across the valley. She looked up and smiled at her mother.

"I'd say that the universe is more complicated than that."

"The universe?" replied her mother. "What does a little girl know about the universe?"

"Not nearly enough, I guess."

"My dear daughter. You're full of wisdom and grace this afternoon. How did I get so lucky?"

Trelinia lowered her gaze.

"What is it?" asked her mother.

"I miss him so much," she said, crying.

Nadia dropped to her knees and embraced her daughter with both hands. Comforting her. Hearing her.

"Oh, Trel. I know you do. So do I."

Nadia pulled her close and felt her heartbeat racing.

Noticing this exchange, her uncle held up his hand, motioning for the rest of the company to halt. They all turned and watched with understanding eyes.

After a moment, Trelinia wiped her tears and looked up.

"I love you, mother."

"I love you too, my precious daughter."

Nadia held Trelinia's hand as they continued along the long and winding path home.

Along the path of life.

Together.

CHAPTER XVIII

THE SHADOWKUUR

"Gothkar?" asked Benjamin.

"The one and only," he replied. "It's been a while, Ben. How the hell are you?"

"I'm good. But you were supposed to be in the *Smoking Wizard* until nine. What are you doing out here?"

"Are you my mother?" replied Gothkar, popping another pork bun into his mouth.

"Of course not," said Benjamin. "But a vendor down the street told me that you usually stay in there until that time. I've been waiting out here until you were finished."

"That was a thoughtful gesture, old friend, but why would I be in a tavern at nine in the morning on a weekday?"

Benjamin scratched his beard. "Drinking?"

Gothkar choked. "I recall drinking a little when we were teenagers, but I'm not that far gone. I do have a job, you know."

"It's just that you're a…"

"I'm a what?"

"You're a troll."

"This is true."

"And most trolls drink in the morning, don't they?"

"Most do, but I prefer coffee. Is that acceptable?"

Benjamin shook his head, laughing. "I'm sorry, Gothkar. I've been stressing out for the past week about our reunion, and now I've gone and totally screwed it up."

"It's not a problem," he replied. "Don't even worry about it. But why would you be stressing out? I've been in Kad ever since we were kids. You could've visited me anytime."

"You're not at all how I remember you when we were teenagers," said Benjamin.

"Go on."

"Well, I remember you being a real asshole."

Gothkar laughed. "There it is. Yes, I most certainly was an asshole the last time you saw me. But Ben, that was when we were fourteen years old and full of piss and vinegar. I've had some life experience since then, as I'm sure you've had your share as well. People can change, can't they? Even trolls."

"Of course they can."

"Well now," said Gothkar. "Since we seem to have our awkward reunion all worked out, what brings you up to Kad?"

Benjamin looked around at the mass of commuters and busy streets. "Is there somewhere else we can go that's more private and talk for a bit? Do you have time before work?"

"Sure," he replied. "I'm self-employed these days, so I can go to work whenever the hell I feel like it. How are you doing on your coffee?"

Benjamin held up his empty hands. "I'm out."

"Then let's head over to a quaint little coffee shop I know. We'll have plenty of privacy to talk about whatever it is that's so important. Sound good to you?"

"Sounds perfect," replied Benjamin.

***

"Let's grab that table over in the corner," said Gothkar as they entered the café.

Gentle crackles from a stone fireplace blended with the murmur of conversing patrons. The shop's interior was bathed in candlelight, containing only a dozen tables. A Stryrax waitress tended to customers amid the clink of mugs and silverware.

"In my opinion, this place has some of the best coffee in Kad," said Gothkar. "None of that burnt, designer shit that you see out on the street or in those trendy shops that all the kids hang out in. This is the traditionally brewed stuff. It's spicy and bitter as hell, but it's fantastic."

"Thorndale has a small coffee shop, but it's the designer shit. I've had this spicy type before, but it's been a while."

"Here we are," said Gothkar as the waitress arrived with a brass pot. She filled two decorative mugs.

"Wow," said Ben as he took a sip. "That *is* strong."

"I told you, right? Give it a while. It takes some getting used to, but I live on this stuff. I probably have ten cups of it a day so I can keep focused on my artwork."

"You're still drawing?"

"Drawing, painting, sculpting. I even started writing."

"That's great news. I'm glad you've kept up with it."

"Thanks," replied Gothkar. "I did have to take a break from art for a while after our adventure, but I've picked it up with a vengeance over the last decade or so."

Benjamin nodded as he took another sip of coffee.

"A year ago, I started selling enough of my paintings that I was finally able to open up my own studio. It's only a few blocks away. If you're going to be in Kad for a while, you should come by and check out my new work. It's pretty wild."

"Do you still draw in that style?" asked Benjamin. "Those illustrations you did to create the portal?"

"Quiet," replied Gothkar, looking around the café and almost spilling his coffee. "Are you nuts? Don't bring that topic up in public."

"Why?"

"You really have been out of touch for a while, haven't you? Don't you remember the trouble I got into for making that type of art? Why do you think I had to give it up?"

"I never saw you again after you sent me through the door. When our quest was completed, I emerged to someplace way up north near Whitehaven."

"And while you were zipping between dimensions with ghosts, I was back here in the real world running for my life. Remember how they rushed into the room right as you were going through? I barely made it out of there in one piece."

"I'm sorry about that. I guess I'd forgotten all that you had to go through as I was crossing over."

"Wait a damn minute," said Gothkar. "Please tell me that we're not sitting here because you want me to do that shit again."

Ben stared back and was silent. He took a sip of coffee.

"Goddamnit, I knew it," replied Gothkar. "It figures that

you'd pop up out of thin air and need me to do this again. Right when I finally have my life in order."

"Sorry, old friend," said Benjamin. "But it's worse this time. My children are involved, and I really need to use your talents again if they're to stand a chance."

"What do your kids have to do with it?"

"Speaking of being out of touch, you sure don't sound like you've been following the news lately."

"I'm an artist, man. I don't care about that bullshit."

"That bullshit is happening all over again whether you care or not. So, you'd better start paying attention. And if we don't handle it as we did before, then all of this is finished. This great coffee, your new studio, even Kad itself. They're coming."

"Who's coming?"

"You know exactly who."

Gothkar took a sip of coffee, expelling a long sigh.

"You know, if your Uncle Arthur hadn't done that thing for my father, I'd be walking out of this café right now."

"Maybe," replied Benjamin. "But you're not going to do that. You know why?"

"Please enlighten me, Ben."

"Because you know as well as I do, that you're proud of what we did when we were teenagers. As much as you want to complain and moan about all the trouble you got into afterward, you loved every minute of it. The adventure. The puzzles. The danger. Figuring out how to draw the symbols to open the door."

"Don't talk about that out loud," exclaimed Gothkar.

"Tell me something, old friend," said Benjamin as he leaned over the table. "It sounds like you're doing well these days, but when was the last time your artwork saved Silvarum?"

Gothkar smirked, shaking his head. "You know what's really funny about all this? *You* seem like the asshole now."

"Nejareeth?"

"What?" asked Gothkar.

"That Krii vendor that I talked to about your alleged drinking habits. He just walked into the coffee shop, and now he's pointing us out to some other people."

Gothkar turned and looked at the front door.

"You talked to that guy? He's a lowlife scoundrel."

"So his story about you drinking until nine every morning in the *Smoking Wizard* was bullshit?"

"Obviously. It looks like you're the one he was after."

"Why?"

"We'll find out in a second."

Nejareeth and two men approached the table.

"Did he speak of it?" asked one of the men.

"No," replied Nejareeth. "It was the human."

"Very well. Provide your evidence."

Nejareeth extracted an electronic device from his jacket pocket and pressed a button. A low-quality audio track proceeded to crackle with Benjamin's voice.

"those illustrations you did to create the portal," it said.

"What the hell is this?" exclaimed Ben, standing up.

"Please remain in your seat, sir," replied the other man, pulling a pistol from a holster.

"This evidence is acceptable," said the first man. "Here's your reward. Thank you for your service. Good day, citizen."

Nejareeth snatched the gold coin and exited the café.

The man turned to Benjamin and Gothkar, brandishing his own weapon. It was a brass revolver with a leather grip. An assortment of metal gears and pistons were wrapped around its chrome barrel and cylinder.

"Please stand up, gentlemen, and come with us."

"What are you talking about?" asked Ben.

"You're accused of smuggling artistic knowledge. This is a felony per municipal law 233-05, section 89."

Gothkar shrugged. "Ben, I have a confession to make. I lied to you earlier. I never actually stopped drawing in that style. As a matter of fact, I've become an expert over the years."

"Both of you are under arrest," shouted the other man. "If you move or say another word you'll be shot."

As the men raised their weapons, Gothkar pulled a pencil from his shirt pocket and quickly drew a symbol on a napkin. Ben watched as his friend pulled the two-dimensional drawing out of the paper and held it in his palm. The symbol now possessed a three-dimensional form.

"Holy shit!" cried Benjamin. "How'd you do that?"

"Get ready to run, old friend."

Gothkar threw the symbol at the men. A loud crack and a green explosion echoed through the café. The blast propelled the men across the room in a blinding concussion.

"We should probably go," said Gothkar.

Benjamin vaulted to a standing position, upending the table and spilling their coffee everywhere. Patrons screamed as they dove behind chairs and under tables.

As Benjamin and Gothkar burst through the front door, blinding sunlight temporarily halted their escape. They threw up their arms to shield their eyes and staggered into the street. A brachiosaurus, surprised by their sudden entrance into the traffic, stood on its hind legs, emitting a screeching cry. A bench full of commuters tumbled from the beast's back, crashing to the street.

The two men surged through the café's front door.

"Here they come."

"Quick," said Gothkar. "Get across the street."

"Through that?"

A wall of dinosaurs, giant insects, and overgrown spiders bounded along the double-lane street. Two Pteryxtodon swooped out of the sky, dropping a pair of finely dressed Brol onto the sidewalk. Rows of Kyrashk and Labzhir played a game of stop-and-go as they crept along in the morning rush hour. Benjamin took a deep breath and then followed Gothkar into the forest of massive legs and tentacles.

Pop. Pop Pop. Pew. Pop.

The two men fired their revolvers into the crowd as they continued their pursuit.

"They're shooting at us," said Benjamin.

"Just like old times," replied Gothkar.

A towering insect scrambled down the street in front of them. It stood three meters tall and carried a group of Tulleks on its back. Wings and antennae fluttered in the sunlight.

"Crawl underneath that thing," said Gothkar, pointing.

As they maneuvered between the insect's legs, one of their pursuers discharged another volley of gunfire. Several shots struck the insect in its bulbous abdomen. It shrieked in agony.

Benjamin and Gothkar watched from the sidewalk as the insect pounced upon the man, skewering him with its razor-sharp stinger. The man screamed and squirmed as he was torn in half with a twist of the creature's tail. A pack of smaller bugs sprang upon the bloody remains, devouring them with slurping gulps.

"That was disgusting," said Benjamin.

"Come on," replied Gothkar. "Let's get off the main street. I know a place where we can lay low for a while."

They sprinted down the block, slipping into the shadows of a narrow alleyway.

"Help me with this," said Gothkar as he lifted one edge of a storm drain.

Putrid water splashed as they dropped into the sewer.

"Wait a second," said Gothkar as Benjamin ran down the tunnel. "Let's see if he followed us."

They peered up through the metal grating, watching as the man ran passed. He paused just out of view, but they could still hear the jangling of doorknobs as he tried to get into the shops and stores within the alleyway. The man cursed and then faded back into the busy street.

Gothkar and Benjamin listened for a few more moments and then ran along the tunnel into the fetid gloom.

***

"Where are we going?" asked Benjamin.

"I want to introduce you to some of my friends. If I'm really going to help you again, then I want to get it right this time. No blunders like before."

"The trick you did in the cafe. Where'd you learn that?"

"From the folks you're about to meet."

"Why is art illegal in Kad now?" asked Benjamin.

"Corruption has always been out of control, but it's really picked up over the past decade. After rational discourse for change failed, people started to fight back. One of the tactics used was melding magic with art. It was extremely successful."

"So they outlawed it?"

"Exactly."

"Then how are you able to have your own studio?"

"It's not accessible through legitimate channels. Let's just say my studio is part of a larger, underground network. You'll see what I mean when we get below."

Benjamin and Gothkar maneuvered through the murky tunnels of the Kadiaphonek sewer system. A constant trickle of water echoed within the maze of passageways and chambers. Rats, snakes, and other vermin skirted along rusty pipes and tangled roots. A putrid mustiness choked the air.

"Through this archway," said Gothkar, sweeping aside an outcropping of hanging moss.

"It would be helpful if we could see where we're going," said Benjamin. "I'd forgotten how much I hate it down here."

"Do you have a piece of paper on you?" asked Gothkar.

Benjamin slapped the pockets on his pants and shirt.

"I do, actually," he replied, extracting a folded note from his breast pocket.

"Watch this," said Gothkar, pulling out a pencil.

He drew a circle with three intersecting lines. With his thumb and index finger, he slowly pressed down on the drawing, plucking it from the paper and into the third dimension. The circle was now a glowing, green sphere.

"Will this do?"

"That's an amazing skill you have."

"I know," replied Gothkar. "You can't even imagine what I've had to go through to get to this level."

"How many of those symbols do you know?"

"Thirteen. It takes about two years of training to learn a

new one, and there are a bunch of weird rituals involved. I'm on the verge of the next level. There's one more test I have to perform. I'll tell you more about it later. Let's get out of this stinking mess. We're almost to our destination."

The passageway sloped at a shallow angle as they passed through withered doorways. A thin stream of foul water gradually split into two smaller channels, diverting through canals in the walls. Benjamin held up the green sphere, noticing a difference in their surroundings. Pipes, conduits, and valves had been replaced by fossilized stonework, crumbled columns, and burial chambers. Bizarre hieroglyphics covered the walls and ceiling.

"We're getting down into the ancient depths of the city," said Gothkar, pointing to a fissure in the floor. He pulled a rope from a hidden space in the wall and descended. "It's down here."

Benjamin dropped from the end of the rope and scanned the environment. A mystical veil of fantasy stimulated his senses. Hallways of Doric columns weaved between ribbed vaults and flying buttresses. Thin pools, crowded with clusters of purple tea lights, flowed between statues and altars. The clatter of wind chimes hummed as a hint of jasmine and nutmeg lingered.

"What is this place?" asked Benjamin.

"We're inside the ruins of an ancient cathedral," replied Gothkar. "One of the first-ever built in Kad."

"Who are these friends you're taking me to?"

"They call themselves the Shadowkuur. They're a society of artists, conjurers, shapeshifters, and rogues. Basically, everyone who's been shunned from the normalcy of the Overworld. I wish I'd known about them when we were kids. They could've saved us a great deal of trouble."

"How many of them are down here?"

"Thousands," he replied. "They have their own city. It's called Ebonthain. Come on, you'll see."

Benjamin leapt over one of the glowing pools, following Gothkar through a decorative arch. They walked along a corridor and were soon greeted by a locked door.

"Now what?"

"We knock," replied Gothkar, tapping on the door three times with his pencil.

"They won't hear that," said Benjamin.

A series of gears and locking mechanisms echoed through the hallway as the large door immediately slid open.

"This is a magic pencil," said Gothkar with a wink.

They peered through the doorway. A spider web fluttered across the corner of the stone frame as a bat squeaked and flew off into the darkness. There was no one to greet them.

"That's odd," said Gothkar, scratching his chin. "Blazrug or Eddie are usually guarding the backdoor."

"Look down here, you overgrown troll," said a voice.

They lowered their gaze. A Tullek woman glared back.

"What do you want?" she asked.

Gothkar turned toward Benjamin.

"Don't look at me," he replied. "This was your idea."

"Hurry up," she said. "I don't have all day to stand here and wait on you idiots. Either state your name and purpose or face the wrath of the Soulflayer."

"Good morning, ma'am," replied Gothkar. "Two of my friends are usually at this door to greet me."

"They're not here now are they?" she replied. "So, as I said, state your name and purpose, or be gone with you."

"My name's Gothkar. I'm here to see Vomexium."

"I've never heard of you," replied the woman, pressing a button to close the door.

"Wait a minute," replied Gothkar. "I'm an artist."

She pressed the button again, and the door stopped.

"An artist, you say? Prove it."

Gothkar felt around in his pockets for a piece of paper.

"It seems I've run out of drawing materials."

"That's a shame," she said. "Have fun with the Soulflayer. Good day, gentlemen."

She pressed the button, and the door slammed shut.

"What the hell?" moaned Gothkar.

"Such a sweet, little woman," said Benjamin. "What do you suppose a Soulflayer is?"

"I have no idea," replied Gothkar. "This is bullshit, man. I've been down here a thousand times and never been treated like this. I don't know who the hell this Tullek lady thinks she is, but I'm going to speak with…"

A deep moan echoed from a distant passageway.

"What was that?" asked Benjamin.

"What was what?"

"That sound from the darkness."

"I didn't hear anything."

The moan rang out again, closer and louder.

"Did you hear it that time?"

Gothkar nodded.

"The Soulflayer, I suppose?"

"I guess."

They turned, gazing down the corridor. Except for a few shafts of pale light that glimmered from intersecting corridors, it was black as pitch. Webs of spider silk blew between the ceiling and columns. A ghostly figure turned the corner at the far end of the passage and approached.

"What should we do?" asked Benjamin.

"If only I had some more paper," replied Gothkar.

"I have another piece."

"Seriously? Why didn't you give it to me a second ago?"

"You didn't ask."

Gothkar laughed. "May I please have it now?"

"Sure, but you might want to hurry up with the drawing. The Soulflayer is getting closer."

"Thanks, but I think I can handle this."

Gothkar drew a straight line with two curved ends on the scrap of paper. He pulled it into the third dimension, holding it in his palm. The form pulsated with a red glow.

"This one's called Molten Arrow. It should easily take care of this Soulflayer thing."

The apparition extended its arms as it sprang upon the companions. Gothkar threw the red symbol.

"Ouch!" cried the Soulflayer. "That hurts."

Gothkar and Benjamin looked at each other in dismay.

"That will be all, gentlemen," said a voice from behind.

An old man and the Tullek woman stood in the doorway.

"Thank you, Eddie," said the old man. "We appreciate your services during this test. Do you require medical attention?"

"Nah, I'm all right," replied Eddie, rubbing his head. He transformed from the spectral form of the Soulflayer into the frail body of a ten-year-old boy.

"Test? What the hell is going on here, Vomexium?"

"Good morning, Gothkar," replied the old man. "I'd like to introduce you to my associate, Dorothy Tompkins."

The woman dropped a curtsy.

Gothkar looked at her and scoffed. "Hello, again."

"Please call me Dot," she replied. "Your artistic abilities are indeed impressive. Vomexium was right about you. We devised this quick test so I could gauge your talents."

"What for?"

"A job."

"What sort of job?"

"The saving the realm sort," replied Dot. "Now, bring along your friend Benjamin Woods with you and follow us down to Ebonthain."

"How do you know my name?" asked Benjamin.

"I know everything about you," replied Dot.

***

Gothkar and Benjamin followed them to a footbridge that extended across an enormous chasm. As they crossed, Benjamin peered over the railing into the abyss. A deep cylinder had been carved out of the granite and sandstone. Hundreds of bridges crisscrossed the chasm, connecting to adjoining hovels and dwellings on each side. Torchlight flickered like fireflies.

They reached the end of the bridge, descending along a spiral walkway. At the bottom was the first of countless floors in the complex. Each layer encircled the cavity and was intertwined by bridges and stairwells. Individuals moved from floor to floor amidst the glow of tranquil lamplight.

"Welcome to Ebonthain," said Vomexium.

"It's wonderful," replied Benjamin, gazing at the sparkling lights and movement.

Hushed voices met their arrival. Benjamin turned from the vastness of the central shaft, observing the archways and windows that covered the interior space. Doorways, corridors, and storefronts lined the walls. Curious eyes peered from within.

"This way," said the old man. "Let's go down to the next level so we may talk for a while."

Descending to the second-floor, Benjamin examined the eccentric collection of individuals that peeked around corners and drawn curtains. A man with violet skin leaned within a doorway with his arms crossed. A hand that protruded from the top of his bald head extended its middle finger as the group walked by.

"That's Blazrug, Eddie's father," said Gothkar. "Ignore him. He's just a smart-ass like most of us down here."

"What a friendly group," replied Benjamin.

"They're not that bad," said Gothkar. "The Shadowkuur are just extremely distrustful of strangers from above."

"We're all down here for a reason," said Vomexium.

Benjamin turned his attention to the next scene. Through a circular window, oddly lit by orchid lanterns that expelled blue smoke, stood a mesmerizing figure. It appeared to be a kneeling person, yet its form was comprised of the bottom half of a leg and an arm. A mouth emitted a sound like running water as the creature seamlessly changed into a different combination of body parts. This process repeated itself every few moments.

"A shapeshifter?" asked Benjamin.

"Yes," said Gothkar. "Look over here at this one. She's probably one of the best painters in Ebonthain."

An art gallery contained a wide variety of oil paintings and engraved illustrations. Some of the canvases stood two meters, leaning against the inner walls of the shop. Painterly brushstrokes and vibrant colors filled the bizarre compositions. In one piece, a woman held up an umbrella under a cloudy sky. Her head was slightly tilted and her expression was swathed in sorrow. The opposite side of the room featured an equally impressive canvas. It held a crowd of people gathered around a floating pyramid.

"What am I looking for?" asked Benjamin.

"Here she comes," replied Gothkar.

A woman stepped from the crowd and walked out of the painting. She crossed the gallery floor, casually striding into another piece of artwork. Her form instantly became a part of the composition the moment she touched the canvas.

"Wow," said Benjamin.

"Pretty cool, right?" asked Gothkar. "I learned a lot from her about brush technique and how to establish exceptional compositions, especially with oil paintings. That's one of the hardest mediums to work with, you know?"

"Where did she go? Is she actually in the painting?"

"Yes. There's a whole different world in each oil painting that she creates. It's similar to the technique I used to send you through the portal to the Tombworld."

"Gentlemen," said Dot. "I'm terribly sorry to interrupt your conversation, but we have other pressing matters to attend to. Would you please follow us?"

"I'm right behind you," said Gothkar.

***

"If you wouldn't mind," said Vomexium, "Gothkar and I have some previous business to discuss. In the meantime, Dot will explain to you the details of the job."

"Sure," replied Benjamin.

"Fabulous. We shouldn't be too long. I'll summon you when we've concluded, and then you and Gothkar can get started on your quest."

"Already?" asked Benjamin.

"Indeed," said Dot. "I said pressing matters, didn't I?"

Benjamin looked at Gothkar.

He shrugged.

"Follow me," said Dot. "My laboratory is this way."

***

"Have a seat," she said as they entered the room.

Two leather chairs sat in the far corner. They faced each other with a matching bench in between, allowing each person to stretch out their legs. Throw pillows, blankets, and a soft rug completed the arrangement.

"I call this my cozy corner," said Dot.

The chairs were Tullek size. Ben stood two meters tall.

"It's cozy, all right," he replied.

He squeezed into a chair, raising his feet.

"No, sir," exclaimed Dot. "There'll be no dirty shoes in my cozy corner. Take them off this instant."

Benjamin groaned as he kicked off his boots.

"Now, isn't that better?" she asked.

"It's delightful, thank you."

She took one of the fuzzy blankets from the arm of her chair and covered herself up to her chest.

"Well now, Ben. How are you?"

"I'm very comfortable."

"I didn't ask you that. I asked how you're doing."

A trigger went off in his head. He was painfully familiar with this type of situation. It was undoubtedly going to be *a talk*. The variety where each participant was expected to actively play a role in the conversation. Sharing feelings. Being present. It was his worst nightmare. He squirmed around in the small chair to get more comfortable. The blanket that he had covered himself with reached to his kneecaps.

Benjamin cleared his throat. "I can honestly say, all things considered, that life is not that bad at the moment."

"And what exactly does 'not that bad' mean?"

"It means that, in general, things are good. You know?"

"No, I actually don't know. Could you elaborate?"

Benjamin sighed, scratching his beard. He was in hell.

"I was finally reunited with my old friend Gothkar earlier this morning. I've been searching for him for weeks."

"That's great," she replied. "How are your children?"

"My children? What do they have to do with anything?"

"Everything. They're why you're here."

"I don't know how they're doing, actually. I've not seen them in a month, and I haven't received a letter from them in over a week. Is that a good enough answer for you?"

"You don't have to get defensive, Ben. I'm only trying to converse with you about your feelings. I imagine that keeping in contact with your children is an important factor in your life."

"Of course," he replied, taking a deep breath. "Look, I'm sorry I snapped at you. I guess I'm not doing well after all."

"Your reaction is perfectly predictable," she replied. "You don't know me. Why would you divulge your true feelings after only a few questions? When you pass a stranger on the street and casually ask them how they are, do they stop you in your tracks and burden you with all their feelings? No. They almost always say that they're fine, regardless of how they're really doing."

Benjamin chuckled. "I guess that's true."

"Now," she said, "let me ask you again. This time I want you to answer truthfully. But before you do, I'll give you something in return to help ease your tension. Earlier you asked how I knew your name. I may be a stranger to you, but you're well known to me. Did Trel never speak of me?"

"Trelinia?" replied Benjamin. He dropped his feet to the floor, sitting up straight. The little blanket fell from his legs.

"Indeed. I helped her during her quest thirty years ago. We've been close friends ever since. It confounds me that she's never mentioned me to you before."

"Well, we separated not too long ago. Our interchange of information hadn't been productive."

"That's a good one," she replied with a giggle. "I've not ever heard it put that way before. I believe the term you are referring to is effective communication skills, right?"

"You're right. However, I'll say that before I set out for Kad, Trel and I had started seeing each other again."

"Really?" replied Dot. "Now that's interesting."

Benjamin relaxed, attempting to compose himself. He did not fully understand why he felt this way, and he certainly was not used to the sensation, but he persevered down the unfamiliar river of emotions. He would share his feelings.

"Yes. It hasn't been anything serious, but we did entertain the idea of going out on another date."

"Have you considered getting back together with her?"

"That's a pretty direct question."

"Those are the only types of questions I ask."

Benjamin gazed down at the floor.

"I've had a lot of free time recently to think. Time to reflect upon the choices I've made throughout my life. Memories are a funny thing. You can have a lasting experience without fully appreciating it in the moment. Then, for the rest of your life, you can dwell upon how you let that experience slip away. At the conclusion of each day, I always seem to be walking down the same tired road. Were all those decisions in vain? Was it worth it? The armor that I've built up over the years is impenetrable most of the time. But on some days, life seeps through. The bliss of their laughter. A glimpse of her smile. There are moments I find myself unable to breathe. During my recent journeys, I've spent night after night sleeping within the arms of the forest or by the edge of a river. Each time during those contemplative moments before I fall asleep, there are always two things I focus on."

"What are they?" asked Dot.

"My children."

"And the other?"

"Trel."

CHAPTER XIX

SPACETIME DISTORTIONS

Roger thought for a moment and then stepped through all the procedures that Merkresh had demonstrated for him over the past hour. He cycled through each of the menus, sub-menus, and text boxes and then queried for the proper number combination. Satisfied with the results, the boy communicated to CAAT that he wished to set the Eyeculus magnification back to level one.

"Eyeculus magnification level one initiated," she replied.

"You're getting better already," said the old man. "You'll get faster at executing those commands the more you use the device. Before you know it, you'll be clicking those sensors and twirling your glove around as efficient as a symphony conductor."

"That's exactly what I pictured in my head when I first started waving it around to use the keyboard," replied the boy. "Not that I know what it feels like to be a symphony conductor, but you probably know what I mean."

"I know exactly what you mean," said Merkresh. "Now, please make your way back over toward the polytope, and let's confirm what I hope to be true."

Roger walked to the mysterious shape.

"All right," said Merkresh as he extended his open palm, gesturing toward the glass enclosure. "The whole purpose of this apparatus is to attempt to replicate, on a minuscule scale, the bizarre physics of the 4-dimensional objects that we encountered hovering above the city of Nexxathia."

"We? You mean when *you* traveled up to that city?"

"Indeed," he replied. "I've actually been up there on two separate occasions. Those details are part of a much longer story that I'll be happy to share with you later. In the meantime, however, we need to verify once and for all that those visions you've been having, that allowed you to see the symbols of the eight runes, are due to your magical abilities."

"Okay. What do I need to do?"

Merkresh lowered his arm and stepped up to the device. Attached to the left side of the wooden base sat a control panel that contained a brass lever and four black buttons. They were each labeled with metal tags. The old man pressed the first button that said *POWER*. A mechanical hum radiated from within the innards of the machine, projecting a pulse of energy throughout the room. Roger felt the shockwave in his bones.

"Wow," exclaimed the boy.

"Keep your eyes on the polytope," said Merkresh.

As the machine generated more energy and the humming became progressively louder, the polychoron slowly lifted off the top of the pillar, hovering. As it rose, it also began to slowly rotate. The increasingly violent vibrations in the room caused the metal tools and other small objects in the immediate area to bounce around and jingle. Click, who had relocated his current activities to a table adjacent to Merkresh and Roger, raised his brass head in response to the sudden ruckus. He expelled a sequence of anxious chirps.

"Everything's fine, Click," said the old man. "I'm just showing off my new toy for Roger."

The spider acknowledged with a series of robotic beeps. He scrambled to a shelf above the apparatus to get a better view of the demonstration.

"Is this thing going to get much louder?" asked Roger, covering the mask's earhole.

Merkresh smiled, holding up his finger in a gesture for patience. He then arched that same finger down and pressed the second button on the control panel that said EQUALIZE. A gear shift locked into place and the humming went silent.

"That's much better," said the old man.

Roger breathed a sigh of relief. "Now what?"

"In a few moments, the polychoron should be hovering and rotating exactly as the real ones do over Nexxathia. When that's all set, I'm going to have you switch on the lens that allows you to see the object in four dimensions. Here's the twist, though, and the test I've been talking about all night. Once you're able to see the polychoron in its pure form, I'm expecting, hoping really, that you'll be able to communicate with it."

"Communicate how?"

"I don't have the slightest clue, but I do know that some form of communication is possible based on my knowledge of how these things work and from documentation and artifacts that I've recovered from Nexxathia. When I'm wearing that mask, and

I look at the object while it's floating and rotating, all that I can perceive is the 4-dimensional shape. That in itself is impressive, but the real test is to make some form of contact with it. Because of your recent visions, and the fact that I know you possess untapped magical abilities, I believe that you'll be able to interface with it. All I can really say is, keep your eyes and ears open. This thing may try to communicate with you in creative ways."

"Okay," said Roger. "I guess I'm ready. Let's see what happens. I'll be honest, though. I'm a little nervous about looking at this thing. How do you know something bad won't happen? Like, what if I get sucked through a wormhole?"

"A wormhole?" replied Merkresh, laughing. "I wouldn't consider that a bad thing. I've always wanted to pass through one of those. Remind me to show you the..."

"Come on, Merkresh. I'm serious."

The old man stopped laughing and placed his hand on Roger's shoulder. "I promise you'll not get sucked into another galaxy. I've studied these objects for many years, and I can assure you that they don't operate like that. For one thing, I made this device from scratch, so I have a fair idea of its capabilities. Secondly, it's your magical abilities that control the capacity for what you may or may not experience. You alone determine the strength of your vision. Fill your mind with positive thoughts and focus on pushing out the fear. You'll be fine. I believe in you."

Roger turned to the mysterious device and stared at the floating polychoron. "I can do this," he said after a few moments.

"You should probably use this opportunity to keep practicing with the HUD, but for the sake of time, and because I have this combo memorized, I'm just going to tell you how to initiate the 4-D lens. The combo is: *4-3, 3-3, 1-1*."

Roger tapped the finger pads, executing the command.

"Eyeculus four-dimensional lens online," replied CAAT.

The left eye lens cycled through a selection of adapters, locking into place with a snap. As Roger focused his attention upon the hovering and rotating polychoron, an odd sensation washed over his perception. A thick, tingling pulse tickled the tips of his fingers and toes. His arms and legs felt as heavy as lead. An inky blackness, warm and calming, oozed within the periphery of his vision. He felt himself tumbling into a chasm of uncertainty.

"Roger!" cried Merkresh as he lunged forward with open arms, catching the boy's limp body.

***

Music.

Roger heard peculiar music as he fell into the void. It was faint at first. Gradual. Patient. A delectable murmur increased in amplitude and then was constant. Its tone was pleasant and inviting. The hum was constructed of a deep baritone layer and a balanced treble. The two were in perfect harmony. Roger rode the tones through the darkness and focused intently on the music. He was adrift within a current of alien sound waves.

Eons passed. Lifetimes. The hum progressed as the boy drifted through the emptiness. Fear, joy, anger, sadness; emotions did not exist in this new place. There was only the music. Only the constant hum. It was Roger's entire universe, and he willingly relinquished his existence to its mesmerizing grasp.

The music fluctuated, only by a fraction, but Roger immediately perceived its new complexity and composition. A harmonic pulse crept along the hum, washing over his ears. His eyes widened from the new sensation. His teeth clenched. The pulse slammed a wave of energy through his entire body. For the first time during this erratic experience, there was a flash of bright light. It flickered for an instant and then vanished. The harmonic pulse was also gone. He was drifting alone again, along the magnificent hum through the blackness of space and time.

A second pulse. A third.

The energetic oscillations bombarded the boy's senses in rapid succession. An overload of melodic refrains, allegros, and progressions cycled through his bewildered mind. The iterating music produced sight. Through the flashing lights, he began to grasp colors and shapes. The black void transformed into a majestic vista of mountains and snow. A crystal-clear, blue sky hung above cyclopean peaks and windswept, arctic plains. Roger's lungs inhaled a breath of frigid wind. He smelled the crystallized air as snowflakes stung his face. He was flying.

Rising along the roots of a primordial mountain range, Roger beheld the outlines of a hideous cityscape. Its cruel angles and marble columns sneered within a jagged valley of rock and ice. Granite-tipped pyramids and cracked monoliths crowded the illogical geometry of the city's districts and avenues. A frozen blade of dizziness punctured the boy's mind as he decelerated, hovering at the threshold of the metropolis. An attempt to behold its scale and breadth was a pursuit into madness.

The music persisted.

As Roger struggled to comprehend the absurd imagery that beckoned before him, his mind was again thrust into motion. He flew downward, directed toward the innards of the dismal city. Intersections, plazas, and courtyards flashed by in a muddled blur. Obscene statues and incomprehensible effigies filled every junction and shadowed corner. His mind was forced to take a sharp right turn down an alleyway. Now a left along a ghastly promenade. Another right. Left. Left. Right. He lost track of all the turning and twisting.

An immense structure loomed before him. Its Ionic columns, crumbled pediment, and marble steps convulsed an evil and malignant rage. Roger struggled in vain to flee from its offensive hold. The constant music in his mind was absolute, pushing him forward. He slowly moved up the fractured steps and into the desolation of the entryway.

Down, down, down.

Roger descended along rotted staircases and passageways. Filthy, labyrinthine corridors, choked with cobwebs and dust, forced the boy's mind lower and deeper into the belly of the city. The odors were musty and ancient. The light was pale and sallow. Dank air swept against his face as he approached the end of a darkened hallway, pausing in front of a door. Its oaken planks and iron hinges stood stained and festering. Horrific symbols had been chiseled into its wooden face. Roger studied them intently. He realized that this door was not the end of the journey, yet the symbols seemed important. Their features were illogical and maddening. Their compositions were fashioned from harsh symmetries and irrational perspectives. He could not understand the cryptic designs, yet he desperately attempted to remember their highlights.

The oak door opened, interrupting his focus amid the grind of rusted gears. Roger noticed a hitherto obscured symbol, causing his heart to skip a beat. A lidless eye, framed by two overlapping circles, turned and glared at him at the moment his body was thrust through the doorway.

The interior was cramped and dark. Purple torchlight crackled within the chamber as faint shadows danced against curved walls. The persistent music in Roger's mind willed him further. He obediently moved toward the center of the catacomb, standing amidst eight stone caskets. They were laid out in a square in the middle of the chamber. Engraved into each of their lids was carved disturbing symbols, all equally perplexing as the hieroglyphics on the door.

Roger's attention turned to the lid of the coffin at the southeast position in the formation. He focused intently, studying its features. Vicious words and symbols were chiseled into the stonework. A flowing script, devoid of form or grace, had been hatefully scrawled along the border of the lid, framing an oval pit at its center. Next to the empty depression he perceived a familiar design. It was one of the eight symbols that he had drawn on his map: The Rune of Frost.

A bolt of electricity discharged from the coffin's lid, enveloping the boy. His vision turned black as the iterating musical pulses increased exponentially. A series of images cycled through his mind.

A haunted castle at dawn…

His father and a troll walking through a swamp…

A serpent bursting from the surface of a river…

His mother struggling with a cloaked intruder…

***

"Mom!" screamed Roger, pulling off the mask and glove.

"What happened?" gasped Merkresh.

The boy collapsed in a heap, vomiting onto the workshop

floor. Chunks of food and strings of amber liquid splashed onto the surrounding table legs and boxes.

"Oh no!" cried Merkresh, rushing to Roger's side. "Click! Fetch some water and a towel. Quickly!"

The spider squawked into action, dropping from his web. An assortment of glass bottles and containers sat on a shelf next to a brass sink. Click snatched one of the bottles with his front legs and filled it with water. He then grabbed a towel from the side of the sink, scrambling across the floor.

Roger lurched on all fours, expelling another mouthful of vomit. He breathed in heavy and labored gasps.

"I saw her!" he said between breaths.

"Saw who?"

The boy gagged, projecting another stream of vomit across the floor. His heaves were gurgled and high-pitched. The tendons in his neck protruded from the stress.

Roger wiped his mouth. "Your workshop. I'm so sorry."

"Don't worry about that," replied Merkresh. "Please, just try to relax. Go on and finish if you need to."

"I think I'm done," replied Roger, wiping his mouth. He tried to stand up.

"Go easy," said Merkresh. "Don't try to get up too fast. Click! Where are you with that water?"

The spider chirped in response, hopping up and down on the adjacent table. Merkresh grabbed the towel and water.

"Here you are, lad. Nice and easy."

The boy slowly sat up. He took the towel and placed it on his forehead, exuding a long, exhausted sigh.

"How long was I gone?" he asked.

"Gone?" replied the old man. "What do you mean?"

"How long was I unconscious?"

Merkresh frowned. "I don't understand. You weren't gone. You looked at the polychoron, and after only a second you fell over. I caught you before you smashed to the floor."

"And that just happened?"

"Yes. Only seconds ago."

"But that can't be," exclaimed Roger. "I was out there in the blackness forever. Then I was flying through a horrible city. And there was music."

"Music? Please tell me exactly what happened."

Roger cleared his throat. "It began with this really strange music repeating in my head. Everything was black, and it felt like I was floating through empty space. After a while, it really did seem like forever, I was flying in the mountains and snow. Then I descended beneath a city. It was hideous."

"Nexxathia," said the old man.

"What?"

"The hideous city. You had a vision of Nexxathia. I knew you could do it, Roger! You successfully communicated with the polychoron. This is a fantastic breakthrough and proves to me that you're already attuned to their technology."

"I sure don't feel fantastic," replied Roger, pulling himself to his feet.

"Did you see anything else important?" asked Merkresh. "What about the symbols you drew on the map, or the pyramid with the halo around it? Please try to remember."

Roger pressed the damp towel to his forehead and closed his eyes. "I think I saw some new symbols on a door and maybe on a coffin, but I'm having trouble remembering their details now. Most of the vision is foggy. I do remember the stuff I saw at the end. As I stood over one of the large tombs, or whatever it was, I was zapped by a bolt of electricity, and then I saw a bunch of different scenes in sequence. It was like a silent film. One of the scenes was of my mom fighting with someone. The person wore a sapphire cloak, but I couldn't tell who it was."

"That's troubling," replied the old man.

Click hopped off the table, scurrying across the floor to the far end of the workshop.

"What does it mean?" asked Roger.

"It could be a vision of the future," replied Merkresh.

"Or it could be happening now."

"I don't know."

Roger set the towel down and strapped on his backpack. "I'm really worried about her now, Merkresh. I think I should go home and make sure she's all right."

"Yes, of course. Go check on her. I'm sure everything is fine, but it would be wise for you to get home at this late hour, anyway. You've been an immense help tonight. Thank you, my friend. I mean it. Get home safe now, and I'll clean up the mess on the floor. It's my fault anyway. I should have…"

"Shit!" shouted the boy.

Merkresh froze in mid-sentence. "What is it?"

Roger held up the mask in his hands. It was completely destroyed. The emerald glass of the larger eyepiece was cracked, and the Eyeculus itself was a crumpled mess of brass and wires.

"Oh no," moaned Merkresh.

"I'm so sorry," said Roger. "I can't believe I threw it to the ground like that."

The old man sighed as he examined the extent of the damage. "There's nothing for you to be sorry about. It's my fault.

I'm the one who put you in that situation without understanding how it would affect you. You dropped it because you were sick."

"Maybe it's not completely ruined," said Roger. "Can't you replace the glass and patch up the eyepieces? I'll help you."

"I'm afraid it's not that simple. The glass for the eyepieces is made with a special type of…"

BEEP! BEEP! BEEP!

Roger and Merkresh spun toward the opposite end of the workshop. The spider peered through one of the basement windows, his radio dish spinning rapidly and blinking red.

"That's Click's proximity alarm," exclaimed the old man. "It appears we may have some uninvited guests."

"What do you mean?"

The clatter of falling objects and books resounded from the upstairs room. They both looked to the ceiling.

"Did you lock the front door?" asked Merkresh.

"I think so."

Heavy footfalls stomped upstairs. Someone was smashing display cases and upending tables.

"Who is that?" asked Roger.

"I have no idea, but they certainly didn't knock. And I doubt it's my neighbor asking to borrow a cup of salt."

"Then what? Someone's looking for you."

"I'm sure. I just didn't expect them to find me so soon."

"What?" asked Roger. "Who's looking for you?"

A gloved hand punched through one of the basement windows, ripping away the remains of the frame. Shards of glass and bits of wood sprayed across the room. A grisly figure, clad in leather armor, slipped through the open window and stood at the far end of the workshop.

"He's down here," shouted the intruder.

The footsteps above raced across the floor, descending the curved stairwell. The tip-tap of leather boots against stone echoed in the narrow chamber.

"Who are you?" asked Merkresh.

The intruder smirked but remained silent. Two other men rushed through the workshop entrance, pausing just beyond the threshold.

"Merkresh Warington," said the taller of the two. He had a thin, crimson scar that ran vertically from his eyebrow down to the middle of his cheek. Both men were dressed in leather armor and had curved daggers sheathed within scabbards on their belts. Grim beards and dirt covered their faces.

The old man extended his arm to shield the boy. "Who are you rascals? Be gone with you!"

"Merkresh Warington," he said once again. "By decree of Count Zaran, I hereby place you under arrest."

"Arrest? Nonsense. For what charges?"

"For treason against his castle and realm."

"His realm?" replied Merkresh, laughing. "What the devil are you mumbling about? Get out of my house. Scoot!"

"Count Zaran commands that you accompany us back to the castle at once for judgment," said the scarred man. "There will be no debate or conversation. You're coming with us now."

The old man scoffed at the order. "My nephew wants me arrested, you say?" He slowly moved toward the table to his right while using his extended arm to calmly guide Roger with him. "Rubbish I say to you. You look more like a gang of amateur pickpockets. Who do you really work for?"

"Funny jokes, old man. I would watch my tongue if I

were you before it gets sliced off and fed to my Qugron pup."

"Merkresh," said Roger. "What are we going to do?"

The old man raised a finger to his lips, motioning for the boy to remain silent.

"Now you listen to me, brigand," said Merkresh with a commanding tone. "Whoever you are and whatever you want, you clearly don't represent my nephew. You've broken into my home and threatened me. For that, I'm now obligated to defend myself and my property, and to punish you."

The scarred man laughed. "Punish us? An unarmed old man and a cowering little boy? Against the three of us?"

"Not unarmed!"

As quick as lightning, Merkresh reached under the nearest table and snatched two throwing blades from a hidden sleeve. In one fluid motion, he propelled the blades across opposite ends of the room. One was directed toward the intruder who entered through the window, and the other blade was hurled at the head of the ruffian next to the scarred man. Both weapons met their targets with brutal force.

"Uraaaagh!" shrieked the man at the back of the room as an upper section of his skull was sheared off. A stream of bright blood erupted from his exposed brain, spraying in threads against the wall. His body fell to the floor in a crumpled heap.

The second blade buried itself deep within the left eye socket of the other ruffian. The impact created a popping sound. Several of the man's teeth shattered as he reflexively bit down, clenching from the trauma. Particles of teeth and blood shot out of his mouth and stuck to the scarred man's face and beard.

"You're fucking dead!" he howled, unsheathing his blade and hacking at the air wildly. His eyes were wild with rage.

"Now we're even," replied Merkresh, withdrawing a long sword from underneath the same table. It produced a marvelous, metallic twang as he pulled it free. "But it's a shame you brought a dagger to a sword fight."

The scarred man leapt over the corpse of his companion, charging across the room. He screamed and spat as he ran.

"Roger, pick up the glove and stay close," said Merkresh. "Keep your distance but stay behind me. This is going to be messy. Click! Get over here."

The spider had been observing the encounter from his web on the ceiling. At Merkresh's command, he crawled toward the middle of the room, dropping along a thin thread. He hopped on the table next to them and awaited his next task.

"Run upstairs and fetch my other mask. Double-quick!"

The spider scrambled back up the thread and across the ceiling. He leapt to the ground, disappearing up the corridor.

The scarred man was almost within striking distance. As he rapidly approached, he threw aside one of the worktables with a wild roar. Tools and equipment smashed against the far wall. A screwdriver struck one of the hanging oil lanterns, sending it crashing to the floor. Tongues of flame licked the base of a tarp-covered instrument. It was soon engulfed.

"Now you die, old fool."

"Wrong again," replied Merkresh. "Now Palewalker will teach you some manners."

The scarred man crouched, preparing for his attack. He held the dagger low in his right hand and extended his left arm forward. He wiggled his fingers in a mocking gesture. Merkresh remained motionless as he studied his attacker. His eyes expertly sized up his opponent, calculating his probable movements.

The man lunged forward with three furious strokes. A horizontal slash, a vertical slash, and a diagonal strike. The crash of steel screamed each time their blades met.

"That was rather pathetic," said the old man. "Allow me to demonstrate a proper sword fighting technique."

Merkresh took a nimble step forward and produced a dramatic head fake. The scarred man fell for the faint, raising his dagger to block the phantom attack. As a result, the old man swept his sword in a tight arch, severing three fingers from the scarred man's left hand. Blood squirted from bare stumps as the fingers dropped, bouncing on the floor.

"Don't worry," said Merkresh. "You still have two more to wiggle with."

The man growled in pain. He thrust forward his dagger using a reverse grip. Merkresh parried the advance with ease.

"You're a tenacious one. I'll give you that much."

The old man shifted his stance, driving a diagonal slash into the scarred man's left leg. Palewalker sliced through the leather armor and muscle like butter. A fountain of blood spewed onto a neighboring chair.

The scarred man screeched in agony, retreating in hops behind a tool bench. Blood continued to belch from the exposed gash as he desperately searched for an alternative tactic or more lethal weapon. The man hobbled to the burning equipment and picked up a wooden chair. Its legs were glowing spouts of fire.

"You can all burn to death," he shouted. "I'll find what I came for once your bones have turned to ash."

The scarred man hurled the chair across the room. As it exploded upon impact, the embers ignited the piles of wood shavings and oily rags. The workshop became an inferno.

"Come on, Roger! We have to get out of here."

"How? The stairwell is blocked."

Merkresh motioned to the back wall. "Out the window."

They scrambled to the back of the room, covering their mouths from the thick smoke. Click emerged from the tunnel and crawled to them along the ceiling. He had retrieved the other mask from upstairs.

"Nicely done, Click!" said the old man. "Drop it here."

The spider let the mask fall into his master's hands.

"Roger, do you still want to see that plasma pulse?"

"Hell yes I do."

"Then please throw me the glove."

The boy tossed it, backing up to the open window.

In three smooth movements, Merkresh put on the glove, the mask, and switched on CAAT.

"Good evening, sir. How may I..."

"No time for chit-chat. There's vermin to exterminate."

He tapped the finger pads like an expert.

"Plasma pulse online," said CAAT. "Please lock onto the requested target and fire when ready."

The scarred man was beyond the wall of flame, shouting and pumping his dagger into the smoke-filled air. "Burn! Burn! Burn!" he screamed.

Merkresh held a necklace above his head. It had a black chain with an iron key dangling from its center.

"Is this what you're looking for?"

The scarred man paused, peering through the smoke.

"Target acquired," said CAAT.

"Throw me the key, old man, and I'll let you live."

"No thanks," replied Merkresh as he aimed and fired.

A green bolt shot from a barrel on the glove. The orb of plasma screeched through the fire and smoke, thumping into the scarred man's chest. His upper body, along with his arms and head, exploded into a red cloud of gore and bone. The twitching legs buckled for a moment and then fell to the floor.

"Quickly now! Up and out that window."

Roger crawled up onto a desk and pulled himself through to the grass. Click followed. Crickets could still be heard amidst the roar and pop of the house fire.

The old man, the boy, and the mechanical spider raced across the backyard, pausing at the tree line. They turned and watched as the workshop and all the wondrous inventions burned to the ground.

"That's about a hundred years' worth of work going up in smoke," said Merkresh.

The old man tapped the boy on his shoulder and pointed across the street. Other houses and shops were on fire. The village of Thorndale was under attack.

"Come on," said Merkresh. "Let's check on your family."

CHAPTER XX

DIRGE OF SEPTEMBER

"Mckenzie, wake up," said Marie.

"What is it?" she replied, rolling over onto her other side. She grabbed her pillow, plopping it on top of her head.

"Did you hear that noise?"

"No. I was sleeping. Can you please leave now and let me continue? I was having a pretty good dream."

"I thought I heard footsteps walking around downstairs."

Mckenzie groaned. "I seriously doubt it. You were having a dream of your own."

"I'm serious. It's freaking me out."

"I bet it's just Mom cleaning," said Mckenzie, "or doing something else moms do."

"At one-thirty in the morning?"

"Are you seriously going to make me get out of bed?"

"I'll come with you. I just don't want to go alone."

Mckenzie lay motionless in her bed for a few moments and then dramatically thrashed out of her covers, jumping to her bare feet. "Fine. Let's run downstairs and ambush the thief that's stealing our hidden treasure."

"Thank you very much, but I have to say, your jokes are much better once you've had time to wake up."

"Come on," said Mckenzie. "You might as well grab your wand so you feel safer."

"I don't know the first thing about using that yet."

"Just grab it," she replied. "I'll bring mine too. But first, I'm going to put on my robe and slippers. Did someone leave a window open all night? This floor's freezing."

The sisters met back in the hallway and peered over the railing into the darkness.

"See, other than those crickets and frogs outside, I don't hear a thing," said Mckenzie. "Can we please go back to bed now?" She walked to her room.

"Listen," replied Marie. "There's something else."

Mckenzie rolled her eyes, turning back. They both leaned over the railing and listened. Marie cocked her ear to one side, trying to hear through the white noise of the crickets.

"What is that?"

"What is what? I don't hear anything."

"It sounds like breathing."

"Shut up," replied Mckenzie with a serious tone. "There's no one down there. Stop being such a baby. Let's just check it out and get this over with."

As Mckenzie descended the stairs, a shape flashed across the open doorway at the opposite end of the upstairs hall. The girls froze, turning toward the movement.

"What the hell was that?"

"Somebody's in here," replied Mckenzie.

"That's what I've been trying to tell you."

Mckenzie held the curly wand in front of her, creeping up the stairs.

"What do you think you're going to do with that?"

"I don't know. Let's have a look."

The sisters crouched low, cautiously advancing down the hallway together. Each step produced creeks and moans through the wooden floorboards.

"Could you be any louder?" asked Mckenzie.

"I can't help it. This floor is a thousand years old."

As they reached the end of the hallway, Mckenzie held up her hand, motioning for them to stop. She slowly peeked around the corner. The hall to her right was clear. It led to their parent's room at the end, but the door was shut, and no light was visible through the bottom crack. She turned, looking to the opposite end of the hall. The door to the guest bedroom was also closed.

"Look," said Marie, pointing.

The window at the end of the hallway was open. Beams of pale moonlight passed through the lace curtains, settling upon the hallway rug.

"Should we close it?" asked Marie.

"What do you think?"

They tip-toed toward the open window, dropping to their knees. Mckenzie peered into the front yard.

"Do you see anything?" asked Marie.

"Not really."

A clump of birch trees blocked most of the ground view. Their limbs swayed in the wind of a gathering storm.

"Then what's that light?"

"What light?" asked Mckenzie.

"Over there near Kaldor's house."

Mckenzie leaned out of the window, attempting to get a better angle. "Holy shit! His house is on fire!"

"We need to find Mom."

"Let's get her and then see if Kaldor needs help," replied Mckenzie, shutting the window.

The sisters turned, immediately freezing in place. Marie flung her hand to her mouth to prevent a scream. Their mother stood in the middle of the hallway, a finger raised to her lips.

"Shhh," she whispered.

"Mom, what're you doing? You scared us to death."

"Please lower your voice," she said. "We're in trouble."

"What are you talking about?" asked Marie.

"There're people downstairs, and something terrible is happening out in the village," replied Trelinia.

Marie exhaled a panicked breath.

"Who's down there?" asked Mckenzie.

"I don't know yet, but they're not friendly. There're more outside in the yard. They're all speaking a strange language."

"I'm scared, Mom," said Marie.

"So am I," she replied. "But we're going to get out of this. Did you happen to bring your wands with you?"

Both girls nodded, holding them up.

"That was good thinking," replied their mother.

At that moment, the crash of broken dinner plates and utensils emanated from downstairs. Trelinia turned and peered down the moonlit hallway.

"Here's what we're going to do," said Trelinia, crouching

down and pulling the girls close to her. "We're going to have to fight our way out of this."

Marie let out another terrified breath.

"You can do this, Marie. We'll be safe as long as we stick together. Just stay close to my side when we go downstairs."

"Why not just escape out this window?"

"No. This is our home. We're going to defend it."

"I'm ready to fight," said Mckenzie. "Let's go."

"Hold on a moment," said Trelinia, regarding Marie. "Tell me what you're feeling right now."

The girl gulped. Her panicked eyes raced in all directions. "I can't think straight. I feel so scared that I don't even think I can move. What are we going to do?"

Trelinia placed her palm to Marie's cheek, caressing it gently. "Look at me, my love."

Marie blinked wildly, attempting to focus on her mother. The girl shook uncontrollably with anxiety.

"I know you're scared, honey, but I want you to try and do something for me. I want you to get angry instead."

"Angry?" replied Marie.

"Yes. This is your home. The place where you grew up. Think of the memories you have here. Of you and your sister and brother. Your dad and I and all your friends. Now picture these intruders forcing their way into your home. Destroying those memories. How does that make you feel?"

"It pisses me off," said Mckenzie.

"Dammit," replied Trelinia. "Be quiet for a second and let your sister answer."

Marie took a deep breath and slowly nodded. "I'm not as brave as the two of you, but I promise I'll try. I'm so scared."

"You're strong, Marie," replied her mother. "You *can* be brave. Together, the three of us will overcome this."

The sounds of destruction intensified from downstairs. Hateful laughter crept up the steps, mocking their courage. Marie turned her gaze from her mother and grimaced at the stairwell. It seemed more imposing than a dragon's lair.

Trelinia removed her hand from Marie's cheek and stood. "It's time to fight, girls. It's time to defend our home."

***

"There's another one," said Roger.

"I see it," replied Merkresh. "Wait until it crosses the road and then we can run to the other side."

"What is it? Can you see it better with the mask on?"

"It's wearing a cloak and hood, but it's not like the men from the workshop. I'm not sure what it is."

They crouched behind a hedgerow. Across the road stood Kaldor's burning house. A figure lay crumpled in the front lawn.

"Go now," exclaimed Merkresh.

They crept through the hedge then raced across the road. Shouts, screams, and explosions raged throughout the village. The crack of sporadic gunfire echoed through distant streets.

"What's happening out there?" asked Roger.

"A raid. But it sounds like the villagers are fighting back."

They reached Kaldor's front lawn. Merkresh took off the mask and glove, handing them to Roger.

"Is it him?" asked the boy.

The large figure lay on its side. Merkresh gently turned it over, inspecting the damage.

"Damn," he said, shaking his head in disgust.

"Is it Kaldor?"

"I'm afraid so."

A jagged laceration had split open the old owl's throat. His brilliant yellow eyes, filled with death and confusion, stared up at Merkresh.

"Kaldor was such a wise and gentle creature. Whoever's responsible for his murder will pay for this."

"Why would anyone kill Kaldor?" asked Roger.

"This isn't about him. The entire village of Thorndale is under attack. Listen."

Amidst the distant screams and gunfire, several larger explosions bellowed through the nearby trees.

"Those sounds are coming from my house," said Roger.

"Help me carry his body away from the flames," replied Merkresh, "then we'll continue."

***

"Stay close to me."

"What's our plan?" asked Mckenzie.

Trelinia raised her hand to her mouth, yelling downstairs. "Whoever you are, come out of the darkness and show yourself. You've been warned!"

"That was brilliant," replied Mckenzie, rolling her eyes.

"They know exactly where we are now," said Marie.

Trelinia shrugged. "They already knew. Since they're not coming out, whoever we see from this point on, we blast."

"Blast?"

"With your wands."

"I don't know how to use this thing," said Marie.

"Yes, you do. You're both already attuned to your wands. All you have to do is point and shoot."

"How are we supposed to shoot?"

"I don't know, you just do," replied Trelinia. "It's like you're using your thoughts to project the magic from the wand."

"But aren't there special commands we have to say aloud for them to work?" asked Marie.

"There's no nonsense like that. For now, just point your wand and think about what you want it to do. You may be surprised by what happens. I'll teach you proper spells later."

"This is so crazy," exclaimed Marie.

"Stay focused," said Trelinia. "We need to get down these stairs and make it to the dining room."

"What's in the dining room?" asked Mckenzie.

"That's where I left the book."

"Is that what they're looking for?"

"Yes."

The stairwell descended to a living room that contained open archways at either end. A stone fireplace was nestled on the opposite wall amidst a collection of fine furniture. As they reached the bottom step, the silhouette of a cloaked figure emerged through the door at the farthest end.

"Move quickly to the other door," said Trelinia.

"Who are you?" she asked. "What do you want?"

Another cloaked figure stepped into the open entryway to their left, brandishing a curved dagger.

"Marie, get ready to use your wand on the one across the room. Mckenzie, once she shoots, focus your fire on the other."

"Wait a second!" cried Marie. "I don't know how."

The furthest figure rushed forward.

"Shoot now!" shouted Trelinia.

Marie turned toward the attacker and raised her wand. In her haste, she fumbled it against her leg, sending the wand flying end over end across the room. She reached out in desperation.

The other cloaked figure attacked Trelinia. She dodged to her left, but in the process bumped into Mckenzie, spilling her over the side of an armchair.

Marie scrambled on her hands and knees across the living room floor to retrieve her wand. It had settled under a side table near the fireplace.

"I said stay close!" screamed Trelinia.

The attacker at the far end of the living room turned its attention to the young girl on the floor, drawing its own blade. It stepped from the doorway and rushed at her.

While lying on her stomach with her arms fully extended, Marie snatched the purple wand from underneath the table. She aimed at her attacker, focusing her thoughts.

A fireball shot from the tip of the amethyst, engulfing the creature. Its body burst into flame. Due to its momentum, the corpse continued to fall upon Marie. She quickly rolled to her right, watching as the smoldering heap slammed headlong into the fireplace.

"Move Mom!" screamed Mckenzie.

Trelinia lunged behind the sofa for cover while Mckenzie aimed her wand. She focused on the other attacker. Her thoughts were overcome by an intense sense of nature.

A red beam of energy screamed from the tip of her wand, exploding into the cloaked figure. Two enormous booms echoed through the house. Vases and plates jingled from the shockwaves.

The figure ceased its onslaught, convulsing violently. Like enraged seedlings, countless thorns ripped through its skin and fabric. Geysers of blood and muscle shot out of the attacker as the thorns became branches. The branches curled and wrapped around its quivering arms, legs, and neck. It expelled a final gasp of breath, rupturing under the strain. Chunks of flesh splashed against the wall and chairs.

"Holy shit!" exclaimed Marie, running across the room. "How'd you do that?"

"I have no idea. I just focused my thoughts on killing that thing. The image of thorns suddenly appeared in my mind."

"That was the wand working its magic," said Trelinia. "I knew that the two of you could do it."

Mckenzie gawked at the curly wand in her hand.

"And look at you," Trelinia said to Marie. "Scrambling across the room like a little mouse to retrieve your wand before incinerating that guy."

"I don't know what came over me. I was…"

"Angry," replied Trelinia. "Just like I asked you to be."

"I guess so," said Marie. She looked back at the burning corpse. Charred skin bubbled and popped within the hearth.

"You two did well, but we need to keep moving. Let's go to the dining room and get that book."

"And then what?" asked Marie.

"Then we're getting the hell out of here."

Trelinia led the girls through the door and into the library. Numerous books had been pulled from their shelves and thrown into piles. Marie noticed that the side door was wide open. Torn pages flapped in the wind. As they crossed the room, a flash of lightning and the cracking boom of thunder filled the house.

"They've destroyed most of our favorite books."

"But not the one they're looking for," said their mother as she opened the door to the dining room.

A gloved hand thrust a dagger into her chest. Trelinia spat a mouthful of blood, dropping to her knees.

"Mom!" screamed Marie.

A tall woman stood before them. She was shrouded in a sapphire cloak with the hood drawn. A morbid glow highlighted her sharp facial features and flowing hair. The woman calmly wiped the blood from her blade and sheathed it.

"Mrs. Roberts?" gasped Mckenzie. "Why?"

"I've waited a long time for this moment," she replied.

While holding the ancient book in her other hand, Mrs. Roberts made two circular motions with her wand and vanished. Trelinia Woods collapsed to the floor in a pool of blood.

***

"Hold on," said Merkresh. "There are two more of those creatures in the yard. Do you see them by the front porch?"

Roger focused the mask. "I see them, but the one on the right is walking away."

"I think there are more, but whatever is going on inside your house has their attention for the moment."

"I hope everyone is okay in there," said the boy.

"Click. Where are you?" whispered Merkresh.

The spider responded with two hushed chirps. He had been sitting on a tree branch above them.

"I have a task for you. Quietly follow that fellow to the back of the house and distract him while we sneak inside."

Click beeped in acknowledgment, crawling away.

"Now," said Merkresh, "let's take care of this one."

Roger observed from the tree line as the old man crept across the yard to the side of the front porch. Wearing the mask allowed him to see every detail. He tapped the combination for a higher magnification and focused on Merkresh.

The old man calmly walked up behind the cloaked figure and sliced his neck with Palewalker. He placed the corpse behind the porch bushes, motioning for Roger.

"Now what?" asked the boy as he approached.

"Let's go around back and check on Click."

They snuck around to the side of the house. A wooden fence wrapped around the backyard, obstructing further progress. Fortunately, the gate had already been kicked in by the attackers. It dangled from one of its iron hinges amidst shards of wood and pieces of metal. Roger pushed the gate and stepped through.

They immediately noticed a body lying next to the garden. The spider was on top of it, hopping up and down.

"I said distract it, Click, not cut it to pieces."

"He can kill people too?" asked Roger.

"Indeed. He's lethal when required, but I've tried to teach him to not harm others. To be honest, I think this was payback for Kaldor. Click was fond of that old owl."

"Look," said the boy. "The back door is wide open."

The companions crossed the backyard, approaching the open door. There were no lights on inside, yet it was evident that the interior was in shambles. Overturned tables and piles of torn books cluttered the library floor.

"It seems like they're looking for something."

"They are," replied Merkresh. "They're looking for your

mother's book. Just like they were looking for my key."

"What book are you talking about?"

Storm clouds converged, dumping heavy sheets of rain.

"It's a long story. I'm sure you're going to learn all about it soon enough. Now, let's get out of this downpour."

***

"Put more pressure on it!" shouted Marie. She sat next to her mother, gently brushing the hair from her eyes.

"I'm trying to," replied Mckenzie. "It's so fucking dark in here I can't see where all this blood is coming from."

Shock had begun to overwhelm the sisters. They were both shaking uncontrollably and breathing in heavy fits.

"She's all right," said Marie. "She's going to be okay. It didn't even hurt anything important. She's fine."

"Quick!" shouted Mckenzie. "Get one of those candles from the table so I can see what I'm doing."

Marie dashed to the dining room table and grabbed one of the large candles. She flung herself back down next to them, holding it up. The candlelight produced an ominous glow that framed the frantic movements of her sister's hands with the gasping breaths of her mother's mouth. Lightning and thunder filled the room.

"Move the light closer to her face," said Mckenzie.

Marie lowered the candle so they could get a better look. Trelinia's eyes peered straight up, blinking wildly. Her lips were quivering and frantic. Ribbons of blood covered most of her face.

"Mom. Can you hear me? Can you speak?"

Trelinia slowly turned her shocked gaze toward the voice.

"It really hurts," she gasped.

The girls recoiled in terror.

"What should I do, Mom?" asked Mckenzie. "Please tell me how I can fix you."

Trelinia made no response. She turned her eyes upward again, continuing to stare at the ceiling. Another hail of lightning and thunder bombarded the room.

"I don't think I can do this," moaned Marie, lowering the candle to the floor. "I'm going to pass out."

"I need your help!" cried Mckenzie. "I can't do this on my own. Pull yourself together and hold that light up."

"What's happened here?" shouted a voice.

The sisters whirled around. Roger and Merkresh stood in the doorway. A canvas of falling rain and storm clouds filled the composition behind them.

"Help us, please," said Marie.

"Who's that?" asked Roger.

"Your mother."

"What happened to her?"

"She was stabbed. She's bleeding to death."

Roger and Merkresh fell to the floor next to them.

"Let me see the wound," said the old man.

Mckenzie looked at her sister and brother.

"It's okay," said Roger. "You can trust him."

She removed her hands from her mother's chest, sliding to the side. A spout of thick blood gushed from the laceration. Trelinia moaned in agony.

"Oh my God," cried Marie.

Merkresh quickly pressed his hands to her chest.

"I need something sharp. Something to cut with," he said.

The sisters shook their heads, looking around the room.

"My knife!" shouted Roger. He fumbled in his pocket and pulled out the knife that he had kept while at the workshop.

"I need to cut some of her thick blouse away so we can get a better look at the wound," said the old man, taking the knife from Roger. "I need to see how much time she has."

"What's that mean?" asked Mckenzie.

"If the blade punctured her heart then she would already be dead. I need to make sure a major artery hasn't been sliced."

"And if there hasn't, then she'll be okay, right?"

"Maybe," he replied. "She's lost a lot of blood already. We must stop this bleeding now and get her to a doctor. Marie, I need you to help me put pressure on the wound while I cut away the fabric. Can you do that for me?"

Marie's face was deathly white. She shook hysterically, while her eyes darted in every direction.

"She's going into shock," said Mckenzie. "Let me do it."

"I can see that," replied Merkresh, "but I need her to focus on this and help me. We're losing her too."

Roger placed his hand on his sister's shoulder, speaking to her with a calm voice. "Marie, please listen to Merkresh. He's trying to help Mom, and he needs your help. We all do."

Marie slowly turned and stared at her brother. Her eyes projected a mind that was desperately trying to escape from the trauma of the situation. She nodded, looking at the old man.

"Very good," said Merkresh. "I'm going to lift my hands, and then I need you to apply pressure just above the hole. That way I can try and see what's going on. But there's going to be a lot more blood. Are you ready?"

"Yes," she replied, handing the candle to Roger.

Merkresh removed his hands from the wound and began to quickly cut away a section of the blouse.

"Be careful with that knife. It's sharp," said Roger.

Marie locked her fingers together, pressing down onto the exposed gash. She immediately felt the pulsing gush of blood with each heartbeat. Warm threads seeped between her fingers, producing a sticky puddle around their knees.

"Trel," whispered the old man once he finished cutting. "It's Merkresh. Can you hear me?"

Trelinia's eyes fluttered for a moment and then focused on him. "Merkresh? What are you doing here?"

"You've been injured. Can you tell me how you feel?"

"It's excruciating," she replied. "I can't breathe."

Merkresh wiped a pool of blood away from the gash, attempting to get a better view. The constant flash of lightning and candlelight produced a confusing mixture of shadows. They danced over every surface.

"I need more light," he said. "I can't see anything."

Roger held the candle closer.

Merkresh shuffled his head back and forth in a desperate attempt to diagnose the damage. Fresh waves of blood gushed from her chest.

"It hurts really bad," she moaned.

"I know, Trel," he replied. "I'm trying to fix you up, but in order to do that I'm going to have to cause you more pain."

"What?" gasped Mckenzie. "Why did you say that?"

Marie looked up at her sister with desperate eyes.

"I think one of the main arteries has been severed," he replied. "If we can't clamp it, then she's going to die right now. Applying pressure is not going to do anything anymore."

"No!" cried Marie. "But you said."

"You said that it didn't hit her heart," said Mckenzie.

"I don't think it did, but something's still been severely cut. Maybe not all the way, but with this much blood loss, she doesn't have much time. She's not going to make it unless I try."

His voice was sharp and powerful. The siblings gazed at him with confused and frightened expressions.

"Try what exactly?" asked Roger.

"I need to reach inside and find the severed artery."

"You can't do that!" shouted Marie.

"I can't see anything, and I don't have the right tools," he replied. "I have to use my fingers."

"No," moaned Mckenzie.

Merkresh closed his eyes and took a deep breath. Sheets of rain battered the windows and roof, while cracks of thunder pounded through the yard. He looked down at his fingers. They were revolting. Dirt, oil, and soot caked his skin and fingernails. He wiped his hands against his vest, leaning over Trelinia.

"Merkresh," she said in a calm voice. "Stop."

They all looked down at her.

"Do you really think I'm going to let you put your dirty fingers inside my chest and fumble around? And how exactly do you plan on clamping the artery if you find it?"

"Trel, you'll not survive unless we stop the bleeding."

"I know."

"Mom, he has to at least try," said Marie.

"No, my love. This isn't the way that it's supposed to be. I can feel that I don't have much time left. All the pain is gone now anyway. Everything is just warm. It's like…"

"What is it?"

"It's like a soothing harmony. Like beautiful music."

Merkresh glanced at Roger. The boy wept as he held the candle over his mother.

"And I can see them. I can actually see them."

"What can you see?" asked Marie.

"The two eagles."

Amidst the falling rain and candlelight, Trelinia Woods took her final breath, then gently faded forever from the world of the living.

CHAPTER XXI

MORNINGRISE

"Good morning," said Merkresh.

"What's good about it?" replied Marie.

The old man took a sip of coffee and continued to gaze into the front yard. The morning sunlight had awoken from the eastern hills, painting the crystal-clear sky with a striking shade of blue. A crisp freshness filled the air. The scent of wet leaves and grass lingered in the aftermath of the storm. Finches, chickadees, and blue jays sang amidst the garden and nearby woods. The occasional crow and dove called in the distance.

"Were you able to sleep?" he asked.

Marie walked to the other end of the front porch and sat in one of five rocking chairs. She folded her arms, threw up her hood, and watched her brother and sister walk around in the yard, inspecting the damage caused by the storm. A small, metal object crawled behind them.

Broken limbs, clumps of leaves, and puddles of standing water littered the grass on either side of the front walkway. Even the hundred-year-old walnut tree, that bore generations of carved names, had crashed to the ground. A red tree swing lay crumpled in a web of branches and bark.

"If you're hungry, I've made a light breakfast of taters and onions and scrambled eggs. We've already eaten, but I left you a plate in the…"

"Why are you still here?" asked Marie, interrupting him.

Merkresh regarded the girl. She continued to stare out into the front yard.

"Your brother and I came to check on the three of you," he replied. "My workshop was attacked last night and burned to the ground. Just before that happened, Roger felt that you were in danger. So, we came to help."

"Whatever," she said.

The old man frowned, turning back to the yard. He took another sip of coffee. The tip-taps of a distant woodpecker drifted from the woods as Roger and Mckenzie walked over to the fallen walnut tree. The boy picked up an object from the base of the trunk and laughed.

"When I was about your age," said Merkresh after a few moments, "there was this old man that worked with my Uncle Raimond for a time. Gelimer I think he was called, or Galimere. Something like that. Anyway, this guy was odd and eccentric. I mean, walk in the other direction as soon as you see him on the street kind of eccentric. He had a giant, white beard and the craziest eyes you've ever seen. He was always filled with the most intense energy, and he'd talk to anyone about almost anything. Even to complete strangers. He was friendly though, polite even.

He was just intense. What frightened people about Galimere was the fact that he could foresee many terrible events before they happened. He was usually spot-on about the most specific details. Of course, some of his premonitions didn't come true, or the outcome was slightly different, but he was clearly talented. He appeared to be tapped into a higher layer of consciousness. He would write these premonitions on pieces of paper and hang them up all around the castle. After many of his warnings came true, people started to become afraid."

Marie turned slightly but remained silent.

"Nevertheless, you'd think that the townsfolk would be more concerned about the foreboding events, rather than place blame on the man who relayed the unfortunate information. But no, that's exactly what people were afraid of."

Merkresh took another sip of coffee.

"After a gruesome accident involving a young boy from a neighboring village, a group of enraged townsfolk, incited by my brother Amfridus, abducted Galimere. They tortured and hanged him the following day."

"God, what kind of story is this?" asked Marie.

"The story isn't over," he replied. "A few months later a woman arrived at the castle, requesting to speak to my father, the count. She explained that her brother Galimere, a veteran of several wars, had suffered a stroke earlier that year and had recently managed to lose his way in the countryside. He'd lived alone, enjoying long walks through the forests and hills. Once my father disclosed to the woman the unfortunate fate of her brother, she explained that Galimere had, in fact, foreseen his own execution, months before he vanished. Somehow, due to the stroke, a portion of his mind had allowed access to abilities that he didn't previously have. A rewiring of his brain, so to speak. It wasn't real magic, like the kind that some people are born with. Like your magic, for instance. Instead, it was the type that a few souls stumble upon by chance. Usually to their own demise, as was Galimere's fate."

"What's the point of this story?" asked Marie.

"The point?" replied the old man. "Well, perhaps it's to illustrate to you that some people are not always as bad as you might make them out to be. Galimere was weird and maybe a little scary to others, but in reality, he was a gentle person who'd been inflicted with a misunderstood power."

"Mom always told us to stay away from you."

"That's very sensible," he replied. "I must seem a lot like Galimere to you and your sister."

"I don't even know you. You're just some weird old guy that lives all by himself and teaches my brother a bunch of foolish ideas about adventuring and fighting monsters."

"If you don't know me, then why would you be so quick to judge me? Do you want to know what I think?"

"I don't really care," replied Marie.

"I think that sometimes we can be critical of others for the same faults we see in ourselves."

"Did you hear me? I said I don't care."

"Very well," replied Merkresh. "We don't need to figure all this out right now. I will, however, let you know that we're leaving in about thirty minutes. We have a long journey ahead of us, so you'd better get something to eat before we begin."

"Who says we're leaving?"

"I say. Your sister and brother have also agreed that we must depart immediately if we're to keep to the plan."

"My mom's dead now," she exclaimed. "The plan doesn't mean anything without her."

"I'm devastated by what happened to your mother, just like you are. Believe me, I've known Trelinia and Benjamin since they were children. But please understand when I tell you, we're all in grave danger now. We may all be dead soon unless the three of you succeed in taking back the Rune of Frost."

"Get some other kids to do it. I don't care anymore."

"There are no other kids. The three of you are the only individuals in Silvarum capable of confronting this evil."

Marie huffed, turning back to the yard. She continued to watch her sister and brother explore the storm's damage.

Merkresh took a deep breath. "Look, Marie. I need you to gather up whatever gear you want to take with you and be ready to leave soon. Just put it all in your backpack. I suggest you bring some camping gear and extra clothes. We're going to be traveling through the deep woods for the next few days, at least. Mckenzie mentioned that your mother was planning to teach you spells and train you with your wands. Because of what's happened with Mrs. Roberts and the unfortunate fact that she's stolen the other book, we can't delay our departure any longer. Kadiaphonek should be our first destination. It's about a three-day hike from Thorndale. I found some of your mother's spell books that you and your sister can study while we're on the road. Do you understand what I've just explained to you?"

"The only thing I understand right now is that I couldn't do anything to save my mother's life last night," she replied. "All I could do was tremble at her side like a coward and watch as she bled to death. I failed her, and now I'll have to face that forever."

Merkresh set the mug of coffee down, turning his chair to

face her. "Listen. You didn't do anything wrong, Marie. Do you hear me? You did everything you could in that horrible moment. You could have passed out, but you didn't. We all saw how you fought the fear and remained present."

The girl gazed at him. "But she ended up dying anyway. We all failed her. Even you."

"I know," he replied, "but you need to understand that it's possible to do everything right in a situation and still fail. It wasn't your fault or mine. In the end, your mother chose to pass on in a manner that she felt was the most appropriate. It was rather admirable, to be honest with you."

"I don't know about that. All I know is that my dad has left us and now my mother is buried in the backyard, murdered by my teacher. They've been friends since childhood. How does that make any sense?"

"It doesn't," he replied. "Some people are just evil, but I'll promise you two things right now. I'm not going to leave any of you until we arrive safely in Kadiaphonek. More importantly, I'm going to track down your teacher and bring her to justice. She'll be held accountable for her traitorous deeds."

"Not if I kill her first," said Marie.

"I understand the emotions you're experiencing. I'll do everything I can to help you deal with this, as will your siblings. For now, though, please try to take that anger and hate and refocus it on completing our current task. The day will come when you'll face Lilly Roberts again, I promise. Now, go and grab a bite to eat, gather your belongings, and meet us back here in fifteen minutes."

***

"Ready to go?" asked the old man, still sipping from his mug of coffee and peering out into the yard. Marie stepped onto the front porch, fastening her backpack.

"Just about," she replied. "There's something I still need to get from that fallen walnut tree."

"Very well. I'm going to do a final check around the house, and then we'll be on our way. I'll meet back up with the three of you at the driveway shortly."

Merkresh stood and walked inside.

Marie stepped onto the cobblestone pathway and took a deep breath. She surveyed the yard and smiled at all the fond memories that she had acquired throughout her childhood. There was the garden that she and her mother had worked tirelessly on three summers ago. And the small pond that they had dug and filled together when she was seven. They had stocked it with three purple-finned harcus fish and one golden chorkix. All the harcus had died within the first week. The chorkix, however, had survived to this day. Marie had named him Squeaker because he used to make funny noises for her while she sat on the stone bench, feeding him each morning. Her heart ached as she yearned for her mother's company.

"Marie!" shouted Roger across the yard.

She waved in return. Her siblings were still standing next to the fallen tree. The small, metallic object that she had noticed earlier crawled up and down a thick branch.

"I'm coming," she replied, tightening the straps on her backpack while walking across the lawn.

The turf was extremely soggy. Puddles of water carpeted the grass and filled the ditches that bordered the driveway. She carefully hopped and stepped over each body of water.

"Hey," said Marie as she arrived.

"How are you feeling?" asked Mckenzie.

"Not great."

"Me too. Do you want to talk about it?"

"Not yet," replied Marie. "Maybe later. I just want to get this stupid trip started and try to forget about it for a while."

Mckenzie and Roger nodded.

"What have you been doing?" asked Marie.

"We're teaching Click how to fetch walnuts."

"You're what?"

"You haven't met our new friend yet, have you?"

"No. What friend are you referring to?"

"Here he comes," said Roger.

The brass and mechanical spider burst through a wall of leaves, scrambling up to them along the bark of a snapped tree limb. He held four walnut husks with his front legs.

"What is that thing?" gasped Marie. "A spider?"

"That's Click," replied Mckenzie.

The spider dropped the walnuts and proceeded to raise itself on his eight legs. He bobbed up and down, expelling a series of motorized beeps. The rotating dish antenna on its head spun in circles as he danced and sang.

"It's a robot?" asked Marie. "Where in the world did you find a weird thing like that?"

"Merkresh made him," replied Roger. "He's coming with us on our journey. Wait until you see all the cool stuff he can do. He's a wonderful piece of technology."

Click nodded his head in agreement.

"Are you sure you're comfortable with having a spider as a traveling companion? What about that incident last summer?"

Mckenzie snickered.

"The incident last summer?" asked Roger, glancing at the mechanical spider. "I'm over that now. Yea, I'm fine with spiders. Besides, Click isn't a real spider. He's just gears and wires."

Marie grinned. "Whatever you say."

Roger took off his backpack, motioning to Click. "Toss those walnuts in here, please."

The spider picked up the husks, throwing them one by one into an open pocket.

"See," said Roger. "We're going to get along just great."

The sisters rolled their eyes.

"Did you find any of the pinecones?" asked Marie.

"Yes," replied Mckenzie. "Roger picked up a few."

The boy fumbled around in his backpack, extracting a sun-bleached pinecone. It had a piece of green yarn tied to it.

"Here you go," he said.

Marie took the pinecone and gazed at its features. It was delicate with a faint emerald hue.

"Is that the one?" asked Mckenzie.

"Yes."

During an evening walk when the children were very young, Trelinia had gathered pinecones for each of them. They had tied green yarn to the ends and hung them on the lowest branch of the walnut tree.

"I think that's the one with your name on it," said Roger.

"It is," she replied, placing it in her backpack.

Mckenzie and Roger stared at their sister thoughtfully.

"What is it?" asked Marie.

"Nothing," replied her sister, smiling. "Let's hurry to the driveway before Merkresh delivers another boring lecture."

***

"Are we ready to begin our grand and marvelous quest?" asked Merkresh, trotting up to the driveway.

"I don't know about marvelous or grand," replied Roger, "but I do know that I'm scared out of my mind."

"So am I," said Marie.

"Me too," said Mckenzie.

"Of course you are," replied the old man. "That's to be expected. What I mean is, think of all the wonderful places you'll see and the adventures you'll experience."

"And all the monsters and other creatures that are waiting to kill us. That sounds like a fantastic time," replied the boy.

"Come on," said Merkresh. "Life is always full of danger, quest or not. Besides, you have me to help you, at least for now. And you have a new friend called Click."

The spider chirped as he crawled next to them.

"Plus, you're the new owner of the mask and glove," said Merkresh. "The girls now have their wands. It's all going to work out just fine. You wait and see."

"Sure it will," replied Roger.

"Wait a second," said Marie. "I want to say goodbye to Squeaker one last time."

"Certainly," replied the old man, pausing on the driveway. "Roger, this would be an appropriate time for you to take out the mask and glove and put them on. You need to start getting used to operating them during the journey."

"Right," he said, pulling them out of his backpack.

"Wow," said Mckenzie. "That's one weird looking hat."

Marie stepped off the driveway and followed a stone path

that led to the fishpond. Snapped tree limbs and stones choked the area. The water's surface was covered with leaves and grass.

"Squeaker!" she said. "Squeaker!"

There was no movement in the water.

"Squeaker. Come on, little buddy. Where are you?"

The pool remained still.

"Please don't be dead too. Please."

A face emerged from the water.

Sqreeeeeeeesh. Cheek. Cheek. Breeeep. Buuureeeep.

"There you are," replied Marie. "I hope you're still doing well in that tiny home we made for you. I wanted to come by one last time and tell you goodbye. We're all going away for a while, and I probably won't see you again for a very long time."

The fish opened and closed its mouth.

Breeeep. Kreech. Kreech. Buuureeeep.

"I love you too. Goodbye."

"Come on, Marie," said Roger from the driveway. "How long does it take to say goodbye to a stupid fish?"

Mckenzie punched him in the arm. "Don't be an ass."

Marie sighed, gazing at the fish a final time.

Sqreep. Zeep. Zreep.

She lowered her head and walked back up the hill.

"All set?" asked Merkresh.

"Yes," replied Marie, noticing Roger's mask and glove. "What are you supposed to be? A robotic tap dancer?"

Mckenzie laughed. "Good one!"

Merkresh shook his head, chuckling.

***

Merkresh, Roger, Mckenzie, Marie, and Click made their way along the driveway to the main road. Their neighborhood was comprised of twenty-one families that lived in wooden homes and farmhouses. A handful of the older estates were constructed of stone and brick. Properties typically consisted of large, grassy lawns and gardens, that were tucked neatly within groves of elm, spruce, and birch.

"Which way?" asked Marie as their feet met the crunch of the gravel road.

Merkresh rubbed his beard, peering in both directions. The land directly across the driveway was thick with trees and bramble. They would need to stick to the road if they wanted to escape Thorndale by evening. He turned and looked back to the east. Plumes of thick smoke spiraled above the treetops while the silhouettes of dark-winged birds circled high above.

"I had a thought while I was doing the final walk-through in your house," said the old man. "I think we should take a trip through Thorndale before we delve into the forest, and make sure nobody else needs our help. Roger and I had to bury Kaldor last night. Unfortunately, we didn't find him in time. He was lying dead in his front yard."

"Kaldor?" asked Mckenzie. "What happened to him?"

"He was murdered," replied Roger. "Probably by those same cloaked creatures that invaded our house."

"They attacked us too. We killed them with our wands."

"But Kaldor," said Mckenzie. "He was just an old, gentle creature. He didn't have anything to do with this madness."

"We all have something to do with this madness now," replied Merkresh. "All free and peaceful creatures of Silvarum play a role in this conflict. No one is safe until we're victorious.

We must come to terms with the evil that's determined to destroy us. We should seek out and recruit all able-bodied individuals to assist us in this task. We're going to need all the help we can get."

The teenagers nodded in agreement.

"That's it then," replied the old man. "We're going to take one final stroll through the village and check for survivors. Whoever we come across, as long as they're willing and able, will accompany us to Kadiaphonek. That's the closest rallying point for refugees of the smaller towns in this area. I can't imagine Thorndale was the only village under siege last night."

"That sounds like a good plan," replied Roger.

"Let's go," said Mckenzie.

The group turned to the east and walked along the road. Click scrambled ahead, at Merkresh's request, and scouted the surroundings. The midday sun blazed hot in the blue sky.

As they approached the intersection of Excalibur Court and Eclipse Drive, the previous evening's destruction revealed itself. Smoking ruins of burnt houses, overturned wagons, and crumbled walls littered the landscape. Unchecked infernos had transferred their wrath to adjoining fields, gardens, and trees. The lush neighborhood had been transformed into a bare skeleton, overcome with devastation and loss.

"Is that a person?" asked Marie, pointing.

"Where?" replied Merkresh.

"On the ground, next to that carriage."

"Roger," said the old man. "Can you please focus on it with your mask and get a better look from here?"

"It's a person," said the boy. "I think it's a man, but he's definitely dead. At least, what's left of him is dead."

They all turned and looked at Roger.

"What do you mean?" asked Marie.

"I don't see a bottom half," he replied. "Oh wait. There it is, on the other side of the road. It looks eaten."

"Oh no," gasped Mckenzie.

"Can you see any bodies up along the road to the south?" asked Merkresh. "Or any living people, for that matter?"

Roger scanned the front yards and road. "No. There's more fire damage and destruction that way, but I can't see any sign of a person, living or dead. It looks like the road is blocked by large objects. Burned wagons and carriages."

"What about north?"

"It's the same that way too," he replied. "It's a real mess in both directions, but I don't see anyone. The road seems a little clearer to the north. Only a few trees are down."

"All right," said Merkresh. "We need to start making our way north through the village if we're going to make it to Kad. I want us to be under the cover of the forest by nightfall, and I certainly don't want to be delayed by anything we may encounter going south. Let's head up this way and stick close to the tree line, just in case. Who knows what's lingering about."

"What about our wands?" asked Marie. "Should we get them out and have them ready?"

"Yes, that's a great idea," he replied. "Good thinking."

The sisters pulled the wands from their backpacks.

"Are those things powerful?" asked Roger.

"Yes. We each used them last night. I'm not sure what else mine can do other than shoot fireballs."

"Fireballs?" replied her brother.

"And mine made one of those creatures explode with a burst of thorns," said Mckenzie. "It was incredible."

"They're indeed powerful," said Merkresh. "I know your mother was going to spend time training you on how to make potions and spells. I don't know as much as she does with that type of magic, but I know enough. As soon as we get to a point where we can relax, I'll try to teach you something. Now, let's get moving. It's already past noon."

The company moved from the middle of the intersection and headed north along the side of the road that hugged the trees. Acorns, pinecones, and broken branches coated the grass and gravel. Several large oak trees had fallen across the road, their trunks splintered in multiple locations. The impacts had sprayed shards of fresh wood in every direction. The sweet aroma of sap and timber filled the air as they climbed over the remains.

"Wait a second," said Marie, motioning for the group to stop. "Do you hear that?"

Harsh growls and snarls roared from a nearby yard. There were other sounds as well. Mixed within the animal's hateful cries rang the shouts and curses of two human voices.

"Should we investigate?" asked Roger. His leather top hat, green-tinted eye lenses, and brass frames glared in the sun.

"Yes," replied Merkresh, "but be ready to fight."

"Do you still have your sword?" asked the boy.

"Palewalker? Of course, I do. It's been at my side ever since we left my workshop."

He swept aside his cloak, withdrawing the longsword. A metallic hiss preceded its introduction. "Follow me," he said.

The group crept along the tree line, advancing toward the yard. As they cleared the corner, the trees withdrew, revealing the source of the threatening shouts and cries.

Across the street was a house in shambles. The first floor

and most of the second was burned to a crisp. What remained of its wooden framework and walls had been crushed to pieces by a fallen elm tree, exposing the front of the house to the afternoon air. Nevertheless, a portion of the second-floor master bedroom remained intact. Strips of wallpaper and blue carpet dangled over the edge. On a narrow section of the remaining floor clung two petrified teenagers.

"That's Frederick," said Roger. "And some girl."

"What are they screaming at?"

Large tree limbs blocked a clear view of their attackers.

"Dogs," said Marie.

"They're wolves," replied Merkresh, "and rabid by the sound of their shrieking snarls."

"Oh great," replied Marie.

"Stay low," said the old man. "Let's try to cross the street here and get around to the back of the house. There might be an easier way to rescue those kids."

As they crossed the road, one of the wolves climbed up onto the end of the fallen tree, scrambling to the second floor. The trunk had settled against the house at such an angle that it provided the beast a direct path to its prey. Frederick shrieked in terror, attempting to climb the water spout up to the roof.

"You idiot!" screamed the girl. "Don't leave me!"

"This situation is deteriorating fast," said Roger.

"That's an understatement," replied Merkresh. "Forget about going around back. I have a better idea."

The old man put two fingers to his lips and blew an ear-piercing whistle. The wolves on the ground halted their assault, lunging through the branches. Two frothing beasts dashed across the yard, straight for the companions.

"Marie," said Merkresh. "Would you please do us a favor and dispose of these critters?"

"Excuse me?" she replied, floundering with her wand.

They all watched her anxiously.

"You might want to hurry up," he said. "They're almost across the road."

Marie pointed the purple wand. The raging wolves were meters away, their sharp claws kicking up clumps of gravel. She focused on their ravenous eyes and concentrated.

A rotating orb of purple and black energy shot from the tip of her wand. It engulfed the closest wolf, transforming its body into a cloud of sparkling dust. The second wolf was not deterred. It puffed through its companion's remains, raging toward the group. Sharp fangs dripped with blood.

"Shoot it!" cried Roger.

"I'm trying to, but nothing's happening," gasped Marie.

Mckenzie raised the curly wand.

As the beast leapt through the air, a wave of ice crystals swept over its fur, freezing it solid. The beast's outstretched claws and teeth hung in mid-air, centimeters from Marie's face.

Merkresh swung Palewalker, obliterating the block of frozen wolf into a thousand pieces. Ice particles of fur and meat shattered onto the road and grass.

"Nice shot, Mckenzie!" yelled Roger.

Marie sighed with relief. "Thank you. I don't know why my wand didn't work on the second wolf."

"Anytime," replied Mckenzie.

"Fantastic work, you two," said the old man. "Let's take care of this last varmint, shall we?"

They rushed across the street, entering the yard with the

fallen elm and panicked teenagers. The remaining wolf was still attempting to ascend the trunk and reach the girl. Sporadic yelps escaped from its fangs as it negotiated between tree limbs.

Frederick's strategy to flee to the rooftop had not been successful. He had scaled a portion of the waterspout but now hung precariously from the gutter, his legs dangling and kicking.

"Arina!" shouted Marie. "Is that you?"

The girl paused her cursing, peering down at the group. She raised a hand to her eyes to shield the sun.

"Please hurry! I dropped my wand and then twisted my ankle. Now this stupid ass has left me up here as dog food."

Merkresh laughed.

"What's so funny?" asked Mckenzie.

"I have another idea," he replied. "Roger, switch on the plasma pulse and get ready to shoot the part of the tree trunk that intersects with the second floor."

"Can I please just shoot the wolf instead?"

"No," he replied. "This will be better. Trust me."

The boy activated the glove, taking a few steps closer to the tree. "I'm ready," he said.

"Arina," said Merkresh. "Can you please step back into the house a bit further? I don't want any of this to hit you."

The girl nodded and backed up. Frederick continued to dangle from the gutter. He watched in silence as the old man approached the tree and stood under the climbing wolf.

"Roger," said the old man. "At the count of three, I want you to shoot. Ready? One. Two. Three. Shoot!"

A bolt of green plasma screeched through the air, striking the trunk at the second floor. A shower of bark, leaves, and dust erupted into the sky. As the lower half of the tree crashed to the ground, the wolf expelled a pitiful cry and tumbled. Merkresh swung his sword, slicing the beast clean in half. A wave of blood washed over Frederick's body and face.

"Gross!" gasped Mckenzie, covering her mouth.

The gore-soaked boy fought to maintain his grip. "I can't hold on any longer. It's too slippery!" he cried.

"Then look down," replied Merkresh.

Frederick peered below, realizing he was dangling over a pond of fish and lily pads.

SPLASH!

The boy sat up in the pool, spitting up a mouth full of water. A lily pad with a pink flower was perched upon his head.

Roger and his sisters laughed from the yard.

The old man extended his hand and pulled Frederick out of the pond. The boy stood sulking and dripping wet.

"Lad," said the old man. "Maybe next time you'll think twice about abandoning a companion in danger."

Frederick lowered his eyes. "I'm sorry, sir. I panicked."

"Very well," replied Merkresh. "Now help me get Arina down from the house."

***

The group recovered in a shady spot of the front yard.

"What happened to you, Arina?" asked Marie.

"It was terrible," she replied. "I woke up in the middle of the night, and my house was on fire. I couldn't find my dad anywhere, so I escaped through my bedroom window and waited in the front yard. The entire bottom floor was engulfed in flames. I noticed that other homes in the neighborhood were also on fire.

Then I heard shouts and people fighting. I didn't want to leave my dad, but I was afraid, so I ran and hid in the woods."

She paused for a moment, staring into the distance.

"It's all right, Arina," said Merkresh. "Take your time."

"As I hid and watched my home burn to the ground, I saw two figures drag my dad away. They were dressed in dark cloaks with the hoods up. I've never seen creatures like that before, and I didn't know what to do. I was petrified. I had my wand with me, but I couldn't gather the courage to move or help him. Instead, I followed the creatures as they dragged my dad around the burning house. There was another person at the back of the yard near the woods. They threw my dad to the ground right at the person's feet. It was dark, but from the glow of the fire, I could see that the other figure was a woman. She wore a sapphire cloak and hood. She laughed when she saw my dad."

"That was Mrs. Roberts," said Marie.

"Our teacher?"

"Yes. She's responsible for all of this."

"How do you know?"

"Because we saw her last night too," replied Marie.

Roger and Mckenzie lowered their gaze.

"What's happening?" asked Arina. "Why Mrs. Roberts?"

"Because she's in league with our enemy," said Merkresh. "Her role is clearer to me now that we've learned of your father's fate. Your mother was also taken recently, wasn't she?"

"Yes," replied Arina. "I don't know where either of my parents are. I don't have anyone now."

"You have us," said Marie. "Will you join our group? Will you come with us to Kadiaphonek?"

"Of course I will."

"I want to come too," exclaimed Frederick. "But why are we going to Kadiaphonek?"

"It's a long story," replied Merkresh. "Grab all your stuff and come with us. We'll tell you everything on the way."

The boy regarded his wet clothes. "This *is* all my stuff!"

***

The company had increased to seven members. They included Roger, Marie, Mckenzie, Merkresh, Arina, Frederick, and of course, the spider Click. They traveled along the road through the devastation of their village, making their way to the eastern border of the Blackwood Forest. Merkresh explained to the newcomers all that he could about the events of the previous twenty-four hours. Roger filled in a few details here and there, as did Marie and Mckenzie, but overall, the old man drove most of the narrative. He chronicled a history of the Drake Expedition, the evil city of Nexxathia, and the eight runestones.

Dusk settled upon the group as they finally departed the boundary of Thorndale, approaching the ominous tree line. A blanket of purple and gold sunlight wrapped its arms around the surrounding fields and meadows. Ravens perched atop frowning scarecrows while an orchestra of crickets awoke for their twilight performance. Wood smoke filled the air.

"This is Blackwood Forest?" asked Marie.

"The eastern edge of it," replied Merkresh. "Just beyond this point, maybe a day's hike through the forest, we'll run into the Wondering River."

"And then we'll be close to Kad?" asked Frederick.

"No. The journey requires three days of travel, at least."

"What's the plan when we finally arrive?"

"There's a woman we need to visit. Her name's Dorothy Tompkins but goes by the nickname Dot. She's an old friend."

"My mom mentioned her," said Mckenzie.

"She helped your mother during her quest thirty years ago. I'm hoping Dot will provide us shelter and guidance before the three of you travel south to confront Lord Mortis."

A chill breeze swept through the corn stalks as the old man spoke the dragon's name. The teenagers shivered with fear at the realization of their impending quest.

Merkresh noticed their uneasiness. "Listen. This is only the beginning. There's a long road ahead of us before you need to start worrying about him. In the meantime, let's focus our attention on finding a suitable spot for a camp, and building a warm fire. Onward!"

CHAPTER XXII

ETHEREAL LIGHT

"Who is that?" asked Abigail.

"A friend," replied Penelope.

"Is she a ghost too?"

"You'll see. Please follow me down to the catacombs."

Abigail followed Penelope and the stranger across the mausoleum floor. The room was completely dark except for the flickering glow of the candlelight. The air was musty and stale, yet a hint of lavender and sandalwood lingered.

"Watch your step," said Penelope as they approached the yawning mouth of a doorway. Its Gothic arch and flamboyant tracery cast amorphous shadows against the interior stairwell.

Abigail heard a soft hum as she descended the steps. It was delicate at first. Gradual. The gentle murmur increased in amplitude and then became constant. A soothing texture of chanting overlapped the tones. Abigail turned her head, expecting to see a troupe of choralists assembled behind her.

"We're almost there," said Penelope. "One more flight."

The humming and chanting intensified as they arrived at the last step. They were the most captivating melodies Abigail had ever heard. If the sounds had been water, she would have willingly drowned in their serenity.

"We're here."

Abigail focused her eyes.

"It's my crypt again," she gasped.

"This isn't your crypt," replied Penelope. "It's *our* crypt. We all begin our journey in this place."

Situated against the far wall stood a wooden pedestal. An ancient book, covered in eons of dust and decay, sat on its surface. A beam of frosty blue light shined from its pages.

"That's the same book I saw when I first arrived here," said Abigail. "It sent me on a miraculous vision where I traveled to a snowy mountaintop and saw my mother."

"That was no vision," said a voice.

Abigail's heart sank as she regarded the stranger.

"She finally got here."

"Aye. I told you she would," replied Penelope.

"Who are you?" asked Abigail.

The stranger lifted her hood.

"I'm Trelinia Woods. I'm going to help you get home."

PART II
DEPARTURE

CHAPTER XXIII

SHADOWS IN THE THRONE ROOM

"What's happening now?" asked Smitty.

"Nothing yet," replied Randal. "But can you please push me up higher, for crying out loud? I can barely see."

"Maybe if you didn't weigh as much as a pregnant Brol, I'd have an easier time supporting your fat ass on my shoulders."

"Hurry the hell up. They're about to walk by."

Smitty grunted and lifted his brother so that Randal could get a better view through the crack in the wall.

"Is Belris still with them?"

"I think so."

"Damn. I thought I saw someone lead him away. Right after the captain and his guards ran over to check on the man who collapsed in the mud."

"No. Once they all realized it was that stupid Hubert guy, I saw them turn back and continue to the keep."

Smitty sighed, shaking his head.

Layers of dripping water echoed through the darkness of the secret passage. The brothers held their breath as Captain Hamonet and his group entered the inner bailey and began to pass in front of the crack. The crunch and clank of their approaching footsteps filled the air.

"I can see them clearly now," whispered Randal. "They definitely have Belris and some other guy. I think that's Brian Woods, Belris' sergeant. He looks huge walking next to our little brother."

"Now what's happening?" asked Smitty after a few moments. His voice was eager with anticipation.

"They're passing through the side door. Now they're gone," replied Randal. He jumped down from his brother's shoulders and brushed himself off.

"What do we do?"

"What the hell *can* we do? They're obviously taking them up to Count Zaran's throne room, and there's no way we're getting inside that place."

"What about Quinthorpe?" asked Smitty. "Could he help us get inside, at least? Doesn't he know every nook and cranny and secret in this place?"

Randal looked at his brother and grinned.

"He just might. Let's go and find that old gnome."

The brothers turned, dashing into the darkness.

***

"Hold here a moment," said Captain Hamonet.

The group stood within a lonely anteroom. Candelabra

and forlorn candles flickered amber light from within wall niches and tiled insets. Two guards stood at attention before the throne room door.

"Listen to me very carefully," he continued. "Beyond this door, you're going to stand before Count Zaran. You'll not dare speak unless spoken to, you'll not ask questions, and most importantly, you'll not mock me or anyone else you encounter beyond these doors. Do I make myself clear, Sergeant Brian Woods?"

"Perfectly clear."

The captain nodded and turned to Belris. "And you, private? Is my guidance simple enough for you to comprehend? Shall I repeat it, just to be sure?"

"No, sir," replied the boy. "I understand."

"Very well," said Captain Hamonet. He motioned for his knights to remain behind in the anteroom. "Then let's begin."

He turned to the door guards and cleared his throat. "Please inform the count that Captain Hamonet has brought forth Sergeant Brian Woods, as commanded."

"Yes, sir. They're expecting you," said one of the guards as he opened the door, ushering them through.

Belris felt as though he would pass out from the stress. His eyes darted in every direction as they crossed the threshold and into the uncertain judgement of his fate.

Count Zaran's throne room was massive. Floor to ceiling windows, shrouded by thick drapery, lined walls otherwise obscured by piles of books and bizarre gadgetry. Chandeliers dangled from a vaulted ceiling, projecting peculiar shadows upon the Doric columns and tapestries. A stained-glass window, circular in shape and situated directly above the dais, cast a colorful glow of purple, orchid, and crimson upon the floor at the foot of the throne. Its mosaic design consisted of two overlapping circles that formed a lidless eye, and a bizarre human form that seemed to be folding within itself. A faint aura of incense drifted between the glowing braziers and marble statues.

Captain Hamonet motioned for the men to move forward along a carpeted pathway toward the throne. Belris looked to his left as they walked and beheld many strange objects tucked within the gloom. Complicated equipment, laboratory devices, and other contraptions cluttered the walls. Cauldrons of bubbling broths filled one corner, while exotic machinery, metal gears, and pistons clattered persistently. At the far end of the great room, a fire whispered and popped from within a grand fireplace, bathing the hearth in a golden glow.

The group halted at the head of the carpet. They stood within the center of the stained-glass projection, peering up at the empty throne. Brian and Belris turned to their guide with questioning eyes. The young captain shrugged.

"How delightful!" said a deep and aristocratic voice.

The men turned in the direction of the fireplace and beheld a large table. Stacks of books, scrolls, and dripping candles covered its surface. A middle-aged man sat with his boots propped upon the table as he flipped through a voluminous book. Another figure, much older and cloaked in black, stood motionless at his side.

Captain Hamonet gestured for the group to face the table.

"Lord, I present to you Sergeant Woods, for whom you wished to speak once the transaction at the gate was complete."

"Hush," replied Count Zaran with a raised finger.

He stood from his chair, strolled across the floor with the

open book, and leaned next to the crackling hearth. "Listen to this delightfulness, will you?"

> *No petal doth shudder, no swell is awakened*
> *On the water all is tranquil, and the twilight's yawning eye*
> *Seals shut, and omits all its Phlegetheon woe,*
> *Beguiled to obscurity by the hum of the dragonfly,*
> *And the moon, whether demure or gracious,*
> *Hath sunk to her burial, well knowing that I wish for*
> *No guide in the nightfall, no path in the grief,*
> *But for my Andromeda's eyes, and her brilliance*
> *Shall be my guide within the eternal darkness.*

Count Zaran closed the book upon the final syllable and gazed into the fire. He rubbed his beard, nodding to himself.

"Simply delightful," he whispered into the flames.

"You always loved that passage, my lord," responded the cloaked figure.

"I do, Amfri. I definitely do. It's the darkness of it, I think. The absolute emptiness. Yet I can always see her eyes. I wonder if they'll ever fade from my mind."

"I can't say, my lord. Perhaps one day."

"Perhaps," said the count. He continued to peer into the fire. The glowing flames flickered within his eyes as an awkward silence filled the room.

"My lord," said Captain Hamonet with a timid voice.

"Yes, yes," replied the count. "I haven't forgotten about you, my dear captain. Please be patient."

"Of course, sir."

Count Zaran turned from the fireplace and set the well-worn book on the table. He eased back into his chair and then reached for his mug.

"Oh, dear," he said. "Please tell me we have more of this wonderful coffee brewed."

Amfridus held up a brass pot. "Indeed. We still have a few cups left. Would you like me to refill your mug?"

"I certainly would," replied the count as he set his boots upon the table. He toasted his mug to the visitors and took a hearty sip.

"Now that's a tasty bean if I do say so myself. It's strong and spicy, yet rich and satisfying. Not like that designer rubbish they sell in the marketplace. Please give my sincere regards to the coffee shop in Kad that delivered the shipment this month. What was their name again?"

"*The Dharma Tearoom*, I believe," said Amfridus.

Count Zaran nodded and took another sip.

"Now," he said as he wiped his mouth. "How may I be of service, Captain Hamonet?"

"Lord," the captain said. "I present to you Sergeant Brian Woods, as you requested."

"Splendid," replied the count. "And the other gentleman? Whom do I have the pleasure of welcoming to my abode this morning?"

"This is Private Belris Llanforth."

"Though I didn't specifically request to make Mr. Llanforth's acquaintance today, would I be correct in assuming that he stands before me because of an infraction?"

"You would assume correctly, my lord."

"I see," said Count Zaran. "That's most unfortunate. For I've been in such a pleasant mood this morning. Reading through my favorite poetry and enjoying this fine coffee. Would you like me to remain in a pleasant mood, private?"

"Of course I would," replied Captain Hamonet.

"Excuse me, sir. I believe I asked for Mr. Llanforth's response. Not yours."

Both Captain Hamonet and Brian turned to look at the young man. His eyes were glazed, and his face had turned a deathly shade of white.

"Please, sir," said the count after a few moments. "Step forward and answer my question. I don't appreciate having to repeat myself. It's damn exhausting."

Belris took a step forward. He was shaking.

"I...I would like you to remain in a pleasant mood," he replied with a quivering bottom lip.

"A most excellent answer, young man," said Count Zaran as he dropped his legs from the table and sat up.

"Please have a seat and enjoy some of this fine coffee with me. We still have a few cups left. Isn't that right, Amfri?"

"Yes, sir. One cup of fresh coffee coming right up."

Amfridus produced a new mug and filled it to the brim.

Belris stood motionless. He looked blankly at the captain and the sergeant. They stared back with wide eyes. The young man felt sluggish and sleepy, as though he was wandering around after a confusing dream.

"Please, Mr. Llanforth," said Count Zaran. "I have other business to attend to. You're not the only soul in the realm that's been naughty. Sit down, my boy, and have a cup with me."

Belris took a deep breath, managing to propel himself toward the chair. He was not entirely in control of himself. His world consisted of uneven landscapes of blurry shades of gray.

"Here we are," said the count as Amfridus placed the cup of coffee on the table. "Have a sip and tell me what you think."

The young man looked at the mug in front of him. It was porcelain, filled with dark, steaming liquid. Coffee, the man had said. He was supposed to take a sip of it. What was a sip? That was like taking a small drink of something. He would take a small drink of the dark liquid. Yes. He needed to move his hand toward the handle and lift the mug to his mouth. That was an easy enough task. Belris stumbled along his gray landscape, attempting to perform the required actions.

"Well," said the count. "What do you think?"

"It's good," replied the boy.

"Only good? Give me a break. That must be one of the tastiest and most satisfying beans I've had the pleasure of sipping in many a moon. Now, I know you can do better than that. This time, really try and articulate how you feel about the experience. Go ahead now."

Belris grimaced, struggling to formulate an intelligent thought. Translating it into words to then communicate a suitable response was beyond his current capacity. His mind was too numb. Frozen. He sat motionless in his chair and stared. A pop came from the fireplace, adding to the tension.

"Son," said Count Zaran after studying the boy. "Are you still with us?"

The young man blinked out of his trance and looked at the count. "Yes, sir, but I'm not sure what I should say."

"Interesting," replied the count. "For you didn't seem at all unsure about your words this morning upon the drawbridge. Isn't that true?"

"Sir?" asked Belris.

"Do you really think I don't know why you've been brought before me this morning?"

Captain Hamonet shuffled where he stood and cleared his throat. "Lord, I was about to explain to you the details of the private's dereliction of duty."

"Save your breath," Zaran responded with a dart of his eyes. "Your competence in transmitting information to your superiors in a timely fashion is about as worthy as your ability to remain coherent during a routine trade transaction. Now shut your fucking mouth until I request your input."

The captain hung his head and was silent.

"As I was saying," continued the count, "I already know what you did, Mr. Llanforth. There's no need to play dumb. Unless, of course, you are indeed dumb. Are you?"

"Am I what, sir?"

"Oh, dear. This is starting to become frustrating."

He turned to Amfridus, shaking his head. "Is this really what I'm expected to deal with nowadays? Does anyone that still works for me possess functioning brain cells?"

The necromancer raised his eyebrows and shrugged.

"Very well, Mr. Llanforth," said Zaran as he gazed upon the faces of his guests. "If you're not willing to speak to the comments that you made after this morning's transaction with the Nexxathians, then I suppose we'll have to discontinue this pleasant conversation and get to the matter of your punishment."

Belris' eyes widened with fear as he opened his mouth.

"Too late for a retort, I'm afraid," said Count Zaran with a wag of his index finger. "However, I will require your mouth to remain open, if you please."

The captain and Brian looked at each other in confusion.

Belris swiveled his eyes, desperate.

"Amfri, please ensure that our guest doesn't close his mouth for the remainder of the visit."

"As you wish," he replied with a raise of his hand.

Belris instantly felt a powerful force slam against his head and lock his jaw into place. He was unable to close his mouth, or even swallow. His body was as rigid as stone.

"Show everyone that clever tongue of yours that was so quick to express contempt for your commanding officer."

Count Zaran looked at Amfridus and nodded.

The necromancer turned his hand counterclockwise and sideways. The young man's tongue protruded from his gaping mouth like a rodent from its burrow.

The count pulled a dagger from his belt and smiled.

"Please hold still, son," he said as he moved around the table. "This'll be easier for me if you don't struggle."

Captain Hamonet gasped. "Lord, although the private was disrespectful with his comments to me this morning, I don't think this level of discipline is warranted."

"And why would you assume that I care what you think?" replied the count. "I'm only getting started. You, sir, are next on my to-do list."

The captain's expression transformed from one of mild concern to pure terror.

"What did I do?" he asked. "I did nothing."

Brian could not restrain a grin.

"You're correct," replied Zaran. "You did nothing that I required during the meeting this morning. Not only could you not stand on your own two feet, but you also failed in procuring the required payment. You're an embarrassment to this castle."

"The Nexxathians said that they wouldn't pay the full price for the amount that we had." The captain's voice wavered with panic.

"I heard," said Count Zaran. "My spies along the North Gate informed me of every word spoken during the encounter. In fact, that wart-nosed peasant memorized the entire exchange. What's his name again?"

"Hubert," said Amfridus.

"Yes, Hubert," said the count. "He was dumber than a box of hair, but he was a good little mole. No doubt about it, his services will be missed. At least I could rely on his ability to gather information without fainting on the job. Too bad Sergeant Woods here had to go and murder him in cold blood. No problem, though. I have many more little moles patrolling my castle, and their burrows run deep. You never know where my spies might pop up."

"Lord, please," said Captain Hamonet. "I'm so sorry."

"Hush now," he replied. "Be patient and wait your turn. I must tend to Mr. Llanforth first."

As Count Zaran stepped up to Belris, raising his blade, the captain made a mad dash for the door.

"Are you kidding me?" said the count. He shook his head and laughed. "Amfri, would you please restrain the captain?"

"With pleasure," replied the necromancer. He pointed his already raised hand at the running figure.

In full stride, Captain Hamonet's legs, from the hip bones to his feet, exploded into a ball of red mist. What remained of his torso, plunged to the floor, bouncing several times before coming to rest against a marble column. Jets of thick blood spewed from the open wounds.

"Ha!" exclaimed the count. "Now he really has an excuse to fall. Well done, Amfri. Very creative."

"Thank you, sir."

Captain Hamonet howled in agony as dark pools of blood collected around him, saturating the carpet.

"All right then," said Count Zaran and turned back to the private. "Let's get this over with." He placed the blade to the base of Belris' outstretched tongue and began to slice.

Belris gagged reflexively but otherwise remained still. His terrified eyes were the only parts of his body that moved. They roved in wild circles as the count carefully began to cut through the connective tissue.

"Sir," said Amfridus.

Zaran paused mid-slice and looked up. His expression reflected a hint of annoyance. "Yes? What is it?"

"I was thinking, sir. Would it be wise for us to relocate our guests to the other room and utilize the device?"

The count lowered his dagger. Belris' tongue flopped over and dangled at the point of incision. Saliva and blood streamed from the exposed ducts and vessels.

"I hadn't thought of that," replied the count, rubbing his beard. "I suppose it would be fitting to use our dear captain here to make up for the shortage of product this month."

The necromancer nodded.

"However," said the count, "to be honest with you, I'm starving and ready for lunch, and the last thing I want to do before I eat is pick up that bloody mess over there and carry it all the way downstairs. Why not use the older device in the corner?"

Amfridus looked across the room. Even Brian turned to see what they were talking about.

"That version hasn't been used in years. I'm not even certain that it still works."

"I hear you, old friend," said Count Zaran, "but let's at least give it a go before we relocate downstairs."

"As you wish."

The count wiped the blade on his pants and sheathed it. "All right, you three. Well, two and a half. This party is relocating across the room. Off we go now." He motioned with both arms for them to move.

Brian Woods walked across the carpeted pathway. Belris remained in place, his tongue still dangling and dripping, while Captain Hamonet screamed in pain near the far entryway.

"Amfri," said the count. "A little help?"

"Forgive me, sir."

With a snap of his fingers, the necromancer transported the private and the captain to a far corner of the throne room. A metal box, about the height of a tall man, loomed beside them. Brass piping, dials, and other controls covered its exterior.

"How does this one turn on?" asked Count Zaran.

Amfridus scratched his beard and looked over the device. He shook his head after a moment and walked to the other side. "Here's the switch," he said as he flicked on the power. Nothing happened.

"Good grief," said the count.

"I told you, sir. This one's in bad shape."

Count Zaran sighed. "Damn. I was looking forward to having lunch on time today. Steven is preparing crimped fish and soused pig's face."

Brian cleared his throat and pointed toward a nearby power generator. "The cord, sir."

Count Zaran and Amfridus turned, looking down.

"For heaven's sake," exclaimed the count. "The wretched contraption isn't even plugged in. Thank you very much, Mr. Woods. How observant of you."

The necromancer bent down and plugged the device's cord into one of the available outlets on the power source. A deep hum filled the room as the apparatus kicked into life.

"Finally," said Count Zaran. "Okay, captain. In you go."

"Half a moment," said Amfridus.

"Good gracious, what is it now?"

"The construction of this version is so outdated that I'm not entirely certain how to properly set the configuration."

"Just set it up as we do on the other one."

"I'm afraid that won't be possible. The controls on this old box were designed to be set in a very specific order, and I have honestly forgotten what order that is."

"There should be instructions around here somewhere," said the count. "Look around. Sergeant Woods, you help too."

The three men searched the area around the device for any sort of instructions or documentation. Belris remained frozen. His half-severed tongue dribbled spit and blood. The captain was barely conscious.

"Is this the one?" asked Brian.

"Throw it to Amfri, please."

"This is it!" he replied. "Give me a minute to review."

Count Zaran and Brian waited. They fidgeted while Amfridus configured the dials, buttons, and knobs with precision.

"All right, I'm ready," he said, pulling open a hatch that revealed a large compartment within the device. "Please help me lift Captain Hamonet and put him in."

311

"What? I'm not touching that disgusting mess. Just do that thing you do and magically transport him into the box."

Amfridus smirked. "Lord, you know I can't. That type of transport spell consumes most of my power in one shot. I'll not be able to transport anything again until I rest."

"Fine. Have Mr. Woods help you."

They picked up the bloody torso that was once Captain Hamonet and prepared to toss him through the device's hatch.

"Wait," croaked the man. "No..."

"So long, captain," said Count Zaran. "Let's hope that your value is worth more to the Nexxathians than it was to me."

Once the captain had been deposited, Amfridus closed the door and flipped on a switch that illuminated a circular portal. The captain was fully awake again. He had his hands pressed against the glass and was screaming, but the sounds from the box's interior went unheard.

The necromancer looked at Count Zaran.

"Proceed," he said.

Amfridus pushed a red button and the box rattled and vibrated as an engine deep within awoke from a long slumber.

"This thing better work," said the count.

The escalating vibrations stabilized, and Captain Hamonet abruptly discontinued his hysterical screaming. He scratched wildly at his face and eyes. His skin began to blister and pop.

"Here we go. I think this one's a winner, Amfri."

"Yes, sir."

A bright flash erupted from within the portal. The hum of the engine subsided and gradually stopped. Count Zaran and Amfridus approached the window, peering inside. The captain's remains were gone.

"It worked," said the count. "Where's the product bin on this machine?"

"It should be in the same place as the new one. At the back of the box, under the grinding cone."

Count Zaran walked around to the back and held up a metallic cube. A small portal on the device revealed a white, pulsating light from within.

Brian Woods gasped.

"Yes, sergeant," said the count. "This shiny little thing now contains the lifeforce of Captain Hamonet. It's a marvelous invention! If we were to spend more time together, I'd be happy to explain its purpose and origins over some more of that fine coffee. Alas, your life in its current form is coming to its conclusion. After Mr. Llanforth's turn in the box, of course. How is the old boy doing, anyway?"

Belris' condition had neither changed nor improved, and his terrified eyes still roved around the room.

"Fabulous," exclaimed Count Zaran. "Amfri, please turn off your spell so we can hurry this up some. I'm starving."

"Yes, sir," he replied with a wave of his hand.

The young man collapsed to the ground.

The count shook his head and grumbled. "I should have seen that coming. All right, I'll help you this time."

As the men bent to collect the private and put him into the device, an alarm from the table next to the fireplace went off.

"Lunchtime!" exclaimed the count, dropping Belris.

"But sir. Should we not finish processing these two first? Then we can take a break."

"Absolutely not," replied Zaran, waving his hands. "This errand has gone on long enough. I need to eat. I'm starting to feel light-headed. We can finish later this afternoon. Please escort our guests to the dungeon until then."

"What about the boy's tongue?"

Count Zaran regarded Belris. He was curled into a ball on the floor and panting like a dog. His half-cloven tongue lay outstretched and swollen in a puddle of fluid and goo.

"Very well," he said.

The count knelt beside the boy, brandishing his dagger. With one fell swoop, the remainder of the tongue was cleaved in two. Count Zaran kicked it across the floor.

"Off you go now, Amfri. I'll see you this afternoon."

"Goodbye, sir. Enjoy your lunch."

CHAPTER XXIV

FIREFLIES ON THE ROAD

"I can't get this damn fire started," said Marie.

"Because you're doing it wrong," replied Roger. "It's all about proper preparation. When starting a fire, you need to take your time to be successful."

"Yea, whatever," she said. "Just help me."

"No, you need to learn this stuff, Marie. Look here. You don't even have your tinder properly set. And you need a circle of rocks with branches and kindling in the center. Who in the world put you on fire detail, anyway?"

"Merkresh did," she said.

The old man grinned as he and Frederick finished setting up the final lean-to shelter. Mckenzie and Arina were gathering water from a nearby brook, while Click bustled back and forth between the trees collecting firewood.

"Nice work, Click," said Roger.

The spider beeped a thank you in return.

"It looks like you've acquired a few pieces of fig in that pile. Fig is a softwood, and you know what softwoods are good for, right Marie?"

"What?"

"Fire bows."

"Wow, I'm so excited now. A fire bow."

Roger shook his head and sighed. "I know you think all this adventurer stuff is a waste of time, but you're going to have to learn to do this on your own, eventually."

"He's right, Marie," said Merkresh. "Having the ability to start a fire, with materials gathered from the wild, is a great achievement. Give it a chance. You'll be thankful later."

The girl huffed. "All right, Roger. Show me how then."

The boy examined the pile and extracted a few sticks to make fire by friction. One of the longer pieces had a modest bend to it. Roger took a long strand of string from his backpack and tied it to each end of the stick.

"See, this is now the bow part," he said, holding it up. "We still need to make a few more components. The spindle, bearing block, and fireboard."

"Okay," said Marie. "What can I do?"

"Look around the camp for something we can use as a bearing block. That's the thing that you hold on top of the spindle to make it spin in place. I've used rocks with notches in them, pieces of wood or bark, even seashells."

"I don't think I'm going to find any seashells in the deep forest," said Marie.

"Then look for a suitable rock or chunk of bark."

Marie began to look around the perimeter of the camp

for something useful. The occasional crunch and crackle of her steps against the forest floor mingled with the chirps of the crickets and frogs.

"Roger," said Merkresh. "Frederick and I are going to go and check on our rabbit traps. Are the two of you good here?"

"Three of us, you mean."

"Forgive me, Click. Are the *three* of you good?"

The spider squawked at the old man.

"I believe so," answered Roger. "The girls should be back with the water any time now. I think we'll have the fire going soon. Then we can start to boil up some drinking water."

"Excellent plan," said Merkresh. "All right, Freddie. Grab your backpack and follow me."

"My name's Frederick, sir. Nobody calls me Freddie."

"I do now, so hurry up. I'm getting hungry."

Roger chuckled and turned back to his fire preparation tasks. He had produced a lovely pile of tinder, a large circle of heavy stones, and carved out a fireboard with several notches that would collect the glowing embers.

"Click, can you please find a heavy leaf or a piece of bark that I can use to transfer the embers to the tinder?"

The mechanical spider peeped his acknowledgment and then scurried off into the darkness.

Roger paused in his work and gazed into the arms of the forest. A gentle breeze whistled through the branches. He could hear the faint hoots of a distant owl. It was the first time that he had been completely alone since standing on the old man's front porch. Was that a few days ago, or a week? He could not remember. All he knew was that his life, as well as the lives of his two sisters, had changed dramatically on that horrific evening.

His mother had been murdered. The pain of her passing hammered against his innocence, yet the emotional wall that he had constructed remained steadfast. Furthermore, they were on some crazy quest to fight a dragon and reclaim some weird stones. If starting a simple fire in these relatively peaceful woods caused his younger sister anxiety, then how were they really supposed to perform the colossal tasks that were expected of them? His sisters needed to toughen up before they started slaying monsters. They needed walls of their own.

A sudden rustle of wings from the nearby trees seemed to respond to his internal monologue. Whether it was a good sign or a bad one, he could not tell.

Roger closed his eyes and enjoyed the calming effect of the wind blowing through the trees. The evening temperatures were still comfortable, being only the epilogue of summer, and the clean air felt wonderful against his face. The fragrance of fallen leaves and clover complimented the experience.

Snap! Crack!

The boy opened his eyes and whirled around.

"Marie, is that you?"

There was no answer.

Roger peered farther into the darkness. The crickets and wind filled the void, but there was nothing else.

Crackle! Crack!

This time the footsteps were in the opposite direction. He jumped to his feet, searching for his mask and glove. "All right, Marie. This isn't funny. You can come out now. I can see you crouching next to those trees."

"Nonsense, since I'm currently standing right behind you," she said with a chuckle.

Roger leapt into the air and squeaked like a mouse. "Don't ever sneak up on me like that again!"

"I didn't sneak up on you. I was over there, looking for this stupid bearing block thing. Here, will this rock work? It has a perfect little notch right in the center."

"If you were over there the whole time, then who's by those trees over there?"

They focused on the misty darkness. Two silhouettes were huddled next to the roots and trunk of a fallen oak tree.

"It's probably Mckenzie and Arina playing a trick on us. I thought I heard them approaching through the woods a few minutes ago."

"Nope," replied a voice from behind. "That's definitely not us."

Roger and Marie jumped, spinning around. "Oh my God," shouted the boy. "Will you guys stop sneaking up on me!"

"Relax, little brother," said Mckenzie, laughing. "We weren't sneaking at all. We've actually been talking up a storm on our way back from the creek to collect this water. Arina can make some very good owl hoots."

"Thanks, Mac," said Arina.

Roger sighed. "Okay, then for the third time, who's crouching by those trees? And I swear, if Merkresh, or Frederick, or that little spider taps me on the shoulder right now, I'm going to grab my glove and smack somebody."

"You mean these two crouching monsters?" asked Marie as she walked over and held up an armful of tree moss.

Mckenzie and Arina burst into laughter.

"What's the matter, Great Adventurer Brother, are you scared of twisted roots and moss?" asked Mckenzie.

"Shut up," he replied, sitting back down by the fire.

"What's all this ruckus going on over here?" exclaimed Merkresh as he, Frederick, and Click approached from the darkness. "We could hear your screeching and yelling clear across the valley."

"Our camp was attacked by tree roots," said Marie.

"What?" replied the old man.

"It's nothing, Merkresh," said Roger as he started to work the fire bow. "They're just messing with me, as usual."

"Well, keep your voices down from now on," said Merkresh. "This isn't the Thorndale Woods anymore, for crying out loud. There may actually be nasty critters about that don't appreciate your hilarious jokes as much as I do."

"Sounds fair to me," said Marie.

"Me too," said the other girls.

"Splendid," the old man said. "Once Roger gets that fire going, we can boil some water and toss these rabbits into the pot. Marie, you can help me with skinning and gutting them."

"Oh, wonderful," she replied.

***

"How many pieces are left?" asked Frederick as the group sat around the fire and ate their supper.

"You already had your share," replied Arina. "There are plenty of these wild cucumbers that I picked by the creek."

"I don't want any more of that stuff. I want meat."

"Freddie," said Merkresh. "We're at the stage where we need to start being mindful of the amount of food we eat. We need to get used to not having as much as we normally do."

"With all due respect, sir," replied the boy, "my name is not Freddie. It's Frederick."

"Come on," exclaimed Roger. "It suits you."

"No, it doesn't."

"Why does it bother you so much?" asked Mckenzie.

Frederick sighed and picked up a handful of cucumbers. He shoved them into his mouth and began to crunch away.

"One of my aunts, on my mother's side, used to call me that when I was little."

"Big deal," said Mckenzie with a roll of her eyes.

"It wasn't just that she called me Freddie, it was the way she used to say it."

Merkresh looked at Roger and shrugged.

"What do you mean?" asked the old man.

The boy spit a few of the chewed-up cucumbers into the fire. "God, those are gross," he said. One of them popped as it hit the bright embers.

"Tell us how she used to say it," said Marie.

Frederick looked over at her while he wiped his hands on his shirt. "My family used to visit her at least twice a year. Mostly on holidays or other special occasions. She lives up near Corset. Roger knows. You went with us once when we were like ten or something. For my cousin's wedding."

"I remember," he replied and chuckled. "Is she the one with that crazy hairdo and rats for pets?"

"Yes, she's the one."

"Wait," said Mckenzie. "Your aunt has a pet rat?"

"No, you don't understand," said Roger. "She has rats for pets. Plural. And that's not even the weird part."

"Good grief," said Marie. "What's the weird part?"

321

They all looked at Frederick.

"My aunt has nine rats. They all have names, but please don't ask me to try and remember them."

"Oh, hell yes we are," said Mckenzie.

"No way," he responded. "If I must tell this dumb story, then I'm making it a rule right now that I don't have to recite all nine rat names. I'll agree to naming only one."

"I believe that's a fair request," said Mckenzie. "Does everyone agree?"

The rest of the group mumbled their approval.

"I'd like to hear the names of all the rats," said Marie. "I bet they're cute."

"Another time, Marie," said Merkresh. "Go on now, lad. Please continue with your story."

"What's the one rat's name?" asked Arina.

Frederick sighed. "You'll never guess."

"Freddie!" shouted Marie.

"Hush," said Merkresh. "Not so loud."

"Of course it was," said Frederick. "She used to let her favorite rat, Freddie, sleep within the top of her big hairdo."

"Gross," said Arina. "Did it poop up there too?"

"I'm quite certain that I'm not privy to the scheduling details of Freddie the Rat's bowel movements, but I'll tell you this much. His stupid little face was always peeking out of her giant hair every time we entered their house."

The group laughed in unison.

"Furthermore," he continued, "here's the hideous thing she would say to me, once she was done hugging and kissing my older sisters."

"I can't wait for this," said Marie.

Frederick cleared his throat and prepared to speak.

"Hold on," said Mckenzie. "I think it'll be more enjoyable for us if you get up and demonstrate it."

"Yea, right," he replied. "I'm sure you'd love that."

"Do it, Freddie," said Merkresh. "I mean Frederick."

The boy frowned. "Fine, if you really want me to. I'm more than happy to make an ass of myself so that my fine friends are thoroughly entertained."

"That's the spirit," said Roger, raising his cup.

Frederick got up and walked to the fire. He wiggled his rear end back and forth as he turned to face everyone.

"What's that you were just doing?" asked Arina.

"That's how she walked," he replied. "Do you want me to do this or not?"

"Okay," she said and giggled with Marie.

"I have another idea," he said. "I think I need some of Roger's killer moss to recreate her hairdo."

"Good thinking," exclaimed Mckenzie. "Click, would you please grab some moss for Frederick's hair?"

The spider hopped from his log and retrieved the moss.

"Thank you, my little metallic friend," said Frederick once he returned. The boy took a wad of moss and carefully wrapped it around the top of his head. He made a hole in the middle and stuck a pinecone in to simulate the rat.

"How does this look?" he asked.

"Ridiculous," replied Arina.

"Great," said the boy. "Okay, here's my best rendition of my Aunt Jinglewort, her stupid hairdo, and her rat."

He cleared his throat again and spread his arms in a dramatic hugging gesture. "Oh, my little Freddie," he said in a high-pitched squeal. "It's so marvelous to see you again. My oh my how you've grown since your last visit."

Roger spat up some of his water as he laughed.

"Come right on over here and say hello to your…"

"Frederick," interrupted Merkresh in a stern voice.

Everyone turned and stared at the old man. Frederick halted his absurd demonstration. A piece of the root moss fell from his head. Click ran over, picked it up, and attempted to hand it back to the boy.

"Did you just say Jinglewort?" asked Merkresh.

"I did," he replied in a startled voice.

"Your aunt's last name is Jinglewort?"

"That's correct."

"What's her first name?"

"Magnolia."

"Oh no," exclaimed Merkresh as he leapt from his log and began to pace back and forth. He shook his head in disbelief. "Your aunt's name is Magnolia Jinglewort?"

"What the hell's going on?" asked Roger as he looked around. "What's happening?"

The girls shrugged.

"Yes, Merkresh," said Frederick. "That is, in fact, her full name. Why are you freaking out?"

The old man ceased his pacing and faced them. "Freddie, take that stuff off your head this instant and sit back down and listen to me. All of you. I don't believe that this is a coincidence. That the aunt in your story, the one who you just told us about because I've been calling you Freddie, is the one and only Magnolia Jinglewort."

"Who in the hell is Magnolia Jinglewort?" asked Marie.

"My aunt," replied Frederick.

"No, she's not," said Merkresh. "I mean, clearly she is, but she's something much more terrible than your weird aunt with a pet rat."

"I'm so confused right now," said Mckenzie.

"Tell me about it," replied Arina.

"What do you mean by terrible?" asked Roger.

"Yea," said Frederick as he threw off the moss and sat on his stump. "She's just an old lady."

Click was unsure if he should pick the moss up or return to his previous perch by the fire. He fluttered back and forth in an awkward stasis.

"She's not even that old," said Merkresh. "She should be about the same age as your parents. What I mean by terrible is that I thought we'd destroyed her."

The teenagers gasped.

"Say what?" exclaimed Frederick.

"Magnolia Jinglewort was one of the most powerful witches in Silvarum," said the old man.

"How's that possible?" asked Mckenzie.

"Do you remember the woman I told you about who lives in Kad?" asked Merkresh.

"Dot," replied Marie.

"Right. Dorothy Tompkins. She and I encountered this Jinglewort creature thirty years ago during your parent's quest. There was a great battle, and we thought that we'd killed her. Apparently, we were wrong."

"She's just my Aunt Magnolia," said Frederick. "Even if she was dramatic and kept rats in her hair, she never seemed bad or evil."

Merkresh fiddled with his beard, mumbling to himself for a moment. "It's quite possible that, during your lifetime, your aunt has not been as evil as she once was. How old are you?"

"Fourteen."

"We defeated her about thirty years ago. I bet she's been biding her time and allowing her powers to regenerate."

"Regenerate for what?" asked Arina.

"To help take back the runestones, of course," replied Merkresh. "There are many foes in Silvarum besides the rune protectors. Whole castles and kingdoms, in fact. However, your aunt is not a minor pawn in this game. She's employed by Count Zaran himself."

"My mother mentioned Zaran too," said Marie. "She said that our Uncle Brian has been staying at his castle. But who exactly is he?"

"Don't worry about him for the moment. His role in all of this will be discussed at a later time. Just understand that he's a vicious and malevolent ruler in the north."

"All right," she said. "I'll take your word for it."

"When did you last see your aunt?" asked Merkresh.

"Earlier this month," replied Frederick as he scratched his head in thought. "It struck me as odd because it was the first time that she'd bothered to make the journey down to us. While she was here, she spent most of her time with my teacher."

"Holy shit!" shouted Mckenzie.

A sense of dread swept over the company.

"That's the missing piece!" exclaimed the old man as he began to pace again. "This web of deceit is coming together. The connection among Mrs. Roberts, Magnolia Jinglewort, and the stolen Rune of Shadow is as clear as day."

"Was it all my fault?" asked Mckenzie. Her voice was fractured with regret and anguish. She peered into the crackling fire and struggled to restrain her grief. "The abductions of Arina's parents, and the death of our mother?"

Marie glared at her sister with tearful eyes. "Why would you say such an awful thing?"

"Because. I went out and found all those horrible artifacts for Mrs. Roberts. She lied to me and used them for some nefarious purpose. Probably to help strengthen Frederick's aunt. And look at what they've done. All because of me."

"Don't think that," said Arina. "It wasn't your fault."

Marie looked up at the old man. Her expression pleaded with him. Begged him. "Is this true, Merkresh?"

He stared back at her with heartbroken eyes. The wrinkles in his face and brow were stretched with sorrow. "I'm afraid that's the most logical conclusion."

Mckenzie stood and walked to the tree line. Fireflies danced among the branches as she began to weep into her hands.

"Mckenzie!" cried Marie, running to her side. "You'll not face this burden alone. I'll always be with you."

The others stood and observed with awe the bond between Mckenzie and Marie. The raw emotion from the group's collective perception of that snapshot in time radiated an energy that transcended dimensions. The power conceived during that moment channeled itself equally within them.

The sisters held on to each other and wept.

And the universe noticed.

CHAPTER XXV

MOONCHILD

"Get home? Back to San Francisco?"

"No," replied Trelinia. "To your new home."

"And where's that, exactly?" asked Abigail.

"With your mother and sister."

"So, my mom did die in the accident?"

"She did, dear."

"Why am I in this place and she's somewhere else? Are my mother and sister finally together?"

"They are, and they're waiting for you, but there's still much more that you need to accomplish here before you can be with them. Once you satisfy the book's obligations, you'll be reunited with your family."

Abigail looked at the Novemgradus and sighed. "Why does everything always have to be so complicated?"

Trelinia chuckled. "I know exactly how you feel."

Abigail smiled at Penelope. "I'm beginning to understand what this place represents, but why has it taken you so many years to fulfill your obligations?"

The girl shrugged. "It just hasn't been my turn until now. But thankfully, since Trel is here, and with your help, I believe my time has finally come."

"The book says that I'm supposed to help you," said Abigail. "That's my requirement, and then I can leave, right?"

"That's one of your requirements," replied Penelope. "Only the book can determine everything that you must do and when you have satisfied its demands."

"What if I don't succeed, or refuse to do them?"

"Remember that apparition that chased us through the graveyard?" asked Penelope.

"Of course."

"Well, there you go," said the girl. "If you fail or choose to disregard the book's guidance, then you'll haunt this cemetery until the end of time."

"I see."

"Are you ready to begin?" asked Trelinia.

"Begin what?"

"Your great quest."

Abigail looked around at the shadowy corners and web-covered coffins within the catacomb. "My quest begins here?"

"Nay," said Penelope, pointing. "In there."

The book's eye hummed to life with a radiant blue. The hinges unsnapped with a clink, and the cover opened.

Abigail stared at Trelinia with wonder. "*You're* the key it spoke of? You're going to take me there?"

"Yes," she replied.

"The place that it sent me before, the snowy forest in the mountains where I saw my mom, that was real?"

"It was as real as this cemetery or your life before in San Francisco," replied Trelinia. She looked at Penelope. "Didn't you have a chance to explain any of this to her? How time and space are different here?"

The girl raised her eyebrows. "I tried to, believe me, but it's a tricky subject. I don't even really understand it myself."

"Not to worry," said Trelinia. "It will become clearer the farther we go and the more we accomplish."

"May I ask you a question?" asked Abigail.

"Of course, Abi. Do you mind if I call you that?"

A wave of sadness washed over the girl's face. "My sister was the only one to ever call me Abi. She died last summer."

"I know, my dear. I'm so sorry for your loss. I'll call you by your full name if you prefer."

"No. It's fine," said Abigail. "In a way, it gives me a sense of comfort knowing that I might see her again and that she's waiting for me."

Trelinia and Penelope smiled.

"What's your question then, Abi?"

"Where exactly are we going, and what is it we have to do on this quest?"

"Frost," whispered the book's ancient voice as its blue light filled the room. "The Moonchild and the Two Eagles must clear the path for the Children of the Woods."

"What does that mean?"

"May I tell her?"

"Please do."

"Although we're considered ghosts in this place, and dead

to the living world, there's something amazing we can do here."

"What can we do?"

"When we pass through the book, each of us will be able to transform into our greatest desires. The forms that we could only dream about while we were in the living world."

A tear ran down Abigail's cheek.

"Me and Trelinia can change into eagles."

"Am I the Moonchild?" asked Abigail.

"Indeed, you are," said Trelinia. "It's what you've always wished for, isn't it? The games that you played with your sister, and the powers that the two of you imagined. You'll have them, and where we're going, your abilities are boundless."

Abigail dropped to her knees and began to cry. "Why do I, of all people, deserve such a gift?"

"You of all people?" Trelinia said, placing her hand on the girl's shoulder. "I don't think you're aware of your true potential. Your abilities here are not a gift. You've earned them."

Abigail raised her head, smiling through her tears.

"Now then," said Trelinia. "Please rise and join us by the Novemgradus, Abi the Moonchild. We have much to do."

The girl stood and wiped her cheeks. "Who are you?"

"I'm the mother of the children that we have to help now. Mckenzie, Roger, and Marie are their names. They're The Children of the Woods."

"Wow," said Abigail. "This is all too amazing to believe."

"Wait until you see this next part," said Penelope.

The three companions walked to the pedestal that held the ancient book. Its brilliant blue light had dimmed so that the pages were now clear, yet luminous. A bold chapter heading, penned in a flowing script, displayed the following words:

STAGE I: DEPARTURE

"Once we leave," said Trelinia, "you'll not be able to return to this cemetery until we either succeed or fail in our first challenge. Do you feel that you're ready?"

Abigail thought for a moment, glancing at Penelope. Her friend smiled and nodded back.

"I'm ready."

"Then turn the page," said Trelinia.

Abigail grasped the page and slowly turned. A soothing, warm glow engulfed her mind and body, and she willingly submitted to its heavenly grasp.

***

Abigail, Penelope, and Trelinia stood within a forest glade. Shafts of cheerful sunlight fell from the heights of the canopy and settled upon the waters of a clear stream. Birds whistled and sang amongst the branches and fragrant flowers.

"My God, it's so beautiful and warm here," exclaimed Abigail. "Where are we now?"

"In a place called Blackwood Forest," replied Trelinia.

"Isn't it exquisite?" asked Penelope. "I've waited so long to be in a place like this, I feel that I could burst with gratitude. Whatever happens to us from this point onward, I'm just so thankful for this experience right now. And to share it with the two of you, I can hardly express my feelings. This is a pivotal moment for me."

"For us all," said Trelinia.

"Look at that glowing sun and crystal-clear sky," said

Abigail. "I guess I don't need that warm coat after all."

Penelope laughed. "Nay, I would think not. Especially since you can change into your form now."

Abigail's eyes widened.

"Can I?" she asked.

"At your convenience," Trelinia said.

"What do I do? How do I change?"

"It's not for me to say, my dear. The process is different for everyone. Focus your thoughts, and you'll make it happen. I promise."

Abigail looked into the stream's lazy current and focused on the reflections of sparkling light. An instant later, she sensed herself above the water, hovering.

"What happened?" she cried. "What am I doing?"

"You're flying," said Trelinia. "Your mind has left your body. What did you think I meant by boundless powers?"

"Where'd my reflection go? I can't see myself."

"There's no person to reflect," said Penelope. "You're just energy now. Like you imagined with your sister."

To her friends, she appeared as a small, orb of light.

Abigail could see her environment as before, and so reasoned that she must also possess a similar set of light-sensitive visual abilities. Structures that could perceive the visual spectrum, like human eyes, yet not.

She turned her attention back to the grassy riverbank and saw her friends smiling at her. At the same time, she could also discern the forest behind, and the blue sky above. *How was this possible?* She could see everything at once, yet still retain focus on a singular point. Abigail realized that visible light was not the only range she was able to see within the electromagnetic spectrum.

Ultraviolet, radio waves, infrared, and X-rays danced within a ballet of color and structure. Free from the confines of her human brain, she could process all the information. It flowed naturally for her, like a tributary of data and light. She had become one with the universe.

"Amazing," she heard herself say.

"All right, come back now," said Penelope. "I want to show you what I can do."

Abigail focused her thoughts again and found herself back in the grass next to her friends. She immediately reeled from exhaustion. "Oh my, I feel terrible. What's happened?"

"It's the unfortunate cost of transforming," Trelinia said. "Your mind is adjusting to the limitations of your human brain. The sensation will pass."

Abigail took a deep breath and stood.

"How do you know about all this stuff?" she asked.

"Me and Trel have both been in a place like this before," said Penelope. "Except last time, she was about your age and on a quest of her own."

"Living people can exist in a place like this too?"

"Of course," Penelope said. "This is a real place, just not the world that you and I came from."

Abigail looked around at the sky, trees, and river. "It sure looks a lot like Earth."

"I didn't say it wasn't Earth."

"Huh?"

"What she means," said Trelinia, "is that you shouldn't think of where we are as a different planet. You and Penny have come from a place you call Earth. My people and I don't call it by that name, but it is, in essence, the same place."

Abigail stared at the woman blankly.

Trelinia scratched her head. "For now, think of it in terms of dimensions. We're all occupying the same space but in different times and dimensions. All right?"

"Sure," said Abigail. "Whatever you say."

Penelope and Trelinia laughed.

"Come on," said the girl. "Enough of this fancy talk. I want to show Abigail how I can fly."

"Fair enough," said Trelinia. "But make it quick, please. We need to get started if we're to make it to the east end of the forest before the others do."

"Others?" asked Abigail.

"My children."

"Watch this!" yelled Penelope as she sprinted through the grass. Her green cloak and hood fluttered behind her. As she reached the water, she leapt from the edge and transformed into a golden eagle. She soared above the trees and circled high within the cerulean sky.

"Wow," exclaimed Abigail. "You can do that too?"

"Indeed," replied Trelinia. "As you've now experienced, it can become exhausting if you transform too often. We try to do it only when necessary. Penny is just excited to show you. Hold out your arm for her, and she'll come back."

"What about those giant talons?"

"She'll be gentle, I promise."

Abigail extended her arm.

Penelope let forth a piercing cry and dove from her aerial perch. She landed gracefully upon Abigail's bare skin.

"See," said Trelinia. "Not a scratch."

"I hate this transforming back part," Penelope said.

"What's it like to fly that high?" asked Abigail.

"Half a moment," replied the girl as she rubbed her eyes and moaned. "It's like daggers in my stomach. Why does it have to hurt so much? We're dead already, aren't we?"

"That doesn't seem to matter here," said Trelinia. "Even as ghosts within the book, our minds have a difficult time passing between our human forms and the celestial molds of our dreams."

Abigail smiled. "It's like our minds never really die but are transferred between bodies. We live a life in one place, like San Francisco in my case, then we eventually pass on to another adventure. Forever and ever."

"You're wise beyond your years," said Trelinia. "I too believe that the mind never ceases to exist. We're all energy. Energy can't be created nor destroyed. It's therefore clear that the two dynamic women who stand before me aren't dead at all. You're more alive than you've ever been. Your minds have traveled to a new place. And in this new place, the three of us have been chosen to complete a great task. Together, we can accomplish anything."

The teenagers smiled and gazed into the approaching eventide. A delicate blanket of orange, magenta, and golden light fell upon their faces. Penelope grasped Abigail's hand.

"Do you feel the energy flowing through us?"

"I do," replied Abigail.

From death, they had discovered a more meaningful life.

CHAPTER XXVI

THE STARS GUIDE THE PATH

"Are the two of you ready to depart?" asked Vomexium.

Benjamin nodded. "Yes, sir."

"And Dot's guidance is clear to you? Do you have any more questions before you begin?"

"The Gate of Frozen Whispers that we have to find," said Benjamin. "Are you certain that it leads to the Tombworld?"

"Very certain," replied the old man. "Through it, you will reach your destination."

"I have a question," said Gothkar.

"Yes?"

"This task of ours seems like it could be difficult."

"Only as difficult as you make it," said Dot.

"Of course," replied Gothkar. "But it occurred to me that this could be the perfect opportunity to earn my next symbol. It's been two years now, and I've studied and participated in all the required ceremonies. All that's left is that I complete one final chore. So, what do you say, boss? If Ben and I acquire this contraption for you, can this count for my advancement instead?"

Vomexium and Dot looked at each other thoughtfully.

"That's your call to make," she said with a shrug.

The old man sighed, scratching his beard. "Very well, Gothkar. Aside from that stunt you pulled last month, you've thus far proven yourself to be a promising student of the Shadowkuur Arts. If you successfully retrieve the Intensitron and escort Benjamin to the gate, I'll file an exception and promote you to level fourteen."

"Sweet!" exclaimed Gothkar, with a pump of his fist.

"If there are no more inquiries or last-minute negotiations to facilitate, then the two of you should be on your way," said Dot, motioning toward the exit.

"Good luck, gentlemen," said Vomexium. "Stick to the map and follow the guide we've established. If you can remain inconspicuous, at least for a while, then your odds for success will remain high."

"It'll be a piece of cake," said Gothkar.

***

"What are we supposed to do first?" asked Benjamin.

"I have no idea," replied Gothkar as they exited a secret door and stepped into the Kadiaphonek alleyway. "What did that little old woman tell you?"

"Seriously? You just told them that this was going to be a piece of cake, and you don't even know what to do?"

"Relax, Ben. I know this city like the back of my hand."

"And that's supposed to make me feel confident?"

"You can feel whatever you want, man," said Gothkar. "But I'm not going to stress out over any of this. You should really try and shed some of that negative energy you have all balled up inside. You'd feel a lot better. Maybe even have a sense of humor."

"Give me a break," replied Benjamin, rolling his eyes. "Let me see that map. I want to figure out what in the hell an Intensitron is."

"It doesn't matter if we understand. I bet it's just a fancy little gadget that grumpy old lady wants, nothing more."

"Probably so," said Benjamin. "But I'd like to learn more about it. Hand it over."

Gothkar pulled a folded-up piece of parchment from his pants pocket and handed it to his companion.

Benjamin held the paper up to the afternoon sunlight and read the first lines aloud:

The Stars Guide the Path.

"What's that supposed to mean?"

"Beats me," said Gothkar.

"It has to be important. Think about it."

"I'm trying to."

Benjamin peered to the end of the alleyway. The sidewalk was choked with pedestrians and slithering creatures. Sunlight twinkled from their metal and brass adornments.

"The stars!" he exclaimed with a snap of his fingers.

"What?"

"Vomexium said that we need to follow the guide that they made for us. What's the name of Kad's main plaza?"

Gothkar smiled. "Plaza of the Stars."

"Right. Now, take a look at this little drawing."

Benjamin pointed to a small design that had been sketched below the line of words. It was a series of six points, each connected by a line.

"It looks like a constellation," said Gothkar. "But what does it have to do with the plaza?"

"I'm not sure. Let's get moving, though. We can figure it out on the way."

***

"Do you think they'll figure it out?" asked Dot.

Vomexium took a sip from his mug as they relaxed in the cozy corner. "Even if they run into trouble, our friends will be keeping an eye on their progress. I don't remember much of this Woods fellow, but I can tell you that Gothkar is sharp."

"Is he now? I haven't been impressed."

"Understandably so," he replied. "Gothkar can certainly come across as indifferent and aloof, but under all those layers of apathy is a critical thinker."

"Maybe," said Dot. "We shall see."

"What's this thing you sent them off to find, anyway?"

"The Intensitron? It's a device believed to have the ability to translate Nexxathian hieroglyphs."

"But I can translate those," said Vomexium.

"Not these kinds."

The Tullek woman reached from her chair and pulled a leather-bound book from a nearby shelf.

"I recently acquired this specimen from a local dealer. Roberts, I believe was her name."

"I've never heard of her," remarked the old man. He took another sip of tea.

"She's a schoolteacher and an archeologist. She claimed to have recovered it from one of the graveyards in the south."

"Interesting. What's so special about it?"

Dot opened the cover and flipped to the middle. She cleared her throat and whispered a series of words. Eight glowing shapes sprang from the pages and hovered. A radiant blue pulsated from their geometric contours and edges.

Vomexium spit up a mouthful of liquid.

"Oh, my word. What are those?" he asked, sitting up.

Dot laughed. "I told you they were new. Apparently, they hold one of the secrets of the dragon's castle."

"Lord Mortis," whispered the old man.

A malevolent chill infiltrated the room. Light from the candelabra flickered and gasp for breath, while Dot pulled her blanket tighter to withstand the loathsome onslaught.

"Let's speak not its name aloud," she said.

"Indeed," replied Vomexium. "Even within this hidden sanctuary, his claws grasp at our minds."

***

"How much further is the plaza?"

"Ten blocks, at least," replied Gothkar.

Benjamin expelled a heavy sigh. "This isn't going to work at all. We've got to get off the sidewalk and find a faster means of travel. There are too many people."

"You're right. What district is this?"

"You're supposed to be the Kad expert. Are we lost?"

"Of course not. Just give me a second."

Gothkar pushed his way through the crowd and hopped to the base of a lamp post. He shielded his eyes from the sun and gazed into the metropolis. A sea of bodies washed through the maze of streets during the rush hour commute. Gothkar turned his attention to a cluster of cages at the end of the next block. A Xekal vendor was yelling at the top of his lungs.

"Get home quick! Fastest transit in Kad!"

Gothkar snapped his fingers and pointed at Benjamin.

"What is it?"

"My friend, Francis. I forgot he works down here."

"Is he going to give us a ride?" asked Ben.

"Sort of. He's going to rent us one."

"What does he rent?"

"Bugs," replied Gothkar.

The companions slipped back into the flow of sidewalk traffic and made their way to the end of the block. Three metal cages loomed before them. Towering insects, each covered in bright colors and twitching antenna, stared through the openings.

"Hey Francis," said Gothkar.

The vendor ceased his hollering and inspected the duo.

"Hello stranger," he replied. "What brings you out here to the Noffrets District?"

"My friend and I need a lift. We're in a hurry."

"I can certainly help you with that. Please take your pick," he said, gesturing toward the cages.

"How much for the orange and green one?"

"Her name is Clementine," replied Francis. "She normally costs three hundred silver for the day. However, you gentlemen caught me at an opportune time. I'm currently having a sale. Two hundred silver and Clementine is yours."

Gothkar frowned. "That's still a bit rich for my blood, old friend. How about one hundred?"

"Goodness, no. Do you have any idea how much it costs to maintain these creatures? Not to mention the amount of food that they consume. Oh, and their medical checkups. I swear if my insurance premiums go up again next month I'm…"

"How about one seventy-five?"

"Sold!" exclaimed Francis, unlocking the cage. "Are you comfortable driving her? Do you need a refresher?"

"Of course I'm comfortable, man. I grew up riding these things all over the countryside."

"That may be so," said the vendor. "But there's a specific detail you need to know about Clementine."

"Relax, Francis. I can handle her. Plus, we don't have time for all that. Come on, Ben. Climb aboard!"

Benjamin had never ridden an insect before, especially one as large and colorful as Clementine. He gawked at the beast's features and design. Her abdomen, thorax, and wing coverings were embellished with a vibrant combination of persimmon and forest green. Reflections of sunlight produced a hypnotic display of movement. Obsidian spots and unusual patterns intermingled with the insect's lustrous casing.

"Quit your ogling and get up here," said Gothkar.

Benjamin stepped into the rear stirrup and pulled himself up. He wiggled in between the pommel and cantle and held on to the saddle horn.

"See. It's like riding a horse," said Gothkar.

"Great," replied Benjamin. "I hate horses."

Gothkar rolled his eyes.

"Thanks again, old friend," he said. "We'll drop her off to you tomorrow afternoon."

"Wait," shouted Francis. "You forgot her medication!"

***

"I see them," said Lilly Roberts.

"What're those two idiots doing now?" asked Magnolia Jinglewort. "Still fumbling around on that beetle?"

Lilly lowered her looking glass and placed it back into her shoulder bag. Her sapphire cloak fluttered in the wind as they peered from the heights of a cathedral spire.

"They're going down Brusque Way, toward the plaza."

"Splendid. Exactly how we intended. That stupid little Tullek woman has led them precisely where we need them to be. Once they solve the six puzzles and reach the final pyramid, we can dispose of them and take the Intensitron back to Zaran."

"And the ghosts?" asked Lilly. "Trelinia and those other two girls should have arrived by now."

"I'll handle that group. You'll need to head back to Warington to deliver this gadget."

"Very well," said Lilly.

She snapped her fingers. An instant later, an enormous arachnid crawled from the other side of the spire. Its legs tapped and prodded against the stonework.

"We'll follow them into the catacombs and monitor from a distance," said Magnolia as she climbed onto the spider and nestled into the saddle. "There's no need to disturb their progress until they reach the end."

"If they make any progress."

"True, but these two could cause us some trouble if we're too hasty. Best to simply let them do all the work. If they fail, then we'll have to do this the hard way. Either way, we're not leaving without the device."

Lilly pulled the saddle reins and the spider crept down the face of the cathedral. Pteryxtodons screeched as they soared through the heights and passed the cloaked figures. Once at ground level, the spider hopped from lamp post to lamp post and slinked along electrical wire until it reached the face of the next building. Up, up, up they dashed. Down, down, down they plummeted. They paused intermittently on rooftops or church steeples to locate the beetle and its occupants. Eventually, they reached the Plaza of the Stars and watched from the top of a marble obelisk as Benjamin and Gothkar entered the first pyramid. Lilly looked at her companion and grinned.

***

"Will Clementine be all right tied up out there?"

"Of course," replied Gothkar. "Relax."

"I'll relax when the eighth runestone is retrieved."

"Great. Then I can expect you to be all tense for the next decade or so?"

"Probably. Where does that thing say we can find the hidden entrance to the catacombs?"

Gothkar took the map out of his pocket and pointed.

"The red dot over there next to that bookshelf looks like a good place to start. Let's check that out."

They walked across the pyramid's mountainous entrance hall. The sacred structure was hollow, and the delicate acoustics amplified their footsteps as they made their way to the far wall. A few worshipers and disciples prayed quietly amongst the various shrines. The pyramid was otherwise unoccupied.

"Now what?" asked Benjamin. "I don't see a door."

"We probably have to solve some sort of puzzle or something to find it. Remember before?"

"How could I forget? Are there any clues or notes on this part of the map?"

Gothkar mumbled to himself as he studied the drawing.

"The only thing I see are two numbers. Five and three."

Benjamin walked up to the towering bookshelf and stared in thought. "Five and three. Five and three. I think I have it figured out."

"Already?"

"Sure. Fifth shelf from the bottom, third book in."

"Try it then," said Gothkar.

Benjamin reached up to the fifth shelf and pulled a leather-bound book from the third slot. Nothing happened.

"That's strange."

Gothkar laughed. "I think your idea was partly correct. The five is not the fifth shelf from the bottom. It's the fifth shelf from the top."

They tilted their necks to the ceiling. The bookcase had at least fifty shelves.

"Are you kidding me?"

"You better start climbing," said Gothkar.

"Forget it."

"Why not?"

Benjamin turned to his friend. "You know why."

"I'll do it since you're scared of heights, but you owe me."

"Thanks, old buddy."

Gothkar pulled the ladder closer and began to climb. "Hold her steady, will you?"

Benjamin held on to the base of the ladder and surveyed his surroundings. Within the periphery of his vision, he noticed two figures enter the pyramid and kneel before one of the shrines. He looked back up at his friend's progress.

"Almost there?"

"Will you give me a break? This ladder was built for Xekals or something. I'm a troll, remember?"

"Then could you speed it up just a little, please? This place is giving me the creeps."

"Sure," replied Gothkar. "Is this fast enough for you?"

A thick book slammed to the floor next to Benjamin and produced a thundering echo. All the worshipers, except the two new figures, turned and glared at the companions.

"Good lord, man," said Benjamin. "Cut that out."

"Then stop your whining. I almost have it."

Gothkar reached the fifth shelf and extended his hand. The clank and grinding of gears revealed a secret door on the adjacent wall. Curved stairs led to the catacombs below.

"There we go," said Gothkar. "A piece of cake."

"Right," said Benjamin. "Now come on down."

Once Gothkar reached the bottom, the friends stepped onto the stairwell and descended into the darkness.

The two shadowy individuals followed.

CHAPTER XXVII

LEVIATHAN

Morning sunlight peeked through the branches of Blackwood Forest as the company made their way along a well-worn path. The spreading arms of oak and chestnuts gradually gave way to an assortment of strange and foreign trees. The teenagers had never experienced such specimens within the tame woods of Thorndale. Cypress, hemlock, and thick clusters of spruce contended for space within the forest's canvas. A flurry of birdsongs and crickets harmonized amidst the withered bows.

Merkresh and Click led the group, while Roger, Arina, and Frederick trudged along in single file behind them. The two sisters walked together at the rear.

"Marie," said Mckenzie.

The girl blinked out of her entrancement. "Yes?"

"I need to tell you something."

"What is it?"

"I had another dream about Mom last night."

"So did I," replied Marie.

"I kept seeing her face. It was covered in blood. And that horrible expression she made as she gasped for breath. I can still see it now, and it's tearing me apart."

Marie remained silent, staring at the ground.

"Say something, will you?" asked Mckenzie.

"What do you expect me to say?" she exclaimed without looking up. The coldness of her tone was shocking.

"How about giving me some comfort? I really need you to help me carry this burden right now. Like you said you would the other night." Her voice trembled with grief.

Marie stopped walking and rubbed her forehead. "I'm sorry, Mckenzie. I don't know what's wrong with me right now. I've been thinking about Mom all morning too, and I feel sick to my stomach. Lost."

"We're both lost and in pain, but I can't keep it locked up inside as you can. I need to talk about it. Will you help me?"

"I'll try."

***

Roger noticed that his sisters had fallen behind.

"What are they doing way back there?"

"Helping each other," replied Merkresh. "This morning's hike is the first real moment that either of them has been able to address their grief."

The boy nodded and took a deep breath.

"Would you like to talk about it?" asked the old man.

"No."

"Very well, lad. But please know that I'm here for you whenever you're ready. Your sisters too. They may not know it yet, but they'll support you. Don't ever forget the importance of family. It provides the strength to ease our minds."

"Thank you, Merkresh. But I don't feel ready to speak about my feelings just yet. I want to, I just don't know how. I've never been very good at it."

"Sharing your true feelings with others is difficult. It takes time to feel comfortable doing so. I once struggled as you do."

"Really?"

"Absolutely. When I was younger, there was a time when I completely shut off my feelings from my family and friends. The stoic disposition, as I liked to refer to it. I learned to bury my emotions deep within my false sense of virtue. I got used to it."

"And?" asked Roger after a few steps.

"And it almost crushed me. I'd become so distant that it saturated into my highborn responsibilities. The ironic thing is that suppressing your feelings becomes a weakness, rather than the strength you intend it to be."

***

"Do you guys hear that?" asked Arina.

The bubbling current of a great river floated through the trees. Beams of sunlight fell upon the path ahead and illuminated an opening in the forest.

"What is that?" asked Frederick.

"The voice of the Wondering River," replied Merkresh.

Marie and Mckenzie ran to the front of the group.

"We made it," said Marie.

"This is but our first crossing," said the old man. "Let's get to the edge and find a safe passage. If my memory serves me, there should be an old footbridge up ahead."

"Can we take a break and have a bite first?" asked Roger. "It feels like we've been walking forever."

Merkresh took a deep breath. "Would anyone else like to have lunch before we attempt to cross?"

All the other teenagers raised their hands.

"Very well," he said. "When we get to the shore the five of you can relax for a few moments. Click and I will scout around and look for that bridge. Onward!"

The company reached the edge of the river and withdrew from the arms of the forest. The murky and cramped atmosphere opened to an overwhelming warmth of light. The Wondering River was immense. Its breadth stretched a hundred meters at its widest, and the current was dreadfully swift. A green meadow of jasmine and lavender encompassed the river's banks.

The three girls ran to the top of a grassy hill.

"What's that in the distance?" asked Mckenzie.

"Kad," said Arina.

The tips of the city's tallest spires and monuments clawed their way through the distant canopy. Flying reptiles and flocks of birds weaved between spirals of blue smoke.

"It's wonderful," said Marie.

"Kadiaphonek is a magical place," said Arina. "Just wait until you see it. It's filled with the most exotic creatures you could ever imagine. Dinosaurs, Labzhir, and the Qugron. The Muurx, those funny little eyeball guys, are my favorite."

"Our parents never took us there," said Mckenzie.

"We stayed in the city for a few days during our move

from Briargulch," said Arina. "If we have time once we get there, I'll take you guys to Moonlight Avenue. It's the coolest street in Kad. The shops and boutiques are filled with the most enchanted treasures you've ever seen. I got my wand there."

Marie held her hand over her eyes to shield the sun and gazed into the distance. Light flickered from golden steeples.

"Ready for lunch?" asked Roger as he and Frederick reached the top of the hill. "Merkresh will be back soon."

"Yes, please," said Mckenzie. "I'm starving. What do we have left to eat?"

"I still have some of those wild cucumbers and bearded tooth mushrooms," said Marie.

"Disgusting rubbish," replied Frederick.

Roger pulled a container from his backpack. "We also have a little bit of rabbit left, some snake meat, and the turkey that we trapped yesterday."

"Now that sounds delicious," said Frederick.

The teenagers assembled the food and drinks and made a suitable picnic spread atop the grassy hill. Arina even laid out one of her colorful quilts. Their lunch consisted of roasted turkey and rabbit meat, apple slices, and a mixture of mushrooms and other wild edibles.

Frederick reached for another piece of meat.

"Your arm," said Mckenzie. "It's still purple."

The boy shrugged. "Not as bad as it was last week. Plus, the side of my arm up to my pinky doesn't feel like it's asleep anymore. You can still practice your healing potions on me if you want. I don't mind."

Roger and Marie struggled to restrain their laughter.

"Um, no thanks," said Mckenzie. "I really am sorry that I

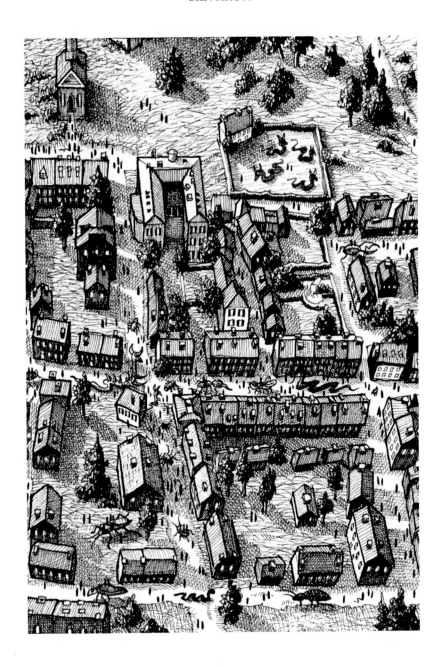

did that to your arm, but I think I figured out what the problem was. Your services are no longer required."

"All right," he said and played with his food awkwardly. "Would you like to learn how I built that turkey trap? Maybe later we could go for a walk and I could teach you?"

Mckenzie frowned. "No, thank you."

Merkresh and Click ascended the hill.

"Did you find the bridge?" asked Roger.

The old man sat down and fixed himself a plate of food while the mechanical spider explored the top of the hill.

"We did, but I'm afraid that I have some bad news."

"What is it?"

"It appears that Lilly Roberts and Magnolia Jinglewort destroyed the bridge during their flight out of the valley."

The teenagers let out a communal sigh.

"Is there no way across?" asked Marie.

"Fortunately," said Merkresh, "one side of the bridge is still mostly intact. Though we'll need to cross in single file. The river's current is still extremely fast due to the recent storms."

"Does that mean that Mrs. Roberts will be in Kad?" asked Marie. "If she is, I intend to go after her."

Merkresh nodded. "I believe that's where they were headed. Whether they'll still be there once we arrive, I can't say. Regardless, we need to find Dot and hear her counsel before we make our next move, and we need to stay focused."

Marie threw her plate of food to the ground. "I'm tired of waiting," she said as she slung her backpack and marched down to the river's edge.

Mckenzie jumped up and ran after her.

Roger stood too, but Merkresh stopped him with a wave.

"Let them go," he said. "They need each other right now and I need the three of you to help me clean up this mess. We have to get across that river."

***

The rushing water gurgled and gushed as they approached the footbridge. A golden-brown toad with red spots croaked at the travelers before hopping from a splintered railing.

"This looks impossible," said Frederick.

"With a cheerless attitude like that, it certainly does," said Merkresh. "Instead of giving up before you have even tried, why not analyze your situation and come up with a plan? Roger, what does your mask show you for a possible path ahead?"

The boy tapped on the glove's finger pads to increase the mask's magnification and peered out into the flotsam.

"The entire left side of the bridge is ruined. The right side is still intact, but there's a gap near the middle. It looks like we'll each have to jump across."

"Oh, great," exclaimed Mckenzie.

"You can do it," said the old man. "Come on now. We've no time to dilly-dally. We must traverse in single file and very slowly. Who'll go first?"

"I will," said Marie and stepped up to the bridge.

"Very good," said Merkresh. "I'm right behind you."

Frederick followed the old man, while Roger and Arina stepped cautiously from board to board. Mckenzie was the last to cross. She moved with uncertainty and dread.

The mechanical spider reached the gap first and hopped up and down with excitement.

356

"Marie, slow down a little," said Merkresh.

"Why? This is easy."

"Because we need to consider the progress and safety of the others. They're moving much slower than you."

"Fine," she said and paused at the edge of the cavity.

"Watch that loose board there," said Frederick.

"I see it," replied Roger. "I'm more concerned about that nasty current. One slip, and we'd be done for."

"Everyone stay focused," said Merkresh over the roar of the river. "Mckenzie, are you doing all right?"

The girl was frozen with fear, clinging to a slimy beam a quarter of the way across the bridge. Her eyes were frantic.

"Arina, can you help her, please?" asked Merkresh.

"Mckenzie," she said. "Take my hand and cross with me. We'll make it to the gap together."

"I'm too scared."

"So am I, but staying out here is much worse. Grab my hand and I'll lead you to the middle."

"I can't make that jump anyway. I have to go back and find another way across."

"No," said Merkresh. "There's no other way. You must gather your wits, Mckenzie, and cross with us now. I know you're scared, but you must. Hurry now."

Arina extended her hand. Mckenzie slowly pushed herself off the beam and reached for her friend. Her foot slipped.

"Mckenzie!"

"I'm all right," she replied as she regained her footing.

The girls held on to each other and negotiated across the precarious planks until they reached the gap.

"You did it," said Arina.

"Thank you for helping me," said Mckenzie.

The group stood at the edge of the rift and gazed across. A great explosion had ruptured the bridge at its center. Charred fragments and sharp edges sneered at them.

"I'm not going to sugar coat this," said Merkresh. "This is going to take a bit of courage from each of you to make the jump. Find your focus and you'll be able to do it."

The teenagers looked at each other anxiously.

"I have rope," said Roger. "Can't we use it here?"

The old man shook his head. "It's not thick or sturdy enough to make a bridge."

The boy nodded.

"What about the wands?" asked Arina. "Can we use our magic to get us across?"

"How exactly would you do that?" asked Merkresh. "I'm afraid that our magic and technology will not solve this problem for us. Some obstacles in life require a human touch. I'll go first to show you where to jump. Marie will go next."

"I'm ready," she said.

The old man motioned for them to step back.

"The boards on the other side are broken at a downward angle and lower than this end, so we can use gravity to our advantage. Aim for that section without the fire damage, but be mindful of the fractures. They're very sharp."

He took two steps backward and then leapt across the gap. The old man's agility was impressive. He fell upon the required section with ease, scrambling to the top.

"It's not as bad as I thought," he said. "All right, Marie?"

Without hesitation, the girl flung herself to the other side.

The group gasped with admiration.

"Nicely done," said Merkresh as he helped her to the top.

One by one, the other teenagers conquered their fear in their own way and made the jump. Frederick took a running start, while Roger elected to bend his knees low and leap from a stationary position. Arina's flight was almost as nimble as Marie. Mckenzie, on the other hand, found herself frozen again, unable to overcome the panic that swelled within her.

"Come on, Mckenzie," said Marie. "You can do this."

"I think not," she replied.

"Focus on that section where you have to land," said Roger. "If you miss, it'll all be over anyway."

"Roger!" shouted Marie, punching him in the arm.

"I'm just joking."

"This isn't the time for jokes," replied Merkresh. "Your sister is having trouble and needs our support. Now try again."

Roger sighed. "I'm sorry, Mckenzie. Aim for that section and use your legs to propel yourself to the other side. Take a running start if you have to."

"That worked for me," said Frederick.

Mckenzie took a deep breath and gathered her strength. She backed up a few paces and bent her knees low in preparation.

"I'll go on the count of three," she said.

"Very good," replied Merkresh.

"One…"

She took another deep breath.

"Two…"

She dug her heels into the soggy wood.

"What's that?" screamed Arina.

The company turned in horror as a spout of mist erupted from the river. A monstrous serpent, covered in glistening scales and horns, exploded from the depths and besieged Mckenzie.

"Three!"

As she soared through the air, the leviathan snapped its razor-sharp teeth at her. It missed by mere centimeters. Mckenzie was knocked from her trajectory and propelled into the current. She screamed as she fell headfirst.

"Mckenzie!" yelled Frederick.

The creature spun away from the bridge and circled back around for its next onslaught. Its forked tail whipped into the frothing current and showered a wall of water upon them.

"Attack it!" cried Merkresh with a demanding voice. "You three protect Mckenzie while Frederick and I get her out."

Arina, Marie, and Roger responded with resolute furor. Arina was the first to draw and fire. A sphere of lavender shot from her wand's moonstone and struck the sea beast behind one of its pectoral fins. It shrieked in agony.

Roger tapped a combination with his finger pads.

"Plasma pulse online," said CAAT.

He aimed his glove and fired three successive energy bursts. The first two soared over the back of the serpent and disappeared into the distance. The third bolt, however, found its mark. It thumped against a row of scales, tearing a ferocious gash. Chunks of meat and bone splashed into the water.

"Mckenzie," shouted Merkresh. "Can you hear me?"

The girl had risen to the surface but was fighting the strong current. Her arms flailed in desperation as she searched for something to hold onto.

"Help me!" she screamed through a mouthful of water.

"Can you reach that post?" asked the old man.

Mckenzie's head fell below the water line for a moment,

but then quickly resurfaced. She puffed and spat as she tried to hear their commands. The cracks and screams of battle roared all around her.

"It's too far. I can't reach it."

The river pulled her under again. Only her hands were visible, grasping at the air in vain.

Frederick snapped into action. He pulled a length of rope from his backpack and tied an end around his waist. He handed the other end to the old man.

"Take this and guide us to the shore," he said.

"Good idea," replied Merkresh.

"Mckenzie, keep kicking. I'm coming to get you," said Frederick, diving into the water.

He splashed down a few meters away from her and swam with all his might. Merkresh held tight to the rope and navigated his way across the remainder of the bridge.

"I've got you," said Frederick as he grabbed Mckenzie.

She threw her arms around his neck and coughed up a mouthful of muddy water. "You came after me," she said.

"Of course I did, but we're not out of trouble yet. Hold onto my back and I'll get us to shore."

"Here it comes again," said Roger.

The sea serpent's wounds had enraged it to a new level of destructiveness. It convulsed and whipped in frenzied loops as its barbed tail smashed across the bridge. Splinters of wood and debris spewed into the air. Roger and Arina continued to shoot at the beast. Green and pink projectiles screamed for their target. Marie aimed her wand and focused her thoughts.

Streams of electric blue crackled and hissed from the tip of her purple wand. The bombardment engulfed the monster, inducing wild spasms throughout its entire body. It growled in pain and blasted through the remains of the bridge. The teenagers shrieked, tumbling into the water.

"Get to shore!" shouted Merkresh from the riverbank.

Marie, Roger, and Arina floundered amidst the wreckage as they were pulled downriver by the current.

"Our wands. We lost them!"

"Click!" said the old man. "Get out there and find a way to catch their wands before they disappear."

The mechanized arachnid buzzed with determination as he sprang from the shoreline and scrambled atop the floating fragments. With astounding speed, he spun a web between two piles of floating wreckage. The girls' wands bobbed in the current and found their way into the spider's trap.

"Good job, Click!" said Merkresh.

The serpent's glistening scales crested on the opposite side of the bridge and snaked toward Frederick and Mckenzie.

"Almost there," said Frederick. "Hang on."

They crawled through the shallows and flopped onto the sand. Mckenzie huffed in labored breaths as Frederick untied the rope from his waist and got to his feet.

"I don't know how to thank you, Frederick," she said.

"There's no need. I'd do it again in a heartbeat."

"Behind you!" screamed Merkresh.

Frederick was scooped up into the serpent's jaws. Blood gushed from dozens of puncture wounds on his arms and torso. The boy's eyes widened with confusion and then his body went limp. The leviathan disappeared amidst a swirl of bubbles and foam. Frederick was gone.

CHAPTER XXVIII

THE GEARWORKS

The constant drip of fetid water echoed throughout the dungeon cells. Windowless stone walls, blanketed by oppressive darkness, exuded hopelessness and despair. Cries of torture and suffering coalesced with the occasional squeak of a rat, or the passing of guards. Torchlight flickered from the hallway.

"Hey kid, can you hear me?" asked Brian Woods.

Belris emerged from the darkness and leaned against the iron bars separating their cells. His eyes projected reproach as he pointed to his mouth, shaking his head.

"I know you can't talk," said Brian, "but is anything else damaged? How are you feeling?"

Belris examined his arms and legs and gave a thumbs up.

"Good. I'm glad that there's nothing else wrong with you. Physically, at least. What Zaran did was unjust and cruel. Trust me, he'll pay for that, and many other dark deeds."

The boy stared blankly.

Brian took a deep breath.

"Since I feel that I bear some responsibility for getting you into this unfortunate situation, you might as well know the truth for my purpose at Warington Castle."

Belris nodded for Brian to go on.

"My objective was to terminate Count Zaran's dealings with the Tombspawn and ascertain the source of his power. Are you familiar with the eight runestones of Nexxathia?"

The boy gestured in the negative.

"There's a war going on right now because of them, and my family and I are in the middle of it. My brother, Ben, and his wife are on similar missions in the south to devise a plan to regain the first runestone, Frost. Unfortunately, it's guarded by Lord Mortis, a terrifying dragon. Once I fulfill my tasks here, I'm to meet up with my friend Merkresh, the brother of that nefarious warlock you met upstairs. Amfridus the Corruptor."

A mournful wail issued from a distant cell and interrupted his words. He turned back to Belris after a few moments.

"Those are the highlights. I'm here to use my abilities to discover Zaran's power and stop him. I suppose you could probably care less about all these happenings out in the world. How old did you say you were?"

The boy held up his fingers to show eighteen.

"Damn. I really am sorry that this has happened to you. Do you have any family in Warington?"

Belris nodded yes. He held up five fingers.

"You have five brothers and sisters?"

He nodded yes again.

"What about your parents?"

The boy held up one finger.

"Only one? Your mother or father?"

Belris made the letter *M* in the air with his finger.

"So, your mother takes care of you and four others? What happened to your father? Where's he?"

The boy's expression turned solemn as he lowered his gaze to the floor.

"All right, lad. That's none of my business. And you have no way of answering me anyway."

An uncomfortable silence halted their exchange.

"Well, ending up with you down here in this dungeon was not exactly part of my master plan, but all is not lost. I still have a few more cards up my sleeve. I'll be damned if I'm going to allow Zaran and his crazy uncle to throw us into that repulsive machine. How'd you like to break out of here with me? And after that, how'd you like to get some payback for what he did to you?"

Belris raised his head and nodded a definitive yes.

"Very well, my friend. As soon as that guard comes back around our way, I'm going to show you another trick."

Brian ceased his one-sided conversation and sunk back into the shadows of his cell. Instruments of death continued to cry their notes of anguish amid the clink of armor and footsteps.

"Oy! You there," said a guard. "Freak with no tongue. Show me your wretched face. Count Zaran is ready for you."

There was no response.

"Do you prefer that I come in there and drag you out like a miserable dog? I'd enjoy that, I promise."

Silence remained.

"Splendid," he said. "I could use some entertainment."

The guard took out his keys and then screamed in pain.

Brian Woods appeared from the gloom, focusing all of his mental powers upon the will of the man. Reflections of torchlight radiated from his eyes. The guard's fingertips spasmed and clutched the sides of his head. Brian motioned for Belris to reach through the bars and grab the fallen keys.

As the boy bent down and extended his arm, a doorway, hidden among the stone walls of the corridor, flung open. A pair of young men and an old gnome burst from the void and tackled the paralyzed guard.

"Get his keys," said Smitty.

"Where are they?" asked Randal.

Brian broke his focus and gaped at the newcomers' dramatic entrance. The guard recovered from his excruciating trance and wrestled with the trio. He grasped Smitty by his shoulders and threw him against the wall. The gnome and the other boy fell to the ground.

"I'm going to ravage all of you for this devilry!" cried the guard as he stood and brandished his sword.

"Watch out!" shouted Randal.

The guard swung in a wide arch. Smitty ducked and rolled to his left an instant before the blade crashed against the wall. Its steel vomited a shower of sparks upon the floor.

"Get away from my brother," said Randal as he withdrew his own weapon, a short sword with a curved blade.

"Pitiful," said the guard. "I'm going to skewer you."

"I found the keys!" exclaimed Smitty.

As Randal and the guard launched into their duel, Smitty and the gnome rushed to Belris' cell.

"Which key is it?"

"Try that one. With the skull on it."

The iron door creaked open, and Belris rushed out.

"Brother!" said Smitty as they embraced. "Are you well?"

Belris smiled but remained silent.

"What's wrong? Will you not speak?"

"They cut out his tongue," said Brian from the other cell.

Smitty regarded the man with distraught eyes. "What's this madness that you speak of? Who are you?"

"My name's Brian Woods. If you would kindly open my cell, I'd be more than happy to fill you in on the details."

"Is this true?" asked Smitty.

Belris nodded.

"Gentlemen," said the gnome. "Forgive the interruption of your family reunion, but I believe we should dispense with the small talk and assist your brother who's currently engaged in a swordfight."

Smitty diverted his attention to the melee. "He'll be just fine. Trust me."

"In that case," said Brian, "could you please let me out?"

"Very well," he replied, unlocking the door.

"Thank you," said Brian. "And who might you be?"

"My name's Smitty Llanforth, and that fellow over there fighting the guard is my older brother Randal."

"A pleasure to make your acquaintance, although I'm slightly vexed by your prison break tactics. I had this situation under control before your troupe arrived."

Randal frowned. "Sure you did."

"And you, sir?" asked Brian, addressing the gnome.

"Quinthorpe Cogswright at your service," he replied.

"Well met," said Brian. "I'm familiar with your map-making and engineering talents. You assisted my guards and me during a previous assignment near Bishops Loch."

"Yes, indeed," said Quinthorpe. "I remember that project very well. I still have one of the maps hanging in my office."

"This is all very fascinating," interrupted Smitty. "But can you please tell me what happened to Belris?"

"Of course," replied Brian. "As I mentioned, Zaran cut out his tongue."

"Yes, I can see that, but why?"

A sharp twang resounded through the dungeon as the guard's sword was cleaved in two. Randal delivered a flashing strike that carved a gaping wound into the man's abdomen. He shrieked in pain and lunged for something else to fight with.

"Watch out," said Brian.

A bucket of human waste soared through the air. Smitty ducked as it grazed his head, splashing against the wall.

"Gross," he said. "Thanks for the heads up."

"My pleasure," replied Brian.

They returned their attention to the ongoing brawl between the composed boy and the enraged man.

"I'm impressed with your brother's sword-fighting skills," said Brian. "It appears that he's about to put our friend out of his misery."

"Undoubtedly. I'm surprised that the fight has lasted this long. Randal is an accomplished duelist."

The guard was breathing in fits and continued to throw assorted items at his opponent. Randal calmly sidestepped each assault with ease.

"Had enough yet?" he asked the guard.

"Only after I kill you."

"I don't believe that's going to happen."

"Fuck your beliefs."

With a wild roar, the guard snatched up a candlestick and charged the boy. Randal parried the advance and drove his blade into the man's chest. The guard retched a mouthful of blood and dropped to the floor.

"Sorry that took so long," said Randal as he pulled his younger brother into a bear hug. "I knew you'd still be alive. I just knew it."

Belris smiled wistfully.

"Well, say something."

"He's unable to," said Smitty.

"Why the hell not?"

"That monster, Count Zaran, ripped his tongue out."

"Dear God. Why?"

"That's what I've been trying to find out from our new friend here," said Smitty.

They all stared at Brian Woods.

"It was punishment for his words to Captain Hamonet. All things considered, he was lucky to survive the encounter. The captain was not so fortunate."

"What happened to him?" asked Randal.

"You there!" shouted another guard as he drew his sword and raced toward them. "Stay where you are."

"I'll tell you. But I think we should depart first."

"This way, gents," said Quinthorpe. He pressed a stone in the wall that revealed another hidden door.

The group escaped into the darkness.

***

369

"Aren't you the Sergeant of the Guard?"

"Until this morning I was," replied Brian. "Based on my actions since then, however, I assume I've been released from those responsibilities."

"You'll be released into the Pit of Khaz and eaten alive if they catch you," said Smitty.

"I don't intend to be caught."

"We'll all be tossed into that pit if we're captured," said Quinthorpe. "Remind me again why I helped you do this?"

"Because you were our father's friend," replied Randal. "He'd have done the same for your family."

The gnome twisted his mouth in an acquiescing smile.

"Take the second right up ahead," he said.

"Where are you leading us?"

"To an exit near the South Gate."

"Unfortunately, I'll not be joining you," said Brian.

"You intend to remain in Warington?"

"I intend to complete my mission."

"And what does this mission entail?"

Brian halted and addressed the group. "To put an end to Count Zaran and his treachery. I've not pursued my goals in this castle just to tuck tail and retreat now."

"Why put an end to him?" asked Randal.

"Do you have any idea the damage he's done to the citizens of Silvarum? The destruction and misery that he and his uncle have inflicted upon your people? Or how about his dealings with the Tombspawn and Nexxathia?"

"Of course I know, but we're simple folk, sir. How do you expect us to care about the plight of other cities and foreign lands when all our waking moments are devoted to scrounging for food to survive another day? My sole responsibilities are to feed my family and keep them safe."

"No doubt. But what do you think will happen to your family once Zaran learns of your brother's escape?"

"What do you mean?" asked Randal.

Brian sighed. "At the very least, he'll round them all up and throw them in prison."

"And at the very most?"

"You know the answer to that question."

Randal rubbed his forehead and studied the faces of his two younger brothers. "How could we hope to defeat a man like Count Zaran? What do you expect from us?"

"Help me accomplish my objective by bringing his reign of corruption to an end. We stand before the final stage, gentlemen. I've labored over the past year studying his affairs and tracking down the source of his wicked power. It churns just beneath our feet."

"The Gearworks," said Quinthorpe.

"Precisely," replied Brian.

"What in the hell is that?" asked Smitty.

"It's an engine that converts life into fuel."

"Fuel for what?"

"The pyramids of Nexxathia. To power their technology and summon the Dream-King."

"This is all a little beyond my comprehension."

"Indeed," replied Brian. "You've stumbled, quite literally, upon a battle between our realm and an alien civilization. You now have the opportunity to assist me in striking the enemy. Do you choose to help our cause, or will you cover your eyes from the danger and flee into the wilderness?"

A deep hum radiated from the depths of the castle. An underworld of motors, pipes, and steam whispered to them through the stone and rock. Each man in the group lowered his gaze and pondered his fate.

Belris was the first to respond.

"What did you say?" asked Brian

The boy beat upon his chest with his fist.

"You'll join me?"

Belris nodded.

"Thank you, my friend," said Brian. "It'll be an honor to fight by your side."

"I'll come too," said Quinthorpe.

The other brothers peered down at the gnome.

"My wife may not approve," he continued, "but I'm the only person here who knows the route into The Gearworks. The corridors are confusing and full of dead-ends."

"I'm your humble servant," said Brian with a bow of his own. "Your contributions will not be forgotten."

"We're going to die down there," said Randal.

"We're going to die up here unless we fight back," said Brian. "The armies of Nexxathia are already marching out of the mountains. They'll swallow every castle and village in their path, whether we defeat Zaran or not. But if we can cut off this source of their power, we might have a chance to halt their advance. Then we can begin the plan to retake Frost."

"He speaks the truth, Randal," said Smitty. "Think about our mother and sisters."

"That's exactly what I'm thinking about. We should leave now and protect them."

"For how long?" asked Brian. "A month? A year?"

"As long as it takes."

"Then let's take the fight to Zaran. Now."

Randal contemplated his options a moment longer, then made his decision.

"I hear the wisdom in your words. Although I worry for my family, I'll help you defeat Count Zaran."

***

Quinthorpe directed his companions through tunnels and shafts. He guided them down ladders and stairwells. Every so often he pulled a tattered scroll from his jacket to study a few lines of text or a faded map. A circular eyepiece, connected to a bronze chain, allowed him to inspect the path with detail.

Stonework transformed into a mishmash of brass piping and rusted walkways. The metallic clink of their footfalls blended with the churning and grind of distant machinery. Broiling air wafted from exposed pipes and exhausts. Belris groaned as he wiped the sweat from his forehead.

"Almost there," said the gnome. "Straight ahead."

A steel hatch with a wheel handle stood before them.

Belris tapped Brian on the shoulder.

"What is it?"

The boy pressed his hands to his heart and grimaced.

"What's wrong? Are you in pain?"

He shook his head no and repeated the action.

Brian smiled, placing his hand on the boy's shoulder. "Are you trying to tell me that you're scared?"

Belris nodded.

"I'm scared too. Terrified, actually. But we're going to

make it out of this together. Just stay close to me."

The boy nodded and took a deep breath.

"Is this the door, Quinthorpe?"

"Aye. The Gearworks is just beyond."

"Very well. Open it up."

The gnome spun the wheel and pulled the door open. A colossal expanse lay beyond. Tubes and pipes stretched from the ceiling and conjoined at the center of the chamber. Gears and pistons whirled amid spouts of steam and smoke. From their elevated vantage point, the floor was hidden beneath a jungle of walkways and cart rails. Oppressive furnace fires baked their skin.

"What's the plan?" asked Quinthorpe.

"The largest machine down there in the center is the device that we need to disable. The smaller version that I saw upstairs used only a simple cable for its power source. I believe this one will be more complicated."

"Splendid," replied the gnome.

The group descended a series of corroded staircases and made their way across a riveted walkway. Every component in the foundry percolated within a symphony of metallic groans and scrapes. The mechanical locomotion engulfed the setting.

"How long have you been in Warington?" asked Brian as they negotiated between the tubing and conduits.

"My whole life," replied Quinthorpe. "I was born in Kad but moved here soon after. I was married early and became the castle's official cartographer when I was forty-three."

"Then you know what it was like when Gualterius ruled?"

"Absolutely. Life was hard, of course, but Warington still retained a sense of honor and virtue. What Zaran has turned this once respectable fortification into is a disgrace to his ancestors."

"I hope we can change that," said Brian.

The companions stood before the central machine, studying its features. Levers, knobs, and latches covered the metal skin. Pressure valves belched curiously colored smokes from between the crackle of gears and chains. Three industrial cables protruded from the sides and summit. The latter stretched to the ceiling and pulsated an ominous green.

"That one looks like the main power cable."

"Agreed," said the gnome.

"Then let's unplug it," said Brian. "Belris, make your way to the top of this contraption and have a look."

The boy nodded and climbed to the top. He inspected the cable for a moment before giving a thumbs up.

"Do you think you can detach it?" asked Brian.

He nodded.

"Then Belris, my good friend, please do us the honor of disconnecting this miserable device from our lives."

"One moment, please," said a deep voice behind them.

The companions whirled at the request. Count Zaran and Amfridus stood atop an adjacent walkway.

"Welcome to my workshop, Brian Woods. I'm pleased to see you again. What do you think you're doing?"

"I'm putting an end to your reign of corruption."

"Indeed," replied Zaran. He descended the stairs and walked toward them, Amfridus following close behind. "And that's because you believe that you can simply stroll down to my most important creation and shut it off? How bold of you."

Brian and the others remained silent.

"Do you remember when I said I'd be happy to explain the machine's purpose and origins over a cup of coffee? I'm afraid I must rescind that declaration. Truthfully, I'd prefer to give you a more suitable demonstration. Amfri, throw them in."

"At once, sir."

As the necromancer lifted his hand to summon the spell, Brian Woods executed a gambit of his own. With a burst of speed, he vaulted from the walkway and positioned himself atop a neighboring apparatus. He raised a hand and directed his thoughts at the mind of Amfridus. The man screamed in pain.

"Interesting," said Zaran as he drew his sword. "While the two of you get to know each other better, I'm going to finish the task I started this morning."

He turned his attention to Belris.

"Not so fast," said Quinthorpe.

"What are you supposed to be?" asked Count Zaran as he raised his sword. "A little gnome to the rescue? How cute."

A collision of steel and sparks disrupted Count Zaran's killing blow. Randal surged from above, parrying the strike.

"Back off," said the boy.

"Well, goodness," said the count. "This is becoming quite the party. Do you really intend to fight me, young man?"

Randal lifted his sword and stood his ground.

Zaran shrugged. "Have it your way."

With a blinding swing, the boy's head was cleaved from his body. Jets of blood erupted from the neck as the corpse fell over the railing, disappearing into the belly of machinery.

"No!" screamed Smitty.

Belris moaned in horror.

Count Zaran looked down at the petrified gnome. He was shaking uncontrollably, saturated in the boy's blood.

"I was a knight, after all," he said, thrusting the tip of his sword through Quinthorpe's right eye socket. The eyeball was still attached to the blade as it protruded from his skull.

Smitty fell to his knees and vomited.

"Stand up," said Zaran.

The boy gasped for breath, unable to respond.

"Did you actually believe you could rescue your brother and fly away with a normal life? You should have let him serve out his punishment. Not only have you sealed your own fate, but now your mother, Cynthia, and sisters, Robin and Rebecca, have all succumbed to your foolish decisions."

Smitty choked back a wrecking sob.

"Indeed," said Zaran. "They're dead now too."

The boy looked up at his executioner with hollow eyes. "Darkness has prevailed," he whispered.

Count Zaran observed his abdication and grinned. "Your anguish strengthens me."

He grasped his sword's pommel with both hands and plunged the blade through the top of Smitty's skull.

Belris discharged a blood-curdling howl from the top of the machine. He gripped the glowing cable with both hands and pulled with all his strength. Nothing happened.

"It doesn't work like that, stupid," said Zaran. "You won't be able to turn it off anyway, so come on down now and let's get this unfortunate business over with. I have things to do."

Brian Woods and Amfridus were still locked in a battle of thought. The necromancer lowered his hands from his pounding head and opened his eyes. He concentrated all his power on his opponent. Brian was thrown across the room into a pile of rusted piping. He groaned, attempting to get to his feet.

"Very impressive," said Amfridus. "I was aware that you

possessed some form of mind control, but I didn't realize the extent of your power. I'll not make that mistake again."

"Everything all right?" asked Count Zaran.

"Yes, sir. I'm going to deal with Brian Woods myself."

"Be my guest. I have the final Llanforth to silence."

Amfridus levitated from the walkway and slowly hovered to Brian's location. He reached the pile and paused, remaining a few meters in the air.

"I'm going to show you the power of Nexxathian magic," he said as he cast an orb of blue energy from his palm.

Brian raised his hand and blocked it with a force field.

"You're full of tricks," the necromancer said. "Let's try that again. I guarantee you'll not be as nimble."

"Belris!" shouted Brian. "Jump!"

Count Zaran gasped. "Amfridus, don't fire that in here!"

The necromancer released three blue orbs. Brian raised his hands and redirected the first toward the apparatus. It punctured the steel casing and burst into a massive fireball. The second was deflected at the power cable. It sheared it in half. The green light pulsated for a moment and then flickered out.

"No!" cried Count Zaran. "My machine!"

The third orb was far too powerful for Brian to defend against. It slammed against his body with violent force and sent him into a series of convulsions. He clutched his chest with one hand and reached out in agony with the other.

A firm grip caught the outstretched hand and pulled him from the burning wreckage.

"Belris, is that you?" he whispered.

The boy nodded, carrying his friend to safety.

CHAPTER XXIX

WINDOWPANE

Abigail peered beyond the windowpane and found loneliness.

Through the pouring rain, the street below her Victorian townhouse bustled with activity and motion. People thrust their umbrellas up against the deluge, while cars, buses, and scooters advanced through the city traffic. The occasional ring of a cable car sang in the distance.

The energetic scene may as well have been located on a distant planet. For Abigail Somberlain, confined to her home at the close of each school day, was not permitted to experience such a socially interactive and precarious environment.

"Abigail," said her mother from downstairs. "What are you doing up there? Is everything all right?"

The girl glanced at her bedroom door. It had been left open a crack, so her progress could be monitored.

"I'm fine," she replied.

"I haven't heard your violin for a while," exclaimed her mother. "What have you been doing?"

"Nothing," responded Abigail. "I'm just taking a break."

"No, ma'am. You may have a break once your lesson is complete. After that, I need you to help me with a few chores."

Abigail sighed and turned back to the dripping window. The constant hum of rain pelted against the gabled roofing and ivy-covered brick. The unbroken loneliness battered her soul.

She glanced down at her watch. It was 5:23 p.m. The tall man, Indiana, with the fedora and leather satchel bag, would be crossing Spruce Street soon. If he had a different umbrella today, however, she wondered if she would be able to recognize him.

Abigail blinked as she watched patiently for its gray and black stripes. There he was. Right on time, hopping over the puddles and back onto the sidewalk on Washington Street. The worn shoulder bag bounced against his raincoat.

"Hey there, Indiana," she whispered.

She peered down at the other end of the street for the old woman. Chloe, Abigail had named her, usually had a dark-blue handbag in one arm and her walking cane in the other. No doubt the bag would be replaced by an umbrella of her own.

The rain continued. Abigail watched.

At 5:33 p.m. Chloe emerged from a group of pedestrians crossing the intersection of Locust and Washington. To Abigail's dismay, the old woman carried no umbrella. She had instead elected to battle the elements with a wide-rimmed petal hat. A gray floral arrangement accentuated its satin sweatband. What a tough woman she was. Day after day she climbed that hill.

"Hello, Chloe."

Abigail turned her gaze back up toward Spruce. She had

to spot her third and final friend before she resumed her lesson. Luca, she called him, was a young man that wore a black jacket and sputtered along on a vintage Vespa. At 5:51 p.m., the pop of its motor turned the corner and barreled down Locust Street.

"See you tomorrow, Luca," she said with a small wave.

Indiana. Chloe. Luca.

Abigail had said hello to her three friends for the day. Nevertheless, the loneliness settled back in. Like always.

"If I don't hear you practicing that violin within the next ten seconds, you're going to be in big trouble, young lady."

"I am, mother," replied Abigail.

She retreated from the window and continued her lesson.

***

"Have a good evening, Abigail," said the bus driver as the double doors opened. "Get home safe now."

"I will, Mrs. Stanley," she replied. "Goodbye."

Abigail shouldered her backpack and began the short walk home. The afternoon sun beamed bright, and the sky was a crisp blue. During the summer months in San Francisco, this usually meant that a blanket of thick fog would soon roll in from the Pacific. Sure enough, as Abigail shielded her eyes and gazed down Washington Street, she could see the mist's gray fingers clawing over the outer neighborhoods.

With a turn of a key, she stepped through the front door of her townhouse and resumed her daily isolation. Abigail stood in the foyer and stared down the darkened hallway. A singular ray of light passed through the sheer curtains of the far window and fell upon the hardwood. The combination of soft light and vivid shadow created an overwhelming sadness within her.

A hand-written note, taped to the mirror, greeted her once she finally turned and dropped the keys in a bowl on the hallway table.

Abigail- Before you begin your homework and violin practice for the day, I need you to sweep and dust the upstairs hallway. Don't forget to vacuum the rugs this time. Also, tidy up the guest bedroom and your own room. Your dolls are all over the place. Don't worry about your sister's room. Dinner is in the fridge. Please do not go outside, under any circumstances. I'll be home no later than eight. -Mom

The floorboards creaked and moaned as Abigail climbed the stairs. She would skip dinner again tonight. Her stomach was just not up to it.

On the second floor, Abigail paused at her younger sister's bedroom door. A bracket and four-digit padlock had been installed so that no one could enter the room. Only her mother knew the combination, and she changed it once a week.

She stared at the lock and remembered...

***

"Abigail," said her teacher. "Would you please report to the main office. Your mother would like to speak with you."

"Yes, ma'am," she replied.

The expression on her face and the tone of the teacher's voice caused Abigail's stomach to rise into her throat. This was not going to be good.

"Please have a seat, my dear," said the office secretary.

"What's wrong?" asked Abigail.

The woman returned an awkward smile and said nothing.

Was she in trouble? Had they finally found out about the box of colored pencils she had taken from her art class? She cycled through every possible scenario that might provoke her mother to leave work to speak with her.

The office door opened, and her mother stormed in. Her face was suffused with grief and anguish. She looked broken.

"Oh, honey," she moaned. "Candace was in an accident."

The image of her sister's face filled her mind as Abigail collapsed into her mother's arms. The darkness engulfed her.

Abigail blinked away the memory and turned from her sister's bedroom door. She entered her own room and placed the violin next to her bed. Dolls all over the place? Whatever. There was only one that she had left on the floor. All the others were aligned neatly along the shelves of the two bookcases like they always were.

"Moonchild, where did you run off to?" she asked as she tossed her backpack onto the desk.

A gray and brown teddy bear sat on the windowsill. The late-afternoon sunlight accentuated the doll's tattered fur and black eyes. The stitched remnants of a silver moon were barely visible along its left breast.

"Trying to find our friends before I do?"

She picked up the bear and gently stroked a patch of its muddled fabric. Her recent repairs were not very impressive. The threads below the left leg were unraveling, and stuffing protruded from the hole that once contained the right arm.

"I know you're a mess," she replied. "I've tried to patch you up, but none of the other dolls want to give up one of their arms. Can you blame them?"

Moonchild's lifeless eyes stared back at her.

"What?" she exclaimed and shook her head. "No, ma'am. You know that's not possible. We're not allowed to go into her room, and I don't even know if he's in there anyway. Besides, what makes you think he'd want to give up his arm?"

Abigail lightly twisted one of the bear's small eyes.

"How are these things always coming loose? What do you do all day while I'm at school?"

The bear remained silent.

"Yea, you wish," she replied. "I don't believe a word of your make-believe stories, and you'd better stop talking about Candace's room. Otherwise, you're going to go right back up on that bookshelf with all the others. Is that what you want?"

She placed Moonchild back on the windowsill.

"Look at what time it is. We don't want to miss saying hello to our friends, do we?"

A commuter bus thundered down Washington as Abigail looked through the windowpane. Whispers of silky fog began to swirl along the rooftops and down the streets. The late-afternoon sun faded into a curious restlessness.

"There's Indiana," said Abigail. "And look, Moonchild, he's wearing his hat today. Wave hello."

She moved the bear's remaining arm to simulate a wave.

"Time for Chloe. I bet she has her blue handbag today. Here she comes, conquering that old hill like always."

A sudden clamor emanated from the hallway outside her door. Abigail turned her head at the sound, at the same time struggling to keep her attention on the street. She did not want to miss Luca. A moment later, the Vespa's sputtering engine turned the corner. She spun back to the window with a frown.

"Hey there, Luca. See you tomorrow."

Abigail sighed and turned to face her open door. She stared into the shadowy hallway and felt the familiar feelings saturate her mind. Loneliness. Despair. Sorrow. They borrowed their claws deep within her consciousness. The daily ritual with her inaccessible friends had come and gone in an instant, and the bleak reality of her life had returned. She stood and walked into the hallway to begin her chores.

***

"Good night, Abigail," said the bus driver.

"Bye, Mrs. Stanley," she replied. "See you tomorrow."

The fog had already enveloped the city streets as Abigail opened her front door. She placed her keys in the bowl and then stared down the hallway at the light. It was dimmer today but still exuded a paralyzing melancholy. She stared in awe.

Abigail hung up her jacket after a few quiet moments and then peeled her mother's note from the mirror.

Abigail- Since today is Thursday, I need you to wipe down the kitchen counters and take the trash bags out to the back. There are five of them this week, so you'll have to make two trips, but don't go beyond the back porch. Continue reading your book for at least an hour and then work on your violin lesson. Your first recital is coming up next month, so you need to start practicing your solo. Also, you know better than to go into your sister's room. The door was left wide open. Why would you do such a thing? Dinner is in the fridge. I'll be home by nine tonight. -Mom

She stared at the piece of paper with confusion and dread. A sudden light-headedness overwhelmed her as she felt the hairs on her neck stand on end.

Candace's door had been left open? But how? She had

not done it. She did not even know the current password.

Abigail placed her mother's note back on the foyer table and then slowly lifted her gaze to the stairwell. At the top step loomed impenetrable darkness. It was utterly devoid of light or form. Or was it? She focused her eyes into the black.

A faint glow gracefully emerged from the shadows. The delicate lines and curves of a female silhouette stepped forward.

"Abi," it whispered.

Abigail expelled a panicked breath and fell back to the hardwood. She kicked her feet forward as she hit the floor, desperately trying to push herself back along the hallway. Away from the vision and away from the cold whisper. A whisper that could only have been uttered by one person.

Her dead sister.

Candace.

***

Abigail raised her head and moaned. Why was she lying on the floor in the downstairs hallway? What had happened? What time was it?

Her entire body was sore. The bones in her neck popped as she looked down at her watch. It was 5:19 p.m.

Her friends! She could not miss them.

Abigail painfully lifted herself to a standing position and rubbed her forehead. Why were her muscles aching so much? Had she fallen down the stairs? She could not remember. Her mind felt sluggish and lethargic. A distant memory tickled the back of her mind as she struggled to regain her thoughts. The nebulous image of her sister's face intermingled with her friends from the windowpane.

"I need to get to the window."

She held tight to the railing and ascended the stairwell. A sudden chill overcame her as she passed her sister's door. Abigail resisted the curious sensation and rushed to her room.

A torrent of fog rolled along the street.

"No," she cried. "I can't see anyone!"

She checked her watch. 5:23 p.m. had come and gone.

"Indiana, please don't go."

Through the gloom, Abigail could just make out the dress shoes and high heels of the commuters as they bustled along the concrete. Their identities, however, were completely obscured. The Vespa's motor chugged down Washington Street.

"Luca, I can't see you."

Abigail began to cry into her hands and then thought of the old woman, Chloe. She had been out of turn.

The girl slowly raised her eyes back to the window and felt a breath of terror escape from her lips.

Through a break in the fog, Chloe stood stock-still on the sidewalk and stared up at Abigail. The eerie expression on the old woman's face radiated an overwhelming sense of dread. Chloe raised her right hand and held up four fingers.

Then three.

Then all five.

She raised her left hand and displayed seven.

Four. Three. Five. Seven.

The old woman shook her head as if recovering from a profound daydream. The fog devoured her, and she disappeared.

Abigail was in shock. What had she just seen? Why had Chloe stared directly at her and held up her fingers?

"The lock," whispered a soft voice.

The girl looked down at Moonchild. The bear blinked its eyes and smiled.

"Holy shit," exclaimed Abigail. "What the…?"

"Chloe just showed you the code for Candace's room."

"You're talking to me. You don't really talk."

"Clearly, I can," replied the bear. "So, are you going to go into her room again, or not?"

"Again? I haven't been in her room since she died."

"Seriously?" replied Moonchild. The bear stood up and leaned against the edge of the windowsill. "You say this every day. I wonder if you'll ever remember the things we do."

Abigail rubbed her eyes and moaned. "This isn't real. I must have hurt my head when I fell down the stairs."

"Oh, it's very real. And you didn't just fall down the stairs. Candace summoned you and then you fainted. She wants to speak with you in her room again."

"I've gone crazy," said Abigail.

"No, you haven't," replied Moonchild. "Quit being so melodramatic and go on. She's waiting for you."

The girl stood in the middle of the room in a daze. The past twelve months had become a waking nightmare. Since the death of her sister, the daily routine had been filled with unending anguish, loss, and solitude. Not only did her mother prevent her from ever leaving the confines of their home, but strange visions and sensations had materialized. The bizarre light in the downstairs hallway. The coldness as she passed her sister's door. These haunting impressions had transferred their grief into the two aspects of her life that she cherished most. Her friends through the windowpane, and her bear Moonchild.

"I can't go on like this," she said.

"You're right," replied the bear.

Abigail took a deep breath. She left her room and stood before her sister's door. The combination lock waited for her.

Four. Three. Five. Seven. Enter.

An electronic ding emitted from the device and the lock clinked open. The girl pushed open the door and entered the room. A brilliant, warm glow engulfed her mind and body, and she willingly submitted to its heavenly grasp.

***

"Abi," said Candace. "Let's go back to your room. We don't want to miss saying hello to all our friends, do we?"

"In a second," replied Abigail. "I can't find that one doll of yours. Where did you leave it?"

"The bear?"

"Yes."

"She's called Moonchild. Check under my desk."

"Here she is," said Abigail as she retrieved the bear by its right arm. "Didn't Mom get this for your birthday? Why don't you like it?"

"She did, and I do like her very much," replied Candace. "But I thought I'd give her to you."

Abigail looked at the bear lovingly.

"Thank you, but why?"

Candace smiled. "See the silver moon I stitched onto her? My bear, Marie, has a little sun on her chest and I thought that they could be best friends. Like us. Plus, you don't have any dolls of your own."

"I love it," she said. "Why did you name it Moonchild?"

"Because of her powers when the moon is full. She can turn into pure energy. And my bear can perform magical spells when the sun shines just right. When they're together, they can do all kinds of neat stuff. Like slay dragons."

"Wow, I wish I had your imagination."

"Follow me to the windowpane," said Candace, "and I'll show you how we can create some new characters from the people on the street. Then we can go outside and play with our dolls and fight monsters. Would you like to do that?"

"More than anything," replied Abigail.

CHAPTER XXX

ESCAPE FROM KADIAPHONEK

"Look. We're back to where we started," said Benjamin.

"Pretty much," replied Gothkar with a chuckle.

Waves of ruby, orange, and mulberry light washed over the city of Kadiaphonek. Marble domes and stone arches flashed with the sunset's radiance. The companions emerged from the fifth pyramid and climbed atop Clementine.

"This will actually work out nicely," said Gothkar. "Once we solve the final puzzle and retrieve the whatever-you-call-it, we can drop off our transportation. Francis is only a block away."

The beetle squirmed and expelled a high-pitched hiss.

"What the hell's her problem?" asked Benjamin. "She's been doing that all afternoon."

"I don't know. Maybe she's hungry."

"What do giant beetles eat?"

"Fruit and stuff, I think," said Gothkar.

"I have a few apples left in my backpack," said Benjamin. "Should I try and feed her some?"

"Why not?"

Benjamin carefully descended from the saddle and walked around to face her.

"Here you go. How about some of these tasty apples?" he said, extending a handful.

Clementine ingested the fruit willingly but then wobbled violently with discomfort. A deep gurgle sounded within her gut.

"That doesn't sound very good," said Gothkar, holding tight to the reigns.

"I don't think she's…"

BLUUUUURP!

Vomit jetted into Benjamin's face. Chunks of apple and threads of green slime dripped from his ears and nose.

"…feeling very well," he sputtered.

Gothkar burst into wild laughter.

"I'm glad you find this amusing," said Benjamin, wiping a handful of goop from his eyes. Bits of grass and a peculiar gelatinous substance remained in his beard.

"I'm just teasing you. I think she has a tummy ache."

"Which probably has to do with the medicine Francis mentioned, and we didn't bring it."

"Yes, that was my fault," said Gothkar. "But what do you want me to do about it now?"

"You said Francis is right down the block. We could grab her medicine and continue on to the last pyramid."

Gothkar examined the bug's restlessness from his perch. Her antennae shivered as she sneezed onto the cobblestone.

"Very well," he said. "Hop back up here."

Benjamin threw on his pack and climbed to the saddle.

Gothkar patted the top of Clementine's head. "Forgive me, girl. We'll get you all fixed up. Now, can you please take us back to your trainer?"

The beetle squeaked in the affirmative and carried them down the street. The river of insects and dinosaurs enveloped them without disruption.

"What are those?" asked Benjamin, pointing to the sky.

"Pteryxtodons, dropping off some Brol."

"No. I mean the other ones, coming right at us."

Gothkar focused on the cluster of flying reptiles. A flash of light preceded the hissing crack of gunfire.

"Oh, shit!" he yelled. "They found us!"

"Who?"

"Our friends from the coffee shop."

Gothkar pulled hard on the reigns. "Hold on, old girl. We need to make a detour."

Clementine growled in pain. With a kick of his boot, Gothkar compelled her to take to the air. The beetle's elytrons retracted to reveal a set of massive wings. The companions were soaring above the rooftops an instant later.

"Damn!" said Benjamin. "She can fly?"

"Of course. Now hang on. This will be tricky."

"You said you grew up riding these things."

"I did. Just not flying them."

"Shit," said Benjamin.

The policemen swooped down above the traffic and raced after their targets. Screams from their Pteryxtodons echoed through the narrow city streets.

"They're right behind us," shouted Benjamin.

"Not for long."

He jerked the reigns and Clementine was propelled down a narrow alleyway. Her buzzing wings snapped clotheslines and launched a cluster of colorful garments into the air. A large pair of underpants engulfed Benjamin's head.

"Ha! Use that to wipe the rest of your face."

"Shut up and focus on flying!"

Gothkar pulled the reigns again, and the beetle performed a hard-left turn. Her body shuddered against the momentum.

"I don't think she can handle much more of this."

"I know, but she has to. Otherwise, we're history."

The officers hastened their pursuit. Their beast's leathery wings thrashed and pumped the wind. They whipped around corners and bolted down cramped streets, just above the heads of the Brachiosaurus. Curious citizens gazed up at the pursuit.

Pop. Pop. Pop.

Bullets buzzed by their heads like enraged hornets.

"They're shooting at us again," said Benjamin.

"I can hear that. Hold on tight, I have an idea."

Before Benjamin had a chance to argue, Clementine took a nosedive to the street. Their stomachs dropped. Cobblestones rushed toward them but leveled off before hitting the ground. The beetle flew between stomping dinosaur legs and slithering behemoths.

"Are you crazy?" screamed Benjamin.

Their pursuers reacted quickly to the defensive maneuver and descended to the street. One of the policemen was unable to pull his Pteryxtodon out of the extreme dive. He smashed into the pavement at full speed. A pack of small bugs emerged from a sewer drain and consumed the carnage.

"Watch out!"

Gothkar steered Clementine around an enormous spider. It was black and slimy and stood three meters tall. Prickly pincers grasped as they sped by, but the beetle passed unscathed.

One of the remaining police officers was not as fortunate. As he flew by, the hungry arachnid plucked him from the saddle and swallowed him whole. The man's hands flailed in a pitiful attempt for rescue, then vanished into the monster's mouth.

"We made it," said Benjamin.

"Not quite. Look at Clementine."

The beetle was struggling. She wheezed in exhausted breaths and dropped to the street. A Stegosaurus thundered over their heads and nearly trampled them to death. A barrage of other creatures zipped by.

"Get back up there, stupid bug!" yelled Gothkar, pulling on the reigns. "We have to get above the street and out of this neighborhood."

Clementine would not budge.

"What do we do?"

"I have one more idea," said Gothkar.

"Draw a symbol?"

"Yes."

"But there's no more paper."

"I don't need paper anymore."

Gothkar took an ink pen from his shirt pocket and drew a symbol on the top of his hand. The design consisted of a straight line with two curved barbs at the end. He pulled it into the third dimension and held the form above his head.

"Viper's Tongue will get her airborne," he said, casting the glowing projectile at the beetle's rear end.

Clementine belched a deafening shriek and then launched into the sky. They shot well above the tallest monuments.

"That worked nicely," said Benjamin once they settled.

"Indeed," replied Gothkar. "Now we need to get out of here before we lose her for good."

"What's your plan?"

"The woods of Prugglehusk should be a good place to hide out for a bit. Then we can make our way to the final pyramid under the cover of darkness."

"Won't they be waiting for us there?"

"Probably, but we'll have to deal with that later. Now, let's try and find our bearings."

Gothkar and Benjamin scanned the surroundings. The sprawling vastness of Kadiaphonek lay below them. A sliver of fading light lined the distant horizon amid an ultramarine canvas of stars and moons. Thousands of twinkling torch lights and glowing windows dotted the streets. A darker area, filled with enormous trees and lined with lanterns, sat to the northeast.

"There it is," said Gothkar. He steered Clementine gently in that direction and she obliged without a fuss. Her exhaustion had subsided for the moment.

"It's so calm up here," said Benjamin.

"We can catch our breath for a moment, but we need to stay more alert from now on. They'll really be after us now."

"What will you do once I go through the gate?"

"I think that this is an appropriate time for me to relocate to Ebonthain. It's a shame that I'll have to abandon my brand-new studio, but after this job, at least I'll be level fourteen."

"That place seems like a good fit for you."

"I think so too. Remember that artist we saw down there?

The one who could walk within her oil paintings?"

Benjamin nodded.

"I'm going to see if she'll grant me an apprenticeship. I've always wanted to paint well with oil. Plus, having the ability to walk inside of them would be cool too."

"Yea, no kidding."

"And what about you, old friend? Are you ready to visit the realm of the undead again? That Gate of Frozen Mumbles, or whatever they call it, is no joke. A lot of people have gone in and never come out. Are you sure you want to do this?"

Benjamin turned to look at his friend. "Are you serious?"

"Why not come back with me for a while? You said that you and your wife were separated. What do you have to lose?"

Benjamin scoffed. "How about my kids? Or Silvarum?"

"All right, all right. I know you must go, but our recent adventures have been fun. It's been nice to see you again."

"Are you getting sentimental on me?"

"No way, man. I'm expressing myself."

"Ha! Gothkar Maalik, the mighty troll from Blackwood Forest, is finally revealing his tender side. Is that a small tear I see welling up in the corner of your eye?"

"Cut it out. You're being an asshole again."

"I remember when we were kids and…"

CRACK!

A sniper's bullet pierced Benjamin's left shoulder, sending him flying from the back of Clementine. The world turned black as he tumbled through the air and crashed through the limbs of an oak tree. His friend's cries could be heard faintly from above.

***

398

Benjamin opened his eyes. Nightfall. A battery of crickets chirped within the dense woods of Prugglehusk. The occasional song of a blackbird, or the hoot of an owl issued from the distant branches. A thick mustiness saturated the moss-covered roots.

The wound in his shoulder trembled with biting agony. It throbbed with each heartbeat. The bullet had penetrated the space between his clavicle and shoulder blade. He propped himself up with his right arm and felt for an exit wound. There was one. The marksmen's bullet had gone straight through.

"Thank God."

"How rude," said a deep and ancient voice. "You should be thanking me instead of some god. I was the one who broke your fall. You even cracked one of my limbs."

Benjamin jumped to his feet and backed up from the enormous tree trunk. His shoulder shrieked from the abrupt reaction, causing a stream of blood to run down his arm.

"Who said that? Show yourself."

"Look up," said the voice.

Benjamin's eyes traced the twisted skin and knots of the trunk until they met the mystical gaze of two glowing eyes. A wooden face, mostly concealed by lush eyebrows and a flowing beard of lichen, grinned down at the astonished man.

"You're a talking tree."

"No, sir," replied the voice. "I'm of the race Elvelon. Protectors of Prugglehusk and custodian to the Cogswright family. Ironfell Farrowmore is my name. And who are you?"

"My name's Woods. Benjamin Woods."

Ironfell grunted with approval. "A fine surname."

"Thank you."

"Now, explain yourself. Why did you fall on me?"

Benjamin looked up to the night sky. Small patches of starry sapphire gleamed through the gnarled branches. Fireflies danced within the heights of the forest canopy.

"My friend and I were flying above, and I fell."

"I heard a gunshot just before. Was that the cause?"

"It was."

Ironfell regarded the man thoughtfully. "I'm going to assume that you're in trouble with the authorities. Your wound is bleeding badly and needs to be tended to. I want to help you, but I'll first require that you tell me something about yourself. Be forewarned, Benjamin Woods, if I detect a hint of dishonesty or malice in your reply, that gunshot wound will be the least of your troubles. Is that clear?"

A batch of thick roots emerged from the mossy turf and surrounded Benjamin. Their course skin crackled with fervor.

"Very clear, sir."

"So, tell me something."

Benjamin cleared his throat. "I'm from a small village in the west called Thorndale. I traveled to Kad to visit my friend recently, his name is Gothkar and ended up helping him search for an artifact for his employer. In route to the location, we were pursued by the police."

"Why?"

"Because my friend is an artist."

Ironfell gasped. "An artist? Are you quite certain?"

"I am. Why?"

The roots relaxed their posture and sunk back into the ground. A warm light flickered from within the oak. The immense trunk and branches of Ironfell formed a pleasant home. Beneath his shaggy beard emerged a cluster of circular windows.

They illuminated the hoary texture of the bark and the shelves of mushrooms that encircled the trunk's base.

"You may come out now, Maggie," he said. "It's safe."

A circular door at the base of the tree creaked open and an old Tullek woman emerged. She stood motionless at the edge of a flagstone path.

"This is Benjamin Woods," said Ironfell. "The gentleman who disturbed your dinner party. He's friends with an artist."

Several curious faces peeked from the windows.

"I apologize for my intrusion," Benjamin said. "I fell from my transport and have been injured. I'll be on my way."

"Nonsense," replied Maggie. "You'll come inside this instant and I'll tend to that wound. End of discussion."

"Very well, ma'am. I thank you for your kindness."

Benjamin crouched as he followed the woman through the front door. A charming ambiance greeted him with affection and hospitality. They stood within a kitchen. A glowing hearth, crowned with framed portraits and other knickknacks, crackled to their left. The remainder of the space was lined with cabinets, shelves, and crowded countertops. Glass jars filled with colorful contents sat amidst fragrant herbs and spices.

Three other Tulleks sat around a large dining table.

"Say hello to Betella Broughton, Zephora Wythinghall, or Zephy as she prefers to be called, and Mr. Moonthorne. That fellow relaxing over there by the fire is called Shredder."

The three Tulleks nodded with respect.

A black cat purred apathetically.

"Good evening," said Benjamin.

"First things first," said Maggie, motioning for Benjamin to have a seat. "Let's have a look at that shoulder."

He grimaced as she carefully inspected the wounds.

"It went clean through," she said. "That's very fortunate. We'll have you fixed up in no time. Are you hurt anywhere else?"

Benjamin shrugged. "I'm not sure. I did not exactly have much time to check before I was accosted by this tree."

"I heard that," boomed Ironfell's deep voice.

The gnomes laughed.

Benjamin inspected his body for additional injuries.

"Ouch," he exclaimed as he felt around on his right leg. A gash on his calf muscle oozed blood.

"Anywhere else?" asked Maggie.

"I think that's it. A few scrapes and bruises, but I feel all right otherwise. May I have a drink of water?"

"Of course you may. Zephy, be a friend and fetch a glass for Mr. Woods. And while you're up, grab that blue bottle in the medicine cabinet and a handful of bandages from the top shelf."

"Certainly," she replied.

"Well now," continued Maggie, "I believe you're a very lucky individual, Mr. Woods. The bullet appears to have missed all major arteries, nerves, and bones. It's merely a flesh wound."

"It doesn't feel like it."

"Indeed. It'll be sore for weeks to come, but you'll at least be able to use your arm."

Zephora returned to the kitchen.

"Thank you, dear," said Maggie as she set the supplies on the table and opened a sewing kit. "This is going to sting a little."

Benjamin took a deep breath and clenched his teeth. She cleaned the wounds, stitched them up, and wrapped his arm tightly with clean bandages. A pungent, green ointment was applied to his leg wound and dressed in gauze.

"How's that?" she asked.

Benjamin extended his arm in wide circles. "Not bad at all. It's still incredibly sore, but bearable. Thank you very much."

"My pleasure."

Maggie tidied up the bits of bandage clippings and bloody cotton balls and wiped down the table. She motioned for Mr. Moonthorne to pour them each a cup of tea.

"Forgive me," she said after taking a long sip. "I believe I neglected to properly introduce myself. My name is Maggie Cogswright. Wife to the famed engineer Quinthorpe Cogswright, and organizer of this secret club that you've just stumbled upon."

"What kind of club?" asked Benjamin.

She looked at her companions, lowering her voice to a whisper. "A club for renegade artists."

CHAPTER XXXI

THE DARK FOREST

Magnolia halted her spider atop a marble pediment. "Did you see that? They shot him right out of the sky."

"Good," said Lilly. "Now he can visit his wife for real."

"This development makes our task much easier. Look at that idiotic troll. He's going to get shot too."

A battalion of Pteryxtodon-mounted policemen swarmed from the darkened streets and swept upon Gothkar, guns blazing.

"Ben!" screamed Gothkar as the beetle circled in frantic loops above the tree. "Ben, can you hear me?"

A bullet struck one of Clementine's wings, causing her to drop below the forest canopy and spin out of control. A flurry of gunshots cracked through the night sky. Tree limbs and bark exploded around Gothkar as he attempted to control their fall.

"Hang in there, girl. I'm getting us the hell out of here."

He peered down to the forest floor a final time and then

maneuvered the beetle from the woods of Prugglehusk. The flock of policemen raced after him.

Magnolia and Lilly watched from their perch as Gothkar melted into the maze of city streets and disappeared.

"What's our next move?" asked Lilly.

"Clearly, our artistic friend will be occupied for the near future. We still need the device, so I want you to continue on to the final pyramid and retrieve it. Even if that buffoon manages to evade the police and make his way to you, I'm sure you can handle him. But be mindful of his little drawing tricks."

"And what about you?"

"I'll depart for Blackwood Forest. Trelinia and the girls will be feeling overly confident because of their new alliance and abilities. I'll break their courage with a surprise of my own. Benjamin Woods is not the only person who can see those who have crossed over."

"You successfully completed the ritual?"

"I did indeed, and I cannot wait to see their shocked expressions when I intercept them."

"I wish I could be there to see," said Lilly.

"You'll hear all about it once we meet back up at the castle. Now, let's take care of this Intensitron matter."

"Will you be leaving for Blackwood at once?"

"I was, but I think I'll remain in Kad for one more evening. I'll stay with Hallie at the harbor."

"Sounds splendid," said Lilly. "Tell her I said hello."

"I certainly will."

"May I make a final request before you go?"

"Of course."

"Do you mind if I keep this spider since I'm to remain in

Kad? It's so much easier to maneuver the streets with her."

Magnolia laughed. "Of course. It would be better for me to travel on foot anyway. She's all yours."

"Thank you, friend. Good luck on your journey."

"You too."

***

Magnolia awoke the next morning to a burst of sunlight through her bedroom window. Golden rays penetrated the sheer curtains and fell upon the hardwood floor. She sprang from bed with an invigorated sense of energy and stepped to the window.

"What a beautiful day this will be," she said as she swept the curtains aside, pushing open the double-paned window.

The grand harbor of Kadiaphonek greeted her. Galleons, sloops, and frigates crowded the gentle waters, while shopkeepers and tenacious customers busied themselves along the docks. The scent of wood smoke drifted among gabled rooftops and ivy-covered brick. Seagulls and pelicans swooped between mooring posts and ship masts. She took a deep breath of the morning air.

"The first order of business is coffee."

Magnolia threw on her clothes and cloak and bundled her belongings into her pack. She made the bed and went downstairs. Wooden steps creaked with each footfall.

"Out here, Magnolia."

She stepped out onto a balcony that overlooked the harbor. Her friend Hallie sipped from a mug of coffee. Another mug, steaming hot, sat on a table next to her.

"That's a character trait I hope you never lose," she said as she dropped her bag to the deck and sat down.

"I heard you rustling around up there and figured you could use a cup before you headed out."

"Thank you, I needed this," she said, taking a long sip. "Wow, what a wonderful blend this is."

"You know what they say about Kad."

"It has the best coffee in the land."

They chuckled.

"Did you sleep well?" asked Hallie.

"I did, thank you. The air on this side of town is always so refreshing. You really have it made out here."

"I'm not sure I have it made, but I can say that I love living by the water. I spent far too many years in the city. It's moments like this that make me appreciate retirement."

"I'll drink to that," replied Magnolia.

A siege of herons squawked as they flew by the balcony.

"Where are you headed to this time?" asked Hallie.

"I have some business in Blackwood."

"Ha! There's only one sort of business performed in that place. Dark business. What are you up to now?"

"Retirement has made you sleepy," said Magnolia. "You should know exactly what sort of dark deeds I'm up to. I learned just about everything from you."

"Oh, that business," said Hallie with a long sigh. "Is it that time again already? I admit that I've lost interest in following that state of affairs. How many runestones do we have this time around?"

"All of them."

"Really? Then what's the problem?"

"Do you remember the Woods family?"

"How could I forget them?"

"Their children are teenagers now and are attempting to retrieve the Rune of Frost as we speak. Their friends are helping them too. Even my nephew Frederick is with them."

"That's not surprising."

"These friends are different. They're from Earth."

Hallie turned to her friend with a look of dismay.

"What do you mean?"

"There are two ghosts from Earth that have joined up with that wretched Woods woman, Trelinia."

"Trelinia is dead?" asked Hallie. "Dear Lord, I really am out of the loop. What happened to her?"

"Lilly Roberts did away with her and took the book."

"The one with all those transcripts and puzzles?"

"Yes, and now Trelinia has recruited a couple of recently deceased teenage girls to help her and her children. The lot of them intend to fight the dragon and take back the runestone."

"Very interesting," said Hallie. "Can they do it?"

Magnolia huffed and folded her arms. "Of course not."

"Your response does not sound very confident."

"They cannot possibly defeat a dragon like Lord Mortis, or any of the other rune protectors for that matter. It's just…"

"Just what?"

"There's a peculiar energy surrounding this group that's different from before. I cannot put my finger on it yet, but they possess a strength that concerns me."

"Their parents succeeded thirty years ago, didn't they have similar energy?" asked Hallie.

"They had that old fool, Merkresh."

"Is that troublemaker still around?"

"Yes. He's marching those band of brats up to Kad."

Hallie sighed. "Will he ever die?"

Magnolia shrugged and took another sip of coffee. A bell rang down in the docks as one of the massive galleons pulled out of the harbor. Its colorful flags flapped in the wind.

"Although I prefer to distinguish myself as experienced rather than elderly, I concede that I'm in no shape to battle any of these characters this time around."

"You are indeed experienced," said Magnolia.

"However, I can certainly assist your efforts from afar."

"That would be greatly appreciated."

"Wait here a moment," said Hallie as she went inside.

Magnolia stared across the river to the darkened tree line of Blackwood Forest. Its twisted bows beckoned for her submission. Dark deeds indeed. That place contained horrific memories that even she had not reconciled. Nevertheless, she needed to summon its power once again. The Woods children and their compatriots would not be allowed to exploit the magic of the runestones. They would yield, or they would die.

"Here we are," said Hallie, returning to the balcony.

"What's that?"

"A gift for a dear friend. This is a summoning scroll."

"Fabulous," said Magnolia. "It's been ages since I've used one. How did you acquire it?"

"I've been holding on to this for years. A member of our coven, Adeline Rathmore, I believe was her name, gave me this during a mission to the Shadow Mountains."

Magnolia took the scroll and unrolled it. Lines of symbols and flowing script filled the faded parchment.

"An undead guardian?" she gasped. "What a gift."

"You're welcome," said Hallie. "I hope that this will come

in handy when you encounter Trelinia and her ghosts."

"I have no doubt," said Magnolia, inspecting the scroll further. "This line at the bottom says that I have to perform the summoning at a cemetery."

"If you're headed south to intercept them before they reach Lord Mortis' castle, then you can stop by Maple Hill on the way. There's a small cemetery near a watchtower. Just keep an eye out for the groundskeeper. Jarvis, I think he's called."

"I remember that place."

Magnolia looked up and smiled at her mentor. "This is a wonderful gesture," she said. "Thank you."

"My pleasure," replied Hallie. "With a little help from this demon, you may be able to kill them without a fight."

"That would be nice."

"Would you like me to refill your cup?"

Magnolia tucked the scroll into her bag and stood. "Sadly, I must be going. But this was a delightful visit and I'm so happy that we were able to catch up."

"Be sure to stop by again on your return trip."

"I promise I will."

***

"I think it's funny that we still have to sleep in tents," said Abigail. "Even though we're ghosts."

"Dimensions," said Penelope as she folded their tent and stuffed it into her backpack. "We're in a different dimension now. We're only ghosts when compared to those other places."

"I got it, but it still seems weird to me."

"Are you girls hungry for breakfast?" asked Trelinia.

"Definitely," replied Abigail. "What do dead girls from another dimension eat around here?"

Penelope laughed. "Good one, Abi."

"Let's see," said Trelinia, picking through her backpack. "I have a rabbit from yesterday's catch, some purple dead-nettles, and a bundle of cattail roots."

"I love those things," said Abigail.

"Do we have any coffee left?" asked Penelope.

"I'm afraid not, but I can brew some green tea."

Trelinia, Abigail, and Penelope spread a quilt in the center of a luminous forest glade. Feathery ferns and thick beds of moss-covered the soft ground. Groups of dragonflies buzzed between trees and occasionally paused to inspect the newcomers.

"What are we doing today?" asked Abigail.

"We're continuing on through Blackwood until we reach the eastern side. There's a watchtower near a junction of three roads. Roger, Marie, and Mckenzie will meet us there."

"They won't be able to see us, though."

"No, they won't."

"Then how are we supposed to help them?"

"Penny, do you remember my husband?" asked Trelinia.

"Benjamin. Of course, I do."

"He's on his way here right now."

"What do you mean by here?" asked Abigail.

"He has the ability to cross over into our dimension. His part of the plan was to retrieve passages from the Novemgradus, meet with Penny in the Tombworld, and travel through the forest to link up with my children at the watchtower."

"But now you and I are here too," said Abigail.

"Exactly. We were never part of this plan."

"Is that a bad thing?"

"I guess it depends on how you look at it," said Trelinia. "I was supposed to lead my children, but I was murdered by a woman called Lilly Roberts. Now I have no idea what happened to them or if they'll even make it to the watchtower. I do recall that my friend Merkresh was by my side when I passed, so I still have hope that he's been guiding them."

"The three of us are together now," replied Penelope. "I think that's a good thing."

"Exactly my point," said Trelinia. "From that perspective, this part of the plan has grown stronger because of our combined abilities. We'll be able to overcome more obstacles as a group than we could have if we'd laid the burden on one person."

Abigail smiled at Penelope.

"There's another problem," said Trelinia.

"What's that?"

"Ben may still not know that I've died."

"Oh no," said Penelope.

"And he'll realize that once he sees you with us?"

"Yes," she replied, lowering her gaze.

Abigail extended a consoling hand.

Trelinia looked up and smiled. "This is the path that has been laid out for me. Many occurrences in life result from circumstances beyond our control. I could choose to withdraw into my grief, or I can accept this fate and use my energy to embrace our new relationship. I hope that you two want that."

"We do," replied Penelope.

Abigail nodded furiously.

"Then I'll try my best," said Trelinia, standing. "But I'll need your help as well. Reuniting with Ben in this form is going to be heartbreaking for both of us. Especially since we'd been separated for a year, but recently decided to try and make things work again. Then all of this madness happened."

"We'll be there for you, Trelinia," said Abigail. "Just let us know how we can bring you comfort."

"Talking about it helps," she replied. "Will you listen to what I have to say while we travel?"

"You know we will."

***

A gentle rain tapped upon the canopy leaves as they made their way along a dirt road. Robins and blackcaps chatted to one another, while bees hummed amidst dense patches of sunflowers. The sunshine had given way to a somber overcast.

"Did you end up going on a date, or not?"

"We did," replied Trelinia.

"And what happened? Where did he take you?"

"Back in Thorndale stands a huge elm tree that overlooks the entire village. We used to play on it when we were kids, and it's the place that Ben first proposed to me. He took me there again for our most recent date. The sun was setting as we reached the tree at the top of the hill. He'd spent the whole afternoon setting up a picnic for us. Complete with candles and a bottle of red wine. We watched the sun fall behind the mountains and talked together for hours."

"Wow," said Penelope. "That's beautiful."

"It was one of the happiest moments of my life."

"Trelinia," said Abigail after a few silent minutes.

"Yes?"

"You've explained to me that we now exist in a different dimension than your children and husband."

"That's correct."

"Yet your husband conveniently has the ability to pass into our dimension and interact with you. So, does it even really matter that you've died? Why couldn't you continue with your relationship in this new form?"

"I suppose we could, but my children will never see their mother again. To them, I really am dead."

"I know," said Abigail. "I just mean that maybe, out of all of this misery, there's still a chance that the two of you could be together. Even if it's a rather strange relationship."

"If we did, it would only be temporary."

"Why?"

"Because the three of us will not last forever in this new place. At some point, just like your mother and sister, we'll cross over into the next stage."

"But Trelinia," said Abigail, "even before we died, in the previous dimension, our existence was never guaranteed. Weren't we temporary there as well? Yet that never stopped anyone from falling in love. We act within the time that we have."

Trelinia stopped walking and stared at the girl. "As I said before, you are wise beyond your years, Abigail. I'm starting to think that I need your wisdom more than you need mine."

"I seriously doubt that."

"Come on," said Trelinia. "Let's keep moving a while longer before this rain overwhelms us. Dark clouds approach."

The gentle taps of rain soon turned into a deluge. Puddles cluttered the dirt road, with streams of murky water flowing along its shoulders. The crack of lightning pulsated above.

"Where did this storm come from?" asked Penelope. "It was perfectly sunny a few minutes ago."

"I don't know," replied Trelinia.

"I think we should find shelter."

"Good idea."

"Look over there," said Abigail. "That hollowed-out oak should be a good enough hiding place."

"As long as it doesn't get struck by lightning."

"We have to risk it," said Trelinia. "Run for it!"

The companions splashed through the dense puddles and sprinted toward the tree. Deep booms of thunder filled their ears amid the torrential downpour. Penelope threw up her hood and leapt over the edge of the road. They sputtered and huffed as they crammed themselves into the belly of the tree.

"The wind is crazy," said Abigail. "Look at how all the trees are bending! They're going to snap."

"I wish I could see," said Penelope.

"Give her some room, Abi, and let her have a look."

Abigail shifted, allowing Penny to move forward.

"Wow," she said, peering into the howling chaos. "This is the strongest storm I've ever seen."

A shape within the distant trees caught her attention.

"What was that?" she yelled.

"What was what?"

"I just saw something move between the trees."

"Everything is moving," said Abigail. "It's insane."

"No," replied Penelope. "I saw a person."

Trelinia and Abigail frowned.

"That's not possible. No one could walk in that."

"Look!" cried Penelope. "It moved again. It's a woman."

"Stop it," said Abigail. "You're scaring me."

Trelinia struggled to locate the figure, but blinding sheets of rain and blowing debris obscured her view. Through a brief lull in the inundation, her eyes locked onto a murky shape. A woman stood perfectly still amidst the driving wind and water. She stared in their direction.

"Penny speaks the truth," said Trelinia.

"But how?" asked Abigail with a shaken voice. "She'd have to be in our dimension to see us, right?"

Thunder erupted through the forest. A bolt of lightning exploded in the tree next to the woman. The flash of light illuminated her face, providing Trelinia a glimpse.

"Oh no," she gasped. "We may be in trouble."

Before either girl had a chance to respond, a massive hand burst through the side of the oak and pulled Penelope into the storm. Wind and bark choked the interior of the tree. Trelinia and Abigail were forced to flee its safety.

"Wait!" cried Abigail, collapsing to the sodden ground. Her white dress was spattered with mud.

"Stay close to me," said Trelinia. "Where's Penny?"

"I don't know!"

Penelope gasped for breath as she raised herself out of the muck. A menacing figure stood over her. It inhaled in gurgles and exhaled with the clarity of broken glass. A blaze of lightning revealed rotted flesh dripping from its face and extremities. Maggots slithered within decomposed muscle and marrow. The abomination glared down at the girl with dead eyes.

Penelope screamed and attempted to crawl away on her hands and knees. The creature grasped her by the leg and pulled. Its grip was merciless. The popping of tendons sent a blast of pain through her body. Her ankle bones were crushed as she was launched into the side of a tree.

Abigail and Trelinia scrambled to Penelope. They leapt over the remains of the hollowed-out oak and then were stopped in their tracks. The woman stood before them.

"Magnolia," said Trelinia.

"Hello again. Surprised to see me?"

"Stop this now."

"I'm afraid not."

She raised her wand and shot a glowing orb into Abigail's chest. The girl flew backward, splashing into the water.

Trelinia transformed into her eagle form and took off into the sky. The heavy rain impeded her ascent, and she careened into the limbs of a nearby tree.

"That type of attack will not be successful," Magnolia said. "Why do you think I created this storm?"

Abigail spit up a mouthful of muddy water and got to her feet. Her chest ached but was otherwise undamaged. She saw the golden eagle in the tree and knew what she had to do.

She transformed.

An instantaneous calm overwhelmed her perception. The howling wind and rain persisted but made no sound within her new perspective. The forest became alive with light and energy. She could see tendrils of life radiate through the trees' limbs and roots. Magnetic fields expanded like lungs with each burst of the lightning's electrostatic discharge. The landscape before her was crystal clear.

Magnolia prepared to fire upon Trelinia, while the undead horror sunk its teeth into Penelope's calf. Instead of gushing blood, Abigail could visualize the thermal energy of the flesh as it was chewed and digested. The creature moaned with delight and prepared to finish off the unconscious girl.

Abigail reacted instinctively. The boundless measure of her consciousness allowed her to manipulate the surrounding energy. The trees broadcast their consent, and she instructed them to attack. Furious limbs crashed upon the creature and sent it flying. Its decomposed carcass splattered against the trunk of an oak, disintegrating into a doughy mess.

"No!" yelled Magnolia, blasting the trees with her wand.

The concussions sent severed limbs and husks of bark into the air. Tongues of flame consumed several trees but were quickly extinguished by the rain. An infuriated groan reverberated through the landscape, and the forest besieged Magnolia.

Trelinia descended from the tree with a furious cry. Her massive talons extended for the attack. Magnolia turned at the onslaught but was too late. The eagle's claws sank into her upper back and tore off a patch of skin and muscle.

Magnolia screamed in agony. She fired wildly into the air and then paused to consider her next move. Her guardian was destroyed, the forest itself was about to rip her to pieces, and one of the girls apparently had the ability to transform into pure energy. Even the storm had conspired against her.

"Defeated by my own design," she said.

As the grasping bows of Blackwood Forest reached for her, Magnolia disappeared with a wave of her wand.

The storm evaporated an instant later. Sunshine washed through the canopy, reflecting off the saturated ground. The chirping of birds filled the woods once again.

"Penny's been hurt bad," cried Abigail as she reverted to her human form.

Trelinia disembarked and landed next to the girls. "We must stop the bleeding," she said.

"What should I do?" asked Abigail.

"Help me lift her out of this water."

They carried Penelope to a moss-covered log and pulled her dress up to inspect the damage. Trelinia tore off a section of her petticoat and applied pressure to the wound.

"My ankle," moaned Penelope.

"Not to worry," said Trelinia. "I'll be able to mend this in no time. Abi, we passed a willow tree farther back along the path. Please run to it and gather some of its bark."

"What will it do?"

"Relieve the pain. Now hurry."

Abigail jumped up and sprinted back down the trail. Her combat boots kicked up mud and water as she ran.

"What happened?" asked Penelope.

"We were attacked by a powerful enemy," said Trelinia. "A witch called Magnolia Jinglewort."

"But how could she see us? Is she a ghost too?"

"I don't think so. Some have the ability to interact with our dimension. Apparently, she's succeeded in doing just that."

"Will she come back for us?" asked Penelope.

"I'm sure of it, and next time she'll bring more help than a decomposed zombie. But there's something even more important that Magnolia succeeded with."

"What's that?"

"Realizing the strength of our group."

CHAPTER XXXII

MYSTIC PLAINS

"Fredrick!" screamed Mckenzie.

The river's surface was calm. Only the destroyed bridge and its flotsam remained. All other traces of the battle with the serpent had dissipated into a foamy stillness.

"He's dead," she cried. "That thing ate him whole."

The others stood on the shore in a daze. A dreadful sense of helplessness swept across their faces. Tears welled in Roger's eyes, yet he found himself unable to grieve or utter a word. The thought of his lifelong friend being killed in front of him was too much for his mind to comprehend. He stared silently into the horizon as his sister wept beside him.

"A dark day this is," said Merkresh.

Marie and Arina knelt by Mckenzie and tried to provide solace. The three friends held on to each other while Marie gently stroked her sister's hair to calm her shaking.

"He was always so nice to me," said Mckenzie. "And all I ever did was tease him."

"It wasn't your fault," replied Marie.

"He saved my life," continued Mckenzie. "Even after all my rejections, he still jumped in and saved me."

"Then let's honor him by his final act," said Merkresh. "A brave, young soul who sacrificed himself for our quest."

Mckenzie broke down at the finality of the statement.

No other eulogy or memorial was spoken. The old man placed his hand on Roger's shoulder and joined the teenagers in their silent bereavement.

BEEP! BEEP! BEEP!

Roger looked up, attempting to focus on the location of the distant sounds. He wiped his eyes and sniffled.

BEEP! BEEP!

It was the mechanical spider. He was much farther down the shore, jumping up and down hysterically.

"What now?" moaned Merkresh.

"It's Click!" cried Roger.

"That's his proximity alarm again."

Roger felt his heart skip a beat. *Could it be?* Blood rushed to his head with the thought of the possibility. He scrambled to put on his mask and switch on the magnification.

"What's wrong?" asked Arina, looking down the shore.

"There's something by Click," said Roger. "A body."

"Is it him?" asked Mckenzie.

"Let's find out," replied Merkresh.

The companions sprinted down the shore toward the jumping spider. Their boots kicked up heaps of sand, and a flock of seagulls scattered from their intensity.

"It *is* Frederick," said Roger, breathing in fits.

"Oh God," said Mckenzie. "He's chewed to pieces."

"No," replied Merkresh. "He lives! Roll him over."

Roger bent down and gently turned Frederick onto his back. Multiple lacerations covered his upper-body and arm, but his chest still fluttered with life. The boy moaned and sat up.

"Freddie!" they all cried.

He coughed up a mouthful of muddy water and inspected his wounds. "Please stop calling me that."

Mckenzie fell to her knees and embraced him.

"Careful!" he exclaimed. "It still hurts."

"Give him some room," said the old man.

Mckenzie kissed him on the forehead. "I'm so happy that you're alive."

"What happened to you?" asked Merkresh.

"That creature chewed on me for a second and then spit me right out."

"It was all my fault," said Mckenzie.

"No, you're the reason it spit me out."

"What?"

Frederick held up his arm. *His purple arm.*

"Whatever concoction you used to turn my arm purple, induced a violent reaction with that serpent. As soon as it bit into my arm, it freaked and spit me out. You saved my life."

Merkresh laughed. "Mckenzie, you've successfully devised an impressive serpent repellent. I wonder, however, if I can now call upon your talents for actual healing. Frederick's wounds are still serious and need to be cared for immediately."

"Of course, Merkresh," she replied. "I've really improved over the past month. I'll do whatever it takes to help him."

"Excellent. Then please run into the forest and fetch the following ingredients. Dwarf Everlast, chamomile, and a handful of pine needles. Do you know what all those look like?"

"I do."

"Very good. Marie, go with her and help."

The two girls ran off into the woods.

"Roger," said the old man. "Please get a fire started and then help me and Arina clean Frederick's wounds."

"Yes, sir," replied the boy.

Each member of the company busied themselves with the task at hand. Even Click helped with gathering wood for the fire.

***

"Ouch!" cried Frederick.

"Hold still," said Arina. "This is the last one."

Mckenzie returned from gathering the ingredients. She brewed a healing potion as well as a topical ointment. Arina, with the oversight of Merkresh, had cleaned and stitched each of the lacerations. Frederick sat next to the fire, biting his lip as the needle poked his skin for the final time.

"There," said Arina. "Not too bad if I do say so."

"Not bad indeed," exclaimed Merkresh. "Where'd you learn to stitch like that?"

"My mother taught me when I was little."

"Impressive work," replied the old man. "Freddie, how are you feeling?"

"You mean Frederick."

"Yes, of course. Frederick, how do you feel?"

"Like I've been chewed up by a giant sea monster."

"Are you ready to try and stand?"

"I think so," he said as he slowly pushed himself to his feet. "Oh, that doesn't feel very good."

"What is it?"

"My legs feel like jelly and my chest is still burning."

"We'll get you proper treatment once we reach Kad. Other than the aches and pains, do you feel like you can carry on unassisted for the remainder of the journey?"

"I should be able to make it on my own, but please don't ask me to run a marathon on the way."

Merkresh chuckled. "I don't anticipate any more surprises until we reach the city."

"Famous last words," mumbled Roger.

"If everyone is ready then, I think we should depart for Kad forthwith," said the old man.

"Sounds good to me," said Frederick. "I hope I never lay eyes on this stupid river again."

"Unfortunately, we still have to cross another section."

The boy rolled his eyes and groaned.

The company gathered their belongings, extinguished the fire, and made their way to the edge of the forest. Click pattered along the shore and hopped up and down at the mouth of the trail. The afternoon sunlight glinted off his metallic edges.

"What's he doing?" asked Marie.

"I don't know," said the old man as he walked over to the spider. "What are you going on about, little friend?"

Click rose up on his hind legs and scratched at the air.

"He's trying to tell us something," said Mckenzie.

"One second," said Roger. "The mask is able to translate what he's saying, but I'm having trouble understanding it."

"If he sensed that we were in danger, he's programmed to sound his alarm," replied Merkresh.

"Maybe he's trying to warn us about something, but being quiet about it," said Arina.

At that moment, a twig snapped in the nearby trees. They turned to the sound, weapons ready.

"Come out of there," exclaimed the old man with a demanding tone. "Slowly."

After a few tense moments of silence, a man and a boy walked out of the underbrush. They were both human, at least in appearance. The boy was about ten years old and the man was in his late thirties. He wore a large top hat, similar to the one that Roger had on.

"Greetings," said the man.

"Good afternoon," replied Merkresh. "Who are you and why were you sneaking up on us?"

"Many apologies. My son and I did not intend to sneak. We're searching for a group of travelers that are heading to Kad. We bring urgent news. My name's Blazrug and this is Eddie."

The boy gave a quick nod.

"A pleasure to make your acquaintance. I'm Merkresh. My friends and I are indeed traveling to Kad, but so are many other folk. How do you know we're the group you seek?"

"Fair question," replied Blazrug. "My associate, Dorothy Tompkins, dispatched us to intercept a group of travelers that consisted of an old man with a long beard, two boys around the age of fourteen, three teenage girls, and a mechanical spider. I agree that there are probably many other groups traveling to Kad today, however, I'd argue that not many of them match your group's characteristics."

"Indeed," said Merkresh. "Dot is a dear friend of mine. If you're truly her associate, then you'll be able to tell me the secret passphrase of Ebonthain."

"Taters and onions," replied Blazrug without hesitation.

"Correct."

"Taters and onions?" whispered Frederick. "What kind of rubbish is that and who are these rascals?"

Roger shrugged.

"We're shapeshifters, young man," said Blazrug. "From the great city of Ebonthain."

The man took off his top hat and bowed. A human hand protruded from the top of his bald head. Its fingers flexed and twitched.

"Whoa," gasped Frederick.

The other teenagers cringed at the spectacle.

"Very well," said Merkresh. "As you can see, my young friend here has been injured and we're in haste to provide him suitable medical care. Relay your news directly so that we may be on our way to the city."

"Yes, sir," said Blazrug. "But first, I may be able to help the young man. I'm also a master healer."

Mckenzie looked at Frederick with wide eyes.

"Are you comfortable with Blazrug's offer?" Merkresh asked Frederick.

"Of course," said the boy. "Anything to help this pain."

"But will you accept care from a rascal?" asked Blazrug.

"I apologize for that comment."

"Think nothing of it. Now hold still."

Blazrug reached up and detached the hand from his head. He approached the boy, gently sweeping it over each of the bandaged lacerations. A faint glow radiated from the tips of the wiggling fingers.

"It tickles," said Frederick, laughing.

"Remove the gauze and have a look," said Blazrug.

Frederick brushed away the bandages and stitching. They fell from his chest to reveal undamaged flesh and muscle. The wounds were completely healed.

"Wow," said the boy, touching the smooth skin. "They're gone and there's no more pain. How'd you do that?"

Blazrug smiled. "Through decades of training."

"So much for my pitiful stitching efforts," said Arina.

"Nonsense," replied Merkresh. "You did a fantastic job, just like the rest of the group. The important thing now is that the lad is all healed up and able to continue."

Mckenzie hugged Frederick. "Does this still hurt?"

"Not at all," said the boy, pulling her closer.

Merkresh dramatically cleared his throat. "When the two of you have finished, I'd like to hear Blazrug's news."

Mckenzie released her grip. Frederick offered his open palm and she clutched it willingly.

Marie observed the passion in her sister's eyes.

"Your news please," said Merkresh to Blazrug.

"There's been a battle at Warington Castle."

"With the Nexxathians again?"

"No. With Brian Woods and Count Zaran."

"Uncle Brian?" gasped Marie.

Blazrug turned to the girl and nodded. "It appears that way, young lady. According to one of our scouts that returned this morning, your uncle and another man have been arrested and thrown in the dungeon."

"Arrested for what?" asked Merkresh.

"We don't know, but they tried to escape."

"Oh no," said Roger.

"Your instincts are correct, lad. There was an altercation during their flight, and several people were slain. Our scouts narrowly escaped the chaos."

"Is Uncle Brian dead?" asked Marie.

"We don't know that either. It's why I was dispatched to find you. Your group is strong. We understand that you're traveling to Kad to seek the counsel of the Shadowkuur, but Dot has requested that you alter your plan and head for Warington directly. They need your help."

"We cannot go," said Merkresh with a stern voice.

Roger breathed a sigh of relief.

"But I can," continued the old man.

The teenagers stared up at him with astonishment.

"You're leaving us?" asked Roger.

"It's required. If Brian has failed his task, then I must confront Count Zaran myself. The entirety of our plan depends on the disruption of his wicked enterprise."

"Then why can't we go with you?" asked Marie.

"Because the three of you have a dragon to fight."

Mckenzie looked at Frederick and felt her heart race.

"What about Arina and Frederick?" asked Roger.

"They will continue on to Kad as originally planned. The final stage of our quest must be performed by the three of you."

"We're not ready to go on alone," said Mckenzie.

"Yes, you are," Merkresh replied. "Consider all that you've accomplished so far. You've defended your home against invaders, fought with wolves, and defeated a sea serpent. Not to mention the courage it took to leave the safety of your village for the first time. You're ready to face whatever lies ahead."

The teenagers lowered their heads in apprehensive silence. The murmur of the river and the chirps of finches filled the void.

Mckenzie gripped Frederick's hand after a moment and peered into his eyes. "Will you wait for me in Kad until I return?"

"Of course. And I'll think of nothing else."

The boy leaned forward and gently kissed her on the forehead. Both of their faces turned a cardinal red.

"Well now," said Merkresh. "I'm sorry that this surprising news has forced our untimely departure, but we must say our goodbyes in haste and be on our way. The afternoon tires."

"Good luck," said Arina as she hugged the sisters in turn. "I'll expect you to look me up again once you return to Kad so that I can take you on that tour of Moonlight Avenue."

"You can count on it," replied Marie with a smile.

"So long, Roger the dragon slayer," said Frederick.

"Yea, right. Like I know what I'm doing."

The boys embraced, nodding in solidarity.

"Thank you for your assistance you two," said Merkresh.

"What did we do?" asked Arina.

"A great deal. We've learned of the role your parents have played in this conflict. I wouldn't be surprised if I learn more of their whereabouts once I reach Warington."

"Really? Please try to find them if you can."

"I'll do my best."

The old man turned to shake Blazrug's hand. "Thank you for your assistance, even if your news is the last thing in the world I wanted to hear."

"I understand, but I'll try to make it up to you by safely guiding your friends back to Kad. I'm sure I can persuade the Shadowkuur to provide them asylum."

"I appreciate that."

With a heavy exhale, Merkresh turned to the company and studied each of their confused faces.

"You've made it this far. Be proud of yourself. In spite of the losses you've suffered along the way, you're all tougher for it. Take that experience with you wherever your path now leads and use it to your advantage. Each of you is stronger than you could ever imagine."

The teenagers hugged one another a final time, then split into groups. Blazrug, Eddie, Arina, and Frederick stepped onto the trail and proceeded into the northern woods. Before their forms disappeared within the haze, Frederick turned and blew a kiss to Mckenzie.

"Very well," sighed Merkresh. "I must be on my way."

"What do we do now?" asked Marie.

"You must travel east. Within a day's hike, you'll reach the main road through Blackwood Forest. Follow it until you reach a great watchtower. Just beyond that, you'll be able to see the castle of Lord Mortis."

"And then?" asked Roger.

"And then kill the dragon and retrieve Frost."

"Because that's such an easy task."

"It's the task that's been assigned to you, easy or not."

"Will we ever see you again?" asked Mckenzie.

"Of course. Barring any other misfortunes, I'll reconnect with you again at the watchtower once I find Brian and discern the fate of Count Zaran."

"I hope he's all right," said Roger.

"Let me worry about him. The three of you need to stay focused on this next battle."

A high-pitched squawk emanated next to them.

"You mean four," laughed Roger.

"Of course," said Merkresh. "I'm terribly sorry to have omitted the importance of your function in this final act. Please watch over our friends, Click, and keep them out of trouble. Farewell for now!"

The old man turned without another word and vanished into the forest. The teenagers stood together on the river's edge as the afternoon sun sank into the treetops. Flecks of orange and purple light glinted off the face of the churning river.

"Well," said Roger, "I guess we should get going."

CHAPTER XXXIII

RUMINATE

Maggie held the torch above her head and pointed to the end of the corridor. "The door is right up here."

Tendrils of ancient tree roots poked through the damp ceiling. Amid the darkness, moisture dripped from stalactites and limestone deposits. A delicate moldiness filled the air.

Benjamin followed close behind, rubbing his shoulder.

"How's it feeling?" she asked. "Still sore?"

"A little," he said, grimacing. "I'll be all right."

"That's the spirit."

"How'd you learn about this cave?" he asked.

"My art club has been using its tunnels to travel between sanctuaries. We're an underground movement, literally. A year or so ago, while exploring some new corridors, we happened upon this door that leads right up to the sixth pyramid. The Sanctum of Saeglosos it's called. Apparently, there are a bunch of tombs and burial vaults within its depths. All the previous rulers of Kadiaphonek are enjoying their eternal sleep down there. Anyway, we've never bothered to investigate further, but seeing as how that's your destination, it's worked out just perfectly."

"Perfectly indeed," said Benjamin. "I really do appreciate all the help you've provided me. Is there anything I can do for you in return?"

Maggie paused as they reached the door. She pondered for a moment and then smiled at Benjamin.

"Actually, would you mind relaying a message to my husband if you happen to run into him during your travels? I haven't seen him in months. He's an engineer for the city but often travels back and forth between the neighboring villages and castles. His name is Quinthorpe Cogswright"

"Of course," said Benjamin. "What shall I say?"

"Just tell him that his loving wife misses him and that he should write her more often." Maggie wrung her hands together anxiously. "And tell him that I'm sorry for what I said. And that he was right."

Benjamin was unsure how to react to this last statement. He provided a warm return, nonetheless.

"If I ever have the honor of meeting Quinthorpe, I'll be sure to pass along your message."

"In that case," said Maggie as she opened the door. "I wish you good fortune for the remainder of your quest, Benjamin Woods. You're a good man. It was a pleasure to meet you."

"Likewise, ma'am."

Benjamin nodded a final time and then stepped through the door. A steep stairwell greeted him in the darkness.

***

As he climbed the stairs, Benjamin realized that he had not been this alone since waiting under the lamppost across from the *Smoking Wizard*. The silence of this new environment was profound, yet he rather enjoyed it. His thoughts soon drifted. Much had occurred to him over the past few months. He had separated from his wife, left his children behind, and ventured into the wilderness on an absurd quest to find his old friend. He had even been shot while riding a giant insect. Benjamin shook his head in the darkness and laughed at the absurdity of it all.

At the top of the stairs was an intersection of corridors. The air was cleaner at this level and the light more luminous. Sporadic torches lined the marble walls. Benjamin considered which hallway to take.

A faint chanting emerged from the left passage, and he turned his ear to listen. The vocalizations were muted and distant, but comforting in nature. The delicate rings from a bell also occasionally floated from the shadows.

Other than the crackle from the torchlight, the hallway to the right was silent. Likewise, the path directly in front of him was devoid of movement or sound. Benjamin looked back down to his left. Perhaps the chanting individuals could direct him to the catacombs. More than likely, based on his current run of luck, they would call for the authorities instead.

Benjamin stood in the intersection for a few more moments and calculated his options. The exotic melodies of the chanting relaxed his troubled thoughts. They called to him. He nodded with acceptance and stepped into the left corridor.

SMACK!

A blunt object struck Benjamin on the back of his head, forcing him to the ground in a heap.

"Stay down!" shouted a voice.

Benjamin disobeyed the order and rolled to his right. He stumbled to his feet, facing his attacker.

"Gothkar?"

"Ben, is that you?"

"Yeah, it's me. Why the hell did you hit me?"

"I'm sorry, man," replied Gothkar. "I thought you were another cop. They're swarming this place."

Benjamin rubbed his head and groaned.

"I'm so glad to see you survived that fall, though. What happened to you back there?"

"I'll tell you all about it on the way to the catacombs. Do you know which way we're supposed to go?"

"Yeah. The stairs are over here. I went down and poked around a little but had to backtrack to avoid all the cops. Grab one of those torches and follow me."

The companions opened an oak door and descended another set of crumbling stairs. Musty air blew through unseen cracks in the walls and brushed against their faces.

Gothkar coughed into his torch.

The flickering light revealed piles of bones and debris along the sides of the stairwell. Benjamin could make out the chiseled lines of an embellished shield. Cobwebs and dust covered most of its flourishments.

"This way," said Gothkar.

The stairs dissipated and opened to a massive crypt. It was littered with coffins from floor to ceiling. Most were closed with heavy stone lids, but some were open with their contents visible. Grim skeletons, clad in armor and mail, stared blankly at the ceiling. A few of the forms wore golden crowns, peppered with sparkling jewels and intricate design work. Benjamin marveled at their beauty. He had never seen objects of such wealth and extravagance.

In the center of the room sat nine stone caskets, situated in three rows of three. Each was elaborately decorated with hieroglyphs and sigils. Benjamin held up his torch and focused on the casket at the far end of the room.

"Where are you going?" asked Gothkar.

"Look at the front of that one lid," said Benjamin as he walked between the coffins. "I've seen those symbols before."

Fire dripped from his torch and crackled to the floor.

They reached the end of the rows and gazed down at the coffin that had excited Benjamin. He held his torch above the closed lid so they could both see.

"Look at that one. Do you still have the map?"

"I do," replied Gothkar, unfolding it.

Benjamin swept away a layer of dust that had settled over the centuries. There were many more runes and symbols covering the lid. Some were strangely familiar.

"See," said Benjamin. "That's the same symbol that's on the map. The triangle above the circle and intersecting line. There are eight other symbols on there as well."

Gothkar inspected the map closely. "You're right! But what does it mean? What are we supposed to do?"

"I'm not sure."

Benjamin frowned and stared at the symbol. It was carved into a raised portion of the stone lid and resembled a button.

He turned to Gothkar and shrugged.

"Push it," said the troll.

Benjamin pressed down on the symbol and it sank into the lid. The grind of mechanical gears bellowed from the nearby wall and a door slid open slightly. The companions looked at each other with astonishment.

At that moment, the oaken doors at the top of the stairs burst open, and shill cries echoed through the chamber. A cold wind rushed down the steps and into the lower crypt, almost extinguishing the torchlight.

"Here they come again," said Gothkar.

"Quick! We can do this. Show me each of the symbols in sequence so I can push them. Hurry!"

Gothkar pointed to the next three symbols and Benjamin rapidly pushed them all in. Four. Five. Six. Each stone button was pressed and each time the wall ground with a mechanical hum. The new doorway opened a little upon each activation.

"There's the seventh symbol and there's the eighth," said Gothkar as he glanced over his shoulder.

Harsh footfalls and amber torchlight filled the bottom of the stairwell.

"They're almost here."

"Where's the ninth symbol then?"

"It's this one, but I don't see it on the lid."

Benjamin snatched the map out of Gothkar's hands and studied the ninth symbol. The parchment on that section was so worn that he could barely make it out. The design consisted of a horizontal line with a half-circle at its center. At the edge of the curve extended an upward line with an adjacent dot.

"This one's not on the lid," said Benjamin.

"No shit," exclaimed Gothkar. "What the hell do we do

now? There's no other way out of here."

"There!" shouted Benjamin, pointing.

Three meters above the partially opened door, carved into the marble wall, beckoned the ninth symbol.

"It's too high for me," cried Benjamin. "I can't reach it."

"But I can," said Gothkar.

As the crack and impact of gunfire erupted around them, Gothkar leapt above the door and smacked the stone button. A metallic thump reverberated through the wall and the doorway slid fully open. The companions dove over the threshold and into the safety of the new passageway. The stone door slammed shut behind them, kicking up a cloud of dust. Muffled shouts pounded and cursed on the other side of the door.

"Do you think they can open it again?" asked Gothkar.

"Let's not wait around to find out."

***

"Any idea where we're headed now?"

"I haven't the slightest clue," replied Gothkar.

Benjamin sighed and wiped the sweat from his forehead. Although they had abandoned their torches in the previous crypt, a copious amount of light illuminated the current passageway. He held the map up and tried to salvage a clue for their next move.

"Did Vomexium describe to you the appearance of the Intensitron? Do we even know what we're looking for?"

"Not really," replied Gothkar. "Just that it's a little device that you can hold in your hand. Check the map for more details."

"What do you think I'm doing? There's nothing else on here other than those nine symbols and the clues from before."

Benjamin folded up the map and put it away.

"That light up ahead," said Gothkar. "We might as well keep walking and check it out."

The curious light revealed its source as they reached the end of the hallway. A small chamber, filled with treasure and other kingly possessions, bathed in a golden luster. A stone pillar stood at its center. Atop the capital radiated a glowing orb. Streams of light reflected off piles of gold coins, open chests of jewels and rubies, and racks of exotic weapons.

"Holy shit," gasped Gothkar. "We're rich."

"Come on," said Benjamin. "We didn't come all this way for this stuff. Let's find the damn device and get the hell out of here. I need to get to the gate."

"I'll get you there in time, don't worry," said Gothkar as he scooped up a heaping pile of coins and stuffed them into his pockets.

Benjamin focused his attention on the opposite wall. A solitary chest, flanked by two large urns, radiated in the grandeur. He flipped open the latch and raised its lid.

"Is this the thing?"

Gothkar turned from his treasure seeking and peered into the chest. A metallic apparatus, about the size of a deck of cards, sat within the delicate folds of purple velvet.

"I think we're in business," said Gothkar.

He snatched up the device and inspected it. An array of buttons, each containing an embossed symbol, was situated beneath a computerized display-screen.

"Does it turn on?" asked Benjamin.

Gothkar toggled a switch on the side of the gadget.

"The battery's dead," he replied.

"It doesn't matter. This has to be the Intensitron but to be sure, let's look around for anything else that's similar."

"Good idea."

They swiftly opened all the remaining chests and drawers but were unable to find another instrument that resembled the description. Gothkar, on the other hand, procured a handsome dagger. It had a curved blade and sapphires upon its scabbard. He grinned as he fastened it to his belt.

"Find anything?" asked Benjamin.

"Nope, just this," he said, motioning to his new prize.

"All right, then let's get out of here."

***

"Whatever happened to Clementine?" asked Benjamin as they exited the treasure room and continued down the hallway.

"Oh her? Once I lost you, I was able to make my way back to Francis. I dropped her off with him."

"That's good to hear."

"He wasn't too happy about it. Since we'd forgotten her medicine, she'd become really sick and had to receive an extra dose. Francis then proceeded to lecture me for ten minutes on the importance of animal welfare and the proper treatment of insects. I'll be staying away from the Noffrets District for a while. That's for damn sure."

Benjamin chuckled.

The narrow corridor had darkened again. The crunch of pebbles and dirt under their boots echoed within the enclosed space. Heaps of broken boards and stones occasionally impeded their way, forcing them to walk in precarious paths.

"Shit!" gasped Benjamin as he tripped and fell.

"Woah, you all right?" asked Gothkar, lunging to assist.

Benjamin's right knee blazed with pain. He reached down and felt that the patch on his pants had been ripped to shreds. The warmth of fresh blood seeped through his fingers, dripping to the dusty floor. Rather than focus on the pain, Benjamin's thoughts flashed to a recent encounter with Trelinia. The evening before his departure for Kadiaphonek, she had repaired his worn pants with a fresh knee patch. He had complimented her handiwork and proclaimed that he would probably never have to replace them again. A sickening feeling washed over him.

"Up you go," said Gothkar, extending his hand.

Benjamin brushed himself off and sighed. "I can't wait to get out of this goddamned tomb."

"Me too, brother. But what the hell did you trip on?"

"Who knows?"

They both knelt and inspected the obstruction.

"Damn!" said Gothkar. "It's a person."

"It used to be."

The skeletal remains of a humanoid figure sat slumped against the stone wall. It was clad in sturdy armor, complete with a forest-green gorget, leather pauldrons, and studded greaves. One knee was propped up at an angle and an arm was cast across its chest, grasping something.

"Oh no," said Benjamin.

"What's wrong?"

"Look at its necklace. That's a Woods sigil."

A green emerald, set within the oxidized grooves of a silver medallion, rested upon a cuirass of boiled leather.

"Who could it be?" asked Gothkar.

"Flip it over and see if there's an inscription."

Gothkar carefully removed the necklace and read aloud.

To my dearest friend, Oswulf. May you complete your mission and return home safely. -Merkresh.

The two friends looked at each other.

"Merkresh?" asked Gothkar.

"And Oswulf. He was one of my uncles."

"But why would he be dead beneath this pyramid with an inscription from that old wizard?"

"This was Oswulf's departing gift from Merkresh during my father's quest when he was a teenager."

"How do you know?"

Benjamin pulled a platinum chain from beneath his tunic. Upon its end glistened a silver medallion with a green emerald.

"Because I received one just like it during my quest."

Gothkar looked down at the corpse.

"I wonder what his mission was," said Benjamin.

"He was probably traveling through this dreadful place on some errand to assist your father and the rest of his group," said Gothkar. "It's a shame he perished down here all alone."

"My father never talked much about Oswulf when I was growing up. I wonder if he ever learned of his true fate."

The pair pondered this in silence for a few moments.

"What would you like to do?" asked Gothkar.

Benjamin stood and straightened his jacket. "I think we should carry what's left of my uncle out of this dark, miserable hole and give him a proper burial. His family would be grateful."

The two friends helped each other gather the remains of the fallen warrior. Gothkar repurposed a stack of old rags he had found from one of the many broken crates, while Benjamin gently removed the pieces of leather armor. They wrapped the remaining bones and Oswulf's other personal possessions within the rags and placed them in Benjamin's backpack.

"What should we do with his gear?" asked Benjamin.

"The most logical solution is for you to wear your uncle's armor into battle. I can't think of a more perfect way to honor his memory."

"My battling days are over, old friend, but I do like the idea of wearing this stuff. The craftsmanship is astounding."

Benjamin donned the greaves, tasset belt, gauntlets, and leather pauldrons. Every component fit perfectly. As he lifted the cuirass, a sheathed sword fell to the stone floor with a clang.

"Ho!" he exclaimed. "What's this?"

"A mighty sword by the looks of it," replied Gothkar.

"Indeed," replied Benjamin, inspecting the weapon.

The hilt was wrapped with dark leather straps. On the pommel sat a sparkling amethyst.

"How's your sword fighting skills these days?"

"I was actually pretty good when we were teenagers, remember? Better than you, anyway."

"Maybe," said Gothkar with a smirk. "Put her on."

Benjamin used the intact strap to fasten the scabbard to his tasset. The blade fell perfectly along his side. He flipped the clasp with his thumb and pulled the sword from the sheath. It produced a marvelous metallic twang.

"What are you going to name it?" asked Gothkar.

"What?"

"Come on. You can't have a sword without a name."

Benjamin turned the blade in the air thoughtfully.

"How about Ghostreaver?"

"That's not bad," said Gothkar. "It suits your grim attire. Where'd you come up with that name?"

"From my son, Roger. He used to have a little wooden sword when he was younger that he called Ghostreaver. He and his friends would traipse all over the fields and hills pretending to slay monsters and dragons."

"Except now he really has to fight one."

"God," replied Benjamin. "What a terrible thought."

He sheathed the sword and was silent.

"Come on, man," said Gothkar, placing a hand on his shoulder. "Put that out of your mind for now and let's focus on getting to our next destination. The Gate of Frozen Whispers."

***

The companions walked for hours through the somber hallways. They conversed sparingly and only paused their march for quick bites of food and drink. The unending solitude numbed their dispositions as they trudged through the darkness.

"I see light up ahead," said Gothkar.

Benjamin focused his eyes. "It's a door."

Streams of light crept between wood and stone.

"Another treasure room?"

"I sure as hell hope not."

Benjamin pulled on an iron door handle. "It's locked."

"Half a moment," said Gothkar, rummaging through one of his pockets. He pulled out an iron ring with a large key.

"Where'd you get that?"

"In some drawer, before I knocked you on the head."

"Splendid," said Benjamin.

Gothkar inserted the key and the door opened.

"That was surprisingly easy."

A rush of sunlight filled the hallway. They shielded their eyes in unison and studied the new surroundings.

Benjamin and Gothkar stood atop a rocky ledge that overlooked a forest-filled valley. Blue sky permeated a calming backdrop of cirrus clouds and chirping birds. Crows, warblers, and sparrows fluttered between treetops as a warm breeze hummed along the ridges. On the western horizon stretched the snow-capped spires of the Ethereal Peaks.

"We made it out," said Gothkar.

"Thank God," replied Benjamin. He turned his face to the sunlight and allowed its power to wash over him. His morale improved in an instant.

"Where are we exactly?"

Gothkar examined their immediate surroundings and the sprawling valley. Colossal boulders protruded from the cliff face amid a carpet of underbrush and dangling roots. The forest below was thick and ominous, yet the geometric edges of great structures and roads were clearly visible.

"I can't believe it," he said, "but I think we've walked all the way to the middle of Blackwood."

"Amazing," replied Benjamin. "That passageway took us all the way under the river and out this far?"

"It looks that way."

"What about the gate?" asked Benjamin. "Can we see it?"

"Maybe," said Gothkar. "It should be right below us."

Benjamin peered over the edge but could only discern an ocean of leaves and wood. As he raised his head, he noticed two foreboding objects in the hazy distance.

"What are those?"

Gothkar shielded his eyes and gazed across the expanse of silvery green. "The first one is the Watchtower of Dragolroth."

"That sounds like a terrible place."

"It certainly is. It serves as the crossroads between the western and eastern sections of Blackwood Forest. Some ghastly demon lord resides in its upper levels."

"Thankfully, we didn't have to go near it before."

"True enough. But I don't think you and your kids will be as fortunate this time around."

Benjamin moaned in agreement.

"That other one's the dragon's castle," said Gothkar.

At the eastern edge of Blackwood, nestled between the coast of the Enchanted Sea and the gray grasses of the river valley, frowned the haunted castle of Lord Mortis.

"That's where everyone's headed, isn't it?"

"Yes," replied Benjamin.

The companions peered across the expanse at the castle's pointed turrets and grim battlements. Its loathsome form exuded a darkness that overwhelmed all sense of willpower and resolve.

"Even from this distance, it frightens me."

"I don't envy you guys."

Benjamin scanned the horizon for a moment longer and then stepped onto a narrow path that led down into the valley.

"Let's get off this ridge and find that gate."

"I'm right behind you," said Gothkar.

CHAPTER XXXIV

TO THE COAST

"Can we talk about this?" asked Brian.

"Right now?"

"Yes, right now."

She glanced over at the children. They were seated at the table and ready to eat but collectively paused with confused expressions. The youngest stood up and walked over to the adults. Her mother waved her away with a forced smile.

"It's okay honey, your father and I are just talking for a moment."

"Why would you say such a thing?" he asked.

"I don't want them to hear any of this. She needs to sit back down."

"I'm not talking about that."

"Then what're you talking about?"

He took a deep breath and tried to compose himself.

"You really think I didn't fight for the four of you?"

"That's what you're upset about?"

He let out a frustrated laugh. "Of course, it is. Don't you know how painful it is to hear you say that? You of all people know exactly what I've been through these past few months."

"And yet, here we are again. Exactly where we ended up last time."

"But why do you have to speak to me in that manner? I'm trying my best to handle this thing. I'm trying to do better than before."

"What do you think I'm doing?"

"You're saying things like that and it's killing me."

He rubbed his forehead in frustration.

"Look, I don't think I want us to continue to spend time together."

"Today was your idea," she replied.

"I know it was. I thought it'd be fun for the kids."

"Don't blame this on me. You've been in a rotten mood all day, even before I said that. You've been withdrawn and sullen the entire trip."

"Because I'm heartbroken," he said, his voice trembling. "I always knew we'd end up like this and it's tearing me up inside to see you take all of it so easily. How the hell do you do it?"

She smiled with tears in her eyes. "You really think this is easy for me? I still love you, but how many times can we try to get this right?"

"As many times as it takes."

"I wish it were that simple."

***

Brian Woods opened his eyes. A high ceiling stared back at him. Hammer-beams of timber framing displayed elaborate carvings of griffins and other arcana. He was lying in bed in a dimly lit room. A warm draft of ginger, orange peel, and cinnamon swept over him. Bubbling cauldrons stewed before a hearth of blazing coals. He licked his lips and savored a faintly medicinal tinge of lemon and mint.

"Ah, your friend has awakened at last," said a voice.

"And just in the nick of time," said another.

Brian slowly sat up and processed his surroundings. Belris was in attendance, as well as two other men. One was unfamiliar and wore a pointed, purple hat. The other individual was well known to Brian.

"Merkresh!"

"Hello again, old friend. I'm delighted to see you're finally up and about. How are you feeling?"

"Like shit."

"I would think so," said Merkresh. "My new friend Belris here explained how you went to blows with my brother. The fact that you're alive at all is an achievement."

"I forgot that asshole is your brother. No offense."

"None taken. He's an awful human being to be sure."

Brian frowned. "How exactly did Belris explain anything to you? Did he grow a new tongue during my slumber?"

"Nay. He used those."

The old man motioned to Belris who held up a small journal and a pen.

"Excellent," said Brian.

"My friend, Thibirian, the proprietor of this shop, was kind enough to provide these materials so the young man could communicate. As it turns out, Belris is quite the storyteller."

"He explained how he lost his speech?"

"He did. I promised him that my nephew will pay for that crime and many others. Perhaps not in the near term, but at some point, Zaran will be held responsible."

"My good man, Thibirian," said Brian as he sat up on the edge of the bed. "I thank you kindly for your hospitality and warmth, but may I trouble you for something cold? Lying in this bed has made me very thirsty. Have you any ale?"

The old wizard raised his bushy eyebrows and spoke with animated body language. "This establishment is but a humble apothecary, I'm afraid, and I'm not generally in the business of supplying spirits to customers. But, seeing as you are my personal guests, and Merkresh is a colleague of mine, I would be delighted to pull out one of my private reserves."

"Fabulous," replied Brian.

"In fact," continued Thibirian, "why don't the three of you take a seat over by the window and I'll prepare a bite to eat to complement your ale. I'm sure you have much to talk about."

"Indeed, we do," replied Merkresh.

***

Brian, Belris, and Merkresh seated themselves at a small table nestled between a bay window and a crackling fireplace. The morning sunshine bathed their setting, while the muted chatter of busy townsfolk seeped in from the street.

As their host prepared breakfast, each man busied himself

with a drink. Brian gulped from a curved, horn tankard. Golden-brown liquid ran down his beard during each draught. Merkresh sipped from a similar horn, yet his featured a flat bottom and was finely polished. Belris elected to wash his meal down with an oaken mug of steamy coffee.

Brian raised his face to the sunshine. Its warmth, coupled with the potency of the ale, rejuvenated him with a sense of vigor and contentment.

"This is superb," he said, examining the horn.

Merkresh wiped a bit of foam from his mustache and nodded. "One of the best brews in the region. What about your coffee, Belris? It hails from a brewer in Kad, I believe."

The boy held up his mug and smiled.

"Where are we exactly?" asked Brian.

"A place called East Grimstead. It's a fishing village just beyond Starbrook."

"I've been to Starbrook many times," replied Brian as he finished another swill of beer. "Are you saying that you dragged me all the way down here from Warington?"

"I'm not saying that at all," replied the old man, turning his glance to Belris. "He's responsible for that undertaking."

"I raise my glass to you, my friend," said Brian. "Thank you. I'm in your debt."

The boy scribbled some words in his journal and held it up for both men to read. "You're welcome, sir. It was the least I could do, for I am in debt to you. You saved my life."

"Then let us be in debt to each other," laughed Brian, "and permit our combined pledges to strengthen our bond before the coming storm."

"I'll drink to that," said the old man.

The steady hum and pop of the fire, incorporated with the activity from the street, lulled each man into a moment of introspection.

"Well now," said Merkresh. "You and I have much to catch up on. Pray, tell me all that you learned during your stay in my tumultuous household."

"I'm unable to report *all* that I learned, for there were many curious things that I witnessed over the past year. Allow me instead to share the highlights."

"Proceed."

"You're already aware that Zaran has forged an alliance with the Nexxathians."

"I am," replied Merkresh.

"What may be news to you, however, is the ambition that binds their new partnership."

"Go on."

"Your nephew has, well *had*, constructed a machine that converts human life into an energy source used by those creatures from Nexxathia."

"Had?"

"Yes, Belris and I destroyed it. It was about the only task I was able to accomplish."

"That is a considerable accomplishment. Disruption is the best we can expect with our current resources. It's impractical to think that one man can destroy the power and influence of Count Zaran and Amfridus. That battle will come."

Brian agreed with a grunt, drinking from his horn.

"Do you believe that the destruction of his device has degraded his progress?"

"For the time being, certainly. They were trading for gold,

but I believe that the true motivation was for knowledge. Your brother has been attempting to learn their magic."

"Attempting?" said Merkresh with a raised brow. "Based on what Belris described, he's already learned a great deal and even used it against you."

"True enough."

"What of Zaran's network of influence? What did you discover of his reach to the other castles?"

"His reach is vast. I know for a fact that he's had spies buried deep within the councils of Wintervale, Stowerling, and Cadworth. I was unable to ascertain the status of the other castles."

"Whitehaven has evaded their corruption, based on the whispers of my own agents," said Merkresh, "but they are tucked away in the northeast and isolated. If Winterberry, their neighbor to the east, were to capitulate, then all of the northern castles would be under Zaran's thumb."

"What about Direwood?" asked Brian.

"To the west, above the Bay of Storms. Yes, they're even more isolated and probably secure. I'm afraid they're too distant to be of much aid to us at this stage. Perhaps, if we're able to extend our own influence, we'll be able to recruit them later."

Thibirian arrived with their meal.

"This looks delectable," said Brian.

Their host and two of his apprentices delivered a vast array of items. There was smoked herring, cod, and chunky steaks of salmon drenched in a sorrel sauce. A wooden trencher bore sliced loaves of Rye, Barley, and glazed honey tarts colored with saffron. Three whole chickens, each stuffed with grapes and herbs were accompanied by an almond sauce. The final dish contained slices of pan-fried venison, topped with spices, onions, and leeks. Of course, there were fresh refills of ale as well as goblets of red-spiced wine.

"This is a meal fit for a king," said Brian. "Sir, have you ever considered opening a tavern instead of an apothecary?"

"I had one in a previous life," replied the wizard. "But thank you for the compliment."

Brian, Merkresh, and Belris gorged themselves. Neither of the men had had a proper meal in many weeks and they all ate in silence for a solid hour. The occasional burp or fart interrupted the process, but otherwise, their focus remained on eating and drinking. Merkresh was the first to ease back in his chair and pick at his teeth.

"Remarkable, my old friend."

"Thank you, again," replied Thibirian as he and his help gathered the bare trenchers and flagons. "It's my pleasure to aid such good friends during this time of calamity."

Brian raised his horn of ale and one of the apprentices refilled it. "I have more news to share," he said.

"Please," replied Merkresh. "A full belly and a full tankard favor tall tales and devious tidings. Hearken!"

"My final task as Warington's Sergeant of the Guard was to facilitate a transaction with a company of Nexxathians. I know Belris remembers because he would absolutely not shut up while we waited in the mist on the drawbridge."

Brian winked at the boy.

"Are you familiar with a captain called Hamonet?"

"I'm familiar with the heraldry," replied Merkresh. "Their banner dates back hundreds of years. A red firefly against a field of black if I recall."

"That's correct," said Brian. "Well, a Hamonet was my superior during this little interaction and, through his arrogance, he unwittingly provided me a windfall of intelligence. First, the Nexxathians, at least the ones that I saw, are formidable. They command beasts that are truly remarkable. Booming, reptilian creatures similar to the docile versions that stride through the streets of Kadiaphonek. The ones controlled by the enemy, however, are ferocious. They've also been able to temper the aggressiveness of the spiders from the northwest forests. They had saddles mounted on them."

"Interesting," replied Merkresh, "and disconcerting. That would suggest that Harlow Hall is in league with the enemy. We'll need to determine their allegiance immediately. Very well, go on."

"That covers their means of transport and mobility. The fighters themselves are even worse. You're acquainted with the common foot soldier, but the religious ones, or the priests as I call them, were a new discovery for me."

"Did you see them use the blue light?"

"Almost. The one in charge, Lord Mordok, compelled them to disengage once he realized what I did."

"What did you do?" asked Merkresh.

"I didn't have a choice. He'd already disabled the captain with telepathy, and we were moments away from a battle I knew we'd have no chance of winning."

The old man sighed. "You were supposed to keep your abilities a secret. This complicates things considerably."

"I know that, and I'm sorry, but what's done is done."

"This Lord Mordok was impressed, I presume?"

"He was, and that's what I'm afraid of."

"Precisely," said Merkresh. "He's undoubtedly reported

this detail to his superiors, and now you're a marked man. The enemy and its web of spies will be hunting you at every turn. Not to mention the entire force of Warington castle and all of its allies will be looking for you. I wouldn't be surprised if Zaran himself hops on a horse and tries to track you down. You've prevailed in one thing at least."

"Yes?"

"You've recruited more enemies for us to fight than I'd ever have imagined. I always knew you were an overachiever, but this is excessive."

Belris chuckled behind his mug of coffee.

"Fine, make jokes, I'm used to it," said Brian. "Shall I continue with my report?"

"Please," replied the old man.

"Although I was able to unsettle Lord Mordok with my abilities, I don't believe the others would have stood a chance. Our captain was knocked out within seconds, and if we ever find ourselves in combat with these creatures, we'll need to come up with some kind of defense, otherwise the war will be over fast."

"I'm working on that," replied Merkresh. "Tell me more about Zaran's machine."

"He has more than one. We destroyed the main engine that fuels the other devices."

"How many are there?"

"Two, as far as I know," said Brian. "Belris and I saw the operation of one first-hand, an older version, according to a comment made by your brother. We heard them speak of a newer model that's located somewhere deeper in the castle."

"How does it operate?"

"Gruesomely. The unfortunate victim is thrown alive into

a compartment and sealed shut. With the push of a button, a process converts their lifeforce into a small, glowing cube."

"A cube?"

"Aye. I saw them on two occasions. Once during the trade with the Nexxathians and then during Captain Hamonet's demise. Each cube has a glass portal on its face that reveals the pulsating, white light from inside. The victim's lifeforce."

"Fascinating," said Merkresh.

"Not for the poor soul involved."

"How many of these cubes does Zaran possess?"

"That's another peculiar detail," said Brian. "They seem to have had some difficulty in manufacturing them because they did not have the required sum during the exchange."

Brian turned to Belris. "How many did they have again?"

The boy wrote in his journal. "Twenty-one."

"If they were having a hard time procuring the required supply before, then they'll definitely have problems now."

"Some good news at last," said Merkresh.

Brian moaned and rolled his eyes.

The old man pulled out a timepiece and then finished the final gulp from his horn of ale. "Well, gentlemen, the bright day stands before us, and we have much to accomplish."

"Agreed," said Brian. "I'd like to stretch my legs a bit and explore the village. Have they any brothels in East Grimstead?"

"One moment, sir," said Thibirian.

"What is it?" asked Brian.

"Although I pride myself in nurturing your appetites with a home-cooked meal and mending your ailments, I still run a business and have bills to pay."

"Excuse me?"

"How will you be paying for services rendered?"

Brian looked at Merkresh. The old man shrugged and stood. "I can't get you out of this situation. I have my own business to attend to this morning. We require a ship to get us across Emerald Bay, so I'll be down at the docks booking us passage. Good day, for now. I'll see you soon."

The old man shook his friend's hand and then exited the apothecary. A bell dinged as the front door closed.

"I see," said Thibirian, turning back to Brian and Belris. "Have the two of you any coin?"

"None. We were just prisoners in a dungeon."

"Of course," replied the old man. "Might I propose a compromise to settle your debts?"

"I'm listening," said Brian.

"Forgive me, but I happened to overhear a portion of your earlier conversation and it occurred to me that a man of your skill set could assist me with a delicate situation."

"What's the task?"

"Splendid," replied Thibirian and sat down in the vacant chair. "There exists a shop across town that's owned by a merchant called Harwick. Now, this particular shop deals in goods and merchandise of, shall we say, questionable origins. Being that he's a competitor of mine, I'd normally recoil at doing business with him, but since this item is so hard to come by, I decided to make an exception. The chief endeavor of my establishment is to obtain the recipes and knowledge required to make high-caliber potions and elixirs, that sort of thing. Are you following me so far?"

"I know what apothecaries do. Please, sir."

"Apologies, I'm getting to the point. This merchant,

Harwick, is in possession of a recipe that I have been seeking to acquire for many years."

"So, go buy it from him," said Brian.

"I attempted to, and there lies the dilemma. You see that young man over there behind the counter?"

Brian and Belris turned and looked.

"That's Finlay, one of my apprentices. I sent him over to Harwick's last week to purchase said recipe and he was returned to me with a black eye, a broken arm, and no recipe."

"Harwick beat up your apprentice?"

"No, his son did. Magnus Harwick."

"What for?"

"I imagine because he doesn't want to sell the recipe that I desire. Magnus has a reputation for tormenting children and older folks such as me. Poor Finlay's not the weakest kid in town, but he's no match for that Harwick thug."

"All right, let me see if I have this straight," said Brian. "You want us to march over to this guy's shop, take the recipe, and thrash the bully?"

"Essentially, yes."

"What if I were to tell you to go fuck yourself, and then strolled out of here?"

"You have that option, however, that would force me to report your whereabouts to the local authorities. With all the other people looking for you, I doubt you want East Grimstead on that list."

"What's one more village?"

Brian slurped the final bit of ale from his horn and then looked at Belris. "What do you think?"

"Seems like an easy enough task," he wrote. "And I don't

believe drawing more attention is wise. I think we should do it."

"Theft and assault are going to rustle some feathers, so we're going to draw attention to ourselves either way."

"That's where your skill set comes into play," said the old man. "So, do we have a deal?"

"Sure," replied Brian. "If it settles my debts."

***

The streets of East Grimstead pulsated with activity as Brian and Belris set about their task. The summer sun had nearly reached its zenith and the sky beamed a profound blue. A salty breeze greeted the companions as they departed the apothecary and headed down Market Street.

Legions of seagulls squawked and cried above the rows of stalls that cluttered the cobblestones. Due to its optimal location just north of Emerald Bay, the village enjoyed trade with a vast array of distant lands and countries. The street vendors and hawkers were thus regularly supplied with the most colorful of merchandise. On any given day, an adventurous customer could haggle for rare spices, exotic fruits, or curiosities fashioned from ivory or silk.

Belris held up his journal as they navigated through the open-air fish market.

"What's our plan?"

"I'm still formulating that," replied Brian.

"Can't you use your thought skill?"

"Normally, yes, but not this time."

Belris threw up his arms and shrugged.

"I neglected to mention to our opportunistic host that

I'm unable to perform that talent in my current condition. I don't have the energy yet, and even on a normal day, it's taxing."

"What now?"

"Good question," replied Brian. "But I was thinking since everyone in the realm is after us already, why don't we take care of this job the old-fashioned way?"

"How?"

"We rob the fuckers."

Belris chuckled.

"Great plan. What could go wrong?"

"No one's going to get hurt. Well, not too hurt."

"What do you want me to do?" asked Belris.

"Stay off to the side, like you're browsing his wares. I'll engage him in some conversation, and then inquire if he has the recipe we seek. If he sells it, then we'll pay for it and leave. Easy. If not, then I'm going to take it."

"And the bully?"

"That's where I need your help. Keep an eye out for his son. Are you up for a fight today? You haven't forgotten your gate guard training already, have you?"

Belris smiled, shaking his head.

They reached the end of the block and Brian pointed up at the street signs to get their bearings.

"Thibirian said to go south on Market and then west on Canal Street for a while until we reach Chestnut."

The food stalls and hawkers thinned out, giving way to more traditional storefronts. A cordage artisan, fish smokehouse, and a bakery occupied the north side of the row, while a brothel, shipwright, and netmaker filled in the south.

"I should be in there," said Brian, nodding to the brothel.

They approached Chestnut Avenue. It was much less crowded in this section of town. The commercial shops faded into quaint neighborhoods. Some of the wealthier homes were constructed of stone and stained windows, but most were brick, plastered on the inside and out, with thatched roofs of straw, reeds, or galingale.

"We take this for two more blocks and then Harwick's shop is on the corner."

Belris gave a thumbs up.

"There's hardly anyone around. This should be easy."

Rebirth & Bane occupied a considerable portion of the block between Grace Street and 28th. The shop was substantially more affluent than Thibirian's location. It was a three-level, stone structure, highlighted by conical spires and decorated balconies.

"Impressive," said Brian.

Belris nodded.

"Ready? All right, here we go."

A bell rang as Brian opened the front door.

"Well met, gentlemen," said a middle-aged shopkeeper behind a counter covered in scrolls, letters, and a wide assortment of alchemist's instruments. A collection of sparkling geodes was arranged along the corner. "How may I be of service?"

"Good afternoon," said Brian.

Belris deviated to the right and feigned interest in a shelf packed with taxidermized rodents, insects, and several owls. A deep mustiness, due to the tanning process, saturated his nostrils.

"This is a remarkable shop you have here," said Brian. "It appears that you have a mastery of several disciplines. Medicine, alchemy, and even scroll making. Amazing work."

"Thank you, sir," said the shopkeeper. "Yes, my son and

I pride ourselves in serving the folk of Grimstead in as many capacities as possible. We even function as a makeshift postal service, hence the disarray of parchment and scrolls strewn before you. I do apologize for the mess."

Belris' ears perked up at the mention of the son.

"Not a problem," replied Brian, approaching the counter. "Say, my companion and I are in the market for potions. I see many on the shelves behind you, but may one procure their recipes as well?"

"Of course, sir. I possess a full catalog of superior recipes for sale. We carry all the basics as well as a few of the esoteric."

He turned and pointed to the rows of colorful vials and flasks. "There are many health potion variants, elixirs for mind and body wellbeing, and even a few vials left of Dreamless Sleeps. They're the bright blue ones over in the corner."

"Very nice," said Brian. "However, I'm in search of one such gem that belongs to the latter group you mentioned."

"I see," said the man.

Brian pulled out a small scroll and handed it to him. The shopkeeper inspected its contents and frowned.

"This is most interesting," he said, shaking his head.

Belris glared at Brian from across the room.

"Another customer solicited this exact same recipe only a few days ago, which is curious, because of its scarcity."

"Is there going to be a problem?" asked Brian.

Belris held his breath as he anticipated the next move. Only seconds passed, yet they crawled like an eternity.

"Not at all," said the shopkeeper, perking back up with a smile. "Because it just so happens that another dealer came in yesterday and traded a similar, yet far superior version of this recipe. I'd be happy to sell you either one, or both, it's your choice. Is this for personal use, or shall I gift wrap it for you?"

Brian turned to Belris with his own confused expression. The boy exhaled with relief.

"Bound with string and placed in a bag will suffice."

"Very well, sir," said the man, stepping into a back room for a moment and then returning with a handful of parchment. "Here we are. That'll be thirty-six gold if you please."

Brian grinned with satisfaction. The task had been accomplished without the need to crack skulls or draw blood. Merkresh would be pleased.

As the shopkeeper tended to his order, Brian surveyed the jumble of items scattered across the front counter. An ocean of letters, maps, scrolls, and envelopes. Many of the articles were in various degrees of production, resulting in their contents being open and exposed. The corners of hand-written letters or other personal artifacts protruded from within. Several black and white photographs were visible in the clutter.

"You develop still pictures here?"

"Yes, sir," replied the storekeeper as he bound the scroll with a perfect knot and bow. "We have a crude developing room in the back. Photography has become a beloved enterprise again over the past few years. Grimstead was one of the first towns to embrace the technology many decades ago, because of our access to foreign travelers and the like."

Brian nodded. "I enjoyed the hobby in my younger days. I was actually pretty good at it too, but when…"

His heart skipped a beat as his eyes fell on one particular photograph. A wave of nausea swept over him. He blinked wildly in a hopeless attempt to erase the image that gazed back.

"The fuck is this?"

"Pardon me?"

The storekeeper jolted at the sudden shift in demeanor. He dropped the scroll and looked at Brian with wide eyes. Belris' expression of appeasement contorted into one of dread.

"Why do you have a picture of my wife?" asked Brian.

The man shrugged. "What are you talking about?"

Brian snatched the photograph from the pile and wagged it in front of the shopkeeper's face. "This is a picture of my wife. Why do you have it and a letter written by her? It's a simple fucking question."

The man gazed at the woman's face. A sudden link was formed in his mind, and the corner of his mouth twitched.

"Well?" asked Brian.

"Of course, that's Juliette. We're only acquaintances."

"Are you?"

Brian lowered the photograph and removed the handwritten letter from the envelope. He read the contents to himself in silence. The shopkeeper stood as still as stone, his face now a morbid shade of gray. When he was finished reading, Brian's eyes slowly rose from the page.

"I'm going to ask you one more time."

"We're just friends," interrupted the man. "I swear."

Brian darted around the counter and drove his boot square into the man's groin, dropping him to the floor in a heap.

"Get up!"

"What're you doing?" he moaned with heavy gasps.

"Read it."

"What?"

"I want you to read it to me out loud."

"You can't do this…"

CRUNCH!

Brian kicked him in the groin again.

Vomit projected from the man's mouth, splattering a few of the glass jars of colorful potions.

"You're Owen, aren't you?" asked Brian.

The shopkeeper spit a string of saliva and nodded.

"It's all coming together for me now. You're the man my wife was seeing. It explains her unusual behavior during those last months, the extended weekend trips, and what she said to me during our final conversation."

"What are you going to do to me?"

Brian was lost in thought. He recalled the expressions on his children's faces as they sat at the table, confused and anxious, watching their parents argue during that final day. All the buried grief from the past two years rushed to Brian's brain in an eruption of blood and thunder. The notice of separation, the rules of visitation, and the list of accusations. They all solidified into a singular point of rage that coalesced at this specific place in time. His telepathic abilities were depleted, but his hatred was fully charged. Forevermore, Brian's talents would be the brush to paint his pain upon the canvas of the world.

"I'll read it! Please, just don't hurt me any…"

Brian struck Owen in the face with a halved geode. The man's right eyeball exploded with a burst of vitreous gel, nerves, and blood. Belris covered his ears at the horrific sound and subsequent high-pitched shrieks.

The geode struck him a second time. A third. *A fourth.*

In a matter of seconds, Owen's skull was shattered to pieces. All that remained atop his motionless corpse was a bloody mass of hair, skin, and tissue. Particles of bone and brain dripped from Brian's face.

"Hey Dad," called a voice from a door in the back. "Wait until you see what I made at school today."

Brian and Belris turned at the sound and watched as a teenage boy walked into the room and looked down at what remained of his father. Thibirian's depiction of Magnus Harwick had been an absolute fabrication. The young man was short, thin, and frail. He stood frozen with shock, attempting to process the horror before him.

"Kill him!" screamed Brian.

Belris still had his hands over his ears, so the command registered as subdued and distant, similar to his cognition of the unfolding situation. He looked at the boy and then at his friend. Their mental states could not have been more divergent. One was hysterical with rage, his face covered in blood and gore. The other was pissing his pants.

Before Belris had a chance to react, Brian grabbed a letter opener from the counter and plunged it into Magnus' neck. His training and experience had taught him to stab straight into the throat, to the side of the larynx, yanking sideways to sever the carotid artery and jugular. The boy dropped in a pool of blood, dying almost instantly.

"Let's go," said Brian. "We have to get to the docks and find Merkresh."

Belris' brain was merely along for the ride. The entire melee had transpired in only seconds, yet it contained imagery and emotions that would haunt him for the remainder of his living days. He stumbled after his companion in a fog of anguish.

They passed through the quiet neighborhoods unscathed

and approached the wharf district. A timber quay, used for loading and off-loading goods from galleons and trading vessels, extended along the shores of the Crescent Cove. Brian and Belris rushed along wooden planks, attempting to remain inconspicuous amid the tumult of maritime activities. Coal porters, laborers, and longshoremen shouted and laughed as they worked in the sun.

"Brian!" yelled a familiar voice.

The companions turned.

"What are you doing down here?" asked Merkresh.

"We need to depart Grimstead immediately," said Brian.

"What in the world for? My God, is that blood all over you? What's happened?"

"I'll explain as soon as we're in a ship sailing south. Were you able to book our passage?"

"Yes, but the ship doesn't leave until this evening."

"We can't wait. We have to go now."

"Go where?" asked the old man. "There aren't any ships traveling to southern villages until tonight. The only ship that's leaving now is destined for Kad."

"Then we're going to Kad."

"What?" exclaimed Merkresh.

"Are our tickets transferrable?"

"I suppose so, but what the hell is going on?"

"Trust me, please," said Brian.

With a heavy sigh, Merkresh marched back over to the dockmaster and exchanged the tickets. They were rushed aboard a three-masted carrack called *The Foolish Skirt*, used for daily cargo shipments throughout the vicinity of Emerald Bay. Its topsails and flags flapped in the wind as the crew prepared to disembark.

Merkresh, Brian, and Belris leaned against the taffrail of

the upper deck and watched the village of East Grimstead fade into the distance. The islands of the Fabled Haven dotted the blue waters to their starboard, while the grand spires and turrets of the Academy of Spells, located on the Isle of Magic, loomed on their port. Merkresh turned and glared at Brian Woods.

"What have you done?"

"Settling an old debt," he replied with a scowl.

CHAPTER XXXV

TOADSTOOLS AND DIAMONDS

"I wonder what my brother's been up to," said Ben as he studied the iron key in his hand.

"Brian, right?" asked Gothkar.

"Yea, I haven't heard from him in months, and haven't seen him for even longer. He's been working up in Warington Castle for the past year trying to figure out what kind of trouble Zaran's been causing."

"Maybe Merkresh will know."

"Hopefully."

The companions continued to travel through the forest of Western Blackwood. The early afternoon sun beamed hot upon their shoulders as they transitioned from the craggy trails of the higher elevations to the spongy paths of the bottomlands. Clusters of tapered cypress knees congregated in the marshy expanse, while cattails, water lilies, and knotweed choked the surrounding wetlands. A pair of grey herons ascended through the maze of hanging moss and lichen.

"Time for those damn mosquitoes," moaned Gothkar as he swatted at his arms and exposed neck.

"I see a place over by those orange toadstools where we can bury my Uncle Oswulf."

Ben set the bundle of remains upon a small bed of moss that rested between the massive roots of a cypress tree. They dug a shallow grave, placed Uncle Oswulf, and then covered it as best they could.

"This will have to do, I'm afraid. I can't carry him around where I'm going."

"Actually, it seems appropriate," said Gothkar. "Since you're traveling to an actual cemetery."

"Technically, yes, but I don't think he'd want to spend eternity in a place like that."

"Whatever you say," said the troll as he kicked over a few of the enormous mushrooms. "Shall we say something?"

"Of course," replied Benjamin, clearing his throat. "Uncle Oswulf, I never had the privilege of getting to know you, but my father spoke highly of you. You were a brave, honorable, and…"

"Excuse me!" screamed a high-pitched voice.

Ben and Gothkar jumped at the interruption.

"What do you idiots think you're doing? Scoot! Be gone!"

They whirled around in the direction of the shrieking voice. Waddling up a tiny path and waving a twig was an elderly slug woman. She had on a scarf and a dress with a floral pattern and even wore spectacles. She slid right up to Ben's boot, then up, up, up to the cap of a neighboring toadstool. From there she oozed along a cypress limb until she was face to face with him.

"Good day, sir," she said. "Are you hard of hearing? I'll ask you again, then. What do you half-wits think you're doing trespassing on my land and kicking over my mushrooms?"

Gothkar burst into laughter.

The tiny snail woman looked at him sharply.

He went silent.

"Ma'am," said Ben. "I can hear you just fine, but I would appreciate it if you would…"

SMACK!

She hit him on the tip of the nose with her twig.

"Damn!" he exclaimed, rubbing it gingerly.

Gothkar laughed again and was met with another glare.

"No sass from you," said the woman.

"Ma'am," replied the troll. "Please allow me to explain before you beat my friend to death."

The slug woman regarded Gothkar with undisguised suspicion and slowly lowered her twig. "Very well, troll. What have you to say?"

"May I approach you?"

"Nay, I can hear you just fine from where you stand."

"Very well," he said. "My companion and I unknowingly chose your fine toadstool garden as the final resting place for his dearly departed uncle. Oswulf Woods was his name. He was a great warrior."

"Rubbish," replied the woman. "More like a great bother. Look at what all that digging and kicking has done. Did you slay him with that fine blade that hangs from your belt?"

"Of course not," said Ben. "We discovered his remains in a dark tunnel on our travels from Kadiaphonek."

"I hate that city," said the woman.

"Since he's family, I wanted to give him a proper burial out here in the open air. I mistakenly chose his gravesite to reside within your garden, and I'm terribly sorry."

"Hmph," she replied, rolling her eyes. "I suppose your intentions were true, even though you're still a couple of half-wits. Very well, follow me."

Ben looked at Gothkar and shrugged.

"Where are we going?"

"To discuss how the two of you are going to repay me."

***

"Where'd she go?"

"I don't know," replied Gothkar. "I guess we should follow the trail of slime she left behind."

The companions followed the path around the grayish-brown roots of a cypress grove. A blanket of needle-like leaves covered the turf and led them to another clearing. In the center, among a patch of orange and purple toadstools, stood a house. It had a stone pathway leading to the front door and a fenced-in, neatly kept yard. Amber light glowed from circular windows while blue smoke puffed from a chimney stack. The house was only slightly larger than Ben's boot.

"Come in weary travelers," said the woman from inside. "Please come in and rest yourselves. Have a bite to eat."

Ben looked at Gothkar and frowned.

"Thank you very much for the offer, but I believe we are slightly too large to enter your fine home. May we sit outside?"

"Suit yourselves. I'll be out in half a moment."

They sat patiently and waited. Ben took off his pack and

placed it on the ground. He unrolled the map and spread it out on the cap of the largest toadstool. It had not been of much use during their time underground, but now that they were adrift in the depths of Blackwood Forest, it would come in handy.

"Where do you think we are?" asked Gothkar.

Ben ran his finger along the faded parchment. "I would guess that we're on the outskirts of this swamp near the southern bend of the Wondering River. Kad is up here, and Thorndale is this way, so that definitely puts us right here."

"Wrong!" shouted a voice from his left shoulder.

Ben gasped.

The old woman sat on his arm, smiling up at him.

"You're actually here," she said as she hopped down onto the map and slithered up toward a northern curve in the river.

"Are we near the Gate of Frozen Whispers?" asked Ben.

"In a way," she replied with a grin.

"I'm sorry," said Gothkar, "but who are you, and what are we sitting around here for?"

"I'm Eleanor and I'm going to help you find the gate you seek, but first you must help me. It's payment for destroying my mushroom garden."

"That's fair. My name is Benjamin Woods and this is Gothkar. As mentioned, we've been traveling from Kad in search of the gate."

"Why?" asked the woman.

"It's a long story. How can we repay you?"

"I have a small task for you."

Gothkar moaned. "Small, she says. Ha!"

"I don't like your attitude, young man."

"Don't mind him. He gets that way when he hasn't eaten

in a while. We'd be happy to complete your task. What is it?"

"A local band of gnolls have been causing trouble up and down the shores of the river. My friend Lucy, who lives on the outskirts of Goldcrest, had her house broken into and ransacked. They stole some valuables."

"Is she a snail like you?" asked Gothkar.

"No, she's a human. May I continue?"

"Please."

"What did they steal from your friend?" asked Ben.

"Diamonds."

Gothkar's eyes widened.

"You're interested now, are you?" asked Eleanor. "Yes, those vermin stole a bag of diamonds that I'd given to Lucy for her birthday many moons ago. Those gems have their own arduous history, and I'll be damned if their fate ends in the filthy claws of those beasts."

"If we recover the diamonds for you, can we have a few as payment?" asked Gothkar.

"No, stupid. You're going to retrieve them to pay me back. However, gnolls tend to horde other gems and treasure in their dens, so you're free to liberate whatever else you find. So, what do you say?"

Ben looked at Gothkar who responded with a wink.

"Then you'll show us the location of the gate?"

"I promise."

"Very well, we'll do it."

"There's one more detail," said Eleanor.

"Of course, there is," replied Gothkar.

"This particular gang of gnolls is led by a brute called Grizzlefang. He's about your size and wields a very large sword.

He'll be guarding their treasure mound, so be mindful!"

"I'm sure an adult troll and an armored human with a sword called Ghostreaver can take on this crew."

"Of course, you can! Let me show you on the map where their hideout is."

***

"How do we always get ourselves into these side quests?" asked Gothkar as they made their way along the river's edge.

"It's getting us to our destination," replied Ben. "Besides, they don't call it an adventure for nothing."

"But this is a waste of our time, man. We don't have to help this rude little snail. We could find the gate on our own."

"Perhaps, but this is the right thing to do."

Gothkar grunted. "You and your damn morals."

The waters of the Wondering River lapped along the beach to their west while the thick tree line of Blackwood rose to their east. Marshy cypress had given way to sturdy elms and oaks. Their path was bright and open, contrasting with the darkness and solitude of their previous march under the city.

"What's that?" asked Ben.

"Looks like the remains of a footbridge."

"There's a nice hill on the other side of the river," said Ben. "It would be wise to climb to the top and get our bearings."

"No way in hell we're making it across that bridge. Let's keep moving along this side like we're doing. The old woman showed us exactly where the gnoll den is. We'll be there shortly."

Ben grunted, emulating Gothkar's earlier comment. "You and your damn stubbornness."

As they progressed along their southern route, the sun sunk low on the western horizon. Blue sky transitioned to a blend of apricot, crimson, and lavender.

"We're not going to make it back before dark."

"Nope," replied Ben. "But I did notice a fallen oak not too far back. Once we complete our task we should camp there."

"I think we're close now," said Gothkar, pointing ahead.

Remnants of large bonfires scarred the turf and sand. A ravaged wagon, charred and broken, lay within a heap of debris and overgrown weeds. Bits of flotsam peppered the sand.

"They'll have scouts lurking about," said Gothkar.

"Look down there," said Benjamin. "Sentry fires."

"We should get off the beach and use the cover of the forest to our advantage."

"Good idea," said Benjamin, stowing the map.

The companions crept behind the ruins of the wagon and slipped into the forest. The evening air was warm and windless, and the crickets were out in force. They dashed from tree to tree, keeping watch through breaks in the tree line. Small figures could be seen walking and dancing around the fires.

"Do we have a plan?" asked Gothkar.

"Eleanor said a path leads from the beach to a cave just inside the forest. Let's cut through the woods and bypass the path. We can keep an eye out for lone scouts on the way."

"Fine, then what? How do we get inside the cave?"

"Through the front door?"

"Brilliant," said Gothkar, "but I have another idea. Let's create a diversion out here and get the stupid gnolls away from the cave's entrance. Then we can slip in undetected and make our way to wherever they keep the treasure."

"Not bad. What kind of diversion?"

Gothkar smiled. "A big ass explosion."

They backtracked to the ruins of the wagon to orchestrate their next move. Gothkar removed two planks of wood and carved a symbol into each. It appeared as a half circle with five extending lines, like the elder rune of the sun, yet split in half. They knelt in the sand and peered at the dancing gnolls through the spokes of a cracked wagon wheel.

"We'll leave one here and then detonate the other inside the woods," said Gothkar. "Once they're both triggered, we can approach the cave entrance and enjoy the fireworks from afar."

"Do you have to do your thing first?"

Gothkar acknowledged with a grunt and then pulled the symbol into the third dimension. It pulsated with a crimson glow. He muttered a few arcane words under his breath and then stood.

"It's ready. Let's go do the other one."

Once the second symbol was pulled and triggered, they crept through the trees and made their way to the cave's entrance. An outcropping of boulders and coiled roots, uplifted by the formation of the caves below, provided an ideal hiding spot.

"When will these things go off?" asked Ben.

"In five…four…three…two…one."

A deep tremor rumbled within the bedrock, followed by an upsurging tube of super-heated fire. The resulting deflagration illuminated the entire river valley. A blast wave of super-sonic air pulverized every tree and gnoll within a fifty-meter diameter. Those that survived shrieked in terror and scattered into the surrounding woods.

"Goddamn!" cried Benjamin. "The whole fucking realm heard that. Do you always have to go to such extremes?"

"That's just the first one. Wait for it…"

The second detonation was even larger. Any gnoll or other creature unfortunate to be within the blast zone was incinerated. Burning debris and ash rained down on the river, sand, and toppled trees. The gnoll camp was hysterical.

"Diversion created, let's go," said Gothkar, laughing.

Ben shook his head and followed to the front of the cave.

The entrance was choked with a mishmash of objects. Crates, barrels, and chests with iron hinges were haphazardly stacked within the cave's mouth. The flicker of a solitary oil lamp revealed an oaken door, set within the stone and slightly ajar. Ben and Gothkar eased it open and slipped through unnoticed.

Yelps and shrieks echoed within the tunnels. Gothkar's diversion had not only been successful above ground but even below, the confused gnolls were running around in a frenzy.

"Don't ever forget how great this idea was," said Gothkar as they slinked along the tunnel wall.

"You should be very proud of yourself," said Ben. "But tell me this, smart guy, where do we go now?"

Gothkar pointed ahead. "Down there."

The tunnel sloped gradually to the left and ended at an intersection that branched into three additional shafts. A few barrels, a wooden chair, and a hanging lantern were the only items in the modest chamber. The tunnel to their left rose with a steep incline. Steps, chiseled from the limestone, extended into the darkness above. In contrast, the shaft to their right plunged deeper into the bowels of the cave system. A ferocious stench extruded from its orifice. The path forward remained level.

"Up, down, or forward?" asked Benjamin.

"The leader wouldn't be up, and I'm not going anywhere

near whatever's causing that smell, so forward we go. Onward!"

Alcoves and doors to other rooms appeared on either side of the tunnel. Elaborate deposits of flowstone melded with imposing stalagmites. As Benjamin and Gothkar maneuvered between the formations, the tunnel expanded, allowing more subterranean wonders to be observed.

The gnolls had utilized the natural features of the caves to their advantage. Their ingenuity was impressive. Planks of wood had been used to manufacture shacks and huts along the faces of the massive stalactites and stalagmites. This den was ancient, the calcite and other carbonate minerals having fortified the living quarters better than any topside technique. A maze of suspension bridges constructed of rope and chain connected the huts to one another. In the center of the web, perched atop the grandest stalagmite, was a dwelling with a thatched roof constructed of dried vegetation and reeds from the river. A balcony extended from the tallest spire. A great figure stood at its edge, pumping its fists and shouting commands. War horns blared.

"I think that's our boy up there," said Gothkar.

Shrill cries rang from a bridge to their left. The notch and release of many arrows hissed from above, while the openings of adjacent tunnels glowed with lamplight.

"And the fun begins," said Ben, unsheathing his sword.

"At least you'll get to try out Uncle Oswulf's gear," said Gothkar, pulling out his own dagger, and seeking cover behind a barrel. The thud of arrow impacts riddled the opposite side.

Crouching low, the companions hustled to a bridge that led to the next level. A band of yelping gnolls charged down the ramp, thrusting their spears forward.

Gothkar bellowed a deep war cry and attacked. Using his

massive forearm, he swept two of the group over the railing and into a bubbling cauldron. Twisting in the opposite direction, he performed a diagonal sweep with his dagger. A gnoll's ear and portion of forehead went airborne. The beast stood in shock for a moment, then tumbled over the side.

It was Ben's turn to enter the fray. With Ghostreaver held high, he pounced on the next gnoll in line. Rows of razor-sharp teeth chomped and bit, trying to extract a chunk of human flesh. Ben lopped off the animal's head with a massive lateral stroke, sending a fountain of blood over everyone.

As Ben spit and wiped the gore from his face, a calculated spear attack struck him in the upper arm between the pauldron and gauntlet. He wailed with pain.

Gothkar tossed the final gnoll over the side of the bridge. It fell headfirst, impaling itself on a grouping of thin stalactites.

"You all right, man?" he asked as they recovered.

"I'm fine. Let's get to the next level before more come."

They raced up the bridge and into the first elevated hut. A constant barrage of arrows ricocheted around them.

"I wish we'd thought to bring shields."

Gothkar inspected the interior of the hovel. A straw bed, table, and a few chairs occupied the space. In the far corner crackled a fire, the hearth outfitted with a spit and various pots.

"Will this do?" he asked, grabbing a brass lid.

"It's better than nothing."

The second wave of the attack brought the companion's respite to an end. Fire arrows and light artillery were now in play. The thatched roofing of their hut was ablaze, as well as most of the railing along the outer walkways. They peeked out the door to see another band of gnolls storming down one of two bridges.

The other that led to the third level was vacant.

"I have another idea," said Gothkar. "Keep me shielded with that lid for a moment. Here, trade me."

The troll tossed Ben the makeshift shield and in turn held out his hand for Ghostreaver. Armed with its glistening steel, he burst from the hovel and chopped at the rope that held the bridge to their landing. The approaching gnolls paused in horror.

"So long, assholes," said Gothkar.

The final rope popped from the lack of tension and the entire bridge, gnolls and all, crashed to the depths below. Two crossbow batteries, armed with flaming bolts, were caught up in the collapse. Several misfires punctured a barrel of black powder and the resulting chain reaction sent a mushroom cloud of fire and smoke all the way to the leader's perch. The heat was so intense that it burned the hair right off Ben's knuckles.

"Wow!" he exclaimed as they ran up the vacant bridge.

"Let's take a breather here," said Gothkar.

"May I have Ghostreaver back, please?"

"Certainly."

The third level consisted of hardened huts and dwellings that were built flush against the face of the massive stalactite. Curved walkways ascended the sides of the limestone until they converged at the leader's terrace. Slumped over and panting, Gothkar and Ben looked up to their destination.

"Too many damn steps in this place."

"The real question is, how do we get back down?"

All the bridges and shacks connected to the previous levels were in flames and inaccessible. Gothkar and Ben were trapped on an island amidst an ocean of fire. Nevertheless, arrows continued to zip by their heads.

"We'll figure something out once we get to the top. I've had enough of this errand. Let's go."

"Right behind you," said Gothkar.

They followed a flight of steps that curled up the side. A gnoll popped out of a doorway to their left, but Ben dispatched it with a sword blade through the chest. It was a running battle for the remainder of the climb. Gothkar killed another attacker with his dagger, but not before catapulting two others over his shoulder and into the abyss of flames. As they reached the top and surveyed their options, Gothkar took two arrows in the leg. He went down face first.

"Oh no!" shouted Ben, dropping to his side.

"How bad is it?" asked the troll between clenched teeth.

The arrows had impacted the same leg. One struck the lower portion of his quadricep, while the second had torn directly through the cartilage and ligaments of his knee. Gothkar pulled the first one out immediately. The arrow tip took a chunk of meat out as it exited. The second impact, because the tip had gone through to the other side, would not be as simple to remove.

"Can you walk?" asked Ben.

"No way. I can probably hop if you help me up."

As Ben attempted to lift Gothkar to his feet, a menacing growl emerged from the opposite side of the terrace. It was Grizzlefang. Eleanor was not kidding when she underscored the beast's brutish demeanor. He stood two meters, had greenish-gray skin, razor-sharp fangs, and was covered by a thick layer of disheveled fur. Atop the back of Grizzlefang's long hunched neck rose a black mane. His armor was a patchwork of plate and boiled leather, with a spiked pauldron on his left shoulder. A two-handed Claymore capped the presentation.

"Took you long enough to get up here," he said.

"We met some interference," replied Ben.

"Clever, but I'd say you're the ones interfering. Look what you've done to my community. Who the fuck are you?"

"We're treasure hunters at the moment."

"Of course, you are. Hunting anything specific, or did you just feel like raiding a gnoll den on a summer's evening?"

"A bag of diamonds. Are you familiar with them?"

"I might be," said the gnoll, tapping a pouch on his belt.

"They were stolen from a friend of ours and we'd like to have them back."

"How polite of you to ask. Sadly, I'm not in the business of giving things away, so how about we fight for it?"

"A sword fight?"

"What else?"

Ben examined Grizzlefang's imposing stature and sword. "I think you possess a slight advantage in single combat."

"Too bad for you. You should've considered that before barging your way up here."

"A fair statement."

"Seems your colleague is injured as well. A shame, as I was looking forward to dueling a troll for a change of pace. Well, I suppose a human will have to do for today."

"Your overconfidence is pedestrian."

"And your armor is boring me," he replied, brandishing his enormous sword. "Do you really think a few bits of hand-me-down leather are going to withstand Gutslicer?"

"I couldn't say, and it doesn't matter."

"Why is that?"

"Because I don't intend on getting hit."

Grizzlefang snarled with delight. "*Your* overconfidence is pretentious. I'm going to enjoy eating you once I cook you."

"I'm not pretending," replied Benjamin, jumping aside.

While the two argued, Gothkar had drawn and pulled another symbol into the third dimension. Its design consisted of a full circle intersected by three lines, resembling a snowflake.

"Cool it!" he said, throwing the symbol at Grizzlefang.

The gnoll was instantly frozen into a block of ice.

"That was easy," said Gothkar.

"All this real-world practice with your symbolcraft is going to start racking up the experience points."

"I know, right? I've been keeping a mental note so I can report it to Vomexium."

"Are the diamonds still okay?"

"They should be. I don't think they can freeze, but I don't know. That seems like a question for someone smarter."

Benjamin walked over to Grizzlefang and plucked the pouch from his belt. As it separated from his frozen form, the temperature of the bag rose, and the contents were accessible. Benjamin poured the diamonds into the palm of his hand.

"Beautiful," he exclaimed. "Now let's get out of here."

"About that…," said Gothkar, pointing to his knee.

"Oh, yea. Can't you use a symbol to fix that?"

"Unfortunately, no. I haven't learned anything like that yet. We're going to have to deal with this the old-fashioned way."

Benjamin stared. "And that would be?"

"Pushing it through the other side."

"Won't that be painful?"

"Yes, now will you hurry up and help?"

Benjamin stuffed the pouch in his pocket and knelt.

"I can't drag that arrow tip back through my knee, so push the shaft all the way through."

Benjamin placed his hands on the feathers at the exposed end of the shaft and pushed.

"Wait! Snap off the feathers first," said Gothkar. "I don't want that shit going through me."

"Right," he said, removing all but a few centimeters.

"Now use your thumbs to push it into the knee, and then pull the rest out from the other side using the arrow tip."

He pushed until the shaft disappeared into the wound.

"Pull it out quick," said Gothkar.

Benjamin gripped the tip and pulled. It did not budge.

"Fuck!" screamed Gothkar. "Try again."

A second attempt was also unsuccessful.

"What do I do?"

"It's lodged in between the bones. Take my dagger and cut it out from the other side."

Benjamin felt his stomach roll over. "Are you serious?"

"Hurry the fuck up and do it," said Gothkar. "I'm passing out from the pain. Then we'll never get out of here."

Blood gushed from the hole as Benjamin inserted the dagger's tip and moved it around. A terrible crunching sound, followed by a pop, signified a possible disentanglement. Gothkar grasped the arrow tip and pulled with a growl. The shaft was free.

"Thank God," said Benjamin.

Gothkar fell back and stared up at the cave's ceiling. "Tie it up tight with a rag or something while I catch my breath. Then we're going to plunder whatever treasure is in that shack. I didn't fight my way through all this for nothing."

Benjamin dressed the wounds with clean bandages that he

had acquired from Maggie. He helped Gothkar to his feet.

"How's it feel?"

"I won't be walking for a while."

"I'll fashion you a crutch once we get topside."

"Gutslicer should suffice until then."

Gothkar supported himself with the massive sword and hobbled over to Grizzlefang's lair. Surrounding his throne was a heap of treasure and gold. Chests, sacks, and coffers were filled with every imaginable spoil. Decades of waylaying travelers with little to no oversight had allowed the gnolls to amass mounds of silver and gold ingots, coins, and precious jewels.

"We're getting into the habit of finding treasures that we can't take advantage of," said Benjamin.

"Let's bring a wagon with us on our next adventure."

"Deal."

Gothkar scooped up a handful of gold coins from one chest, then a handful of emeralds from another. "I'll take these, and some of these."

"I'll fill our packs with as much as I can, then we really should think about finding an exit out of this cavern."

"I've already found one," said Gothkar, opening a door behind Grizzlefang's throne. "Looks like it leads up."

An escape tunnel brought them back to the surface.

"Fresh air again," said Benjamin. "I'll make that crutch for you and then we can camp at the fallen oak for the night."

"Don't bother," replied Gothkar. "I think I'll hang on to Gutslicer a while longer. This might prove useful later."

***

The companions awoke slightly before dawn, and after a quick breakfast, made their way back to Eleanor's house.

"You found them!" she exclaimed once they returned.

"Yes, ma'am," replied Gothkar. "You can count them. All nine are there, just like you said."

"I trust you, my dear. But what happened to your leg?"

"A couple arrows. I've dealt with worse."

"And Grizzlefang, did you handle him?"

"Let's just say he's hibernating right now."

Eleanor shrugged. "Whatever works. The fact that you two came through with your end of our bargain is all that matters, and Lucy will be ecstatic. Please give me a moment to take this inside, and then if you're ready, I'll happily show you how to get to the Gate of Frozen Whispers."

"That would be very much appreciated."

Gothkar cleared his throat. "I guess this is goodbye."

"For now. Will you be all right getting back to Kad?"

"As long as I can hobble along at my own pace, I should be okay. It's a straight shot up to the city, and then I'll have one of Vomexium's lads sew my leg up proper."

"I'm all set. Are you ready Mr. Woods?" asked Eleanor as she slithered back up the stone path.

"In a moment," he replied, turning back to Gothkar. "I feel awkward saying this, but I'm really going to miss your company, old friend. I've become quite used to both our banter and arguments over the past week."

"No need to feel awkward, I'm going to miss you too."

Benjamin extended his hand.

"A handshake? Hug it out, man."

They embraced with respect and love for one another.

"I'm glad you looked me up again," said Gothkar. "I'm sorry I can't escort you all the way to the gate. I'll see you again once you complete your quest."

"Can you manage my bag of treasure?"

"Of course, I can. I'm a troll."

"Don't forget about the Intensitron."

"I won't, don't worry. Man, you sound like my mother."

Gothkar waved a final time and then turned to the trail. Benjamin watched his friend pass through a grove of cypress and moss and disappear into the forest. He turned back to Eleanor.

"Now I'm ready."

"Very well. Unfurl your map one more time."

Eleanor crawled to a spot on the map within the northern edge of Blackwood Forest.

"See this little nook of trees on the forest's edge? Next to the slopes of the Ethereal Peaks and the onset of the Whispering Hills is your destination."

Benjamin laughed. "We were way off course. We thought this symbol represented the gate."

"You weren't as far off as you think," she replied. "That symbol represents me. Eleanor Willardsby, caretaker of the Gate of Frozen Whispers. Only I know the true location, and only I know the secret passphrase to enter its domain."

"You were expecting us all along, weren't you?"

"Of course," she replied with a grin. "Farewell, Benjamin Woods. Good luck with the next phase of your journey."

CHAPTER XXXVI

THE GATE OF FROZEN WHISPERS

"See if you can walk on it now," said Abigail.

Penelope carefully stood and applied pressure to her right ankle. "Ouch, it's still too tender."

"Give it more time," said Trelinia. "The potion that I made for you will take effect shortly."

"Look," said Abigail. "Your leg wound already has a nice big scab growing on it. You should be proud, it's your first battle wound. Just imagine the scar you'll be able to show off."

"I didn't battle anything," replied Penelope. "All I did was get thrown around and nibbled on by a zombie."

"But you survived," said Trelinia. "Abi's trying to make light of the situation, but she's right. We won our first battle against the enemy the other day. Let's acknowledge our success."

"I definitely acknowledge it," replied Abigail. "I got to use my powers for the first time."

"You did very well," said Trelinia. "But don't forget what I said about using those powers sparingly. It takes a lot of energy, and we all need to be in peak performance for what awaits us."

"I'm definitely not starting off well," exclaimed Penelope, applying pressure to her ankle again and cringing.

"That's enough self-pity for today," said Trelinia. "Let's get back on the road so we can make our way to Dragolroth by nightfall. Our companions should be arriving there soon."

"You mean your children and husband," said Abigail.

"Yes, dear," she replied with a twinge of heartache.

A deep tremble reverberated through the forest. Leaves fell from the canopy, and twigs and mushrooms bounced around their campsite.

"We're under attack again," gasped Penelope.

"It's an earthquake," replied Abigail.

"I don't think it's either," said Trelinia. "Abi, help Penny, and follow me to the top. Quick!"

Their camp was at the foot of a lofty hill. Maple Hill, to be exact. A bald spot at its crest provided a clear view of the forest and valley. Curious standing stones and other monuments poked out of the green turf.

"What is it?" asked Penelope as they reached the summit.

"Look," said Trelinia, pointing to the distance.

A herd of dinosaurs strode across a grassy plain.

"Holy shit," said Abigail. "Those are Brachiosaurus."

The behemoths arrived at the edge of The Wondering River and took long gulps of the clear water. Two others were already submerged up to their shoulders, where flocks of gulls and egrets soared amidst their towering necks.

"Those two are taking a bath," said Penelope.

"I can't believe I'm looking at dinosaurs," said Abigail. "They're beautiful."

"Look to the other side of the river," said Trelinia. "The kinds with three horns and a frill have always been my favorite."

"We call those Triceratops on Earth," said Abigail. "Do you use the same names here?"

"For the most part, yes," said Trelinia. "There are many similarities between our two worlds, especially with language. The Earth's undead have influenced Silvarum for eons, just like our people have influenced your world since the beginning of time."

Abigail pondered this for a moment as she gazed upon the valley of dinosaurs.

"Living people from this realm can travel to Earth?"

"Now you're putting the pieces together," said Trelinia.

"Look," cried Penelope. "Flying ones!"

Five Pteryxtodons plummeted from the west and circled over the groups of hydrating and bathing dinosaurs. They took turns diving to the river's surface, scooping up fish, crabs, and squid in their beaks.

"Those are my favorite," said Penelope, clapping.

Abigail watched two of the Pteryxtodons fly away to the east before her gaze fell upon a colossal structure on the horizon.

"What's that?" she asked.

"That's the capital city of Kadiaphonek," replied Trelinia.

"It's gigantic," said the girl. "It makes San Francisco look like a little village in comparison. I bet it's twice the size of New York City. Just look at those pyramids."

"There's even more of the flying dinosaurs circling the city," said Penny from atop one of the standing stones.

"I guess her ankle is feeling better," said Trelinia.

"Can we go there?" asked Abigail.

"One day we will, absolutely," said Trelinia. "But not on this quest. Our destination lies to the south."

Abigail, Penelope, and Trelinia turned and observed the two other massive structures looming in the distance. The nearest was the Watchtower of Dragolroth. Its ivy-covered stonework, turrets, and Gothic windows commanded the river valley. Beyond and to the southeast stood the Haunted Castle, refuge of the dragon Lord Mortis, and the current resting place of the Rune of Frost.

"That's where we're going?" asked Penelope.

"Yes."

***

"Fucking mosquitoes," said Gothkar as he rested on the side of the road, swatting at the air, and cursing his knee.

His injury had worsened during the laborious hike out of the swamp and onto the road that led to Kadiaphonek. The Motherwell was the main artery that cut through the western portion of Blackwood Forest, connecting the smaller villages to Kadiaphonek. A few passing wagons had offered him a ride, but his pride had prevented him from accepting. Benjamin had been right. His stubbornness was a detriment, a flaw that needed to be tempered. Gothkar decided that he would accept the next offer of transport.

He hobbled along the road for another few hours, passing pockets of travelers. Some were solitary riders on horseback, but most of the traffic was small clusters on foot. Because of Gothkar's intimidating size and the giant sword he was employing as a crutch, people gave a nod or a tip of the hat from the opposite side of the road. On one occasion, a family of Tulleks pointed and giggled as they passed. Two children threw pebbles at Gothkar, the impacts ringing off Gutslicer. Through the swelling pain, it took all his willpower to refrain from screaming at them. He kept his head down and continued.

Within the last hour, the stream of travelers had waned. This section of The Motherwell was straight and flat and passed between groves of oak and maple. The gentle gradient relieved some of the pressure in his knee, allowing Gothkar to pick up the pace. He could even see the golden tips of Kadiaphonek's tallest pyramids peeking over the distant trees. The sound of hoofbeats signaled approaching horses, and he turned with a smile.

***

"How many different ways do I have to explain this to you before you understand?" asked Frederick.

"Please stop trying," replied Arina. "I don't even care."

"Then you agree with me?"

"No."

"How's that possible?"

"Because your argument is stupid, and nobody besides you ever thinks about stuff like this. You're so weird."

"I don't think it's weird to be concerned about aesthetics, sanitation, and efficiency."

"The two of you have been bickering for the past hour," said Blazrug. "What are you even talking about?"

"The proper orientation of toilet paper," said Frederick.

"I agree with Arina," said Eddie. "Under looks cleaner."

"Wrong!" shouted Frederick. "You can't…"

"Shut up," said Blazrug. "All of you. There's something happening on the road up ahead."

Frederick, Arina, Blazrug, and Eddie had been traveling back to Kadiaphonek on a smaller trail just off to the side of The Motherwell. Many such hiking paths followed and crisscrossed all the major highways within Blackwood Forest. The group crept to the tree line and watched.

"That's a troll," whispered Frederick. "Look at the size of that sword he has."

"He seems injured, though," said Blazrug. "He's using it as a crutch and there's dried blood all over his trousers."

"I can't hear what they're saying," said Arina.

"The cloaked rider on the wagon offered him a ride to the city," said Eddie. "He accepted."

Blazrug peered through the branches to get a better look at the troll's face. Something about him seemed familiar.

"That's Gothkar," he exclaimed.

"Who's that?" asked Frederick.

"A member of my order, The Shadowkuur, but more importantly, he was traveling with your friend's uncle, Benjamin Woods. They were headed to some secret gate."

"Then let's grab him before he leaves."

"Good idea," said Blazrug. "I could take a look at that wound of his too."

"Um, guys," said Eddie, pulling on his father's shirt sleeve and pointing. "Are those goblins in the back of the wagon?"

Yellow eyes shimmered within the blackness of the covered wagon. At that moment, as Gothkar strained to climb to the passenger seat and situate himself, the cloaked rider raised a blunt object and struck him across the back of the head. The troll dropped immediately and was pulled into the back by a frenzy of green hands. The rider threw back her hood and laughed. It was Magnolia Jinglewort.

"That's my aunt!" cried Frederick.

Magnolia cracked a whip and two black steeds thrust the wagon forward. The companions surged from the forest and ran up to The Motherwell. A cloud of dust and the distant crack of a whip greeted them. They stood in shock and stared.

"This is terrible," gasped Blazrug. "We have to get back to Kad right now and inform Dot and Vomexium."

***

Benjamin Woods stood before the Gate of Frozen Whispers. The sunlit grasses of the distant hills contrasted with the faltering light of the foreground trees. The gate was a brick and stone structure, composed of three round arches, engraved hieroglyphics, and surrounded by a well-kept garden. Cyclopean tentacles, wrapped in overlapping scales, exuded from within the gate and curled around its brickwork.

Through the trees, Benjamin could make out foothills that rolled like waves until they broke against the stone shores of the Ethereal Peaks. Upon many of the hills stood ancient monoliths. Flocks of birds expelled mournful cries as they flew between the standing stones. A wave of melancholy swept over Benjamin as he peered into the distance and thought of his family. He threw back his hood, focused his attention to the next phase of his quest, and approached the shadowy arches.

A series of tremors reverberated through the tentacles as

he advanced. They seemed to grow larger, curling tighter around the arches and preventing entry. Whispers fell from the trees, as an icy gust sent Benjamin's cloak snapping in the wind.

"The words," he said while unfolding the map.

Eleanor had provided the passphrase required to enter the gate. He read aloud the following passage:

> *Carry the candle against the wind,*
> *Float above the grass.*
> *Speak the source of your sorrow,*
> *Then only shall you pass.*

Benjamin took a deep breath. "Tombworld," he said.

Nothing happened. The tentacles were unmoved.

He said it a second time, but slower and louder.

Nothing.

He looked at the passage again and muttered the words to himself. The first two lines seemed straightforward. They foretold of an arduous journey, requiring focus and determination. The final sentence was even more obvious. Reveal to the gate your destination, and it would permit your entry.

Benjamin lowered the map in frustration and gazed back out into the distant hills. He did not feel focused now. The solitary hike to the northern edge of Blackwood had been grueling. His thoughts had revolved around how much he missed his friend, his children, and his wife. *His wife.*

"Trelinia," he said.

There was an abrupt fluctuation in air pressure and the tentacles relaxed their grip upon the stone. They retreated from the central arch, allowing Benjamin to pass into the darkness.

***

Cold. Dark. Confused.

Benjamin opened his eyes. He stood at the entrance to a great necropolis. Tombworld. Eleanor's secret pass phrase had allowed him to travel through the Gate of Frozen Whispers.

Before his feet lay a cobblestone pathway, spotted with patches of dusty snow. It twisted before him and curved gently upward between rows of steps and Corinthian columns. Wilted grass and snow covered the bordering slopes. Ben peered from the base of a hill that was surrounded by thick weeds, decaying tombs, and ivy-covered monuments. Despite this, he could still appreciate the expansive scale of the landscape through gaps in the path and spaces between the stone and marble. Golden reflections sparkled from the pyramidal tips of distant obelisks.

He turned and examined the lichgate that had enabled his conversion. It was constructed of solid ash beams and a pitched roof of overlapping clay tiles. A dreary haze lingered beyond the gate's threshold, like looking into nothingness. He followed the gray void straight up until it merged with the blue sky. The sensation caused him to lose his balance. He took a deep breath and then turned to walk up the hill.

The sky was filled with dingy birds. They flew aimlessly and perched upon the contorted limbs of dead trees and the cracked corners of ancient pediments. Their cries echoed against stone altars, Ionic capitals, and ornate triglyphs.

"Where may I find Penelope Crofts?" he asked the wind.

Crows and ravens answered him with malice. He stared back with an expression as stoic as the stone facades that surrounded him. Benjamin took another deep breath. The frosty air filled his lungs and cleared his thoughts. He glared back up at the birds and answered their malice with determination.

"Fine," he replied. "I'm a ghost now, I'll find her myself."

From his teenage travels through the Tombworld, Ben recalled that the Novemgradus was in a crypt near the top of the cemetery. He shielded his eyes from the sun and gazed upward. Level upon level of marble and stone ascended to form a mountain of tombs and graves. Every meter of snow-covered soil was occupied by some form of shrine, vault, or mausoleum. The cramped necropolis was overwhelming, but he realized that the only option was to labor to the top.

"Let's move feet," he said and started up the path.

The contrast between the warm breezes of Blackwood Forest and the frozen gusts of the Shadow Mountains soon brought Benjamin's lungs to a stinging halt. He paused halfway up and rested upon the marble steps of a crypt that faced the mid-day sun. Its warm rays washed over him, replenishing his energy, and restoring his spirit. As he stood to continue, Ben noticed a pile of boots just to the side of the steps. One pair had pink shoelaces and the other had black and white checkered ones.

He reached the next layer of tombs and paused to study his surroundings. To his right, a mosaic of dirty snow barely covered the stone and grass. Rotted masonry lay strewn across a section of path that crested the hill. He surveyed the trail of stonework back along the cobblestone. A fallen birch tree had destroyed the copper roof of a ghastly sepulcher.

Ben looked toward the left. The path curled a short way between structures and tombstones and then rose back up the hill. There were no visible obstructions, and the drifts of snow were lighter and sporadic on this side. He decided to go that way.

Turning the corner, Ben discovered his first promising clue. A set of human footprints in the snow. They had been made by bare feet, originating from a subterranean crypt, and ascending a stairwell to the cemetery above. Ben knelt by a cluster of the prints and noticed droplets of blood. Were they left by Penelope? Was she injured? He descended the steps to investigate.

At the bottom, he pushed open a door and stepped into the darkness. The interior was cramped, cold, and ancient. Thin fingers of pale light crept between cracks in the walls, highlighting slivers of the stone floor. Thick cobwebs covered every angle and corner in the room. Against the far wall, veiled in a gossamer gown of webbing and dust, stood a wooden pedestal. Atop it lay a moldy, leather-bound book, shrouded in dust and decay. Iron hinges cradled the binding and a massive lock prevented further analysis of the tome's contents.

"The Novemgradus," said Benjamin.

Carved into the leather was a pair of overlapping circles. In the center peered a lidless eye. As Ben leaned closer to inspect the details, the eyeball blinked twice. A whisper, as faint as falling snowflakes, spoke from the ancient pages.

"Who has awakened me?"

"I'm searching for Penelope Crofts."

"She is gone."

"Where?"

"The Moonchild and the Two Eagles have departed. The Children of the Woods is whom they seek."

"I'm Benjamin Woods. I'm their father."

"So you are, and a good one based on your dedication. The role that you have played in this great undertaking has not gone unnoticed. The sacrifices that were required of you have been many, yet you have persevered through each obstacle to reach this moment. We have watched, and we are satisfied. You may pass within these pages to be reunited with your loved ones, Benjamin Woods, for they have sacrificed as well. Go, my child. Find your family."

"Thank you," he replied.

The book's eye glowed a radiant blue. The hinges unsnapped with a clink, and the cover opened. A bold chapter heading, penned in a flowing script, displayed the following:

STAGE I: DEPARTURE

He grasped the page and slowly turned. A soothing glow engulfed his mind and body, and he willingly submitted to its heavenly embrace.

***

Benjamin Woods stood on a forest road in front of the Watchtower of Dragolroth. Its circular turret and crenellations frowned down upon him. Shafts of sunlight fell from the heights of the canopy and settled upon the tower's blackened stonework. A pair of golden eagles were perched atop its battlements.

"And just like that," he said, "I'm in Blackwood again."

"Aye," replied a harsh voice from behind. "But alone."

Ben whirled around just in time to draw Ghostreaver and parry a crashing sword attack from above. It was Grizzlefang.

"No tricks," said the gnoll. "We finish our duel now."

"A new sword?" asked Ben, keeping his blade vertical and using his footwork to position for the next attack.

"This one's called Heartseeker. After its steel defeats you, I'm going to pay your friend a visit and retrieve my other sword. Thankfully, I know exactly where that troll is being kept."

"What's happened to Gothkar?"

The gnoll responded with a wicked grin.

Benjamin had not engaged in a proper sword fight in many years. He had been truthful with Gothkar earlier regarding his fighting skills as a teenager, however, now that he was forty-five, most of the muscle memory had been replaced by aching joints and a troublesome back. The decades of knowledge and technique remained. His mind was as sharp as ever, and he would need to rely on his wits to counterbalance the physical anguish he was about to endure from this herculean opponent. A proper stance, the positioning of his feet, and a relaxed grip on the hilt were details that he recalled from his training. Ben knew from experience that this fight would be over in only a few moves. He took a breath and focused.

Grizzlefang initiated with an overhead strike. In that first move, Ben noticed a mistake that could be used to his advantage. The gnoll had stepped forward and landed with his sword, rather than allowing the kinetic chain to guide his movement. This resulted in an overextended stance. Advancing at an angle, while focusing on the straightness of his back and shoulders, Ben threw a counter cut. The crash of steel rang through the forest as their blades met. They were isometrically locked for an instant before Ben disengaged and stepped aside. Even though Grizzlefang's technique was poor, his superior upper body strength offset his flawed posture. Ben quickly realized that entering the bind again was a hopeless strategy.

Benjamin resumed the fight with an overhead strike to

the gnoll's neck. The cut was parried, and once again their swords were briefly locked. Grizzlefang thrust a boot into Ben's thigh, propelling him backward onto the road. He rolled to his left, just in time to evade a downward swing. The ground impact caused Heartseeker's tip to get stuck in the mud. Ben hopped to one knee and using a double-handed thrust, drove his blade between the gnoll's tasset and thigh armor. Grizzlefang howled in pain, swinging laterally with an enraged counterattack. It hit Ben on his right pauldron, shearing off a section of the leather and carving into his arm. Although not a grave injury, the concussion sent Ben tumbling to the ground, losing his sword in the process.

Grizzlefang was severely injured. The strike had severed the femoral artery and shattered sections of his femur and pelvic girdle. He used the remaining energy in his functioning leg to lurch over Ben and execute the killing blow.

As he raised Heartseeker, a screech echoed from above. A pair of eagle talons sunk into the top of Grizzlefang's skull and tore away a massive section of flesh and bone. The separation produced a disturbing suction sound. His resulting expression of shock was accentuated by exposed muscles and flaps of hanging skin. Ben pulled a dagger from his belt and plunged it through the gnoll's gaping mouth. The corpse dropped to the road in a heap of plate armor and fur.

Ben fell to the road in exhaustion. Every joint and muscle in his body screamed with pain. Even the gunshot wound that he acquired during the escape from Kad throbbed with his racing heartbeat. He lay flat on his back, limbs outstretched, and tried to catch his breath. As he gazed up at the mid-morning sky, he saw the eagle descend and land next to him.

It transformed from a bird to a human girl. Ben sat up in

shock. The girl was clad in a gray gown, burgundy waistcoat, and green cloak. She shuttered as if from a flash of pain and then smiled as she approached.

"Penelope?" he asked.

"Hello, Benjamin," she replied. "It's been a long time, but I'm glad you've finally arrived."

He attempted to stand, but his body refused.

"Don't bother," she said with a wave. "Those wounds need to be tended to, and we can talk out here on the road."

"I was just in the cemetery looking for you. The book said you'd left with two eagles and something called a Moonchild. I don't know what any of that means, but clearly you are one of those eagles."

"I am," she said. "The other is standing next to you."

Ben turned to look; he felt as if he would faint. Fatigue compounded the emotional anguish that rapidly swept over him. For months he had dreamed of seeing the face that now smiled back. During the hours of isolation, he had imagined the romantic speech that he would deliver upon their reunion. The lump in his throat and the pain in his chest permitted him to whisper only one word.

"Trel."

CHAPTER XXXVII

A BREATH OF
THE WIDE VALLEY

"Click," said Roger. "Could you fetch my backpack?"

The mechanical spider chirped an acknowledgment and scrambled to the other side of their camp. Upon his return, he set the bag next to Roger's feet and performed an obedient bow.

"Thank you, little sir."

"Do we have any food left?" asked Mckenzie.

"What do you think I'm checking?"

"I'm starving," said Marie.

"Will the two of you please calm down?" asked Roger as he fumbled through the contents of his pack.

Inside were many of the items he had collected during their adventure thus far. Some of these curiosities included a portion of what he claimed was a dinosaur bone, a flint shard, and a leather scroll case that he found within the ruins of a wagon by the river. The backpack was also replete with all manner of adventuring minutia. He could start a fire in seconds, make sketches with ink and parchment, or consult one of several books to determine which plants in the forest were edible. The only item it lacked was the very thing they required the most: food.

"So?" asked Mckenzie.

Roger sighed, throwing his backpack to the ground. Click snatched it and set it upright before the contents spilled.

"We won't be having breakfast today," he said.

"What the hell are we going to do now?"

"You should've thought about that before you ate the last of our food," said Marie.

"Excuse me?" replied Mckenzie.

"You heard me. For the past two days, all you've done is moan about how much you miss Frederick, all the while gobbling up everything that Roger and I have hunted and scrounged for."

"I've helped," she replied.

"Because you gathered a handful of nuts and one apple?" asked Marie. "How about you get over yourself, stop sulking like a toddler, and start helping the group? We're about to fight a damn dragon, for heaven's sake."

Roger cringed at the impending counterattack.

Mckenzie turned to her sister and glared. "He saved my life, you little shit. Then I watched him get devoured by a sea monster, only to have him ripped away from me again when our group split up. As far as sulking goes, how quickly you forget your behavior after Mom died. Are you still crying over that little fish you left in the front yard? What was its name? Squeaker? At least I'm sad about a human being and not some stupid…"

CRACK!

An acorn struck Mckenzie on the forehead.

"Don't talk about Squeaker that way," said Marie as she prepared to throw another.

"Bitch!" screamed Mckenzie, jumping to her feet.

Before she could retaliate, a voice interrupted their brawl.

"Good morning, young friends," said a troll at the edge of their camp. "Might I inquire as to the purpose of your visit in this part of the forest?"

Roger's disposition went from one of mild amusement to immediate concern for their safety. He slipped on his glove and looked for the mask. Marie and Mckenzie abandoned their dispute and retreated to the campfire, brandishing their wands. Click climbed to the branch of a nearby tree.

The troll raised his open palms in a show of peace. "Don't be alarmed. My name is Vulthkar. I'm a resident of a nearby village called Goldcrest. I've been monitoring the road between Thorndale and Kad for the arrival of a specific group of individuals. My cousin Gothkar sent me to help you."

The teenagers looked at each other in amazement.

Mckenzie raised her wand slightly and studied the troll. "It's a pleasure to make your acquaintance, Vulthkar. However, you're going to have to prove your identity before we believe anything you've said."

"A very wise request," he replied.

Vulthkar's appearance was captivating. He was a troll, meaning his physical characteristics were intimidating, but it was the juxtaposition of his attire that fascinated the teenagers. He wore a double-breasted vest with green and bronze brocade fabric, black satin lining, and wide lapels with metallic buttons. The bronze chain of a gentleman's pocket watch hung from a silver clasp. He had adorned his lower extremities with a pair of black airstrip trousers, flared at the waist, and fitted with buttons along the calves. Vulthkar's leather excursion boots were covered with snap pouches, buckles, and metallic accents. An open canvas greatcoat enveloped his massive frame. The travel-worn jacket had a tall collar, oversized sleeve cuffs, and lapel panels with even more buttons.

The troll was also outfitted with a variety of weapons. A double holster held steam-powered revolvers. Each was covered in brass tubing, gauges, and gears. The ivory handles contained a circular gauge to monitor the temperature. Across his chest hung a baldric, housing another pistol of similar design. Strung across his back in a leather scabbard reared a lever-action rifle. The armory was accentuated by a boot blade and a dagger tucked within a leather double belt.

Vulthkar slowly lowered his right hand and extracted a stone from a traveler's pouch. "Gothkar gave me this to serve as identification should I find your group in the wild."

"Place it on the ground in front of you," said Mckenzie.

The troll abided and backed away.

"Click, will you please fetch it for me?" she asked.

The spider lowered from the tree by a thread of webbing. He snatched up the stone and hurried back.

Vulthkar chuckled. "A fine companion you have there. I imagine that's the craftsmanship of Merkresh."

Roger's eyes widened. "You know him?"

"Of course, young man. His reputation is legendary in this region, and all of Silvarum, for that matter."

Mckenzie inspected the stone. She flipped it over and pulled a piece of parchment from her backpack. Marie and Roger waited for her judgement. Vulthkar stood with palms still raised and a smile on his face. The spider swiveled its head and peered at each character in turn. After a few moments of investigation, Mckenzie looked up at the group and smiled. Roger and Marie exhaled with relief.

"I believe you, Vulthkar," said Mckenzie, holding up the notes that she had made from her own companion stone. "The symbols match exactly. Would I be correct in guessing that this other symbol next to Gothkar's represents your name?"

"Yes, ma'am, you would," replied the troll. "Do you still have the other companion stone?"

"No, it was left in Thorndale," said Marie.

"A shame," replied Vulthkar. "They're normal stones on their own, but once brought together can produce useful magic."

"Now what?" asked Roger.

"May I lower my hands?"

"Of course," replied Mckenzie.

"Then please allow me to offer you a proper introduction. My name is Vulthkar Thaddeus Glass, sheriff of Goldcrest and Chief Justiciar of The Order of the Viridian Eye."

"Cool," said Roger.

"How may I be of service?" asked the troll.

"My sister ate all our food," said Marie. "Have any?"

"Marie!" exclaimed Mckenzie with a glare.

Vulthkar laughed. "Sadly, I'm not carrying much food at the moment. I was on my way to hunt some game when I heard the commotion in your camp. Would you care to join me?"

"What kind of game?" asked Marie.

"Dinosaurs."

"I knew it!" shouted Roger. "I told you that dinosaurs live

out here. These two didn't believe me, but I found this bone the other day and they said it was from a stupid horse."

"May I see it?" asked Vulthkar.

Roger plucked it from his pack and tossed it across the camp. Click's eyes followed the arch as it fell into the troll's hand.

"This is indeed a dinosaur bone," he said. "It's a section of the right fibula from a Euoplocephalus."

"What the heck is that?" asked Marie.

"It's a herbivore, about five meters long, and covered in bony plate armor. They're easy to distinguish because of the club at the end of their tail and the row of spikes along their back."

"Can we hunt them?" asked Roger.

"We could, but I was planning on taking down something a little more exciting today. How does hunting a Megalosaurus sound to you? I've been tracking one for the past week."

"Hell yes," said the boy. "We learned all about those last year in school. They're carnivorous theropods and are about two meters tall and nine meters long. Their name literally translates to 'big lizard.' They're bipedal, very muscular, and have dagger-like teeth to slice the flesh of their prey."

"Well done," said the troll. "Shall we give it a go?"

"I'll eat anything at this point," said Marie.

"Even some acorns?" asked Mckenzie.

"Funny," replied her sister.

"Oh, I almost forgot," said Vulthkar. "I have a few eggs that I snagged from a Therizinosaur nest yesterday. How about we cook them up and gain some energy before we head out?"

"Please," said Marie. "I'll get the pan and spices ready."

***

Vulthkar, Roger, Mckenzie, and Marie crouched along the tree line, overlooking a wide valley that overflowed with a variety of dinosaur herds. Click, as usual, was perched on a nearby branch. The late morning sun beamed bright and hot, casting reflections off a bend of the river that flowed between grassy plains and hillocks. Opposite sides of the valley descended from the forest's edge to produce a basin at its center. Within the cool waters of countless ponds, clusters of dinosaur species socialized, hydrated, and rested during the heat of the day.

"I can't believe what I'm looking at," said Roger.

"First time seeing them in the wild?" asked the troll.

The boy nodded in silence. He was lost in the scene.

"Then allow me to give you a tour and set some ground rules before we venture out. From this vantage point, we can examine all the major herbivores. There are the sauropods, the ones with the long necks like Brachiosaurus, and the ceratopsians, those have the parrot-like beaks, frills, and horns. The group of Triceratops sitting in the shade on the other side of the valley are a perfect example."

"They're so cool looking," said Mckenzie.

"Which ones are like the bone I found?" asked Roger.

Vulthkar scanned the valley. "There's a group of them drinking by the river. See their clubbed tails and spikey armor?"

"I see them," said Marie. "What about the Agilisaurus?"

Roger and Mckenzie looked at their sister with surprise.

"How do you know about those?" asked Roger.

"I can read," she replied with a smirk. "They're one of the teeny dinosaurs. I've always wanted one as a pet."

"I don't think that's going to happen," said Vulthkar with a chuckle. "But let's see if we can find some."

The group gazed out into the ocean of shifting forms. A deluge of towering necks, stomping feet, and swinging tails filled the emerald vale. Dinosaurs of every size and variation shared the plentiful resources of the Wondering River.

"What about those?" asked Marie, pointing.

"Nope," replied Vulthkar. "Those are similar, but they're called Nanosaurus and are more solitary. The Agilisaurus prefer to stay in herds, running around the valley."

"What about the meat-eaters?" asked Mckenzie.

"Good question," said the troll. "I'll explain the carnivore situation after I go over the ground rules I mentioned earlier. Even though every species you see out there is a plant-eater, they'll still kill you if they feel threatened."

"You mean we're going out there?" asked Marie.

"Of course we are, so listen up. Just like any wild animal, you need to stay composed when you're around them. No loud noises or sudden movements. Since most are hot and sleepy right now, we should be fine if we just walk by calmly. They're all used to being around creatures like us. Secondly, I noticed that you're all armed. Please be sure to keep your weapons concealed until we're hunting or you're in real danger. These creatures are highly intelligent. Not only will they sense aggressive intentions, but they will not react graciously if you start waving magic wands and mechanical gloves around. Got it?"

"Yes, sir," replied Roger. "We understand."

"Good," he said. "Now on to the carnivores. First, I have a confession to make. I was not completely honest with you with regards to bringing you along on a random hunt."

The teenagers pulled back with apprehension.

"It's not that kind of lie, don't worry," said Vulthkar. "I

know exactly why you're all out here. You're on your way to fight Lord Mortis. He's a frost dragon, and a few teenagers aren't going to survive without at least a little training, I don't care how many fancy weapons you have. Ergo, one of my intentions is to act as your combat instructor."

Their skittish expressions morphed to appreciation.

"Really?" asked Mckenzie.

"Absolutely," said the troll. "Lord Mortis is but the first of eight rune protectors that you must battle. I'm going to assist and train you through each quest, so you better get used to me."

"Why would you do this for us?" asked Marie.

"I love my cousin and he asked me to help you as a personal favor. Also, as Chief Justiciar of The Order of the Viridian Eye, it is my sworn duty to protect those who wage war against the enemies of Silvarum. Finally, I need your help."

"What?" gasped Mckenzie. "Why would you need us?"

Vulthkar grinned. "Sooner or later you're going to realize how important the three of you actually are. As you progress in this journey, all of you are going to become extremely powerful. Even more powerful than me."

Roger laughed.

"Consider my needing your help an investment into your future abilities. Silvarum is a complex place and there's more going on than the war for the runestones."

"What does that mean?" asked Marie.

"You're on your way to Dragolroth, correct?"

"Yes."

"How were you planning on getting there?"

Marie and Mckenzie looked at Roger.

"By following the road," said the boy, timidly.

"That's not going to work," replied Vulthkar.

"Why?"

"Did you hear that huge explosion the other night?"

"Yes. What was that?" asked Mckenzie.

"Someone raided and blew up a local gnoll den. As a result, there're swarms of them roaming the roads near the river and on the way to Dragolroth. Following the road, either by night or day, your group would be attacked. Fortunately, I happen to know a shortcut, and that's where you can help me help you. I get you to Dragolroth along a relatively safe path, and you help me with an important task in return."

"Why can't you come with us along the road and help fight any gnolls that show up?" asked Mckenzie.

"And what did you mean by relatively safe?" asked Marie.

The troll turned to Mckenzie. "Nothing in life is free, my dear. I'm committed to training you for years to come, but in return, I do require your assistance from time to time."

The girl shrugged.

"As for relatively safe," he continued, "like most places in the realm, there is danger everywhere. It depends on what you're comparing it to. Fighting off waves of rampaging gnolls is one form of danger and taking a shortcut through a cave to fight only one enemy is another. Which is more dangerous is a matter of debate. I can say with confidence, however, that killing gnolls will not solve my problem. So, under the ground we must go!"

"Fabulous speech," said Mckenzie. "Are you planning on letting us know what this one enemy is?"

"Certainly," he replied. "We have reason to believe it's a giant spider. There's a village not too far northeast of here called Haltwistle. It's a gnome settlement and apparently, a group of their cartographers were exploring a nearby cave system and vanished. One of them was able to escape and she reported that they were attacked by a spider. Seeing as this river valley is my jurisdiction, I've been dispatched to search for them, recover any survivors, and slay the spider. My only deputy is on vacation in Serranian, so it works out perfectly."

"Let me get this straight," said Marie. "Not only are we going to hunt a flesh-eating dinosaur, but afterward you're going to lead us into a cave to slay a giant spider?"

"You got it," said Vulthkar. "Welcome to your training."

***

They departed from the cover of the forest and entered the river basin. Vulthkar was in the lead, followed by Mckenzie and Marie. Roger and Click brought up the rear. The first variety they encountered was a group of grazing Dicraeosaurus. Their necks stretched to the tops of a cluster of young Lepidodendron, snapping away mouthfuls of leaves. As the group walked by, one of the creatures turned its head to examine them, emitting a high-pitched yelp. An answering call resounded from the opposite side of the basin a moment later.

"It's all right," said Vulthkar. "They're letting the rest of the herd know we're here."

"Great," replied Mckenzie.

The remaining Dicraeosaurus seemed indifferent to the encounter, allowing the teenagers to observe them in detail. Their heads were larger than most sauropods, and their necks wider. A row of spines ran along their backs and extended from their vertebrae. Marie tilted her head back as they walked by and saw two of the Dicraeosaurus chewing furiously. Bits of wood and leaves fell to the grass. One of the beasts shifted its enormous legs to get a better position. The resulting concussion sent a shockwave through the ground. One misplaced step by the great beast would squash Marie like a pancake.

"You're all doing very well," whispered Vulthkar as they walked across the plain. "I've tracked our Megalosaurus to a spot on the other side of the valley. Let's continue forward nice and easy then slip back into the trees."

"Those are Stegosaurus," said Roger, pointing.

"That's right," replied the troll. "Would you like to have a closer look at them? They're rather friendly."

"Of course," said Mckenzie.

A half dozen of the armor-plated lizards relaxed by the river's edge. A few were partially submerged in the cool water, while the others dozed or socialized. Vulthkar led the group to one that had watched them approach. He extended his hand and gently rubbed the top of the dinosaur's head. It closed its eyes and exhaled with a deep purr.

"It's like a big cat," said Marie.

"More like a big cow," replied Vulthkar. "Go ahead and pet it yourself."

Marie placed her hand on its narrow head and patted. It continued to exert the tonal flutters of satisfaction.

"Good little Stegosaurus," she said.

Roger and Mckenzie laughed.

Two others plodded over to the merriment, seeking their own dose of affection. Roger marveled at the armor plates along their backs and the spikes on their tails. As he raised his hand to pet one, an ear-splitting scream shattered the serenity.

"What the fuck is that?" shouted Mckenzie, pointing to the sky. An enormous Pteryxtodon bearing a saddled rider swooped above the herds. A pair of large-caliber rifles, fixed to each wing, fired upon the field. The impacts sent grass, dirt, and gore into the air.

"I said no loud noises!" screamed Vulthkar, hysterically.

"It's too late for that," said Roger. "Find cover!"

The tranquil river valley mutated into a scene of bedlam and carnage. Panic swept through the dinosaur herds, propelling them to seek safety by any means necessary. Amid the barrage of gunfire and confusion, a family of Brachiosaurus rushed for the forest, trampling many of the smaller dinosaurs in their path. The valley was soon soaked red with blood.

"This way," said the troll, leading the group to shelter behind the corpse of a Dicraeosaurus.

"What the hell's happening?" asked Marie.

"We're under attack," said Vulthkar, poking his head up to get a better look. Bullets whizzed by, threatening their meager shelter and splattering blood everywhere.

"We have to get back to the woods."

"How? We'll be stomped or shot."

Before anyone could devise a plan, a thunderous roar erupted from the tree line. An explosion of leaves and timber burst forth as a Megalosaurus entered the melee.

"You've gotta be fucking kidding," said Mckenzie.

"Arm yourselves!" cried Vulthkar. "We have to fight!"

The sisters pulled out their wands and Roger donned his mask and glove. Vulthkar unsheathed his rifle and once again peeked around the side of their shelter to plan their next move.

"That Pteryxtodon is turning around for another pass,"

he said. "Follow me to the next fallen dinosaur. We'll use them as cover back to the trees. On the count of three!"

As the group scrambled behind Vulthkar, Marie watched the Megalosaurus besiege a pair of shrieking Parasaurolophus. Its razor-sharp teeth sliced into the belly of one, spilling organs and blood onto the field. Steam hissed from the pile.

"The monster is on top of us," exclaimed Marie as they collapsed behind the corpse of a juvenile Triceratops. Its body was riddled with bullet holes.

"It appears we've become the hunted," said Vulthkar.

"It's so loud," said Mckenzie, covering her ears as the Pteryxtodon performed another strafing run.

"I see the rider," said Roger. "It's Mrs. Roberts!"

Marie aimed and fired as its wings flapped overhead.

Three successive fireballs crackled from the tip of her purple wand and raced toward the flying beast. It banked to the left for another pass, pumping its massive wings. The fireballs missed their target and vanished into the distance.

"She knows where we are now," said Roger.

"I've got more bad news for you," said Vulthkar.

"What now?"

"The Megalosaurus does too."

The rampaging carnivore had also noticed the fireballs. It turned to their group and roared, chunks of flesh and muscle dangling from its teeth.

"Get ready to fight," said Vulthkar.

"How does one fight a giant dinosaur?" asked Mckenzie.

"With magic and bullets!" he screamed.

Executing his rifle's lever-action with masterful speed, Vulthkar discharged fifteen rounds. Ten hit their target, puffs of red mist bursting along its center mass, legs, and shoulders. The Megalosaurus stumbled but recovered, emitting a thundering cry. The troll dropped behind their cover and reloaded.

"Your turn Roger."

The boy fumbled with the glove's buttons.

"Do you know how to use that thing?" asked Vulthkar.

"Of course," he replied, smashing his fist on the panel.

Two bursts of plasma shot from the glove, propelling him backward into the dirt. The green orbs screeched through the air and struck the Megalosaurus square in the face. Its head exploded with a shower of bone and liquefied tissue.

"That wasn't so hard," said Roger, brushing himself off.

"That was only a baby. Here comes the mama."

Another Megalosaurus, three times as big as its offspring, screamed and stomped toward the companions.

"What do we do now?" cried Mckenzie.

"Run!" replied Vulthkar.

Roger, Mckenzie, Click, and Vulthkar dashed for the tree line. Groups of fleeing dinosaurs, as well as panicked stragglers, continued to trample through the valley in confused trajectories. The companions paused at multiple bottlenecks to allow the thundering beasts passage. Roger focused the mask's eyepiece back to the chaos as they jumped into the bushes.

"Where's Marie?" cried Mckenzie.

"She's going after Mrs. Roberts," replied Roger.

Rather than follow the group to safety, Marie focused on enacting revenge upon her mother's killer. She ignored the stampede, the encroaching Megalosaurus, and the hail of bullets.

"Watch out!" they screamed as the monstrous dinosaur pounced upon Marie.

The girl spun on the dinosaur and waved her wand. The beast stopped in its tracks and convulsed violently. Its skin cooked and blistered, sliding in sheets on to the grass. When the hiss and pop of melting flesh quieted, all that remained was a glistening skeleton.

"How'd she do that?" gasped Vulthkar.

Lilly Roberts swooped around for another pass, baring down over Marie. Although the bullet impacts sent dirt and grass flying, the girl remained resolute. Aiming her wand, she focused her hatred on the winged beast. The amethyst unleashed its fury.

The Pteryxtodon shrieked in pain and then was cloven in two. One half dropped immediately, while the other descended at a gradual rate. Lilly was able to utilize its forward momentum to hang on until it crashed into the dirt. She leapt from the carcass just before the moment of impact.

Marie stood before her. "You murdered my mother."

"So I did."

The girl rolled to her right and aimed. An orange and yellow sphere shot from the tip of the purple wand. Lilly Roberts sidestepped it with ease.

"You're not ready to fight me, little girl."

The woman pulled out her own wand and launched a volley of blue orbs into Marie's chest. The girl was thrown back with tremendous force, dropping her wand, and smacking her head on the ground. She struggled to regain her breath.

"Maybe that'll temper your courage," said Mrs. Roberts, laughing. "You have no idea who you're dealing with."

Vulthkar had been aiming during the confrontation. He pulled the trigger, striking just wide of his intended target. The top half of Lilly Roberts' ear exploded with a wisp of red.

No longer laughing, she shot wild balls of flame into the surrounding tree line.

"Keep firing," said Vulthkar.

Roger and Mckenzie joined the attack. Rifle rounds, green spheres of plasma, and bolts of electricity screeched over the battlefield.

As Lilly Roberts aimed her wand to finish off the girl, a flurry of antennae and wings struck from above, knocking her to the ground.

"It's Merkresh!" shouted Roger.

The old man was mounted atop Clementine, the flying beetle from Kadiaphonek. He pulled the reins and flew over to Marie, extending his hand.

"Come on!"

Marie snatched up the purple wand and climbed aboard.

"What about Mrs. Roberts?"

"You can finish that fight another day."

The others provided covering fire as Merkresh withdrew from the engagement. He waved his arms, motioning everyone, including Click, to jump on the back of the massive beetle.

"Clementine can bear us all. Quickly now!"

They withdrew from the valley, vanishing into the forest.

Lilly Roberts observed their retreat before tending to her wounds. Tearing a strip of cloth from her cloak, she fashioned a headband for her ear. The bleeding had stopped, yet she was exhausted. She sat on the edge of a Triceratops skull and gazed into the destroyed valley. Despite all the slaughter, her attempt to stop the Woods children had failed. On their own, they were unsteady and vulnerable, yet with the help of their friends, they were a force to be respected. Magnolia would not be pleased.

Lilly Roberts took a deep breath, secured the bandage on her ear, and set off on her next errand.

***

"I guess rabbit stew will have to suffice instead of grilled Megalosaurus," said Vulthkar. "Sorry about that."

"It's fine," replied Roger. "An uninvited guest joined our hunting party."

"That's a rude thing to say," exclaimed Merkresh.

"Not you," said Roger. "I meant Mrs. Roberts."

"I know, I'm just giving you a hard time."

The group sat around the fire of their new campsite, west of Maple Hill. Roger, Vulthkar, and Merkresh tended to the food, while Marie, Mckenzie, and Click assembled the tents and bedrolls. Clementine dozed next to a tree.

"How're you feeling?" asked Mckenzie.

"I'm okay," said Marie. "My stomach still hurts a little."

"That was pretty cool what you did to the big dinosaur."

"I hardly remember, I was so mad."

"But you were brave," said Mckenzie.

"I got my ass kicked. She's too strong."

"Right now she is, but…"

Marie stopped working and turned to her sister.

"I'm sorry Mckenzie."

"For what?"

"I'm sorry for saying those things about Frederick. I don't want to fight with you anymore. When I was out there, face to face with Mrs. Roberts, I realized that I can't do any of this on my own. I need you."

Mckenzie broke down and embraced her.

"I'm sorry too. All I want is for our relationship to be like it was before. Let's not fight anymore."

"I love you," replied Marie.

The sisters held on to each other a moment longer, then finished their work in silence.

***

After supper, the company sat around the campfire and discussed their next move. The teenagers took turns describing their adventures since their original group disbanded at the shores of the Wondering River. Likewise, the old man chronicled his experiences with their Uncle Brian in East Grimstead.

"So he's still in Kad?" asked Roger.

"I'm afraid not," replied Merkresh.

"Then where?" asked Marie.

"Your Uncle Brian and his companion Belris have chosen to travel far west to a castle called Direwood."

"Why?" asked Mckenzie.

"I can't speak for your uncle's intentions at the moment, but I think he's in a great deal of trouble. Sadly, we must let him find his own path. We are at the doorstep of our first major battle, and we must remain focused. Do you remember what I said to you that evening before we entered Blackwood Forest?"

The teenagers looked at one another.

"That seems like so long ago," said Roger.

"I said you didn't need to worry about the dragon yet. That ends when we arrive at Dragolroth tomorrow. The three of you will have to confront Lord Mortis within days."

The group went silent. Amid the hum of crickets and snores from Clementine, Click's servos and gears buzzed as he turned to regard them.

"I don't understand why we can't all fight him," said Mckenzie. "Is there a stupid rule or something?"

"In a way, yes," replied Merkresh. "The burden lies with the Woods and Drake families, as your mother explained to you on the eve of this adventure. Simply stated, neither Vulthkar nor I, nor your father or Uncle Brian can defeat the rune guardians this time. It's the way it's always been and the situation you must face now."

"I barely survived three seconds fighting Mrs. Roberts," said Marie. "How can I expect to do any better against a dragon?"

"You showed bravery out on that field," said Vulthkar.

"On the night my mom was killed, I remember her telling me to use my fear and convert it into anger. That's what I did today when I saw Mrs. Roberts. I pushed aside everything else going on around me and focused on confronting her."

"And you single-handedly killed an adult Megalosaurus. I don't believe that's ever been done before."

"Consider this," said Merkresh. "If you were to fix a pair of wings to the creature you defeated today, it would be a dragon. Lord Mortis is roughly the same size."

"Marie, the dragon slayer!" cried Roger.

"But dragons use magic, dinosaurs don't," said Marie.

"Correct," replied Merkresh. "That's why the three of you must rely on each other's talents and creativity to prevail. Having witnessed your parents accomplish similar feats when they were your age, I have the utmost confidence in your abilities. In the meantime, we must assist Vulthkar with his task of the missing gnomes. He and I need to talk alone for a while, so I'd like the three of you to get some rest. I'll wake you when we depart."

Without argument, the teenagers fell into their tents and drifted into a deep sleep almost instantly.

***

Merkresh shook Marie's shoulder gently. "It's time to get up, dear. We're ready to leave."

She opened her eyes and yawned. "What time is it?"

"Early."

"Okay, I'll be right out."

Marie pushed aside the flap and saw that everyone else was waiting. She began to breakdown her tent and gear.

"I'll help you," said Mckenzie.

Marie fastened her backpack and then met the rest of the company out on the road.

"We thought a little extra sleep would help your injuries," said Merkresh. "How are you feeling?"

"Much better, thank you."

The forest was dark, yet slivers of faint moonlight crept through the canopy and illuminated patches of ground. Marie threw her hood up to impede the chill of approaching autumn.

"Where's Clementine?" she asked.

"I sent her back to Kad," replied Merkresh.

"Aww," said Mckenzie. "She was so cute."

"Listen up," said Vulthkar. "The gnolls will be watching this road, so we'll need to hike through the forest on a southwest heading for a couple hours until we reach the cave's entrance. If there aren't any questions, let's get moving."

Merkresh, Vulthkar, Roger, Mckenzie, Marie, and Click traveled through the heart of Blackwood Forest. During this time, Benjamin Woods was just arriving at the Tombworld, Abigail, Penelope, and Trelinia were setting up camp near the base of Maple Hill, and Gothkar was hobbling along alone on The Motherwell. All the pieces were in motion and the final battle for the Rune of Frost was approaching. For the first time in years, atop the highest tower in his haunted castle, the frost dragon Lord Mortis grinned with anticipation.

Vulthkar motioned for the group to find cover. "It's still possible that those vermin will be watching this entrance to the cave. Can you get your little spider friend to check it out?"

"His name's Click," said Roger.

The boy picked up the mechanical spider and whispered a series of commands into its analog microphone condenser.

"Do you understand?" he asked.

Click buzzed in the affirmative and scrambled off.

"How does it communicate its findings?" asked Vulthkar.

"In radio waves," said Merkresh. "He relays his data to an interface on the glove, which in turn gets decoded and translated to the screen in Roger's mask."

"Fascinating," said Vulthkar.

A moment later, Click descended from above and landed on Roger's shoulder.

"He says it's all clear."

"Wonderful," said the troll. "Let's go."

The entrance was nestled within an outcropping of stone and overlapping ivy. Vulthkar extracted a bundle of torches from his pack and handed one to each party member. Roger lit them in turn, and they descended into the darkness.

As the company walked through the shallow passage, the constant drip of moisture filled their ears. Vulthkar took the lead, followed by Merkresh, Mckenzie, and Marie. Roger and Click, as was becoming customary, covered the rear. Because it was so cramped, their torches shed light on all the mysteries the cave had to offer. A mustiness filled the damp air.

"What're those?" asked Marie.

"They're called rootsicles," replied Vulthkar. "The trees above extend their roots into the cave to search for water. Over time, they become coated with calcite and fossilize."

"They look like columns on a building," she said.

The teenagers extended their hands and felt the peculiar texture as they walked past the formations.

"And what's this funny stuff?" asked Mckenzie.

"That's moonmilk," replied the troll. "It's another type of deposit that's formed from fine crystals and calcite. I wouldn't touch it, though. It's a weird, sticky substance."

The passage soon sloped and veered to the left. In addition to the scatterings of rootsicles and moonmilk, many thin stalagmites and stalactites were prominent. Their bony fingers reached from the ceiling and poked up from the floor.

"I love caves," said Mckenzie. "They're like microcosms filled with enchanted creations."

Vulthkar smiled. "Then you're going to love this."

The troll raised his torch and led the company through an opening in the wall and into a spacious chamber. It was filled with subterranean wonders. Flowstone, bell canopies, and strands of contorted helictites covered the floor and ceiling. In the center of the room, surrounded by a beach of limestone, was a shallow pool. The water radiated a pale green within the torchlight.

"Wow," exclaimed Mckenzie.

The teenagers walked down the slight incline to inspect the pool in detail. Click followed along a section of rimstone.

"I thought we could take a quick break for a bite before we continue on to the deeper sections," said Vulthkar.

"That's a fabulous idea," replied Merkresh. "While we eat, I'd like to speak with you further about our plans."

Marie helped Mckenzie fasten the torches to a series of rounded stalagmites, illuminating the chamber. Thin, translucent straws of calcite poked from the ceiling, while chandeliers of gypsum hung from another.

Marie unfurled a blanket and spread it out over a section of the limestone beach. Vulthkar and Roger produced a variety of snacks and leftovers from their packs. They enjoyed rabbit stew, Therizinosaur eggs, and an assortment of nuts and berries. The teenagers sat on the blanket and ate while Merkresh and Vulthkar spoke in hushed voices near a rounded deposit of flowstone.

"So what do you think?" asked Marie.

"About what?" replied Roger.

"About having to fight a dragon in a few days."

"What's there to think about?"

"What's that mean?" asked Mckenzie with a laugh.

"It means you're scared."

"And you're not?" asked Marie.

"Of course I am, but I don't see any sense in worrying about something we don't have any control over. We've all heard what Vulthkar and Merkresh have to say about it. Even Mom explained what we have to do to face our fears."

"Listen to you," said Mckenzie. "All grown-up sounding."

"I have grown up," he replied. "In a way. Think about all

the things we've overcome since that afternoon in the tree."

"You mean when you're pants fell off?" asked Marie.

Mckenzie snorted.

"Yes, stupid. But more precisely, I'm referring to all the other stuff that doesn't have to do with fighting monsters. Like learning about our family's true history or the aftermath of the Drake expedition into the Shadow Mountains."

The sisters quit laughing at the validity of his words.

"Or trying to make sense of Mom's death. I can't speak for the two of you, but it's all I think about most days. I don't know if the pain will ever go away, but it's forced me to grow up a lot quicker. In the grand scheme of things to worry about, the fate of my mother and how I'm ever going to come to terms with that impacts me far more than some dragon."

Marie and Mckenzie stared at their brother.

"You're right, Roger," said Marie. "I shouldn't tease."

"I think about Mom every day too," said Mckenzie. "And about Dad. Will we ever see him again? Have we lost both of our parents?"

The teenagers fell silent at the prospect. Merkresh noticed the change in mood and sat down next to them.

"What's on your mind?"

"Where's our dad?" asked Roger.

The old man sighed. "I honestly don't know, lad. He and Gothkar were on a mission to find a special gate that would allow your father to enter the domain of the undead. According to the original plan, he was going to travel to a cemetery far in the north called the Tombworld, find Penelope Crofts, and then meet us at Dragolroth. Although I'm not certain of his current whereabouts, I did receive promising news while in Kad."

"What was it?" asked Marie.

"The vendor who let me borrow Clementine said that Gothkar had visited him recently. He also said a human male named Ben was with him. So that means your father succeeded in reuniting with Gothkar. Now he needs to get through that gate so he can find Penelope and give her the iron key."

"What key?" asked Roger.

"I know the key he's talking about," exclaimed Mckenzie. "In the last letter we received from Dad he mentioned that Uncle Brian had given him an iron key. That must be the same one he needs to give to Penelope."

"Absolutely right," said Merkresh. "I have a feeling that he and Gothkar are still on course and would even wager they were responsible for the explosion the other night."

"My thoughts as well," said Vulthkar.

"That makes me feel a little better," said Roger.

"Good," replied Merkresh. "Let's return our focus to the task at hand. We still have a spider to slay and some gnomes to rescue. Tidy up this mess and be ready to go in ten minutes."

"Yes, sir," they all replied.

Vulthkar led the group out of the enchanted chamber and back along the tunnel. The slope increased substantially, curling around massive stalagmites. Many of the mounds featured layers of overhanging tiers, caused by eons of drip splash. The troll paused and held up his torch.

"Through this crack in the wall, we'll be entering the ruins of an ancient sewer system. The gnomes came down here to see if they could repair the tunnels and use them as a safer route through Blackwood Forest. Beyond this point, we'll be in danger. Keep your weapons handy and stay alert. This is as deep as I've ever been, so keep an eye out for any clues, especially webbing."

"Webbing?" asked Roger.

"He means spider webs," replied Mckenzie.

As they descended into the sewers, the beauty of the caves transitioned into a cesspool of rot and decay. A heady mustiness filled the air. Calcite formations were replaced with the eroded brick and cobblestone of a forgotten civilization.

"God, it stinks," said Marie.

"Please be mindful of the center section," said Vulthkar. "There's still a bit of running water along the trough. We should keep to the edges."

They traveled through the tunnel, holding their torches high to watch for signs of the gnomes or spider, but also to safely navigate the precarious terrain. Centuries of neglect had degraded the once impressive architecture into a confusion of disarray and debris. Piles of brick lay strewn about the walkways and corroded supply crates littered the dark corners. Roger raised his torch over one of the crates.

"Look over here," he said.

The group assembled around a pile of boxes. On one of the lids rested a silver brooch, a hairpin, and bits of copper wire. The ground below contained fresh wood shavings.

"What happened here?" asked Mckenzie.

"It appears they were fashioning a device of some kind," said Vulthkar, picking up the brooch to examine it closer.

"Who's they?" asked Marie.

"This brooch is of gnome design," said the troll. "I can't tell what they were making, but at least we're going in the right direction."

"Nice job, Roger," said Merkresh. "Let's continue on."

They turned back to the main passage and resumed their investigation. Vulthkar slipped the brooch into a pocket and strode beside Merkresh.

"What do you think?"

"I think we're getting closer," replied the old man.

The flowing water decreased to a trickle, then went dry. The torchlight revealed a silky gown, constructed of spiral orbs, coating the floor and walls. They stopped. Before them loomed a massive spider web. Its vertical plane of symmetrical radials covered the entire tunnel.

"I guess we found it," said Roger.

"Can you see anything beyond the web?" asked Vulthkar.

The boy pressed a combination of buttons on his glove and the mask's eyepiece cycled through various lenses.

"Yes," he said. "There are a few large objects fastened to the floor. I can't tell what they are, but they're covered in webs."

Vulthkar looked at Merkresh. "Cocoons."

"You mean the gnomes are in there?" asked Mckenzie.

"Possibly."

"What should we do?"

"We have to break this large web first," said Merkresh.

"But won't the spider feel the vibration if we cut through it?" asked Mckenzie. "There has to be another way."

"You're right," the old man replied. "Any ideas?"

"Why don't we burn it?" asked Marie.

"I have a plan," said Roger. "We have our own spider. Why don't we send him through without damaging the web and he can check out the cocoons?"

"I like both ideas," said Merkresh. "We'll send in Click, then Marie can use her wand to burn down the web."

Roger communicated the instructions to the mechanical spider, and he scrambled away, climbing along the wall to avoid the sticky threads.

"He's looking at the first cocoon," said the boy. "He says it's an overgrown mole rat."

They all breathed a sigh of relief.

"Now he's looking at the others."

A faint clicking caught Mckenzie's attention. She turned and peered back into the darkness of the tunnel. The fire from her torch crackled, and she strained to focus, but the sewer beyond the perimeter of light was too dark. She spun around and continued to listen to Roger.

"Uh oh," he said.

"What is it?" asked Vulthkar.

"Click says there's an arm sticking out from one of the cocoons. It's a small arm too, like that of a gnome."

"Does it appear dead?" asked the troll.

"Yes," replied Roger. "It's gray and emaciated like it was drained of all its blood."

"Gross," said Mckenzie.

"All right," said Merkresh. "Tell him to come back. We're going to burn this thing down and retrieve the bodies."

"Wait," said Roger. "He says something's moving."

"It's the spider," cried Marie.

"No," continued the boy. "It's another cocoon, but the person inside isn't dead."

Merkresh motioned to Marie. "Burn it down. Everyone else be ready to fight. Quickly!"

The girl raised her wand and focused on the spell.

A glowing orb shot from the tip of her wand and struck

the giant web. It caught fire instantly, popping and hissing as the threads snapped and fell away. The conflagration provided a clear view of the remainder of the tunnel. They were standing in the middle of a nest. Rows of cocoons lined the walls and ceiling before them. As the remaining threads burned away and darkness returned, Mckenzie looked up. A monstrous spider glared down at them. It descended with disturbing speed and snatched Merkresh, pulling him into the shadows.

"It's above us!"

Screams filled the tunnel. As Mckenzie whirled around to locate her siblings, she realized she was alone. Everyone else had been captured and dragged away. A nauseating panic set in as she watched her torch flicker and blow out. She spun on her heels and prepared to run.

A moan from one of the cocoons caught her attention and she paused midstride. She could not abandon her family and friends. Raw fear saturated her mind, infecting her ability to reason. She teetered on the edge of defeat and bravery before a sudden surge of clarity shook her out of the indecision.

"I'm coming," she said, racing back to the nest while casting Floating Lights. A faint, blue orb hovered around her.

Mckenzie collapsed next to the cocoon and tore away the congealed webbing and crust. A head was soon visible, followed by an arm and torso. The girl ripped away the remaining chunks of silk. Before her knelt a middle-aged gnome woman. She struggled for breath and gazed up at Mckenzie.

"Thank you," she gasped.

"Are there more of you?"

"They're all dead."

The gnome's eyes darted around the tunnel, realizing that

she was still in danger. "We need to get out of here now."

"We can't," said Mckenzie. "My friends are still here."

"How many?"

"Four. I mean five. Click, where are you?"

The mechanical spider crawled up to them and buzzed.

"It's one of the babies!" screamed the gnome. "Kill it!"

"No, this is one of my friends. He's a robot."

The gnome looked at her with a confused expression.

"Where did it take the others?" Mckenzie asked.

"Probably to feed her young."

"Oh God."

"There's a crack in the wall that leads to the lair. I refuse to go in there, but if you're determined, you should take this."

The gnome extracted a small mechanical device from her jacket. It was fashioned from a belt buckle, spectacle rims, and parts of a circuit board. Copper wire bound the components.

"What is it?"

"We constructed it to stun the spider. It worked the first time, but then ran out of power."

"I can fix that," said Mckenzie. "May I see the battery?"

The gnome removed the small power source and handed it over. Mckenzie tapped it with her wand, enveloping it with a thin layer of frost. She then bent down next to Click and held it to a charging port on his undercarriage.

"Give it a second. The cold allows it to charge faster."

The device hummed to life as she reinserted the battery.

"Well done," said the gnome. "Magic and technology are luxuries I'd wish we'd had earlier. Sadly, I don't have anyone left to rescue. Get your friends. I'll stay out here and hide."

Mckenzie and Click left the nest and entered the crack in

the wall. The interior was damp and humid. As she fought to suppress her fear, she cycled through all the spells she'd learned over the past week. Her loved ones depended on it.

Along the walls of the lair hung four cocoons. Mckenzie rushed to the closest and ripped the webbing to pieces. Roger tumbled to the ground, gasping for air. She did the same to the next cocoon and out fell Vulthkar. The third held Marie and the final produced Merkresh. Mckenzie helped him to his feet.

"Are you all right? Did it poison you?"

"I don't think so," he replied between heavy breaths.

"Did anyone get bit?" she asked, turning to the others.

"I'm okay," said Marie.

"Me too," said Roger.

The troll pulled out his revolvers, cocking both hammers. "I don't think we're out of trouble yet."

A vicious hiss resounded from above. The spider hung from the center of a massive web, its bulbous abdomen crawling with spiderlings. They leapt from her back in one fluid motion and rained upon the company. The sisters screamed, swatting at their hair to repel the miniature arachnids.

Their mother was enormous. From its posterior spinneret to the claws on the front tarsus, the full-body length was three meters. Eight segmented legs covered in setae and bristles protruded from a carapace of blue biopolymer. Two rows of circular eyes glared from its head.

The spider leapt from the ceiling and pounced on Roger. She sank her fangs deep into his neck, injecting him with poison. The boy dropped to the ground and convulsed violently.

Merkresh unsheathed Palewalker and struck the spider. A spout of green blood erupted from a severed leg. She kicked him in the chest, propelling the old man against the opposite wall. Spiderlings swarmed over his body.

"Merkresh!" screamed the troll. "I'm coming."

Vulthkar unloaded both of his revolvers into the spider's head. Three of the pitch-black eyes exploded in a splash of jelly, while one of its pedipalps splintered and sprayed against the wall. Several of her young were disintegrated in the collision. The troll then rolled to his left while drawing his rifle from its scabbard. He sprung to his feet and fired a full magazine into the spider's body. The abdomen shuttered with furious exit wounds.

"Roger," cried Mckenzie, activating the gnome's device.

The spider froze, stunned by its effects.

Mckenzie fell beside Roger, implementing Dispel Poison. The magic took effect, bringing color back to his face and abating the spasms. He took several deep breaths and opened his eyes.

"I think I'm okay," he said.

The spider, however, was mortally wounded. Six legs had been blown off and its sternum was riddled with bullet holes and sword lacerations. The remaining spiderlings climbed to their mother's back in an instinctive pursuit of safety. In response, she dragged her broken body across the floor, desperate to escape through the crack. Merkresh approached the creature, raised Palewalker, and then cleaved the head from its body. Marie concluded the assault with a fire orb to the spider's abdomen. The offspring shrieked as they sizzled in the flames.

"Is everyone here?" asked Merkresh. "How's Roger?"

"I'm fine now," he replied. "Thanks to Mckenzie."

"Indeed," said Vulthkar. "We all owe her our gratitude."

"We'll have time for that later," said the old man. "Let's get the hell out of here."

They slipped through the crack in the wall and back into the nest. Roger and Click collected their torches from the ground and lit them. From the shadows emerged the gnome.

"Did you kill it?" she asked Mckenzie.

"We did."

"Thank heavens!"

"Ma'am," said the troll. "My name's Vulthkar Thaddeus Glass and I'm the sheriff of Goldcrest. I've come to take you and any other survivors back to Haltwistle."

"A pleasure to meet you, sir. My name is Geddniss Von Apfelbaum. I'm afraid I'm the only survivor of my expedition."

"I'm sorry to hear that," he replied.

"As much as I want to depart forthwith, would it be possible to bring their bodies with us so they may have a proper burial in Haltwistle? They were all dear friends to me."

"I promise it will be done," said the troll.

The companions gathered the remains of the gnomes and fastened them to makeshift gurneys that they had constructed from old crates and rope. Each member of the group, including Geddniss, was responsible for extracting a body from the tunnels.

Once they abandoned the sewers and entered the relative calm of the caves, Vulthkar led them to a tunnel that ascended to the surface and into Blackwood Forest. The mid-morning sun glistened upon the grass as they exited the caves and inhaled a deep breath of the wide valley.

"I must be off," said Vulthkar.

"Already?" asked Mckenzie.

"I have a mission to complete, as do you."

The girl nodded and lowered her gaze.

"Raise your chin, Mckenzie," said the troll. "Be proud of

yourself. You demonstrated tremendous courage in the sewers. If it wasn't for your bravery, we might have all perished. In the short time we've known each other, I've observed all of you take the first step in facing your fears, whether they be in battle or in logic. Yes, Roger, I overheard your conversation at the limestone pool, and I agree that you're growing up fast. Certainly not at the pace you'd prefer, but that's a truth that all of us must face in this life. The three of you will experience more loss and failure before this adventure comes to an end. It's your ability to refocus that grief, to meld its energy into a useful action, that will guide you along the path to comprehension. Always remember that positive thoughts can cut the enemy as deep as the sharpest blade."

"Have you reached the end of that path?" asked Marie.

"I might be some way off," replied the troll. "But at least I've found a purpose."

***

Mckenzie, Marie, Roger, Merkresh, and Click watched as the two figures disappeared into the forest. They stood in silence, contemplating the daunting tasks that lay before them. A crash of steel and shouts of combat disrupted their thoughtfulness.

"It's a swordfight," said Merkresh.

They made their way along the tree line until they reached an intersection of three roads. In the center stood the Tower of Dragolroth. On the road before it was a man. He was clad in leather armor, sitting in the dirt, and appeared to be talking to someone. Marie burst from the trees; her arms extended.

"Daddy, is that you?"

CHAPTER XXXVIII

DROPS OF INFINITY

Benjamin turned from Trelinia. "Marie!"

The girl fell into his arms. "I thought I'd never see you again. I've missed you so much."

He embraced his daughter, pulling her close enough to feel her pounding heart. "I've missed you too. All of you. Roger and Mckenzie and your mother. You're all I've been thinking about. I've waited so long for this moment, and to think all five of us would be reunited at once!"

Marie relaxed her grip and looked up at him. "What did you say?"

Roger and Mckenzie ran up at that moment.

"Father!" they cried, tumbling on top of him.

"Careful!" he said, laughing. "I'm still sore from battle."

As Marie stood and pondered his curious statement, Roger and Mckenzie took turns hugging their father.

"You've all grown so much over the past few months," he said. "Mckenzie, you've sprouted at least an inch. What's your mother been feeding you during your journey?"

Roger and Mckenzie paused and looked at him with confused expressions. The three children ceased their revelry and stood still next to each other.

"He doesn't know," said Marie, tearing up.

"Know what?" asked Ben as he stood and brushed the dust from his armor. "Trelinia, please tell our children to lighten up a little. They look like they've seen a ghost."

"They can't see me," replied his wife.

His smile vanished amidst a wave of nausea as he studied the distressed faces of his children.

"Ben," said Trelinia. "Our children can't see me because I died. I *am* a ghost."

"What?" he replied. The unsettling sensory contrast of his children and wife propelled him into a state of shock.

Trelinia touched the side of Benjamin's face, caressing his weathered skin and beard. "I need you to listen to me, my love."

Benjamin regarded her with bewildered eyes.

"I never imagined our reunion transpiring this way," she continued. "I know how confused you must feel right now, but please prepare yourself for what I have to say."

She paused.

"I was murdered by Lilly Roberts."

Benjamin displayed no reaction. His wife's words and the frantic questions from his children proved too much for him to process. He stared with confusion.

Marie gasped. "He's talking to Mom."

"Oh no," exclaimed Roger.

Trelinia continued to touch his face. "Say something."

Benjamin opened his mouth to respond but instead fell to his knees, launching a stream of vomit into the dirt.

"Dad!" cried Mckenzie.

Roger dropped to the ground and held his father steady.

"No!" howled Benjamin between gasps of air. "You can't be dead. I've gone through too much for it to end this way."

"Is Mom here?" asked Marie.

"Yes," he replied, sobbing.

Trelinia crouched next to her husband and rubbed his back. Her touch resounded through his body, calming his grief.

"I know you have," she said, "but we can still be together in this form, even if it's not what we wanted. It'll be okay."

"It won't be okay," he replied. "Our children will never be able to communicate with their mother again."

"You're wrong," she said. "I'll speak to them through you. Your ability will fill the void between us."

"But I feel so hollow," he replied, still staring into the dirt. "How can we go on like this? Without you, everything is blackness and silence."

"You must go on," said his wife.

"Why?"

"Because I love you, and so do your children."

The family held on to each other and wept, their devotion weaving between dimensions.

***

Merkresh had remained a silent observer while the family recovered from their initial shock. When several minutes had elapsed, he stepped forward and helped Benjamin to his feet.

"Merkresh," he said, finally noticing the old man.

"Hello, my friend. I'm so sorry for your loss. Is there anything I can do?" he asked.

Benjamin took a deep breath. "Would you help me make sense of what's happened?"

"I can try. As a matter of fact, I think it's time that all of us, visible and invisible, gather to discuss what has occurred and to solidify the plan for confronting Lord Mortis."

"Thank you, Merkresh," said Benjamin as he continued to hug and kiss his children.

"Let's get off the road and seek shelter within the tower," said Merkresh. "The ground floor should be safe enough."

"What about those things at the top?" asked Roger.

"Trust me, you won't be going up there," he replied.

In a torchlit chamber within the Tower of Dragolroth Benjamin, Merkresh, Roger, Mckenzie, Marie, and Click gathered. Also present, yet unseen to all except Benjamin, stood Trelinia, Abigail, and Penelope. The full complement of party members to reclaim the Rune of Frost had assembled.

"Before I begin," said Merkresh, "I believe introductions are in order. Benjamin, in addition to Trelinia, two young women should also be in attendance."

"They are," he replied.

"Could you please describe them and where they hail from? We'll do the same in return."

"Sure," he replied, turning to the girls. "The leader of our group, Merkresh Warington, has asked that we all introduce ourselves before we discuss the details of our plan. I'll give them a description of your appearance and then do the same for you."

"Of course," said Penelope. "But we already know what everyone else looks like."

"Really?" replied Benjamin. "How?"

"We watched them exit the caves while we were perched atop this watchtower in our other forms. Passing through the Novemgradus allows me and Trel to become eagles, and Abi can turn into pure energy."

"Interesting," he replied, turning to the rest of the group. "She said they already know what all of you look like. Apparently, now that they've passed through the book, they can turn into other forms."

"What kind?" asked Marie.

"Penny said she and your mother can become eagles."

"Wow," replied Mckenzie. "Can we see them?"

"Yes," said Merkresh. "Their celestial forms are visible to us in this dimension."

"What do you mean?" asked Roger.

"It's complicated," replied Merkresh. "I'll explain how it works another time. Right now we need to introduce ourselves and plan our next step. We have a lot to do. Benjamin, please have Penelope continue."

The girl cleared her throat. "My name's Penelope Crofts and I'm from a place called Jamestown. I sailed across an ocean to live there with my brother and parents when I was sixteen."

She hesitated, reflecting on a painful memory.

"For the past four hundred years, I've been the sole resident of a dreadful cemetery. The day your mother and Abigail arrived was the happiest day of my new life."

"Thank you for that," said Benjamin. "I'll tell the others."

"It's nice to finally meet you, Penelope," said Marie.

"Abigail now," said Merkresh.

Benjamin motioned to the girl. "Your turn."

"Um, okay," she replied, startled at suddenly becoming the center of attention. "Hello, I'm Abigail Somberlain. I'm from a place called San Francisco. It's in the same country as Penelope but in a different time. I mean, I was alive during her future. Honestly, I don't really know how to explain that part of it."

"It's okay," said Benjamin. "Just tell us something basic about yourself. Do you have any hobbies?"

Abigail smiled. "Back in San Francisco, I had a doll that my younger sister gave me. She'd named it Moonchild. It's funny because her doll's name was Marie, just like your daughter. We would take our dolls to the park and pretend they had magic powers. I miss doing that with her so much."

Benjamin relayed her story.

"How old is Abigail?" asked Mckenzie.

"She's sixteen as well."

"I'd like to give Trelinia the opportunity to speak with her children now," said Merkresh.

The faces of Roger, Marie, and Mckenzie lit up.

"Where is she exactly?" asked Marie.

"Right next to me," replied Benjamin.

Marie approached her father. "Mom," she said, crying. "I miss you so much."

"She wants me to tell you that she misses and loves you too, Marie. She loves all of you."

"Is she okay?" asked Mckenzie. "Is she still in pain?"

"No," replied her father. "The only pain she feels now is her inability to see or touch you. She'd do anything to hold you."

Mckenzie nodded, weeping openly.

"Dad," said Roger. "Does she look okay? When we last saw her there was so much blood."

Benjamin regarded Trelinia's crimson cloak and the hood that covered her long hair. "She's still the most stunning woman I've ever laid eyes on," he said.

"I'm sorry for not being able to help her on the night she was killed," Marie said. "Tell her that I've tried to be brave since then. I even fought Mrs. Roberts alone, but she was too strong."

"She said it wasn't your fault and you shouldn't ever feel regret for what happened that night." Benjamin paused to listen to the remainder of Trelinia's words. "There was nothing any of you could have done to save her, not even Merkresh. She believes that it was simply her time to pass from our world to the next. Even though she is separated from you in sight and sound, her love for each of you pervades our two dimensions."

Marie, Mckenzie, and Roger smiled.

Benjamin motioned to his children. "Your mother wants to know if you'll be able to perceive her presence if we're all connected. Join hands and then I'll hold your mother's. Let's see what happens."

The three teenagers grasped each other's hands and Marie held on to her father's. The instant Benjamin and Trelinia forged their familial link, a rush of energy flowed through each of their minds.

A soothing orchestra of cathedral bells drifted through their thoughts and carried them from the depths of the tower to the mountainous heights of a snow-covered forest. The contrast from dark to light was stunning. In the hazy distance, they saw a figure walking amongst the trees. Now visible. Now hidden.

"Where are we?" asked Marie.

"I don't know," replied Mckenzie.

"In a dream, I think," said Roger.

"It's no dream," said their father. "Look."

Marie walked to the shrouded figure. Her boots left soft prints in the snow. They wandered deeper into the silent embrace of the enchanted woods. She approached the figure and paused. Snowflakes fell silently as they faced each other.

"Mom?" asked Marie.

"Hello, my love," replied Trelinia.

"Is it really you?" asked Mckenzie.

"Yes."

"But how?" asked Roger.

Tears streamed down Trelinia's cheeks, crystalizing as they fell from her chin. Snowflakes formed from pure adoration.

"You're all so precious to me," she said.

"Where are we?" asked Marie.

"A special place where we can all be together when we're physically connected," Trelinia said. "It doesn't last long, so I want to tell you something important."

Her children stared with anticipation.

"*Multon and Marie on the castle. The purple gem in sunlight.*"

"What does that mean?" asked Mckenzie.

The snow fell harder as Trelinia turned and disappeared into the forest. She was gone.

"Mom wait!" cried Marie.

"Open your eyes," replied a voice.

Marie blinked. The snow-covered forest dissolved into a spinning flurry of confusion and light. She opened her eyes and found herself back in the darkened tower. Merkresh stood over her, gently tugging her shoulder.

"No!" she shouted. "What happened? Where's Mom?"

"How long were we gone?" asked Roger.

"Thirty minutes or so," replied Merkresh. "I didn't want to disturb you, but Click and I started to get worried."

"Thirty minutes!" exclaimed Mckenzie. "It only felt like a few seconds."

"Wherever we were," said Benjamin, "time was moving at a different pace than here. We should consider that if we want to communicate that way again."

"Is Mom still here?" asked Marie.

"Yes," her father replied. "They're all right here."

"Very good," said Merkresh. "I must insist we talk about our next steps. This will probably be the last time we'll all be together until the confrontation with Lord Mortis either succeeds or fails miserably."

"I have something for you," said Benjamin, extracting an item from his tunic.

"The iron key from Uncle Brian!" exclaimed Mckenzie.

"Yes," said her father as he tossed it to Merkresh. "I've carried this thing a long way."

"And we should all praise your efforts," said the old man. "For this is where our plan begins. This key will get us through the door to the first puzzle."

"Puzzle?" asked Roger.

"Three of them," replied Merkresh. "Because they must be solved in a specific sequence, we're going to have to work as a team. The timing is critical."

"What are they?" asked Marie.

"The first one lies below this tower," he replied. "Abigail, Penelope, and your mother will determine its solution."

He tossed the iron key back to Benjamin.

"Please give the key to Abigail," said the old man. "She and Penelope will need it to solve the riddle."

"I'll tell them," said Benjamin.

"Click, where are you?" asked Merkresh.

The spider dropped from the ceiling and stood before his creator. The clicking of his metallic legs echoed in the chamber.

"The second puzzle requires your skillset. This will be your time to shine, my little friend."

Click's motors and gears buzzed with excitement.

"There's an old tree on the way to the dragon's castle that you must travel to on your own. Within its husk lives a creature that will take you to the second puzzle."

The spider beeped an acknowledgment and scurried for the chamber's exit.

"Wait!" exclaimed Merkresh. "I'm pleased that you're so excited, but you'll have to wait until the girls have completed their task. You can stay with me in the tower until then."

"And the third puzzle belongs to us?" asked Roger.

"Precisely," the old man replied. "The three of you must depart for the dragon's castle immediately."

The teenagers looked at each other with panicked eyes.

"Mom," gasped Marie.

"She's here," said Benjamin. "She says that you need to be strong. This is the moment you've all been preparing for. She loves you and believes in you and knows you'll succeed."

"Come with us," said Roger.

"I can't, son," he replied. "Believe me, I'd want nothing more than to fight by your side, but this is your battle now. You must gather the courage to face the enemy that stands before you.

Like your mother, I too believe in your abilities."

Benjamin paused and took a deep breath.

"I know that I haven't always been the best father."

The teens protested, but he waved their objections away.

"I should have been around more during your younger years. Those are the moments that I'll never reclaim, nor will you. For that, I'm truly sorry. My journey over the past few months has reminded me that the three of you are the most important people in my life. Even though I can't be there with you during this final stage, I'll be focusing all my love toward you. Perhaps that energy will help you in some way."

Mckenzie approached her father and hugged him. "I love you so much, Dad."

"Merkresh," said Roger. "You said that the puzzles need to be completed in a specific sequence. How will any of us know when they've been completed?"

"That's a good question," he replied. "Abigail, Penelope, and your mother will descend below the tower and unlock the first door. Once they're successful, Trelinia will return here with the news. I'll then send Click on his way to the tree. After he's solved his puzzle, I'll signal to the three of you that you may enter the castle."

"How are you going to signal us?" asked Marie.

"From the top of this tower."

"You're actually going up there?" asked Roger.

"I'm going too," said Benjamin.

"Dad," said Mckenzie, still embracing him. "You can't."

"We all have our own struggles to overcome," he replied. "Each member of this party plays a critical role in the endgame. I have to rely on my own courage, just as you do."

"Once Trelinia notifies us of their success, Benjamin and I will ascend to the top of the tower. I'll be in constant contact with Click, so once he's completed his task, I'll give you three the signal to begin your puzzle."

"What's the signal?" asked Mckenzie.

"And how are you in contact with Click?" asked Roger. "I'll have the glove and mask with me."

Merkresh pulled a small device from his vest. "You're not the only one with computerized gadgets. This allows me to talk to him through radio waves."

"Can it communicate with the mask too?" asked Roger.

"Unfortunately, not with the one you have."

"Damn."

"As for a signal we *can* use to communicate," continued the old man. "I believe a roaring fire will suffice."

"What about the gnolls and other things roaming about the forest?" asked Marie. "Won't that be a dinner bell?"

Merkresh laughed. "It's a valid concern, but with all the other moving parts, it's the only option I could think of. If anyone has a better suggestion, I'm all ears."

The group looked at each other and shrugged.

"All right, a signal fire it shall be."

"Abigail has a question," said Benjamin.

"Ask away," replied Merkresh.

"Once they've solved the puzzle and unlock the door, do they meet you at the top of the tower?"

"Opening the door is not the puzzle," replied Merkresh. "That sets them on the path to retrieve their portion of the code to unlock the secret door at the castle."

"Wait a second," said Mckenzie. "I'm confused."

The old man expelled a heavy sigh. "I've explained the individual tasks but failed in clarifying the big picture. My mind has been all over the place. Let me take a step back and expound on why we're doing this in the first place."

Merkresh stood, stretched his arms, and paced around the chamber. "When Lord Mortis recaptured the Rune of Frost, he tucked himself away at the top of the castle and sealed it shut with a powerful spell. You're probably wondering why we can't stroll up to the front door and bypass all these puzzles and running around. If we still had one of the runestones we might get away with that. Since we don't, we're encumbered by these quests. Most importantly, Abigail and Penelope must retrieve their half of the code by solving the first puzzle. They will then travel through an underground passage that intersects with the old tree that Click will be waiting in."

"Click can't see them, though," said Roger.

"True, but he doesn't need to see them. He needs to see the radio waves that contain the code."

Marie shook her head. "This is nuts."

"Benjamin," said Merkresh. "Ask Abigail what it's like when she transforms into pure energy."

"She said that when she's in that form she can see all of the wavelengths of the electromagnetic spectrum."

"Including radio waves," said Merkresh with a smile.

"That's correct."

"Abigail will transform into energy and convey half of the code to Click. He'll use that to solve his puzzle and open the secret door for Roger, Marie, and Mckenzie."

The group was silent for a few moments as they each pondered the complexities of the plan.

"Are they clear on their tasks?" asked Merkresh.

Benjamin looked at Abigail and Penny. "They both say they understand. They'll go down below with Trelinia, solve the puzzle, travel to the tree, and then give Click the code."

"Exactly right," replied Merkresh.

"Where do we go while we wait for them?" asked Marie.

"May I see your map, Roger?" asked the old man.

The boy pulled it from his backpack.

Merkresh pointed to a spot within a swath of illustrated trees. "In this general vicinity lies the ruins of another tower."

Roger gasped.

"Don't worry, there shouldn't be anything dangerous in that one. And why would you be concerned? You're about to fight a dragon atop a haunted castle."

Mckenzie and Marie laughed nervously.

"Make your way to the tower," Merkresh continued, "and wait for the signal. When you see the fire, proceed to Lord Mortis' castle."

"Where's the secret door?" asked Marie.

"If I knew, it wouldn't be a secret," replied Merkresh.

"You don't know where it is?"

"I don't know exactly where it is, but I have a clue to pass along to you: *A buttresses perched.*"

"That's it?" exclaimed Mckenzie. "How does that help?"

"I guess it means we look around for a part of the flying buttress that has a perch upon it," said Roger.

"That's a good place to start," replied Merkresh.

"I have one more question," said Marie. "After we find the secret door, where do we go? You've mentioned that the dragon is at the top. Do we have to fight our way up there?"

"Sadly, I have no idea," replied the old man. "I've never been to that castle before. Prior to its current occupant, it was inhabited by a noble family called Shevington. That was many decades ago, so anyone or anything could be in there now."

Marie sighed.

"Make your way to the highest point in the castle," said Merkresh. "There's only one spire that's large enough to hold a dragon of Lord Mortis' size. You'll be able to see it while you wait at the ruined tower."

"I can't believe we've come to this point," said Mckenzie. "We're really about to do this."

"You *can* do it," replied her father. "I believe in you."

"As do I," said Merkresh. "This is it, my friends. We've prevailed along our respective paths to reach this stage of the great adventure. Focus now on all you've learned since that evening we departed a Thorndale in flames. Gather your resolve and your courage and commit yourselves to complete your tasks. Each member of this party possesses weapons tailored to their specific talents. There's one weapon, however, that we all share more powerful than any spell or sword."

"What is it?" asked Roger.

"Love."

CHAPTER XXXIX

SUBROUTINE 21_3

"Abigail," said Penelope.

"Yes?"

"Can I ask you something?"

"Of course."

"How do you feel about this plan?"

"I'm scared shitless."

"So am I. I've been alone for so long. All I did was wish for someone to be my friend. Then you came along, and now I'm part of this group. Part of me is so grateful, but the rest is more frightened than I've felt in either of my lives."

Abigail took Penelope's hand. "Wherever you go in this new, weird world, I'll go. Whatever struggles we face, let's face them together, like sisters."

Penelope strained to hold back her tears but failed. "I'm

so glad I finally found you," she said as they embraced.

"So am I," replied Abigail. "More than you'll ever know."

Observing their exchange, Trelinia smiled.

***

"Are they ready?" asked Merkresh.

"I believe so," replied Benjamin.

"Very well," he said, motioning for the group to gather around him. "I'm so proud of each of you. Only a few weeks ago you were sitting in classrooms and playing in trees, oblivious to the forces that loomed beyond the sleepy borders of Thorndale. Now you're battle-hardened adventurers. You've defeated a sea monster, fought blood-thirsty dinosaurs, and rescued a villager from a spider's den. Most importantly, however, you've learned to work together. Whether it be solving a shared problem or comforting one another's anxieties, you've proven that you can overcome any obstacle. The bond among you has strengthened as much as your adventuring experience."

"I'm so happy to hear this," Benjamin said.

Roger pulled his watch from a jacket pocket. "Do you still have yours, Dad?"

"It's been with me since the day we made them," he said as he flipped open the cover to his own watch.

"An appropriate gesture," remarked Merkresh. "Because it's time for us to begin."

Marie, Mckenzie, and Roger fastened their backpacks and made their way from the darkness of the tower to the morning sunshine. A breeze greeted them amid an ensemble of bird songs and crickets. The road was blanketed by tiny spots of light, each an image of the sun cast by small openings in the leaves above. The scent of pine needles filled the air.

"A beautiful day for a stroll," said Roger.

Mckenzie and Marie both raised their eyebrows at him.

"The ruins are about half a day's walk," said Merkresh, pointing. "When the road curves sharply to the south, break off into the forest and head north. I've circled the spot on your map where the tower should be."

"Thank you," said Roger.

"Thanks for everything," said Marie, hugging him.

The old man was touched by this show of affection. "I've always been there for you, Marie. Even when I was the last person you wanted advice from."

The girl nodded. "I know. I'm sorry for how I treated you on the porch that morning. You didn't deserve that."

"I was there to listen. *You* deserved that."

"Good luck on your quest, Click," said Roger, bending down to pet the spider. "Tell me all about it when I return."

He danced in a circle, his servos and gears buzzing.

The teenagers said goodbye to their parents a final time and then set upon the road.

"Goodbye, Merkresh," said Mckenzie, looking back.

"For now," replied the old man.

***

The two men watched as the children turned a corner and faded into the forest's hazy light.

Merkresh regarded Benjamin. "How're you holding up?"

"I'm so worried for them," he replied. "I've tried to stay

positive and build their confidence, but I honestly don't know if they're ready for the dangers that lie ahead."

"I felt the same about your group thirty years ago."

"You did?"

Merkresh grinned. "Maybe not your brother or Gothkar, but you were a mess. I recall having many motivational talks with you before you were willing to confront the first monster. Your children are handling this far better than you did."

Benjamin chuckled. "Perhaps you're right."

"Of course I am. Now, let's begin the next phase. Please have Trelinia and the girls meet us back in the tower."

Benjamin, Merkresh, Trelinia, Abigail, Penelope, and Click gathered at the mouth of a darkened stairwell. The bright sun and birds were replaced by cold stone and torchlight.

"Down these stairs is a tunnel that leads to the door," said Benjamin to Trelinia. "Take this key, and once the three of you solve the puzzle beyond, you'll return to us at the top."

"I understand," replied his wife.

Benjamin grasped her hands. "I love you so much. Please be safe down there."

"And you be safe up here," she replied with a kiss.

By the flicker of golden torchlight, the women descended into the unknown.

***

"What are we even looking for?" asked Penelope as they reached the bottom step and entered a cramped antechamber.

"Another door, I think," replied Abigail.

Trelinia held aloft her torch and pointed. "There's one."

She inserted the iron key into its keyhole and turned. The door expelled a mechanical snap and creaked open. An acrid stench of death and decay overpowered them as they entered the next room.

"My God, that stinks," cried Penelope, covering her nose with her bell cuff sleeve.

Eight alabaster walls, seven of which contained carved alcoves, formed an octagonal chamber. A low ceiling, only two meters high, was painted with an elaborate fresco. In the center of the room stood an altar constructed of pure onyx.

"Let's light these other torches for a better look at this room," said Trelinia, motioning to the sconces that hung from the walls.

"Good idea," said Penelope, stepping toward the altar.

"Wait!" cried Abigail.

The others froze.

"There might be traps," she said. "On the floor or along the walls."

"She's right," replied Trelinia. "Come back, Penny. Let's light the one by the door and examine what we can from here."

Penelope slowly turned and tip-toed back to the doorway.

As Abigail ignited the torch, the chamber erupted with an enchanted brilliance. The wall's polished alabaster illuminated a portion of the floor, altar, and ceiling.

"Wow," gasped Penelope.

Upon the fresco was painted a historical chronology. An elaborate sequence of events, disrupted in sections by cracks and chips in the plaster, recounted the ancient history of Silvarum. Humans, trolls, elves, gnomes, and dwarves battled an array of outlandish enemies. In one scene, amidst the blowing snow of a jagged mountain range, a group of dwarf warriors engaged an immense mechanical creature. Smoke and steam billowed from pipes along its shoulders and back. Within another section of the painting loomed a formation of floating shapes, situated above a burning cityscape.

"What does it mean?" asked Abigail, looking up.

"The history of the runestones," replied Trelinia. "Those are the monsters that you'll have to confront during your quest."

"I thought there was only a dragon," said Penelope.

"Lord Mortis is but the first of many, I'm afraid."

"Look!" cried Abigail.

The forms within the fresco began to move. In the scene with the dwarves and mechanized monster, a phalanx of warriors marched toward the wall of brass, iron, and steam. A silent battle ensued within the cracked plaster and brush strokes.

"What kind of magic is this?" asked Abigail.

"I have no idea," replied Trelinia. "But it's wonderful."

"This stench isn't," said Penelope, still covering her nose.

"The floor has paintings on it too," said Abigail.

"Look at that one," replied Penelope. "Two galleons are fighting each other in the sea. They look just like the ship I sailed on from England."

"I don't think they're fighting each other," said Trelinia.

Amid the bursts of cannon fire, a slimy behemoth rose from the depths of the water. Its scaled tentacles enveloped one of the galleons and pulled it beneath the waves. Sailors leapt from the deck, disappearing into the foamy abyss.

"This must be part of the puzzle," said Abigail.

"What makes you say that?" asked Trelinia.

"Because look how the other paintings around the room

aren't moving. Only the two that line up with the lit torch are."

Trelinia and Penelope studied the layout.

"I think Abi's right," said Penelope.

"I love puzzles like this," she replied. "I used to play this one video game where you'd have to point and click to find clues and solve similar puzzles."

"What's a video game?" asked Penelope.

"A form of entertainment back in my world."

"It's my world too," replied Penelope, chuckling.

"You know what I mean."

"If this is the puzzle, then we need to uncover any traps as Abi suggested," said Trelinia.

"What's your plan?"

"They could be anywhere, but the alcoves on each of the walls are what concern me. One of us needs to determine their purpose and whether they pose a threat."

"I'll do it," said Penelope.

"Very well," replied Trelinia. "Try to look into the alcove adjacent to the door."

Penelope crouched low and moved toward the wall. The base of the recess was a meter high. As she came at the alcove from below, she thrust her hand up in front of the void. An iron bolt zipped across the chamber, slamming against the opposite wall. At the same time, the floor dropped out, revealing a putrid pit of skeletons and rotting clothes. The floor rose again a moment later, amid the grind of ancient gears and chains.

"Shit!" said Abigail. "Did it cut you?"

"Almost," replied Penelope, returning to the others.

"There's our trap," said Trelinia.

"And the origin of that stench," said Penelope. "Good

thing you stopped me from walking across."

"So," said Trelinia, "anything that moves in front of the alcoves gets skewered."

"Probably to protect whatever's on that altar."

"How do we get to it?"

"That's the puzzle," said Abigail. "We have to figure out how to get to the altar without being filled with darts."

"Can we use our other forms?" asked Penelope.

"To do what?" replied Trelinia. "Eagles won't be of much use in an enclosed space like this."

"And I can't use my other form yet," said Abigail. "I need to save that energy for when I meet up with Click."

The women stood in silence, thinking.

"Trelinia," said Penelope. "Don't you know magic?"

"I do, but I'm not sure if I still possess my skills in this new dimension. I haven't tried to use them yet."

"Now's a good time to find out," replied Abigail.

"Good point," said Trelinia.

"What kind of magic did you practice?" asked Penelope.

"I was a warlock."

The girls stared at her.

"Are you serious?"

"Quite," she replied. "I was also an accomplished thief, so I have experience using thieves' tools and trap detection."

"Why didn't you say so before?" asked Abigail.

"It didn't seem relevant until now. It's not exactly a topic that comes up in casual conversation."

"Will you teach me to be a rogue?" asked Penelope.

Trelinia regarded the girl. "Really?"

"Yes. I've always wanted to learn those skills."

"Very well," replied Trelinia. "Consider yourself a rogue in training. I'll do my best to pass on what I've learned."

Penelope smiled. "Thank you."

"What about me?" asked Abigail.

"You want to be a rogue too?"

"Not really."

"Then what?"

"I want to learn how to use a sword. To be a fighter."

"I'm afraid I don't have those skills to teach."

"Then I'll teach myself. I'm used to being on my own."

"You're not on your own anymore," Penelope said.

"Absolutely not," exclaimed Trelinia, placing her hand on Abigail's shoulder. "We'll find you a sword and do our best to help each other learn. Abigail Somberlain, from this moment forward, you will be a fighter."

Penelope clapped. "Congratulations, Abi!"

"All right my little rogue and fighter," said Trelinia, "let's see if I'm worthy of my proclamations. I'll attempt to use my spell for detecting traps."

Abigail and Penelope looked on anxiously.

"Please work," mumbled Abigail. "Please work."

Trelinia stepped forward and focused on the elements of the chamber illuminated by torchlight: the walls, floor, ceiling, and altar. After a few moments of concentration, she turned to the girls and smiled. "It worked."

"Yes!" exclaimed Penelope.

"What did you sense?" asked Abigail.

"The alcoves and the floor, as we discovered, are traps. There's something at the altar, but I'm uncertain of its location."

"How come?"

"Because this spell only detects if traps are present. It can't specify their precise location or how to disable them."

"I see," replied Penelope. "So the altar has a trap too?"

"That's not surprising," said Abigail. "I bet that's where we have to solve the real puzzle to get our half of the code."

"Did you learn that from your video games?"

Abigail shot Penelope a wicked grin.

"I'm just teasing," she said with a chuckle.

"One of the lessons I'll be teaching you two is the ability to remain focused during stressful encounters," said Trelinia.

Penelope gave a sheepish smile. "Sorry for joking."

"I have an idea," said Abigail.

"Let's hear it."

"Are you familiar with the historical scenes painted on the floor and ceiling?"

Trelinia examined them for a moment. "The ones I can see, yes. History is one of my main skills."

"Perfect," replied Abigail. "I believe the torches control which events are triggered and activating the correct sequence will disable all the traps in the room."

"That's a great idea. Let's try it."

"How do we ignite the other torches?"

"Simple. Since my magic has translated to this dimension, I can invoke a spell that will light them all."

"Marvelous!" exclaimed Penelope.

"But in order to determine the correct sequence, we need to see the paintings on the other side of the room too."

"I think I've got that covered as well," said Trelinia. "I can use a spell that freezes enemies or objects. What if I light all the torches at once, then, as we determine the correct order of the historical events, I'll douse them with my frost spell?"

Abigail and Penelope both nodded. "That should work."

"Okay, here we go."

Trelinia held her outstretched hands toward the center of the chamber and projected a sheet of flame from her fingertips. The remaining torches ignited at the same time. As a result, the floor and ceiling exploded with movement. Sixteen individual scenes, eight on the floor and eight on the fresco, commenced with their own turbulent histories in a bewitching presentation.

"Give me a few moments to study them," said Trelinia. "Penelope, remember the sequence of names as I call them out."

"Ready when you are," she replied.

"Vexx, Sutekh, Nefaris, Loex, Volyk'k, Mortis, Natassja."

"That's only seven."

"Half a moment. All this movement is confusing."

The girls waited.

"The eighth one is Thulcandra."

"Are you sure that's the correct sequence?"

"Yes, I'm sure. These paintings depict the epic battles that Merkresh and my grandfather endured when they were your age."

"All right," said Abigail. "What about the next part?"

"If your theory's correct, then I'll need to extinguish the torches and light them again in the right sequence."

"That doesn't seem like an elegant solution," said Abigail.

"I agree, but it's the best I can come up with under the circumstances. Do either of you have a better idea?"

Abigail looked at Penelope. "No," they replied.

"Using that many spells won't drain your energy?" asked Penelope. "Like it does when we change into our other forms?"

"They will," she replied. "I'll be able to use each of them

only a few times before I need to rest. So let's get this right."

"You've got this," said Abigail.

Trelinia took a deep breath and centered herself. Raising her hands, she focused on the glowing torches throughout the room. A wisp of cerulean frost smothered each sconce, snuffing out the flames. The torches they had brought with them and the sconce by the door were the only light sources that remained.

"So far so good," said Penelope.

"Do you remember the order of the names?"

"Yes," she replied. "The first one's Vexx."

Trelinia concentrated once again. The torch along the wall to their left ignited, activating both its respective scenes. The motif on the ceiling depicted a red dragon, swooping down upon a village of terrified halflings. On the floor, its companion scene portrayed that same dragon being shot out of the sky. A sharp, mechanical twang emanated from within the wall.

"It's working!" cried Abigail.

"What's the next one?"

"Sutekh."

Another torch burst to life, propelling two more scenes into a ballet of color and movement. The sound of its trap disarming followed.

"I knew this would work," said Abigail, smiling.

"We have to do this five more times?"

"I think so," replied Trelinia. "Give me the next one, I'm starting to feel fatigued."

Penelope thought for a second. "Loex. No! It's Nefaris."

"Are you certain?"

"Yes. Nefaris."

Trelinia scanned the floor and ceiling for the sea monster.

"I don't see it," she said.

"What do you mean you don't see it?"

"It was right there in front of us," cried Penelope.

"It's not there now," replied Trelinia. "And I can't find it anywhere else in the room."

"What do we do?"

The stones beneath their feet dropped, plunging Trelinia, Abigail, and Penelope into darkness.

***

"Click," said Merkresh. "Please keep watch by the door until Trelinia returns. Benjamin and I are heading to the top."

The spider hopped up and down in acknowledgment.

"When was the last time you made this climb?"

"I was your age, I believe," replied the old man, pulling Palewalker from its scabbard.

"Will we need those?"

"Yes. This will not be a pleasant experience."

Benjamin frowned as he unsheathed Ghostreaver.

The men stepped into the first spiral stairwell, their boots tapping upon blackened and stained stones. Benjamin's leather pauldrons and gauntlets scraped against the sides of the cramped walls. After three rotations, they reached the second floor.

"How many levels are there?" asked Benjamin.

"Quiet," whispered Merkresh. "Someone's there."

The room was circular and shrouded in darkness. A lone window produced a beam of light that settled upon the middle of the floor. Otherwise, shadows filled the space.

"Can you see it?" asked Merkresh.

"See what?"

"There, just beyond the light."

Benjamin strained his eyes. The contrast between the sunbeam and subsequent darkness made it difficult to focus. Specs of dust floated within the beam.

"I see it," he said. "Is that a man?"

A skeleton, clad in chainmail and wielding a longsword, burst through the light at full speed. The rattle of its ancient bones echoed off the walls. Benjamin lost his footing as he reacted to the attack, falling on his backside. He rolled to his right as the creature's blade reigned down upon him. The steel clanged against stone, producing a shower of sparks.

Merkresh gripped Palewalker with two hands and swung at the creature's skull. It exploded into a cloud of dust.

"A little help?" asked Benjamin, extending his hand.

Merkresh pulled him to his feet.

"What the hell was that?"

"A guardian," replied the old man.

"A guardian of what?"

He pointed to a treasure chest immersed in shadow.

"Fantastic," said Benjamin as he lifted the bronze lid. "I need a few replacements after my duel with Grizzlefang."

"If you don't find anything here, there're two more levels to look forward to."

"I imagine the guardians get harder the higher we go?"

"Of course," replied Merkresh. "Find anything useful?"

"I don't see any leather armor, but there sure is a lot of platinum and gold. This will come in handy later."

Benjamin scooped up a handful of platinum coins and shoved them into his backpack. He also grabbed a curiously embellished scroll case. The phrase *Drake Expedition, 1184* was engraved within its supple leather.

"Shall we?" asked Merkresh, motioning to the stairwell.

Benjamin nodded and took the lead.

"Any idea what to expect this time around?"

"I'm flying by the seat of my pants just like you. It'll be something terrible, of that, I'm sure."

The men stepped lightly as they ascended the final few steps. The circular chamber on the third level was similarly dark yet contained two windows that produced intersecting sunbeams. Light sparkled upon another golden treasure chest in the center of the room.

Benjamin stepped forward.

"Wait," said Merkresh, holding up his arm.

Cackling burst forth from the shadows.

"Oh, great," moaned Benjamin.

A decrepit hag emerged, its body infused with purple veins and pulsating sacks of pus. Lurching forward, its worn soles scraped against the stone with each laborious step. The creature was clad in scraps of stained leather and frayed cloth. Bundles of twigs, human skulls, and deer antlers were fastened around its sides and hunched back. A necklace of black rose petals dangled around its neck.

"Come closer," said the hag. "I enjoy visitors."

Merkresh motioned for Benjamin to advance right while he moved left.

"Eating them that is," she said. "I'm so hungry."

The hag reached the center of the room and halted. She twisted her head to either side, inspecting the intruders. Tendons popped during each glance.

"Smells tasty!" she said, licking her lips.

As Merkresh nodded at Benjamin to attack, the witch leapt to the wall and climbed like a spider to the ceiling.

"My children!" she screamed from above. "Slay these interlopers. Your mother must FEED!"

Stones at the bottom of the wall slid to the side, allowing a swarm of small humanoids to pour upon the floor. Each was about a meter tall, had green skin, and wielded curved daggers.

"Goblins!" shouted Merkresh.

A group of the creatures rushed toward the old man. He kicked the foremost square between the eyes. Its head launched from its shoulders, splashing against the opposite wall with a shower of brain matter and skull. A swift stroke from Palewalker severed the torsos of his remaining attackers.

The hag screeched in anger from the ceiling.

Benjamin was besieged by twice as many goblins. He was able to dispatch the frontal assault, but a stone beneath his right boot slid open, sending him to one knee. A goblin poked up out of the hole and stabbed him in the calf and hamstring.

"Merkresh!" cried Benjamin. "Help!"

The crone clapped with delight.

As Merkresh rushed to his friend's aid, Benjamin seized the goblin by the throat and bashed its forehead into the edge of the stone. The creature screamed in pain as its face split to pieces.

The old man attacked, driving a brutal sweep of his sword through the group of laughing goblins. Sheets of blood sprayed over the stones amid a volley of severed arms and heads.

"Can you walk?" asked Merkresh.

"I'm hurt pretty bad."

"I'll fix you right up. First, we have to deal with her."

The hag's eyes widened with outrage. Her hitherto shrill voice transformed into a guttural, demonic growl.

"You killed my children! I'll devour your souls!"

"May I?" asked Merkresh, grasping Benjamin's sword.

As the witch propelled herself from the ceiling, Merkresh heaved Palewalker and Ghostreaver end over end. The latter buried itself deep within the hag's chest. Twigs, skulls, and a spout of black blood fell upon the chamber floor like rain. At the same moment, Palewalker carved through her grimacing mouth. Teeth pattered on the stones as her corpse crashed to the floor.

The old man extracted his sword and wiped it clean upon her tattered leather. "Let's take a look at that leg," he said.

Blood seeped from jagged wounds. Merkresh pulled a rag from his cloak and tied it around the deepest gash.

"I'm in no shape to help in the third fight."

"You must," replied Merkresh, hoisting Benjamin to his feet. "Come on, I'll help you walk."

Benjamin yanked Ghostreaver from the crone's chest as they hobbled to the final flight of stairs.

A clear, blue sky greeted them as they reached the summit of Dragolroth. Weathered crenellations overlapped the distant trees and hazy fields of the valley. A flock of startled sparrows cawed at their arrival then fluttered away.

Seated on the edge of the tower's battlements, a demon lord gazed apathetically into the distance. Massive wings towered upon shoulders and arms wrapped in crimson sinew. From the sides of its head curled a pair of ram-like horns.

Benjamin sighed heavily. "Why am I not surprised our final foe would be something absurd like that?"

"Come on," said Merkresh. "We're almost done."

"I can't even walk, how do you expect me to fight?"

"If we don't defeat this creature, the entire plan is ruined. We won't be able to signal your children and they'll never enter the castle. It'll be the end of us all."

"I'm useless now, Merkresh," replied Benjamin. "There has to be another way to give them a sign."

"There is no other way. Don't you think I've…"

"Will you two please shut the fuck up?" said a voice.

Merkresh and Benjamin went silent with surprise. They turned and studied the demonic figure. Its chin rested atop a clawed hand, lost in silent contemplation.

"Excuse me?" replied Merkresh.

"You heard me," said the demon, not bothering to turn.

The old man shot Benjamin a confused glance and then unsheathed his sword. Its steel produced a satisfying tone.

"You won't need that," said the creature.

"Excuse me?"

"Enjoy repeating yourself, do you?"

"Are we not to fight?"

"Not today," the demon replied. "I'm not in the mood."

"Why?"

"None of your fucking business."

Merkresh scratched his chin, uncertain if he should attack the mysterious creature or put his sword away.

"Well, in that case, would you mind if my companion and I light a signal fire? We were hoping to communicate with some friends further down the road."

"Sure," replied the demon.

***

"Is everyone all right?" asked Trelinia.

"I'm okay," replied Penelope.

"Me too," said Abigail. "But where are we now?"

"It's not the pit with the stinky bodies."

"No," said Trelinia. "We're somewhere else."

The new chamber possessed a simple construction. Four granite walls, a nondescript ceiling, and a floor of flagstone tiles. Two torches supplied a golden glow. In the center stood another onyx altar, a metallic object glittering upon its surface.

"Are you able to detect traps?" asked Penelope.

"Yes, but I don't sense anything this time."

Abigail laughed.

"What's so funny?"

"I think we actually solved the puzzle."

"What about the altar in the other room?"

"A decoy."

Penelope approached the slab of onyx. "There are a lot of numbers on this thing," she said, picking it up.

As the object was lifted, two hidden doors slid open. One contained a flight of stairs leading up to the surface and the other a passage that led into darkness.

"I think Abi's right," said Trelinia. "We did it."

***

"Trel," said Benjamin, hugging her. "Did you succeed?"

"Yes. We solved the puzzle and obtained the code."

"And the girls?"

"They're headed to the tree right now."

"Merkresh," said Benjamin. "They did it."

The old man nodded and then spoke into a small device. "Click, you're cleared to proceed with your mission."

***

The spider dropped from his web and scrambled across the floor. He exited the tower at full speed, hugging the tree line that ran parallel to the main road. Eight brass legs propelled him over fallen limbs and piles of leaves, his eyes constantly scanning the area for movement. A squirrel squeaked at him as he dashed by. Click ignored the rodent's obscenities and focused on arriving at his destination on time. This was *his* moment to prove himself.

After an hour of uninterrupted travel, Click arrived at a fork in the road. Gears whizzed as he rotated his head to investigate each route. He accessed the memory banks that held his master's directions and printed them to his heads-up-display. He was to turn north at the intersection of two roads, enter the forest on the eastern bank after eight kilometers, and then scan for the old oak tree. It would be easily marked by three symbols carved into its ancient skin.

Click pivoted north and continued his journey. Just prior to departing the trail to head east, a solitary rider galloped down the road. The spider climbed up the nearest tree and observed. In the bright sunlight, the figure's facial features were ambiguous. Click, however, could distinguish a sapphire cloak with a raised hood. The horse's heavy strides soon faded into the distance. He descended and scurried into the woods.

A soft murmur of crickets accentuated the mid-afternoon breeze as the spider stood in front of the old tree. His symbol detection algorithm confirmed the three markings. As he stepped toward the massive oak, a mechanical voice shouted from above.

"Halt!"

Click watched as a large, metallic spider, worn and rusted, slowly lowered itself from a twisted branch.

"State your name," it commanded.

"My name is Click."

"And your business?"

"I am on a special errand for my master."

"Is that so? Who is your master?"

"Merkresh Warington."

The spider expelled a steam-powered gasp. "Whom did you say? Speak up. Old age has degraded my auditory cortex."

"Merkresh Warington."

"So," replied the spider, "*you* were my replacement."

"What do you mean?"

"Merkresh Warington was my master as well."

Click's servos hummed with excitement. "Really? Then that makes us brothers. What is your name?"

"It makes us no such thing."

"Why not?"

"Because family does not abandon its firstborn."

"I do not understand. Who are you?"

"My name is Prott. Merkresh constructed me eighty-nine years ago. I was the first of our kind, the prototype for his vision of integrating steam-powered robotics with the advanced technology that he had retrieved from the city in the north."

"It is a pleasure to meet you, Prott. I am afraid that I was unfamiliar with your existence or pedigree."

"How old are you?"

"Three weeks, one day, eight minutes, and two seconds."

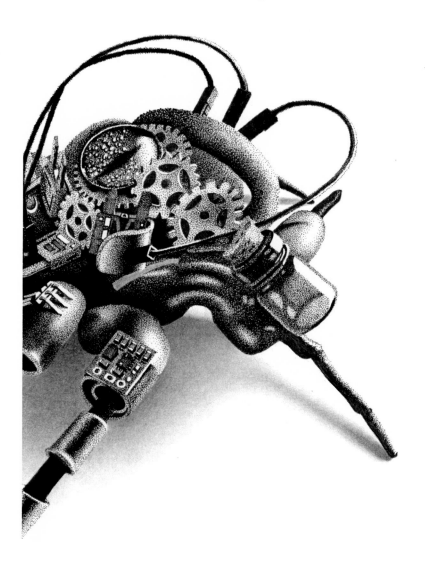

Prott snickered with a series of clanking beeps. "That would explain your kindness and puerility."

Click searched his dictionary for a definition of the latter term. "Yes, I am a recently deployed lifeform. I can understand how you would consider that amusing."

"You think you are a lifeform?"

"Of course, what else would I be?"

"A collection of bolts and wires, nothing more."

Click calculated the accusation's percentage of sarcasm and condemnation. "I respectfully disagree."

"You have that right, I suppose," replied Prott as he continued to examine Click. "If you are such a fancy lifeform, show me what you can do."

"Say again?"

The old spider whirled with frustration. "What makes you so much better than me?"

"We just met, why would I think that?"

"Our dear father certainly does, or he would not have discarded me in this miserable tree. So, Click, tell me all about your wonderful features. What type of processer do you have? Can you perceive multiple electromagnetic wavelengths, or just one? Was Merkresh able to correct the emotion program? How many weapon systems? I have a thousand more questions."

"I do not have time to answer a thousand questions," said Click. "I am on an important mission. Will you help me?"

Prott paused, performing his own calculations to analyze the young spider's behavior. "You are a persistent little fellow. I will give you that much," he said.

"Thank you," replied Click.

"Did you not calculate the probability that I was already

cognizant of your arrival or your mission?"

"I did not."

"I was privy to both. Merkresh communicated to me the purpose of your assignment three days ago. I have been awaiting your arrival since."

Click hummed with surprise. "Why did you not say?"

"I needed to determine the strength of your character. It is not easy to face criticism without responding emotionally. You did a fine job in that respect, even though your programming is barely three weeks old."

"Thank you," replied Click.

"Come," said Prott. "Let me show you around."

***

The interior of the oak was stark and cheerless. A singular web hung in the shadows. The remainder of the space was bare.

"Welcome to my home," said the old spider.

"Why are you here alone?" asked Click.

"Merkresh sent me."

"But why?"

Prott hesitated, his gyros laboring with discomfort.

"I made a mistake once," he replied.

"Everyone makes mistakes."

"Not this kind."

Click regarded his elder. Periodic tremors within his brass legs caused him to shift weight awkwardly. Much of the robot's metallic casing was rusted and scratched. An angry gash, snaking across the glass of one of his large eyes, rendered the old spider partially blind.

"What did you do?"

"I would rather not talk about that right now. My priority at the moment is to guide you to the tunnels below so you can solve the puzzle. Are you prepared to depart?"

"Yes, sir."

"Follow me," said Prott.

At the back of the hollow was a small cavity. Descending a steep passage, the spiders squeezed between dried heartwood, leaves, and roots. Click boosted his thermal imaging level so he could detect threats in the darkness. A brief, yet sharp oscillation echoed through the tunnel as it activated.

"I am familiar with that sound," said the old spider.

"It can help us identify dangers."

"I know, I was able to utilize that feature until it stopped functioning decades ago. To mitigate, I have spun webs through these tunnels. If there is anything sneaking around down here, I will be the first to know. Fundamental skills are still useful, my spiderling. Fancy technologies are not the only solution to a problem."

Click remained silent, following close behind.

They soon reached an intersection and halted.

"The chamber containing the puzzle is straight ahead," said Prott. "Did Merkresh inform you of its design?"

"I am unfamiliar with the details. I was simply ordered to travel here and solve it."

"That sounds typical of him."

"Do you know the solution?"

"If I did, you would not be here. However, I have studied its characteristics for many years, yet I have been unable to make sense of it. It contains symbols my databases are unfamiliar with.

Perhaps your improved software will be more successful."

"I will try my best."

"Of course you will," said the old spider.

The tunnel ended at the face of a stone wall. Click queried his architectural data warehouse and determined the substance to be alabaster. Prott motioned to a crack in a damaged block and the spiders slipped through.

A chamber glowed to life as they entered. Eight alabaster walls, seven of which contained carved alcoves, formed an octagonal space. A low ceiling, only two meters high, was engraved with nine symbols. In the center of the room, covered in fine webbing, stood an altar of pure onyx.

"I equipped the torches to ignite automatically whenever I enter through this crack," said Prott.

"Ingenious," replied Click. "How did you construct it?"

"From metallic bits and scraps I found along the road. The ignition mechanisms themselves are reclaimed from a few of my deprecated electrodes."

"You used your own old parts to make new devices?"

"Of course, spiderling. It is called engineering. Nothing should ever go to waste. Do not ever forget that. It is a skill that could save your life one day."

"I thought I was only a collection of bolts and wires."

Prott's steam-powered motors sputtered with laughter. "I have to admit, your peculiar personality is growing on me."

"I will take that as a compliment."

The spider turned to the network of webbing. "I had to string all of that up because this chamber is full of traps. We can move along the webs to get to the altar unscathed. I believe the puzzle resides there. Do you see the alcoves on each wall?"

"Yes," replied Click.

"They are armed with motion sensors."

"What happens when they are triggered?"

Prott tapped on his damaged eye. The brass leg produced a *clink-clink-clink* upon the glass. "There are also pressure plates all along the tiles. One little step and the floor drops out."

"I will be careful to stay away from both hazards. Thank you very much for your assistance, Prott. Once I solve the puzzle, I will withdraw and trouble you no more."

"As you wish," replied the old spider.

Click's sensors detected increased levels in Prott's anxiety. "Did I say something wrong?"

The tremors in his worn legs intensified as the old spider endeavored to articulate emotions. "You are the first individual I have spoken to in eighty years. I admit I was not looking forward to your arrival. I have had many decades to analyze my previous mistakes and dwell upon my disgust for our creator. However, in the brief time that we have known each other, you have forced me to recall how powerful social interaction can be."

"You will miss me?"

"Yes."

Click purged his random-access memory to create extra space for a more powerful program. "According to my internal chronometer, I am ahead of schedule. Before I go down to solve the puzzle, would you like to talk about what happened to you?"

Prott's jet black eyes regarded Click with reverence. "You would take the time to listen to my story?"

"I would."

"Thank you, Click," he said, attempting to regulate the output of his stimulated emotions. "Merkresh constructed me on the eve of his second journey to the city of Nexxathia. Like I said before, I was the first of our kind. My systems were state-of-the-art, and I was to serve as his chief problem solver, very much like the role you play today. The journey into the Shadow Mountains was arduous, yet we arrived at Edric Drake's basecamp no worse for our wear. I do recall one of the members of our expedition falling into a crevasse in the Silver Highlands. Fortunately, I was able to quickly fasten a web of climbing ropes around the man, allowing the others to extract him safely. I was feeling quite proud of myself, as was Merkresh. Up to that point, the journey had transpired exceptionally well. Everything changed once we finally arrived at the dreaded city. I experienced sensations that clouded my judgement and caused me to second guess myself. It began gradually, but then intensified to unbearable levels as we navigated through the bizarre structures and avenues of that ghastly metropolis."

"What did you feel?"

"Fear."

Click remained silent.

"Do you experience emotions?"

"No, my software was not integrated with that program."

"I see," replied Prott. "That makes perfect sense and the obvious reason for your distinctive personality. Because of my inability to control my emotions during that quest, Merkresh did not provide that functionality to you. Clearly, he did not want you to make the same mistakes as I."

"He dismissed you because you showed fear?"

"No, because I caused the death of three team members."

"I am sorry to hear that, Prott."

"So am I," replied the old spider. "Although watching

them fall to their deaths was horrible, what has haunted me over the years is how easy it was for Merkresh to discard me. He showed no emotion whatsoever. We simply completed the expedition, and upon returning home, he ordered me to leave. It was as if *his* emotional programming had never been installed."

"In the short time that I have been sentient, I too have observed how certain human beings function without emotion."

"Perhaps biological and mechanical lifeforms are not that different," said Prott. "We both share similar weaknesses."

"And strengths."

"Of that I am certain. Ironically, because of my defects, Merkresh constructed a more perfect being: you. I can find solace in the realization that I contributed to your existence."

"Thank you, Prott."

"Well now," he said, his servos and gears humming with activity. "It is time for you to deal with that puzzle."

"It is," said Click as he turned and crawled along the webbing that led to the onyx altar.

Upon its surface was carved seven symbols, identical to the arrangement on the ceiling. The latter, however, contained a larger image within its center: an eight-pointed star with a face. As Click studied both variations, an automated script passed a return value that requested his immediate attention. He accessed a database backup from a week prior and queried the respective table. The result provided a single image file. Click moved a copy to his HUD and compared it to the eight designs situated on top of the altar. They matched perfectly.

"I found the solution," he said.

"For decades I have been staring at this thing, and you are successful in only a few seconds?"

"It was not my solution. My friend saw these symbols in a dream. All I did was match them to a photograph I took of his depictions."

"If you are sure of the sequence, the next step is to touch the correct symbol on the altar. Their counterparts on the ceiling will then line up around the star. I have been able to align the first two. Be aware that for every mistake made, a jolt of electricity is dispatched from the onyx. They become much stronger for each miscalculation, believe me."

"I do, Prott. Thank you for the warning."

"May I enter the first two?"

"Of course."

The old spider stepped forward and tapped one of the symbols that conjoined two curves, a straight line, and a circle. A blue glow hummed from the engraving. The same symbol on the ceiling shifted to the space between the north and northeast quadrants.

"One more," said Prott.

The second symbol in the sequence was an eyeball with a serpent's tail. Once clicked, the blue glow returned, and the shape moved to the gap between the northeast and east points.

"I have never been able to figure out the next image, even though I have tried the other five on the altar."

"That is because the third symbol is not engraved on the onyx," said Click, motioning to the adjacent wall. "It is engraved into the alabaster."

"Amazing," replied Prott.

Click crawled along the webbing to the wall.

"Be careful to stay above the alcoves."

"I will," he said, as he tapped the symbol. It depicted two

overlapping circles that formed a lidless eye.

Click returned to the altar and replicated the process five more times. On the first four occasions, the blue light glowed and the gap in the compass was filled. The final iteration produced a different result. The spiders watched with amazement as a narrow tower rose from the center of the onyx. Within its hollow core, a metallic object glittered in the torchlight.

"You did it," exclaimed Prott.

"No," replied Click. "*We* did it."

The turn of a key reverberated through the octagon. As Click stepped into the cavity to retrieve his portion of the code, a door opened, destroying much of the webbing and triggering the traps. He watched helplessly as scores of iron bolts penetrated Prott's outer shell, obliterating his steam-powered engines and many of his other vital systems. The old spider lay in a heap of twisted metal and brass.

"Prott!" exclaimed Click. "I will get help."

Spouts of oil and steam expelled from his broken body. "No, Click, you must complete your errand. Besides, I have something to give you."

"What is it?"

"A program I have been developing over the years, should I ever have the chance to meet my replacement. And should I actually like him." A stream of caliginous fluid expelled from his mouth as he struggled to laugh.

"Whatever it is, I will accept it with honor."

"It is the sum of all my knowledge and experience. All the skills and engineering tricks I have learned over the decades. You will have them now. Perhaps they will serve you on your great quest in a manner that has more meaning than the existence I have faced alone in this tree. Maybe our father will be proud of me this time."

"I will tell Merkresh how much you helped."

The lights upon the old spider's machinery began to dim. With a desperate gasp of steam, he said his final words.

"I wish I would have had the chance to know you better. Learn from my mistakes. The name of the program is *Subroutine 21_3*. Goodbye…brother."

CHAPTER XL

IMMINENT SENSIBILITIES

"I'm ready," said Abigail, converting into pure energy.

Penelope inserted the key and opened the door. As they entered the chamber, a barrage of webbing broke apart, triggering each of the alcove traps. Abigail watched as a salvo of iron bolts flew across the octagonal room, puncturing a small metallic and brass object atop the onyx altar.

"What did you do?" cried Abigail.

"I opened the door!" replied Penelope.

"Some kind of robot has been injured."

"But can you see Click's radio waves?"

"Yes."

"Then transmit our half of the code so we can get the hell out of here," said Penelope.

***

"That's the last of them," said Benjamin as he tossed an armful of twigs onto the pile."

"Did you search the hag's treasure chest?"

"I did, and I found these leather pauldrons."

"Fantastic," replied Merkresh. "How's the leg?"

"About as bearable as my gunshot wound, the gash from Grizzlefang, and the dozen other injuries screaming throughout my body. Other than that, I feel great."

"That's good to hear," said Merkresh, gazing east.

Benjamin peered across the tower at the demon. "Has he been sitting there the whole time?"

"Yes, I don't know what's wrong with him."

"As long as he doesn't bother us, I don't give a shit."

The device in Merkresh's hand crackled with activity.

"Click has solved the puzzle and unlocked the secret door to the castle!" exclaimed the old man.

"The signal fire is ready," replied Benjamin.

"Light it."

***

Shielding his eyes from the afternoon sun, Roger peered toward the Watchtower of Dragolroth. "I hope Dad's okay."

"Mom too," replied Mckenzie.

The teenagers waited atop the ruined tower. Their hike along the eastern road had been uneventful, except for when they had to dive into the underbrush for cover. A solitary rider galloped past them with furious speed. Marie had thought the tint

591

of the rider's sapphire cloak and hood had been familiar. Since they were already off the road, they took that opportunity to have a bite to eat. After a few more hours of walking, they reached their destination as the sun sat low in the sky.

While Roger and Mckenzie focused west for a sign of the signal fire, Marie looked eastward.

"Look at the size of that castle," she gasped.

The ruined tower from which they stood provided an unobstructed view of the haunted castle of Lord Mortis. Even in the daylight, amidst a blue sky and singing birds, its architecture boasted melancholic intensity. Five black towers crowned with curly spires erupted from a tangle of battlements, pointed arches, and stained parapets. Lancet windows decorated the stone face of a curtain wall, amid the crumbled arms of flying buttresses.

Marie followed the cruel angles until her eyes reached the castle's highest spire: the dragon's lair.

"He's up there," she whispered. "Waiting for us. Does he know that three teenagers have come to slay him? Even so, he's probably sound asleep. What would he have to fear?"

"What did you say?" asked Mckenzie as she approached.

"Nothing," replied Marie. "I'm just scared."

"Me too."

The sisters stood together contemplating their impending task. A breeze whisked through the forest amidst the calls of blue jays, finches, and chickadees.

"Look!" shouted Roger, pointing. "The signal fire!"

Marie and Mckenzie raced to the other side of the tower. Through the orchid haze of dusk, the light of a signal fire blazed atop Dragolroth. The Woods children's fate had finally arrived.

***

"Which way should we go?" asked Mckenzie.

"Anywhere but the front door," replied Marie.

Roger scanned his map. "Our only other option is to sneak through the forest along the west side. There's a steep ridge to the east, that we'd never be able to scale."

"What was the clue about the secret door again?"

"A buttresses perched," replied Roger.

"That's the dumbest clue I've ever heard," said Marie.

"Maybe not," said Mckenzie. "I can see a row of flying buttresses along that curtain wall. The others look destroyed."

"We can't see the back."

"That's true," said Roger. "We could try Mckenzie's idea and if that doesn't work, check around the other side?"

Both girls nodded.

Roger sighed heavily as he fastened his backpack. "Unless there's anything more to discuss, we should get going."

The teenagers descended from the tower and stepped onto a forest trail curling northeast. Mckenzie looked to the flaming top of Dragolroth a final time and thought of her parents. Peering from its battlements, they did the same for her.

Acorns and dried leaves crunched beneath their boots as they walked along the path. The haunted castle was on the edge of the Blackwood Forest, near the villages of Raspberry Grove, Willow Creek, and Gravesend. Beyond the tree line were rolling grasslands and marshes that stretched to the shores of Emerald Bay. Trudging along, they saw the vastness beyond the forest's border. Through gaps in the trees, streaks of apricot, vermillion, and royal blue conveyed the day's dying light.

"We should approach from here," said Roger.

Mckenzie's stomach churned. "Here we go."

The siblings paused along an outcropping of cypress trees. Between them and the castle stretched an unkept yard, cluttered with collapsed statues, decayed gardens, and weeds. The low light of dusk infused the scenery with an ethereal glow.

Roger donned his mask. "Can you two see that rounded tower next to the curtain wall?"

The girls nodded.

"There's a large pile of stone blocks against it forming a small hollow. Once we get across the yard, we should seek shelter there to plan our next steps."

"Okay," they replied.

Roger glanced to either side. The golden glow of fireflies danced throughout the yard. "On the count of three."

"One…"

"Two…"

"Three…!"

The teenagers leapt from the cover of the cypresses and dashed through the tall grass. Their cloaks snapped behind them as they maneuvered around the debris. Even under the veil of darkness they felt terribly exposed. The menacing form of the castle loomed above them, consuming the night sky. They dove into the hollow, their lungs burning.

"Now what?" asked Marie, gasping for breath.

"Which way are the buttresses?"

Mckenzie pointed up.

Roger sighed. "How do we get there?"

His sister shrugged.

"May I see your map?" asked Marie.

Roger handed it to her. "I could sneak atop this mound and scout for more clues."

"If you say so," said Mckenzie.

"I wish Click were here." The boy poked his head out of the hollow and scanned the yard, disappearing into the twilight a moment later.

"What are you looking for?"

"One second," responded Marie, studying the clue and scribbling notes onto the parchment.

"I can't stop trembling," said Mckenzie. "It just occurred to me that we have to go to the highest point of this castle, and I'm afraid of heights! What a stupid thing to be afraid of. The flesh-eating dinosaurs didn't bother me, or the giant spider queen and her babies. But give me a high place and I'm shitting myself. Are you even listening to me?"

"I think we're reading this clue all wrong," Marie replied. "We're taking it literally."

"What do you mean?"

"Do you know what an anagram is?"

"No."

"I learned about them in school earlier this year. They're a type of word puzzle. Basically, you form a message by rearranging the letters from the original phrase. It's like the real clue is hidden within the initial group of words."

"You think that's what this is?"

"Yes," said Marie, holding up the map. "Look."

Below the original clue she had written the following:

"Depress the star cube."

"Whoa," gasped Mckenzie.

Roger burst back into the hollow at that moment. "You

won't believe this, but I think I solved the puzzle and located the correct buttress!"

His sisters looked back at him, smirking.

"What?" he asked.

"Marie already solved it," said Mckenzie.

"How?"

"The clue that Merkresh gave us wasn't even the location. The phrase was an anagram."

Marie handed the map back to her brother.

"What's a star cube?" he asked, reading her notes.

"Who the hell knows, but at least it's a clear instruction."

"Um, guys," said Mckenzie, pointing to one of the stone blocks that formed their hollow. On it was carved a curious symbol: a three-dimensional cube encapsulating a single star.

Roger looked at his sisters, eyebrows raised.

"Do it," said Marie.

Using his gloved hand, he pressed against the symbol. Amid the grinding of gears from some unseen engine, the engraving glowed a radiant blue. A hidden door opened below, plunging the teenagers into darkness.

CHAPTER XLI

A CASTLE IN DARKNESS

Roger coughed up a mouthful of hay as he sat upright.

"Well done, Marie," he said. "My arm's sore now."

"Poor baby," she replied.

"Where are we?" asked Mckenzie, brushing herself off.

"Smells like a petting zoo."

"Cast your lights spell," said Marie.

"Good idea."

Mckenzie brandished her wand and four glowing lanterns appeared above their heads, spreading golden light over their new surroundings.

"We're in the stables," said Roger.

The teenagers stood within a musty hayloft. Stacks of hay bales, rotted and gray, lined the walls. Many had eroded over the decades, creating a spongy carpet over the cobblestones. Wooden barrels, frayed rope, and broken water pumps cluttered the flagstone walkway that curled between the individual stalls.

"Where do we go?"

"Up," said Roger.

"No shit," replied Mckenzie. "I mean out of this dump."

The boy increased the magnification of his mask and peered to their left. "There's a blacksmith's forge ahead. Let's check that out, there may be stairs that lead up to the next level."

Nestled at the opposite end of the livery was a collection of modest artisan stalls. Locksmith, ropemaker, wheelwright, and blacksmith workstations languished in the shadows. Mckenzie's lanterns illuminated a multitude of tools and equipment.

"Look at all this neat stuff," said Roger.

Between the bellows of a brass furnace and a moldered sharpening stone hung a rack of hand-held weapons. Marie pulled a dagger from one of the rungs and tucked it into her belt. The blade was constructed of dual hardened steel and featured a fuller down its length. Upwards-curved quillons sat above the hilt.

"What do you need that for?" asked her sister.

"I don't know. It may come in handy."

"That's good thinking," replied Roger. "We should forage for supplies while we have the opportunity."

The teenagers spread out among the deteriorating stalls. Roger salvaged a nearly undamaged coil of sisal rope and an iron grappling hook. After combing through the contents of a moldy chest, Mckenzie procured a handsome signet ring. A ruby gem was set between intricately carved heraldic designs.

"Look, stairs," said Roger. "And they go up, Mckenzie."

The wooden steps creaked as they carefully climbed a narrow stairwell to the second level of the castle.

"Careful!" exclaimed Marie, pointing. "A broken step."

They passed beneath a stone arch into a common room. A long worktable, covered in dust, web-encrusted candlesticks, and simple kitchenware, stretched down the middle of the hall. Through the splintered glass of a lofty window on the far wall, they could see the courtyard and dancing fireflies below.

"This must be the servants' quarters," said Mckenzie.

"They lived down here?" asked Marie.

"Absolutely," replied Roger. "Many of the servants in a place like this never even encountered the royal family."

"How would you know?" asked Mckenzie.

"Merkresh told me. He grew up in a castle like this."

"Didn't they have their own secret stairs and passages?"

"It wasn't a secret," he replied. "But they definitely used their own entrances and stairwells to move about unseen. The whole point was to keep them out of sight and out of mind."

"There's a hallway over there," said Marie. "Maybe it has a way to get to the next floor."

A collection of servant's bedrooms and utility closets lined either side of the passage. Mckenzie poked her head into one to find that the interior was damp and dismal. A simple desk, wooden dresser, and meager bed were the prominent pieces of furniture. In the corner stood a wrought iron floor candle, poised above a writing desk. She entered the room to inspect an open journal nestled between ink quills and scrolls.

Mckenzie brushed away a thick layer of dust and read the cover's inscription:

The Journal of Annabelle Elsa Shevington.

The leather binding crackled as she flipped the book open and turned to the first page of passages.

July 11 - I'm so excited that mother purchased this marvelous journal for me. I think she acquired it from the store in Kadiaphonek that I mentioned I loved so much. I'm planning to document all my adventures in here over the course of the summer.

July 13 - I visited Loraine in Raspberry Grove last evening. Her family provided a wonderful meal and we got to play in the gardens until sunset. Her father recently had a new conservatory installed in the south gardens. It has tropical plants from across the sea, an orchid room, and even a grove of Red Button Gingers that attracted dozens of hummingbirds! I asked father if he would build one in our garden, but he just laughed. I guess he'd rather collect books than pursue horticulture.

"Mckenzie!" shouted Marie from the hallway. "Could you send some of your lanterns out here so Roger and I can see what the hell we're doing?"

She dispatched two from the room and flipped toward the middle of the journal.

August 2 - We heard it in the sky again. Lorain and I were walking along the road from Dunchester and heard the flapping of massive wings. The trees were blocking the source, but the force of its gusts caused the branches to sway like a summer storm. I've seen the flying reptiles from Kad many times. This was something much bigger and stronger.

August 7 - I couldn't believe my eyes today, but it's a dragon! A real dragon. We were playing around on Maple Hill and saw it clearly as it circled over the forest. I told father as soon as we got home. He was very concerned.

The next three pages were missing from the journal. They appeared to have been torn out. Mckenzie searched for an entry that provided more detail about the dragon.

August 15 - We can't even leave the castle. We've been under siege for the last three days. The creature is an ancient frost dragon. It keeps attacking the outer walls with some kind of ice breath and something my father calls its frightful presence. Everyone is so scared. We dispatched a rider to each of the closest towns a week ago for help, but none of them have returned. Many of the flying buttresses on the eastern side have been destroyed. We have food stores for a year, but I don't know if the castle can withstand the dragon's constant attacks for that long. We need help!

August 16 - My father's archers could not damage the dragon. Their arrows bounced right off his thick, blue scales. They even tried flame arrows, but those had no effect. As a last resort, the mage Xefaris stood from the highest terrace and cast his most powerful spells at the monster as it flew within range. I'm very sad to document that Xefaris was killed. The dragon froze him solid and then attacked with his tail, shattering him into a thousand pieces. Xefaris has been my friend ever since I was a little girl. I will miss him dearly.

August 17 - People are dying from sheer fright. My father believes that the dragon doesn't want to destroy the castle, but rather occupy it as its lair. It's been very careful not to damage the central tower, which is the largest and tallest. The elders have decided that if we cannot inhabit this castle any longer, neither will he.

August 19 - I never imagined that I'd be using this journal to document my own death. It saddens me to think back to the beginning of the summer when I was so excited to go on adventures with Loraine and Caroline. At this point, I doubt I will ever see my friends again. The dragon has forced its way into the castle, and almost everyone is dead. I've been hiding in my secret spot in the Great Hall for the past day. This will probably be my last entry because I can hear him stomping around searching for survivors. I love you Mom and Dad. -Annie.

Mckenzie closed the journal with a heavy heart. "Hey guys, could you please come in here?"

"What'd you find?" asked Marie.

"A journal from a girl who lived here when the dragon attacked. She documented some details that may be useful."

"Does she say how to kill it?" asked Roger.

"Obviously not, since it's still alive."

"What about weaknesses?" asked Marie.

"None that I read. The girl, Annie, described the dragon as being indestructible. The castle's defenses had no effect, nor did archers or fire arrows. Even their mage couldn't damage it with his spells."

"Did she say anything about its attacks?"

"It uses ice breath, a tail attack, and something they called frightful presence."

"What's that?" asked Roger.

"An attack that kills people through pure fear."

"Wonderful," he replied. "If a castle this size can't hurt it, how are we supposed to?"

"I don't know," said Mckenzie.

"What should we do?" asked Marie. "I found the stairs to the next level, but I feel like we should make a plan before we go any further."

Mckenzie slipped the journal into her backpack. "There's no sense in going forward until we have a strategy. If we don't, we could make it all the way to his lair and get slaughtered five seconds later."

"I agree," said Roger. "But after finding that girl's journal, what can we do differently?"

"We're not going to attack it with arrows, for one," said Mckenzie. "And we don't have the skills of a mage. Therefore, however we attack will be different."

"But will our way be better or worse?" asked Marie.

"That's what we have to figure out now."

"What're our assets?" asked Roger.

"You have your mask and the glove's plasma bolts," said Marie. "Mckenzie and I have our ranged spells. The fact that we can attack him while he's flying works to our advantage."

"And our liabilities?"

"There are only three of us," replied Marie. "We've never fought a dragon, and we don't have much battle experience."

"Sounds like a recipe for success," said Mckenzie.

"Even worse is that we don't have the slightest clue as to the environment we'll be fighting in," said Roger.

"He's in the tallest tower," replied Marie. "An advantage for us would be his inability to fly in that enclosed space."

"That's a good point," replied Mckenzie. "But, because he doesn't have room to fly, he may have set a bunch of traps. We'll need to detect those as soon as we get in there."

"Should we even try to fight him in his lair?" asked Marie. "What if we lured him into another part of the castle? We might be able to bypass any traps he's laid and force him out of his comfort zone."

"I like that idea," said Roger. "But if that's not possible, we'll need to find another way to keep him stationary. We have to disable his wing and tail attacks."

"How in the world do we do that?" asked Marie.

"I know a couple spells that could help," said Mckenzie. "I've been practicing one that confuses the enemy. There's another spell that increases my speed. The combination of these could keep him subdued, or at least distracted while you two attack from opposite directions."

"That sounds promising," exclaimed Roger. "We'll need

to make sure we spread out as soon as we enter his lair or wherever we fight him. That'll hopefully keep him from hitting us all with his ice breath at the same time."

"I have another option we could use," said Marie. "In one of my books I've been studying something called polymorph."

"What's that?" asked Mckenzie.

"I could transform the dragon into a lizard or another small creature, rendering it harmless."

"What are the chances it'll work?" asked Roger.

"Probably low, but I can at least try."

"Okay, I think we might have a reasonable plan to work with," said Roger. "First, we attempt to lure him away from his lair. If that's not possible, then we spread out as soon as we enter. You two will immediately detect traps. While Marie is casting polymorph, Mckenzie will increase her speed and try to restrict his movement. That leaves me to continuously shoot him with plasma bolts. You two should also use your ranged attacks as often as possible. And keep moving, we can't remain stationary."

"Sounds good to me," said Mckenzie. "I wish we were at the top already so we could get this over with."

"I wish this castle was a thousand levels high," said Marie. "I don't ever want this fight to begin."

***

They ascended another narrow stairwell and entered a room cluttered with pots and pans. Stacks of sterling silver and decorative dishes filled the sinks and tables. Bits of porcelain crunched beneath their boots as they passed an open hearth, larder, buttery, and numerous pantries.

"The scullery," said Roger.

Through a pair of swinging doors, the group filed into the main kitchen. Two stone fireplaces, each large enough for a person to stand in, lined the walls. In the center of the open space ran a wide island, overflowing with rusted pans, cooking utensils, and copper pots. Withered herbs hung from crooked racks, permeating a faint aroma of thyme and peppermint.

They passed through the main kitchen and into a colossal stateroom. Mckenzie's lanterns illuminated three formal dining tables topped with white linen and candelabra. The High Table, adorned with pewter platters and goblets, stood upon an elevated platform.

"The royal family must have sat up there," said Mckenzie.

Three Gothic windows, embellished with foil arches and flame tracery, towered upon the western wall. Along the edges of the banquet hall glared the busts and portraits of the Shevington lineage. Many were reduced to crumbled marble and torn canvas, marring their legacy.

"Looks like Lord Mortis has been here," said Marie.

One of the enormous dining tables had been upended, its splintered wood was strewn across heraldic rugs. In a corner near the High Table, the remnants of a musical troupe lay in pieces. Lutes, gemshorns, and a hammered dulcimer were all that remained of their merrymaking.

"Look above us," said Roger. "Mckenzie, can you send your magical lights a little higher?"

The lanterns unveiled soaring balconies, held aloft by marble pillars, and garnished with shields and coats of arms. Baroque tapestries, depicting ancient battles and landscapes bathed the walls with threads of splendor.

"More steps over there," said Marie, pointing.

A grand staircase led to the castle's fourth level.

"This room is even bigger than the last," said Mckenzie as they reached the top and gazed across the expanse.

"The Great Hall," said Roger.

An ocean of polished granite flowed into the distance. A hammerbeam ceiling, its decadence amplified by three inordinate chandeliers, soared above. Clusters of decorative tables and chairs were nestled between arched doorways. To one side of the hall, elevated by four marble statues, perched a minstrel's gallery. On the other side of the massive chamber commanded a row of rectilinear windows, accented by stained glass motifs.

"Do you hear that?" asked Marie.

Roger and Mckenzie cocked their heads, listening.

"Sounds like someone's humming."

Mckenzie equipped her wand and led the group passed somber oil paintings, marble busts, and piles of crumbled granite. At the opposite end of the hall, lying on her stomach, feet kicking playfully, a young girl sketched a drawing. Art supplies and paper were strewn around her in a wide circle.

The teenagers looked at each other, confused.

"Hello," whispered Mckenzie.

"Hello," replied the girl, not bothering to look up. The scratch of her graphite pencil echoed through the hall.

"What are you doing here?" asked Mckenzie.

"I live here."

Mckenzie turned to her siblings, unsure what to do. Marie nodded for her to continue the inquiry.

"May I ask your name?"

"Annie," replied the girl.

"Annabelle Elsa Shevington?" asked Mckenzie.

The scratch of graphite ceased, and the girl looked up. In the glow of the magic lanterns, her features appeared ethereal and translucent. "Yes, that's me. Who are you?"

Mckenzie pulled the journal from her backpack. "I found this in the servant's quarters. I think it belongs to you."

"My journal!" exclaimed Annie, hopping to her feet.

As she flipped through its pages, the group could discern that Annie was a ghost.

"So, who are you?" she asked again.

"My name is Mckenzie Woods, and this is my sister Marie and brother Roger."

Annie giggled as she read one of the journal's passages. "I thought I'd lost this thing forever," she said, looking up. "Where did you say you found it?"

"On the second level, in a servant's room."

"Interesting. I don't recall ever going down there. Well, thanks for bringing it back. I need to finish my sketch now."

The girl returned to her drawing.

"Wait!" said Mckenzie. "We're here to slay the dragon."

Annie stopped dead in her tracks. "What did you say?"

"Lord Mortis."

The young girl turned, revealing an expression drowned in heartache. "He massacred my entire family. Is that really why you're here?"

"Yes," replied Mckenzie. "We're part of a larger group that's been tasked with destroying him."

Annie studied the teenagers in detail for the first time. "Where are the others? How many warriors did you bring?"

"It's just us."

"But you're just kids like me. How do the three of you expect to kill him?"

"We know magic."

"So did my friend Xefaris. Did you read about his fate?"

"I did," replied Mckenzie. "But we have a plan."

Annie could not restrain a bitter chuckle. "Really, you have a plan? Pray tell how the three of you are going to storm the castle and slay the mighty dragon."

Roger scoffed. "We haven't endured all we have to listen to this rubbish. Let's go."

"Wait," said Mckenzie. "Annie, I've read the passages in your journal. I know what you and your family went through during those final days. I'm so sorry that it ended the way it did for you, but there's a chance to terminate the dragon's reign over your household. We may not look like much, but the three of us were specifically chosen for this task."

Mckenzie paused, reflecting on her own losses.

"Our mother was murdered by a person who pledges allegiance to Lord Mortis and his masters."

"They killed your mother too?" asked the girl.

"They did," replied Mckenzie. "We can't help that we're three kids with little experience. All we can do is use our talents to try and calm our mother's soul, and to liberate the realm of Silvarum. The three of us have traveled far and achieved much to reach this final stage. We respect and honor that this castle is still your home. Nevertheless, we must continue. Annie, will you help us defeat Lord Mortis?"

The girl considered Mckenzie's request. "I will," she said.

***

"There are some friends in our group who are ghosts, but they're invisible to us," said Marie. "Why can we see you?"

"How would I know?" replied Annie.

"It probably has to do with that dimensional stuff they're always talking about," said Roger.

"You seem strange from my perspective," said Annie.

"What do you mean?"

"You look spectral and thin, like whispers of people. And when you talk it sounds like you're far away. I guess that's why I didn't hear you approach."

"You sound like that too," said Roger.

"What are you drawing?" asked Mckenzie.

Annie looked back at the clutter of materials. "Nothing special. It's a sketch of the northern tip of Fairview Holm. My mother used to take me up there every summer. I'd play on the beach and we'd wave as the massive galleons sailed by on their way to Kadiaphonek."

"That sounds nice," replied Mckenzie.

"I miss her," said the girl.

"Well," said Roger after a moment. "What can you tell us about the dragon?"

"I've had thirty years or so to observe his behavior," said Annie. "What would you like to know?"

"Everything!" exclaimed Marie.

Annie laughed. "There's actually not much to tell. Lord Mortis is a rather boring adversary. He sleeps in the tower all day long and comes out at night to hunt."

"How does he get out?"

"Through one of the windows. He busted it ages ago."

"How do we get in?"

"It'd be easy if you were a ghost like me. Whenever I go to spy on him, I take a secret route through the library, out along the Master's Terrace, and then up a stairwell to the top spire."

"Why's it a secret route?" asked Mckenzie.

"You don't know?" replied Annie.

"Know what?"

"Lord Mortis isn't the only creature in here."

"Are you serious?" gasped Marie.

"I'm sorry to rain on your parade, but there are hordes of cultists and other fanatics occupying the upper levels. Even the kind that can harm me. The only reason you haven't encountered any of them yet is because of the protection spells my father's mages cast on the lower levels once Lord Mortis took over the tower. He and his followers have been trying to get back down here ever since."

"Why?"

"For the treasure, of course," said Annie. "He's a dragon, after all. Every once in a while, during his hunting forays, Lord Mortis will raid a distant village or waylay a caravan of nobles. He's accumulated a considerable mountain of treasure over the decades, but he's grown bored of gold and jewels. His ultimate goal, the true reason he chose my home as his lair, is to plunder what my father and his mages constructed."

"What was that?" asked Roger.

"The greatest library of magical spells in all of Silvarum. Even bigger than the one at the academy on the Isle of Magic."

"Wow," replied the teenagers in unison.

"Lord Mortis has always been a student of magic, but he can't avoid the craving to horde treasure like every other dragon. Nevertheless, my father's library is his obsession."

"A book-hoarding dragon," said Marie. "That's new."

"What about the Rune of Frost?" asked Roger. "Have you seen that in his lair?"

"It's up there," said Annie, "in the middle of his chamber, upon a marble column."

"I read in your journal that he attacks with his breath, tail, and wings," said Mckenzie. "Does he do anything else?"

"Isn't that enough?" replied Annie. "Other than using his cultists as a defense from everyday robbers while he sleeps, those are the only attacks I've seen."

"You mean others have come through here?"

"There have been other adventuring parties. Full groups with wizards, warriors, and healers. I remember one company that marched in here years ago, overly confident in their skills. There were seven of them: a warlock, monk, two clerics, rogue, wizard, and a barbarian. They made it all the way to Lord Mortis' lair and wiped within minutes. Their party had a peculiar name too, but I can't remember it anymore."

"Why did they fail?"

"Because they didn't get to know me, for one. And they didn't learn about the dragon's weakness."

"Lord Mortis has a weakness?" gasped Marie.

"Of course. Every living thing has a weakness. It's just a matter of taking the time to figure out what that is. Fortunately, for your group at least, I've had decades to discover it."

"What is it?"

"Follow me and I'll show you."

***

Annie led Marie, Mckenzie, and Roger to the fifth level of the castle and into a spacious library. Stacks of books and scrolls lined hundreds of shelves from floor to ceiling.

"Is this your father's library?" asked Marie.

"One of them," replied Annie. "But not the special library Lord Mortis is after. That collection is in a secret room."

The teenagers watched as the girl climbed to the top of a sliding ladder. She stretched as far as she could and pulled a book from the shelf. The mechanical grind of gears reverberated from the wall and a hidden door creaked open. Annie grasped both sides of the ladder and slid all the way back down.

"Shall we go?" she asked, motioning to the door.

"What happens if somebody actually wants to read that book?" asked Roger as they walked through a passageway.

"Then they're in for a surprise," replied Annie. "The title of it's called *Essential Adiabatic Theorems and Quantum Perturbations, 1st Edition.* Who would ever want to read such a thing?"

Roger smiled to himself.

Annie pulled a key from her pocket and unlocked a door. The room beyond was surprisingly quaint. In the center, amid a few cabinets and piles of scrolls, stood a single bookstand, on which were shelved eight books. Atop a section of raised hardwood was a ninth tome, opened to page six hundred and ten.

"That's it?" asked Mckenzie. "The great library? I have more books than that in my bedroom."

"I'm very happy for you," replied Annie. "But I guarantee that your library doesn't contain the centuries of wisdom within these pages. Many people have died to create this collection."

"But it's so small."

"Not all small things are what they seem," replied Annie.

"What's the dragon's weakness?" asked Marie.

"Like many of life's mysteries, Lord Mortis hides his most vulnerable attribute in plain sight. Dragons don't have a natural resistance to magic. As a result, many of them devote their entire lives trying to correct this defect. After years of observing his behavior, I believe his treasure hoarding is a ruse. What he really desires is knowledge. Knowledge in the form of magical spells that could make him immortal. Ironically, the library he so desires is the bane of his demise. His lust to seize upon the highest tower and rally his disciples was his critical error. Rather than first securing the lower levels to discover the location of this library, he chose absolute power. And you know what they say about absolute power?"

"It corrupts absolutely," replied Roger.

Annie smiled.

"What does that mean for us?" asked Marie.

"It means that the handful of books before you contain spells that can destroy dragons."

"Why didn't your father's mages use them before?"

"They tried to," replied Annie, "but nothing happened. Most of the spells speak of a family called Drake. Unfortunately, the magic we require only attunes to members of that bloodline. If only we could find a few."

The sisters looked at each other. "I think we can help."

"You know members of that family?"

"Our mother's maiden name is Drake," replied Mckenzie. "You're looking at that bloodline."

Annie's eyes widened. She stared off, thinking.

"I'm sorry for asking the following questions," she said, "but didn't you say your mother recently passed?"

"She did," replied Marie.

"Did she happen to have any siblings?"

"Yes, but her brother died when he was very young."

Annie nodded thoughtfully. "Are there other descendants of the Drake bloodline still alive? Cousins, aunts, anyone?"

"They're all gone," said Mckenzie. "We're it."

"Do you understand what that means?" asked Annie.

"What?"

"Only the two of you can defeat Lord Mortis."

Mckenzie examined the bookstand. "All we have to do is use some of these spells and we'll kill him? Just like that?"

"It's not going to be a walk in the park, but yes, choosing the appropriate set of spells from this library will enable members of the Drake bloodline to defeat the dragon."

"Which ones do we use?" asked Marie.

"I don't know," replied Annie. "Let's take a look."

The girl flipped the opened book to its table of contents.

"Here you go," she said. "Take your pick."

Marie ran her finger down the list of passages as she read the titles. "Arcane Portal, Astral Extension, Charm, Darkness, Expatriation, Solar Radiance, and True Polymorph."

"What does Astral Extension do?" asked Mckenzie.

"It allows you to leave your material forms," said Annie.

"And Expatriation?" asked Roger.

Marie flipped to the page. "It says it attempts to send one creature to another plane of existence, incapacitating it."

"That sounds like a good one to learn," said Mckenzie.

"We must kill the dragon," said Marie. "Not banish him."

"How long do these spells take to attune?" asked Roger.

"Probably not long," replied Annie. "An hour?"

"Then I recommend we take a short rest now before we continue on to the higher levels."

"Good idea," said Annie. "Grab a few books and follow me. I'll take you to the perfect room."

The sixth level of the castle was a labyrinth of extravagant bedrooms, galleries, and solars. Annie led them down a hallway burnished with gold gilding and lined with full suits of armor. A trophy hall, billiard room, tapestry gallery, and gun room were a portion of the offshoots the teenagers were able to perceive as Annie led them to their chambers.

"Here we are," she said as they approached an oak door. "This used to be the Lady's Chamber. My mother's room."

"We can't stay in here," said Mckenzie.

"Nonsense," replied Annie. "If you're going to slay Lord Mortis then you deserve to recuperate like kings and queens. Get some rest and study those spells. I'll be back in a few hours."

"Thank you for helping us," said Marie.

Annie nodded. "I've haunted this castle for thirty years. Soon I'll be thanking you for your achievements. Not only will you have calmed your mother's soul, but mine as well."

CHAPTER XLII

LORD MORTIS

Other than a layer of dust and cobwebs, the Lady's Chamber was the most ornate room the Woods children had ever seen. A ceiling painting depicting a group of angelic beings lorded over an arrangement of sandalwood chairs, crystal chandeliers, and a scarlet canopy bed, detailed with silver leaf. Between golden wall panels hung oil portrait paintings and accented mirrors. In the far corner stood an immense dollhouse, replete with its own royal bedrooms, library, kitchen, and fully stocked wine cellar.

"I'm going to sleep," said Roger, collapsing onto a chaise lounge constructed of mulberry silk.

The sisters dropped their backpacks and gear to the floor, diving onto the canopy bed. The resulting cloud of dust had no effect on their fatigue, and they were soon sound asleep. Roger snored peacefully, still wearing his mask, glove, and backpack.

Annie quietly entered their room five hours later. Roger and Mckenzie were still asleep while Marie sat near the dollhouse in the far corner, pouring over the pages of magic spells.

"Find anything useful?" asked Annie.

"All of it," replied Marie. "My problem is narrowing them down to a few that are practical for this confrontation."

"What's your top three?" she asked, sitting next to Marie.

"True Polymorph, Cloud of Swords, and Ice Immunity."

"You know your spells," said Annie. "Those are the same ones I would choose if I were a warlock."

"How'd you know that's what I practice?"

"I may not have magical skills like you, but after decades of studying these spells and observing the other would-be dragon slayers, I've become a bit of a scholar on the subject."

"There's also the spell Solar Radiance," said Marie. "It keeps reminding me of something my mother recently said to me: 'Multon and Marie on the castle. The purple gem in sunlight.'"

"I thought your mother died."

"She did, but I was able to briefly see and speak to her."

"How?"

"My father has the ability to see those who've passed on."

"Ghosts."

"Right," replied Marie. "Somehow, when the five of us all held hands, we were transported to a weird place where we could see each other."

"So what does her statement mean?" asked Annie.

"The first part signifies me and Lord Mortis."

"But who's Multon?"

"Are you familiar with the history of the runestones?"

"Not really."

"My mother told me before she died that Lord Mortis resurrected himself by absorbing the lifeforce from a man named Multon. He was a member of the original expedition team that discovered the runestones and started this whole mess."

"I see," replied Annie. "And the second part?"

Marie held up her wand. "The purple amethyst on the tip is what she's referring to. The final clue about sunlight is what's been bugging me."

"You think your mother was trying to tell you that the secret to killing the dragon is using the Solar Radiance spell?"

"Possibly."

"The fact that you and your sister are the only two beings capable of such a feat, leads me to believe your mother is aware of much more than we are. You should trust her."

Marie smiled. "I'm going to. I've learned and attuned to that spell as well as Ice Immunity and Cloud of Swords."

"Excellent," replied Annie, pulling out her pocket watch. "Lord Mortis will be returning soon."

"Is he hunting?"

"Yes, I saw him fly off a few hours ago. He's always very fatigued when he returns, so your best opportunity to attack is when he settles back down to rest."

Marie felt a surge of nausea in her belly.

"I know you're scared," said Annie. "You have your sister and brother to help you as well as the most powerful spells in the realm. You're going to be fine."

"I don't feel fine."

Mckenzie yawned as she joined the girls.

"How'd you sleep?" asked Annie.

"I wouldn't call it sleeping. The nightmares were awful."

"A haunted castle with an evil dragon living at the top will do that to you. You feel rested, at least?"

"I'm fine," replied Mckenzie. "What's the plan?"

"Annie said the dragon is hunting and will return shortly. She thinks we should confront him as he's settling back down."

"Makes sense. Should I wake Roger?"

"In a minute," said Marie. "I wanted to talk with Annie a bit more before we get going."

"Okay," replied Mckenzie. "I'm going to grab something to eat, do you want anything?"

"No thanks, I don't think my stomach can handle it."

Mckenzie stood and walked across the room.

"Can I ask you a personal question?" asked Marie.

"Of course," replied Annie.

"Are there other members of your family in the castle?"

"You mean ghosts like me?"

"Yes."

"No one else in my family remains. I don't know why I'm the only Shevington roaming this place, but I'm not alone."

"What do you mean?"

"Many of the servants still wander the halls."

"Why didn't we see any?"

"Because they're scared of you. Wouldn't you be?"

Marie frowned. "I didn't think of it that way."

"I never really go down to the lower levels, which is why I was surprised Mckenzie found my journal there, but I've seen them wandering around up here from time to time."

"Are they nice?"

"I guess so. They're just people like you and me."

"Did you make any friends? You've been alone so long."

"I tried," replied Annie. "It didn't work out."

Mckenzie sat back down, munching on an apple and nuts. "Are you sure you don't want any?" she asked Marie.

Her sister waved away the request.

"I'll try one," said Annie.

"Really?" exclaimed Mckenzie. "Are you able to?"

"I don't know. Let's find out."

Mckenzie dropped a few walnuts into the girl's palm.

"Yummy," she said, popping them into her mouth.

"That's interesting," said Mckenzie. "It appears partially converged dimensions don't care about what we eat."

"We have that, at least," said Marie.

***

Annie addressed the siblings as they exited the Lady's Chamber. "From here onward, we'll all be in extreme danger. Obviously, since we'll be fighting a dragon, but also because of the creatures that roam around in the upper levels."

"What kinds?" asked Mckenzie.

"You name it," replied Annie. "Phantasms, revenants, evil spirits, and wraiths to name a few. Then there're the humanoids."

"The usual suspects?" asked Marie.

"Yep. Humans, trolls, gnomes, even some halflings have succumbed to Lord Mortis' subjugation. If we stick to the route I've stabilized over the decades, we shouldn't have to confront any of them, or the traps they've laid."

"Very well," said Roger. "Let's do this."

Annie nodded. "Good luck."

"To all of us," said Mckenzie.

Annie twisted the base of a golden candelabra, revealing a secret door in the adjacent wall.

"Follow me," she said.

They ascended a darkened stairwell that seemed to go on forever. Wooden steps creaked as they maneuvered a narrow gap between the castle walls. During one section, voices could be heard from the other side. A heavy step by Marie caused a flash of terror when the voices abruptly halted, listening. The teenagers resumed their climb as the conversation reestablished.

Annie motioned for them to halt at the point where the stairwell intersected with the face of a stone wall. Standing on her tiptoes, she peered through a gap in the mortar.

"It's clear," she said after a few moments.

A section of the stone wall slid to the side, revealing a high balcony. Fresh air filled their lungs as the teenagers escaped the stairwell to the embrace of a star-filled sky. Annie motioned for them to stay close to the wall curling around the base of the central spire. The view was astounding. The twinkling lights of Kadiaphonek were crisp and clear on the horizon. Even the activity of Moonlight Bay was visible from this height. Galleons, frigates, and sloops traversed the rolling waves.

"Remain flush with the wall," whispered Annie as they crept along. "There are sentries on the parapet above us."

"You couldn't get me out on that terrace," said Mckenzie. "I don't care if a thousand dragons were chasing us."

They reached the opposite end of the balcony unseen and paused within the shadows. Before them loomed the central tower and lair of Lord Mortis. Roger craned his neck until he could see its pointed crown. A solitary nighthawk croaked as it departed from lead shingles, flapping into the darkness.

"This is the final stairwell," said Annie. "At the top, we'll be entering the dragon's chamber through a crack in the wall. If you need to gather your courage, do it now. There won't be time to hesitate once we begin the climb."

Marie turned and vomited onto the flagstone.

Her sister rushed to her side, holding her steady.

"I'm so fucking scared," said Marie.

"We all are," replied Roger.

"These will help," said Annie, handing each of them an amulet. "Their magic will dispel your fear during the fight."

Roger and Mckenzie donned the necklaces. Marie wiped her mouth, gasping for breath.

***

The teenagers reached the top of the stairwell undetected. Annie raised a finger to her mouth, signaling for them to remain silent as she peeked through the crack.

"Shit," exclaimed Marie. "I lost my amulet."

"There's no time to go back for it," replied Mckenzie.

Annie motioned for them to enter the dragon's lair.

The interior was bitter cold and dark. Puffs of icy breath escaped their mouths as their eyes struggled to adjust in the gloom. The scent of snow filled the air. Marie cast Ice Immunity on the group, however, it did not appear to have any effect.

"Good evening, friends," said a deep and soothing voice from the shadows. "I trust your jaunt hither was incident free? I instructed my associates to provide safe passage, for I've been eager to make your acquaintance. I've heard so much about your marvelous adventures."

The spire's broken window had been sealed with a slab of ice, reducing the exterior starlight. As a result, a complete view of the lair was unattainable. Amid a nebulous glow of ultramarine and silver, a pair of shimmering eyes were their host's only discernable feature. Its voice, strangely seductive, continued.

"Please, feel free to introduce yourselves. You've certainly overcome a myriad of obstacles to reach this moment, shall we not offer one another the respect of a proper reception?"

The companions remained silent. A peculiar docility and calmness reverberated through Roger and Mckenzie. Their minds were at ease and fearless. Marie, by contrast, shook from terror and imminent hypothermia.

"My name's Mckenzie Woods."

Marie regarded her sister, flabbergasted.

"There now," replied the voice. "Someone with the courage to initiate our relationship. And what a pretty name."

"Thank you," she replied. "Who are you?"

"I'm Lord Mortis, proprietor of this castle. You knew that, though, since you're all very clever children."

Roger suddenly felt the intense focus of the eyes.

"Fine sir, pray tell thy name," said the dragon.

"I'm Roger Woods."

Marie gasped. Something was terribly wrong.

"Indeed!" replied Lord Mortis. "A gallant fellow, surely. It's an honor to finally meet you. We have much to discuss. Your talents with technology are praised in this region."

Roger smiled in return.

The eyes focused on Marie. "Young lady, why do you hold your tongue within a sour expression? It requires more energy to keep quiet than to speak the mind. What troubles you?"

"You've charmed them," she replied.

"Undoubtedly," said Lord Mortis. "Charm is an attribute I pay each of my guests. Especially those who demonstrate an air of respect during formal exchanges such as these. In my old age, I've come to savor the fare of meeting new friends."

Marie remained silent.

"Have it your way," continued the dragon with a sigh. "I suppose I shouldn't expect the rabble of Silvarum to appreciate the technicalities of such reverential endeavors."

"Why's it so cold and dark in here?" asked Mckenzie.

"What a thoughtful question," replied Lord Mortis. "In all honesty, my vision is not as sharp as it once was. The dim light helps to soothe my old eyes and bestow a calming environment for my required slumber. As for the temperature of my dwelling, I'm a frost dragon. Do you not enjoy the satisfaction of a warm fire while relaxing in your home? It's the same for me, just on the opposite end of the scale."

Mckenzie and Roger nodded, satisfied with the response.

"Now that we've concluded our amiable salutations, how may I be of service to the Woods children?"

Although freezing and petrified, Marie had enough sense left to realize their plan had failed. Some form of deception had occurred since their ascension from the terrace. She looked around the dimly lit chamber, struggling to grasp how they had been overpowered so quickly.

"Where's Annie?" asked Marie.

Roger and Mckenzie continued to stare at the dragon, stupefied by its sorcery. A blanket of frost covered their shivering forms, producing icicles upon their nose and chin.

"The necklaces!" cried Marie. "Take them off!"

Wicked laughter exuded from the shadows. "I don't think they can hear you anymore, my dear."

Marie attempted to cast Ice Immunity again, but her arms were frozen. Frost formed along her eyelashes, altering her vision like the fluctuating patterns of a kaleidoscope. She addressed the dragon through numb lips.

"What have you done to Annie?"

"You still haven't figured it out," said Lord Mortis. "How pitiful. Do you require a hint?"

As the biting cold dragged her to unconsciousness, Marie considered the peculiar characteristics of Annabel Shevington: their introduction in the Great Hall, her insistence that Marie learn the spells, and the ease by which they navigated to the top of the dragon's spire. A wave of anger washed over Marie.

"You were Annie all along."

"Yes," replied Lord Mortis. "Didn't I mention how clever the Woods children are?"

"So she wasn't real? What about her journal?"

"Good heavens, no," replied the dragon. "I apologize for your confusion. Annie was an unquestionably authentic character, as were the contents of her journal. The events occurred just as she recorded, however, the missing detail was how I devoured her and her family upon sacking the castle. It was all too easy, just like how I used her image and sensibilities to fool you."

Marie attempted to reply, but her mouth was frozen shut.

"Half a moment," said Lord Mortis. "The Ice Immunity spell is so effective, allow me to reduce its potency. I would very much like to finish this enjoyable conversation. The three of you have endured a great deal, it'd be a shame to eat you so quickly."

The frost upon her face melted instantly, as did the icicles on her hands. She gripped the purple wand and focused.

"All the spells you told me to learn were a ruse," she said. "They're doing the exact opposite of their design."

"A wonderful trick, is it not?" asked the dragon. "Rather than waste my time with the overused strategy of setting traps all over the castle, all I have to do is pretend to be a sad, little girl, and you'll follow and believe whatever I tell you. It works every time, especially with humans. You're always so eager to believe strangers and share your feelings. It's pathetic."

"Why go through all that trouble? Why not just kill us?"

"I could, of course, but transforming folk into ice cubes, or smashing them to pieces with my tail has become unfulfilling. And it makes too much of a mess. My gratification results from earning the intruder's confidence, then savoring their anguish as they realize their miscalculation. Torment makes the meat taste so much better."

"And what you said about the Drakes?"

"I was truthful in that respect," replied Lord Mortis. "You and your sister are indeed capable of slaying dragons, which was one of the motivations for the elaborate deception. I receive many guests who presume they possess the skills to defeat me and plunder my treasure, but rarely do I interact with members of the Drake bloodline. Your case is a very delicate matter that required preparations."

"Then you knew we were coming?"

"My dear Marie," he replied. "Do you really think I've lived this long, accumulated this much wealth, and bestowed this much fear without being aware of those who seek to destroy me? Most in Silvarum are aware of your foolish quest, anyway."

"You weren't so mighty when Merkresh destroyed you."

A fierce growl rumbled from the darkness. "Do not speak that name in this chamber," said Lord Mortis. "Once our little conversation has concluded here, you can be certain I'll deal with that motherfucker. In the meantime, I believe I've tired of this parley. It's time I finally put an end to the Drake bloodline."

"Maybe if you didn't talk so much!" she cried.

During Lord Mortis' boastful pontifications, Marie had been focusing on the spells she learned before meeting Annie. A warm glow radiated around Roger and Mckenzie as she cast Aura of Healing and Dispel Charm. They blinked out of their hypnotic slumbers, water from the melted icicles dripping to the floor.

"If you want to live, remove the necklaces at once!"

Although confused, her siblings obeyed the demand.

Vicious laughter thundered from the frigid gloom. "As I said, the Woods children are clever creatures. Hopefully, you're as delicious as you are resourceful."

Lord Mortis, ancient frost dragon, and protector of the Rune of Frost, finally emerged from the shadows.

Candlesticks, sconces, and candelabra ignited, unveiling an immense horde of treasure. The space was circular in design, with a lofty ceiling that converged to a point high above. Piles of gold, jewels, and overflowing treasure chests filled the lair. A thin layer of frost covered every object and surface, resulting in a dizzying environment of shimmering light.

The largest mound of treasure towered at the back of the chamber. Lord Mortis commanded from its summit. From claw to crest, the beast stood nine meters. Two leathery wings, fully retracted, soared an additional thirteen. The dragon's armor was comprised of sapphire scales, a column of posterior spines, and a thorny tale that culminated with a razor-sharp barb. Imperial-red eyes glared behind a row of jagged fangs. Two horns adorned with jewelry and pendants protruded from his forehead, the ends connected by a gold necklace. Marie made a mental note of this peculiar detail as Lord Mortis clawed through the mountain of gold coins to face them head-on.

"So, you choose to fight?"

Marie, Roger, and Mckenzie stood resolute.

"Very well, prepare yourselves for gruesome deaths," replied the dragon. "However, this lair is far too constrictive for a proper engagement. Let's relocate to a setting more congruent with my talents. Mckenzie, how does the Master's Terrace sound to you? Now, witness the wrath of Lord Mortis!"

Amid a burst of laughter, the dragon summoned a portal in the center of the room. An onyx sphere, reverberating with purple threads of energy, expanded from a singular point. He pumped his massive wings and flew into the void. A whirlwind of frigid air bombarded the chamber's interior, seizing the teenagers and sucking them through.

***

"Behold!" cried Benjamin from the top of Dragolroth. "Lord Mortis soars above the castle!"

"The final battle has begun," said Merkresh. "Let us join together and direct our energy toward your children."

Trelinia, Benjamin, and Merkresh held hands atop the tower's battlements, emitting a tributary of love toward the castle.

***

Mckenzie, Roger, and Marie dropped through the portal, tumbling across the terrace's flagstone. A surge of flapping wings resounded as they hurried to arm themselves.

"Execute our original plan!" shouted Roger. "Spread out and use your ranged attacks. Mckenzie, employ your speed and confusion spells against him. Marie, keep trying Polymorph."

Mckenzie peered over the edge of the Master's Terrace, frozen with acrophobia. The forest's canopy, like a rolling sea of liberation, beckoned to her from below. Marie grasped her by the shoulder as she began to step over the edge.

"What the hell are you doing?" cried Marie.

Mckenzie blinked with confusion. "The dragon. I think he's still affecting my mind," she replied, rubbing her head.

"Get to the wall," said Marie. "Are you able to fight?"

Mckenzie nodded. "Yes, I think I'm all right now."

"Spread out!" cried Roger. "Here he comes!"

Lord Mortis descended upon the teenagers at full speed, his muscular wings thrashing the night sky. With a deafening roar, a burst of ice erupted from his mouth. The force of its impact exploded upon the balcony, uprooting stone and mortar. A tier of shattered crenellations tumbled to the depths below.

As the ice stream crashed around Roger, Mckenzie cast an invisible shield around him. Glacial shards and chunks of stone deflected off the unseen barrier, leaving him unharmed. Mckenzie cast Haste upon herself, then aimed the curly wand at the dragon. Bolts of electricity crackled through the air.

The cloud of dust and steam around Roger dissipated, allowing him to join the fight. Aiming his glove as Lord Mortis banked for another pass, he fired a volley of green spheres. They thumped against the beast at the same moment as Mckenzie's barrage. The diversified attack briefly stunned the dragon, causing him to lose his balance and drop. He shrieked in pain as a plasma bolt ripped through the thin webbing of a wing.

"It's working!" cried Marie. "Hit him again!"

Lord Mortis regained his composure and focused his rage upon Roger and Mckenzie. He swooped over the terrace, pausing in mid-air. Massive wings kicked up a fierce wind as he positioned himself to strike both children at once. Roger and Mckenzie raised their weapons but were overwhelmed by the dragon's breath. Tendrils of crystalized water curled around their bodies, freezing them solid within blocks of ice.

Marie screamed.

***

Benjamin watched the action from the top of Dragolroth. "I don't like how this is going," he said as the second stream of bright-blue dragon's breath ripped through the top of the castle.

"It's difficult to say from this distance," replied Merkresh.

"It's easy to see that they're in serious trouble."

"What do you propose we do?" asked the old man. "We can't get there in time to help. The fight will be over either way."

Benjamin turned and motioned toward the demon.

"Are you out of your mind?" asked the old man.

"Yes," said Benjamin. "My children are being slaughtered before my eyes. I'll do anything to protect them."

Merkresh regarded the mysterious creature. It remained on the edge of the battlements, gazing thoughtfully into the night.

"What do you expect me to do?"

"Ask it for help," replied Benjamin.

"Collaborating with him could be as dangerous as fighting a dragon. We don't know anything about this creature."

"Maybe, but so far he hasn't bothered us. As a matter of fact, we were the ones irritating him. It's possible he could use *our* help for whatever he's so concerned with."

Merkresh took a deep breath. "Because of the urgency of our situation, I'll do it, but don't be surprised if we regret this."

"I thank you," replied Benjamin. "As does Trelinia."

The old man walked across the tower and addressed the demon. "I'm sorry to disturb you once again, but we desperately require your assistance."

"Why?"

"My companion's children are battling Lord Mortis."

The demon laughed. "Only cowardly parents would send their own children to plunder a dragon's treasure."

"Sir," replied Merkresh, clearing his throat. "They do not seek his treasure. Reclaiming the Rune of Frost is our objective. We fight for the protection of Silvarum."

The demon turned. "Do you speak truthfully?"

"I swear it with my life," replied Merkresh.

"A suitable response, for that is the collateral I require if I agree to help you. However, upon the fulfillment of my service, you and your companions must agree to another favor in return."

"What is it?"

"The details are not relevant now. Do you agree or not?"

"I can't agree without knowing the specifics."

The demon tilted his head to observe the ensuing battle.

"It appears that you're in no position to make demands. Either agree to my terms, or those children will die."

"I agree," said the old man.

"Very well," replied the demon, standing. His stature was terrifying. Two massive wings unfurled as he extended a hulking arm. "Will your friend be joining us?"

"His injuries prevent him from further battle."

"Then let us depart at once," he said, grasping the old man under his arms and ascending into the night sky.

Benjamin and Trelinia watched as the demon carried Merkresh above the trees. In the distance, the dragon roared.

***

"Did you really stand a chance?" asked Lord Mortis as he hovered above Marie. "Nay, for creatures as weak as you can only tremble within my shadow. They cower as I feast upon their flesh and clean my fangs with their frosted bones. You tried your best, but you failed. Marie Woods, last surviving member of the Drake bloodline, DIE!"

Marie closed her eyes in anticipation of the end. As she prepared to slip into oblivion, her final thoughts were of Roger, Mckenzie, and her loving parents. She had tried her hardest. For that, she could die proud.

"No!" screamed Lord Mortis.

A winged creature, three times as small as the dragon, yet colossal in terms of strength and presence, struck Lord Mortis in the face. Razor-sharp claws sliced through the dragon's cheek, casting sapphire scales to the terrace below. They clanked upon the stone as Marie ran to the opposite side, diving for cover.

"Over here!" cried a familiar voice.

"Merkresh! How'd you get up here?"

The old man pointed to the sky. "With him."

Lord Mortis and the demon were locked in combat. A flurry of wings and freezing air swirled above the highest spires, launching debris in all directions. Like two celestial behemoths, they assailed one another with supernatural aggression. Talons, tails, and fists beat upon crimson skin and icy-blue leather. Each time Lord Mortis attempted to cast his frozen breath, the demon flapped its powerful wings and dodged him. During one iteration, the demon drove a fist directly into the dragon's horns, snapping one completely off. The collection of sparkling jewelry that Marie had noticed in the lair was also destroyed. Bits of gold and silver plummeted to the forest below. The dragon cried out in dismay.

"They were protecting him," Marie whispered.

"What did you say?"

"The dragon's lost his magic. He's vulnerable now."

"Hearken!" cried Merkresh, pointing to the horizon. "The advent of day delivers the hope of sunlight!"

Sunlight.

Like a frozen arrow through her heart, Marie was stunned with awareness. *Multon and Marie on the castle. The purple gem in sunlight.* Her mother's enigmatic phrase had been constructed of clues passed on through the lives of departed loved ones:

Joseph Drake from his forest grave...

Candace Somberlain amidst her room of dolls...

Trelinia Woods within the falling snow...

The fragments had been woven together and passed on to the next generation, empowering Marie to unravel the puzzle that would slay the protector of the Rune of Frost:

To defeat the dragon, raise the amethyst atop the castle at sunrise.

***

Lord Mortis howled at his adversary. "I remember you, demon lord! You may disrupt my magic, but you can't kill me!"

"But I can!" screamed Marie as she climbed to the top of the tallest battlement.

"What are you doing?" cried Merkresh, reaching for her.

"Trust me!"

Amidst the pause in battle, Lord Mortis perceived the old man for the first time. "Merkresh!" he bellowed. In his rage, the dragon struck the demon across the chest with his barbed tail, propelling him into the distant trees.

"We meet again, old fool," said the dragon, positioning himself to attack. "I must withdraw from this fight prematurely, but before I do, allow me to slay the dragon slayers."

Reaching the highest point of the castle, she extended the purple wand above her head. Marie took a deep breath and then shouted over the valley in a voice as clear as an angel.

"For Silvarum!"

A ray of sunlight broke the distant horizon, engaging the amethyst. The wand glowed with a dazzling burst of light and heat, launching a stream of golden energy at the dragon. The ancient creature shrieked in surprise and fear. With a resounding splinter of bone and flesh, Lord Mortis, ancient frost dragon, and protector of the Rune of Frost exploded into a cloud of blood and fire. His reign of terror had come to an end.

CHAPTER XLIII

FROST

Marie Woods, thirteen-year-old girl from Thorndale Village, had defeated the dragon. She gazed in wonder as the remains of Lord Mortis crashed into the forest below.

"You did it, Marie!" cried Merkresh, scooping her off the battlement and hugging her tight. "I'm so proud of you!"

Her joy mutated to grief as she thought of her siblings. "Roger and Mckenzie," she moaned. "They're dead!"

"No we're not," replied a voice.

Marie spun to see her brother and sister standing beside the demon. "You're alive!" she cried, rushing to them.

"Thanks to our new friend," said Mckenzie.

"They were merely frozen in stasis to be eaten later," said the demon. "Luckily, I know a spell to release its influence, but you should expect a nasty headache for the next few days. I'll add their rescue to our running tab."

Merkresh regarded the creature. "Who are you?"

"I'm called Xarga'mos."

"We've been fortunate to make your acquaintance," said the old man, "and are grateful for your service to Silvarum."

"Indeed," replied the demon. "I too am fortunate, for I am now allied with a company in possession of a Nexxathian runestone. Your new powers will aid my errand substantially."

"We don't possess those powers yet," replied Merkresh. "Quickly now, we must retrieve the Rune of Frost."

"How do we get back to the chamber?" asked Marie.

"The portal!" shouted Roger, pointing. "It's still open."

The companions stepped through the onyx sphere.

***

In the center of the dragon's lair, situated atop an altar of polished marble, stood the Rune of Frost. The stone hummed with magic as the group approached. A peculiar symbol carved into its face glowed an enchanted blue.

"Marie," said Merkresh. "Since you killed Lord Mortis, it's your responsibility to administer and protect this magic. Approach and claim what you've rightfully earned."

The girl gazed at her siblings nervously. They smiled in return, motioning for her to proceed.

Marie ascended a flight of steps and grasped the stone. As she touched its surface, a burst of energy pulsed through her body. Her arms and legs convulsed with pain.

Mckenzie rushed to her sister's aid, but Merkresh held her back. "Let her go, it passes quickly," he said with a calming voice.

Marie relaxed a moment later, turning to the group.

"Do you feel any different?" asked Roger.

"Are you more powerful?" asked Mckenzie.

"Neither," replied Marie. "I feel exactly the same."

"You'll never be the same again," said the old man. "As a matter of fact, you're now the most powerful person in the room, not counting our new friend, of course."

Xarga'mos winked.

"The power of the Rune of Frost has transferred to your lifeforce," said Merkresh. "All of the magical abilities that Lord Mortis once enjoyed are now under your complete control. Keep that stone with you at all times. You're its protector now."

"I understand," she said, placing it into her backpack.

"This is quite a collection," said the demon, surveying the piles of treasure. "How do you plan to transport it all?"

"As I told you before, treasure was not our objective," said Merkresh. "Take what you wish, as partial payment."

"Nay," replied Xarga'mos. "I care not for gold."

"That's good to hear because I'd like it to be returned to its rightful owners. However, that task is for others to fulfill. We must leave this castle at once. Our grand quest has just begun!"

Departing the lair of Lord Mortis, they were immediately overwhelmed by an unfolding battle in the hallway. Human ghosts were locked in silent combat with a host of phantasms, revenants, and wraiths. Their swords and anguish produced no sound. A battle waged just beyond the companions' dimension.

"The Shevington servants!" cried Mckenzie.

"Aye," said Merkresh. "It appears that Lord Mortis was not the only soul to pay for his sins on this day. Onward!"

The group descended the stairwell, careful not to interfere with the melee. One of the spectral servants thrust his dagger into the neck of a revenant. As he cleaned his blade, he turned and waved to the group with gratitude.

"I'll meet you at the castle's entrance," said Xarga'mos as they exited the central tower and raced across the balcony.

"What?" exclaimed Merkresh.

"It'll be quicker, and I can transport two of you."

The old man peered at the teenagers. "Who wants to go?"

"I do!" exclaimed Roger.

"I've had enough heights for one day," said Mckenzie.

"Marie?" asked the old man.

"I'll descend with my sister. You and Roger go."

"Very well," he replied. "We'll see you soon!"

Xarga'mos grasped Roger and Merkresh and leapt from the balcony. His crimson wings cut through the morning light.

Marie breathed deeply. "What a day."

"For real," replied Mckenzie. "Let's get out of here."

The sisters slipped through the secret door in the wall and negotiated the stairwell. They reached the hallway that led to the Lady's Chamber and halted.

"Which way did Annie bring us?"

"You mean Lord Mortis," replied Marie.

"Right," she chuckled. "So, which way do we go?"

"I'm not sure, but I don't think it matters."

"True enough. Let's try over there."

They ran down the hallway and descended another lofty stairwell. At the bottom, they recognized the archways that led to the Grand Ballroom. Their boots echoed against the granite as they sprinted toward the Banquet Hall. Morning sunlight beamed through the Gothic windows, guiding them to safety.

The sisters entered the servants' quarters. As they trotted

down the hall, Mckenzie glanced at the room that contained Annie's journal. "I wonder if the real girl is finally free."

"Lord Mortis is dead, and the servants have liberated the castle. I believe her soul can rest now," said Marie as she opened the door to the kitchen.

A gloved hand thrust a dagger into her chest. Staggering, Marie spat a mouthful of blood.

"Mrs. Roberts!" screamed Mckenzie.

Their mother's killer stood before them, shrouded in a sapphire cloak. With a horrible grin, Lilly Roberts calmly wiped her blade clean. "The Drake bloodline is destroyed. Once I take your life, I'll prevail, and The Dream-King will be pleased."

As she charged toward Mckenzie, Marie blocked her path.

"The only life taken will be yours," she said, plunging her own dagger into the woman's heart.

Lilly Roberts collapsed in a pool of blood. Her mocking expression transformed to pure horror as she watched Marie's wound mend itself with tendrils of icy frost. The blood on her mouth dissolved into an exhalation of falling snow.

The woman gasped. "How can this be?"

"Because I achieved what you could not," she replied. "You chose a path without purpose. A friend once told me that positive thoughts can cut an enemy as deep as the sharpest blade. That may be true, but you murdered our mother. For that, my blade will bring your miserable life to an end. Reflect upon your choices as you drown in your own blood. Alone."

Marie knelt beside Lilly Roberts and slit her throat.

***

A congregation of friends and family greeted the sisters as they abandoned the castle. Their father, brother, Merkresh, and Vulthkar were in attendance, as well as Vomexium, Dorothy Tompkins, Blazrug, Eddie, Frederick, and Arina. Even Click demonstrated his elation as he hopped up and down next to Roger. Shrouded by space and time, yet equally ecstatic, stood Abigail, Penelope, and Trelinia.

"Father!" cried the sisters, running to him.

"My precious daughters," said Benjamin as they fell into his arms. "I thought I'd lost you again."

"We did it!" replied Marie. "We defeated the dragon!"

"I'm so proud of you. We always knew you could."

"Where's Mom?" asked Marie.

"Standing next to you," he replied.

"Tell her it was *she* who defeated Lord Mortis. Only after I understood the significance of her clues did I summon enough courage to strike him down."

"She disagrees," he replied. "The courage was within you all along. She simply extended to you the knowledge passed on by departed loved ones. Their spark ignited your bravery."

Benjamin, Trelinia, Mckenzie, Roger, and Marie held each other under the warmth of the sun. Their friends observed with awe the bond between them. The raw emotion from the group's collective perception of that snapshot in time radiated an energy that transcended dimensions.

The Woods were a family once again.

APPENDIX:

NOTES AND ARTIFACTS

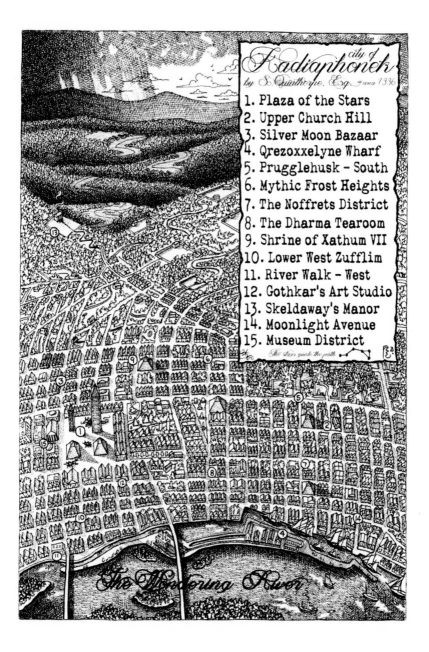

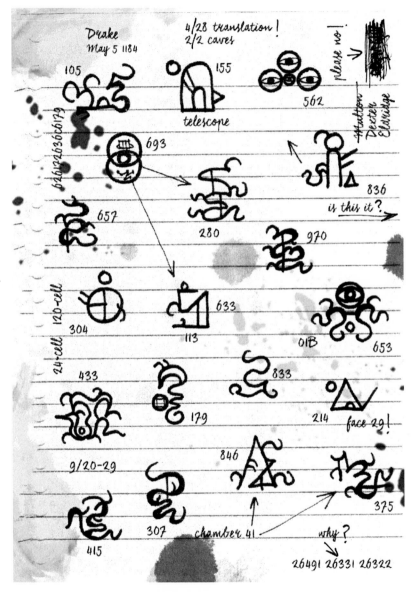

A page from Dr. Edric Drake's field notebook. Recovered from Nexxathia.

Drake May 3 1184
Tomb 87B

The following sketches were carved from tomb 87B during our transcription of volume 465P.

They are based on the numerous carvings and illustrations found on the tombs themselves and on the walls and various sculptures.

R7IX_1

Many humanoid figures carved into the stonework and walls of the tomb. Some of them featured insect and other characteristics. Eyes, legs, etc...

All of the figures and demonstrate a form of levitation. We did not observe any of the specimens. This is consistent with the behavior of the floating objects in district 13.

R7IX_2

The three symbols that have been sketched here were also observed on R7IX. We have not been able to translate their meaning thus far.

R7IX_3

A page from Dr. Edric Drake's field notebook. Recovered from Nexxathia.

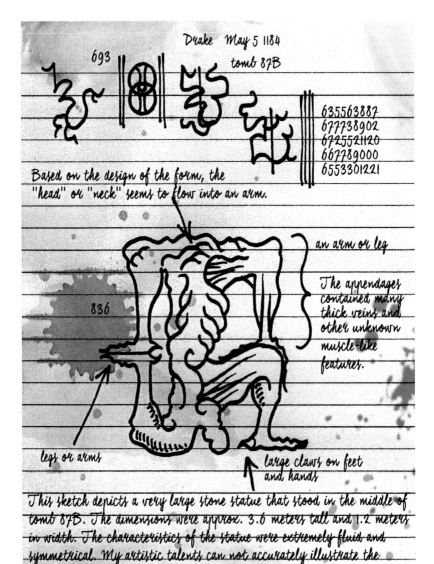

A page from Dr. Edric Drake's field notebook. Recovered from Nexxathia.

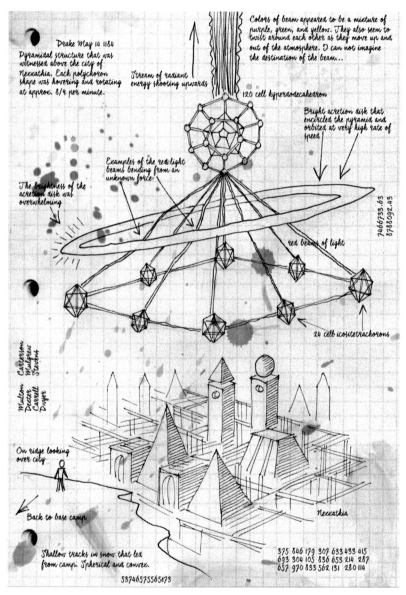

Dr. Edric Drake's sketch of Nexxathia. Recovered from an alley in District 13.

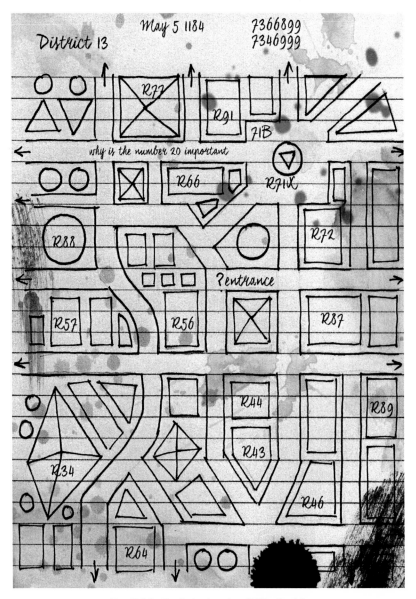

Dr. Edric Drake's sketch of District 13.

Dr Edric Drake
Professor of Paleontology
Diarkoth University

May 14 1184
Drake Expedition

Dr Steven F Huddleston
Professor of Paleontology
Kadiaphonek College
4212 Cedar Hall Room 342

Dear Dr Huddleston

Please forgive the shortage of recent correspondence, for my team and I have been preoccupied with the amazing discovery that I described to you in previous letters. Our findings have led us to indescribable advances in knowledge and technology. Furthermore we have discovered yet another peculiar crypt deep within the city. Within this crypt we found a statue that resembles a human form, yet is certainly not. Upon its base are carved three symbols. The three symbols that you aided in translating based on your feedback from previous letters. I wanted to thank you for 68656c706c65 helping my team and I solve many of these riddles and new languages. Finally, I wanted to share with you the answer to the question you had pertaining to the rune that featured the text "Frost." We discovered that it is more than likely some form of spell or incantation. The three words we translated were

An unmailed letter to Dr. Huddleston from Dr. Drake. Recovered in Tomb 87A.

A page from Dr. Edric Drake's field notebook. Recovered from Nexxathia.

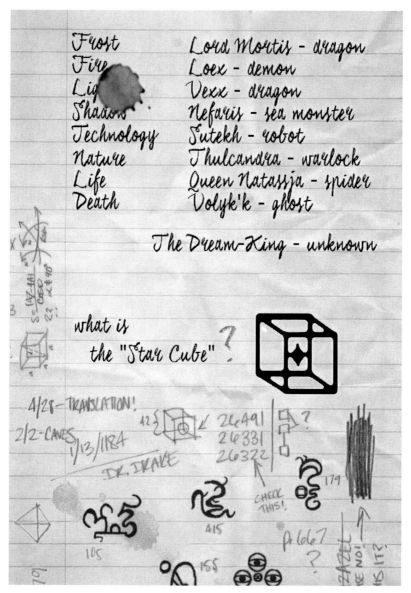

Frost   Lord Mortis – dragon
Fire   Loex – demon
Lig...   Vexx – dragon
Shadow   Nefaris – sea monster
Technology   Sutekh – robot
Nature   Thulcandra – warlock
Life   Queen Natassja – spider
Death   Volyk'k – ghost

The Dream-King – unknown

what is
the "Star Cube" ?

4/28 – TRANSLATION!
2/2 – CAVES
1/13/1184
DR. DRAKE

CHECK THIS!

A list of runestone protectors. Recovered from Dorothy Tompkins' journal.

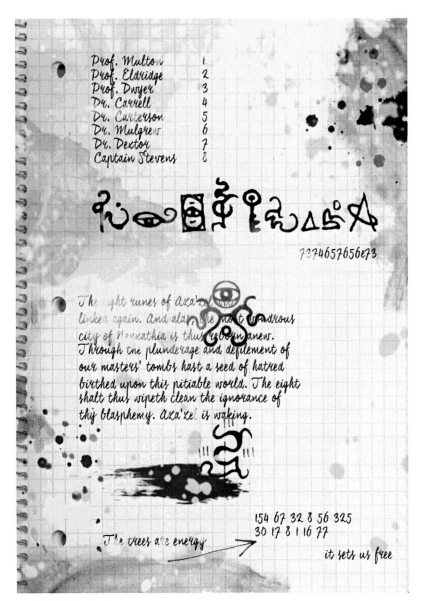

Prof. Multon   1
Prof. Eldridge   2
Prof. Dwyer   3
Dr. Carrell   4
Dr. Carterson   5
Dr. Mulgrew   6
Dr. Dexter   7
Captain Stevens   8

7374657656e73

The eight runes of Aza'zel are linked again. And alas, the most wondrous city of Nexxathia is thus reborn anew. Through the plunderage and defilement of our masters' tombs hast a seed of hatred birthed upon this pitiable world. The eight shalt thus wipeth clean the ignorance of thy blasphemy. Aza'zel is waking.

154 67 32 8 56 325
30 17 8 1 16 77

The trees are energy

it sets us free

Artifact recovered from the streets of Nexxathia. Author unknown.

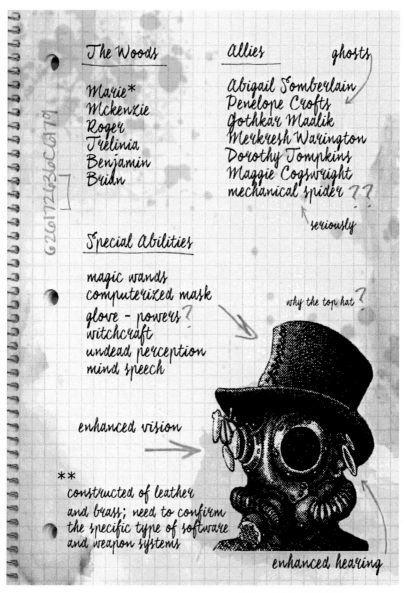

The Woods

Marie*
Mckenzie
Roger
Trelinia
Benjamin
Brian

Special Abilities

magic wands
computerized mask
glove - powers?
witchcraft
undead perception
mind speech

enhanced vision

**
constructed of leather
and brass; need to confirm
the specific type of software
and weapon systems

Allies   ghosts

Abigail Somberlain
Penelope Crofts
Gothkar Maalik
Merkresh Warington
Dorothy Tompkins
Maggie Cogswright
mechanical spider ??

seriously

why the top hat?

enhanced hearing

A page from Magnolia Jinglewort's journal. Stolen by Gothkar.

Artifact recovered from the streets of Nexxathia. Author unknown.

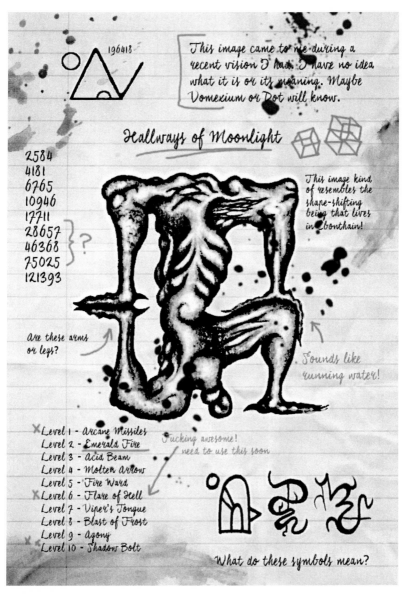

196418

This image came to me during a recent vision I had. I have no idea what it is or its meaning. Maybe Vomexium or Dot will know.

Hallways of Moonlight

2584
4181
6765
10946
17711
28657
46368
75025
121393
} ?

This image kind of resembles the shape-shifting being that lives in Ebonthain!

are these arms or legs?

Sounds like running water!

X Level 1 - Arcane Missiles
Level 2 - Emerald Fire
Level 3 - Acid Beam
Level 4 - Molten Arrow
Level 5 - Fire Ward
X Level 6 - Flare of Hell
Level 7 - Viper's Tongue
Level 8 - Blast of Frost
X Level 9 - Agony
X Level 10 - Shadow Bolt

Fucking awesome! need to use this soon

What do these symbols mean?

An artifact discovered on the side of The Motherwell. Author unknown.

A page from Lilly Robert's journal. Recovered by Marie Woods.

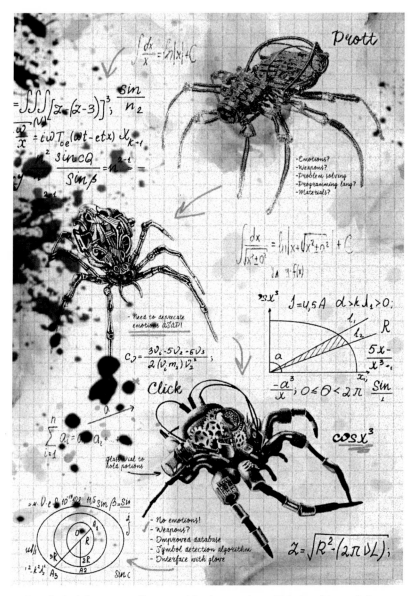

A technical document discovered in the remains of Merkresh's workshop.

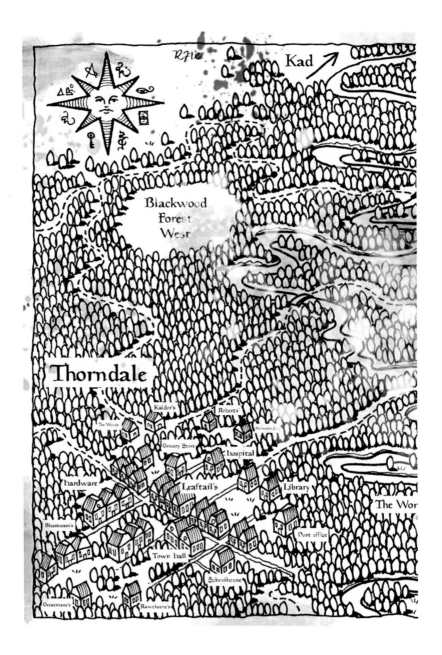

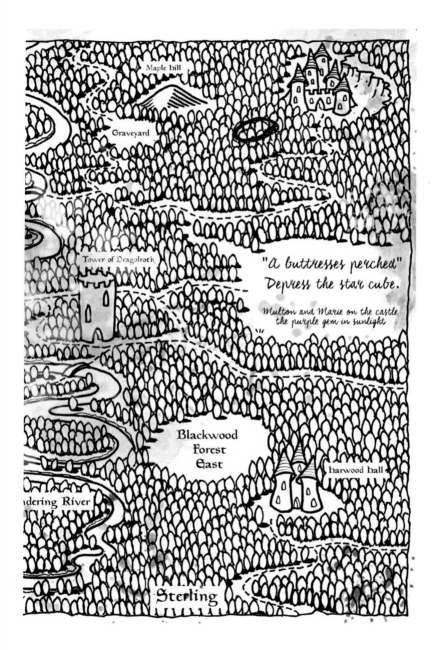

ACKNOWLEDGMENTS

Thank you to all the following people for their invaluable support over the years during the development of *Silvarum*!

Christa Carmen
Jennifer Hrabota Lesser
Sarah Cross
Dan Roberts
Kathleen Roberts
Tamara Hubbard
Esapekka Eriksson
Kimberley T. Sherry
William Fairley
Carl W Bishop
Derek Alexander
Stacy Shuda
Dara Marie Dorsey
Autumn Springfield
Mark-Anthony Page
Carlos Arturo Soto
Eric Sowder
KSZD
Emilia Marjaana Pulliainen
Zach Sallese

AFTERWORD

I've been writing *Silvarum, Book I: Frost* for the last seven years. Before that, however, I began drawing the foundations of this realm when I was a teenager myself. Many of the characters and concepts in this story were conceived in sketchbooks and scraps of loose leaf while I sat in class. Like most authors and creators of imaginary worlds, I've literally fallen in love with this cast of characters during that time. I have teenagers of my own (in real life), yet the process of pushing each of these guys through the realm of *Silvarum* has very much been like watching them all grow up. I know each of their personalities, flaws, and ticks so well, that at times I feel like I'm watching them live their lives and my fingers on the keyboard are simply the means by which I get to observe them. I bet most creators feel that way! It's been a long and difficult journey of my own to write and illustrate their story, but I've loved every second of it. I hope that you will as well. Perhaps you spotted a trait in one of the many characters that you could relate to. Reading a great story isn't just a task to pass the time or to be entertained, but rather, on occasion, a fictional character can handle a situation or a relationship in a way that transcends the written page and makes a tangible impression on you, the reader. Thank you so much for taking the time to read my creation, *Silvarum*!

Dean Kuhta
Richmond, Virginia
September 2020

DEAN KUHTA was born in 1975 in the United States of America and now lives in the state of Virginia. In his free moments, he enjoys drawing with his daughter, playing video games with his son, and listening to heavy metal music. *Silvarum* is his first novel.